BY ANDY WEIR

Project Hail Mary

Artemis

The Martian

PROJECT HAIL MARY

PROJECT HAIL MARY

A NOVEL

ANDY WEIR

BALLANTINE BOOKS
NEW YORK

Ballantine Books
An imprint of Random House
A division of Penguin Random House LLC
1745 Broadway, New York, NY 10019
randomhousebooks.com
penguinrandomhouse.com

2025 Ballantine Books Trade Paperback Edition

Originally published in hardcover in the United States by Ballantine Books, an imprint of Random House, a division of Penguin Random House LLC, in 2021.

ISBN 979-8-217-29946-1
International edition ISBN 978-0-593-59865-8
Ebook ISBN 978-0-593-13521-1

Printed in the United States of America on acid-free paper

5th Printing

Book design by Caroline Cunningham

Title page image: iStock/Roman Kulinskiy

The authorized representative in the EU for product safety and compliance is Penguin Random House Ireland, Morrison Chambers, 32 Nassau Street, Dublin D02 YH68, Ireland. https://eu-contact.penguin.ie.

FOR JOHN, PAUL, GEORGE, AND RINGO

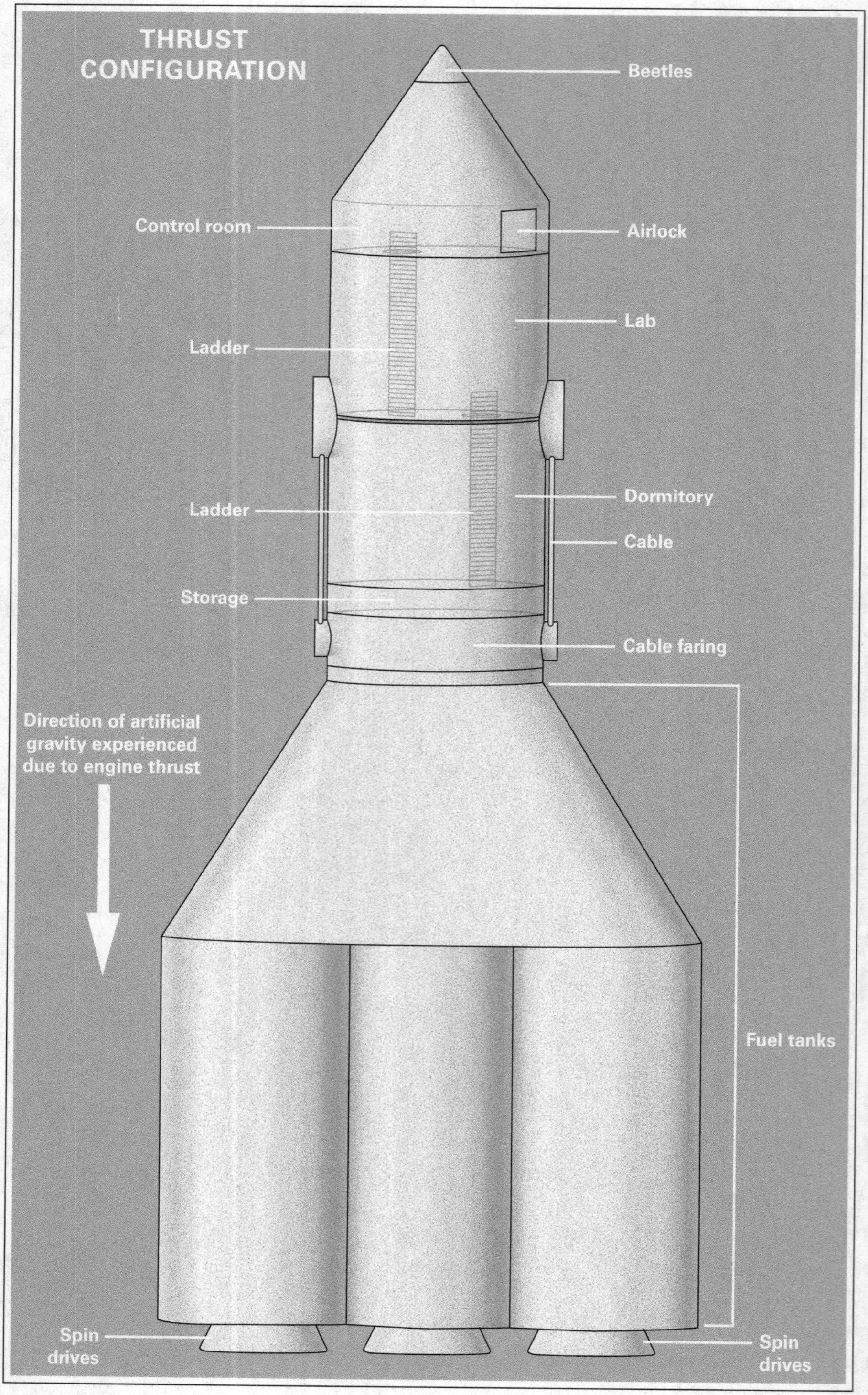
THRUST
CONFIGURATION
Beetles
Control room
Airlock
Lab
Ladder
Dormitory
Ladder
Cable
Storage
Cable faring
Direction of artificial
gravity experienced
due to engine thrust
Fuel tanks
Spin
drives
Spin
drives

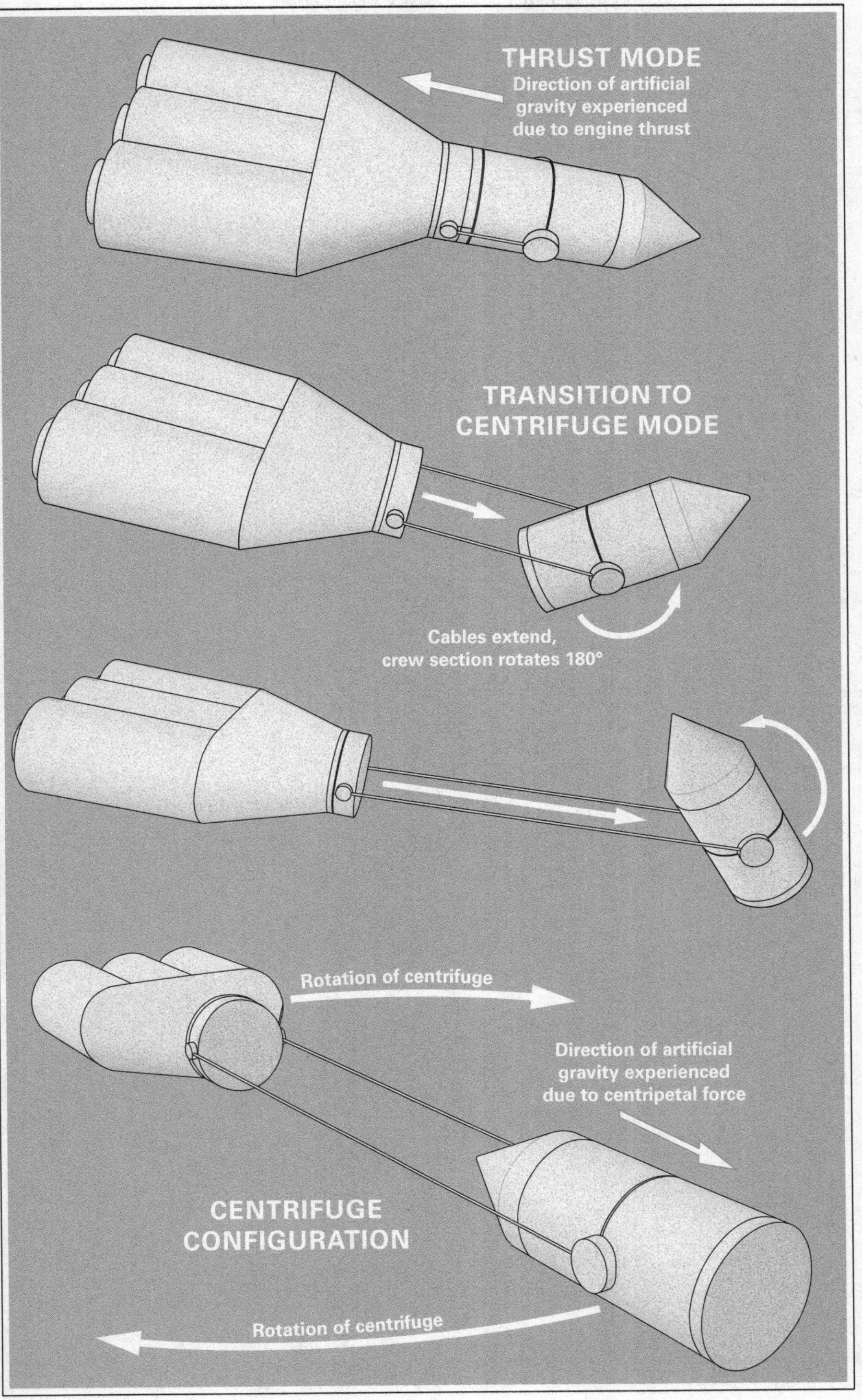
THRUST MODE
Direction of artificial gravity experienced due to engine thrust
TRANSITION TO CENTRIFUGE MODE
Cables extend, crew section rotates 180°
Rotation of centrifuge
Direction of artificial gravity experienced due to centripetal force
CENTRIFUGE CONFIGURATION
Rotation of centrifuge

PROJECT HAIL MARY

CHAPTER 1

"W*hat's two plus two?"*

Something about the question irritates me. I'm tired. I drift back to sleep.

A few minutes pass, then I hear it again.

"What's two plus two?"

The soft, feminine voice lacks emotion and the pronunciation is identical to the previous time she said it. It's a computer. A computer is hassling me. I'm even more irritated now.

"Lrmln," I say. I'm surprised. I meant to say "Leave me alone"—a completely reasonable response in my opinion—but I failed to speak.

"Incorrect," says the computer. "What's two plus two?"

Time for an experiment. I'll try to say hello.

"Hlllch?" I say.

"Incorrect. What's two plus two?"

What's going on? I want to find out, but I don't have much to work with. I can't see. I can't hear anything other than the computer. I can't even feel. No, that's not true. I feel something. I'm lying down. I'm on something soft. A bed.

I think my eyes are closed. That's not so bad. All I have to do is open them. I try, but nothing happens.

Why can't I open my eyes?

Open.

Aaaand . . . open!

Open, dang it!

Ooh! I felt a wiggle that time. My eyelids moved. I felt it.

Open!

My eyelids creep up and blinding light sears my retinas.

"Glunn!" I say. I keep my eyes open with sheer force of will. Everything is white with shades of pain.

"Eye movement detected," my tormenter says. "What's two plus two?"

The whiteness lessens. My eyes are adjusting. I start to see shapes, but nothing sensible yet. Let's see . . . can I move my hands? No.

Feet? Also no.

But I can move my mouth, right? I've been saying stuff. Not stuff that makes sense, but it's something.

"Fffr."

"Incorrect. What's two plus two?"

The shapes start to make sense. I'm in a bed. It's kind of . . . oval-shaped.

LED lights shine down on me. Cameras in the ceiling watch my every move. Creepy though that is, I'm much more concerned about the robot arms.

The two brushed-steel armatures hang from the ceiling. Each has an assortment of disturbingly penetration-looking tools where hands should be. Can't say I like the look of that.

"Ffff . . . oooh . . . rrrr," I say. Will that do?

"Incorrect. What's two plus two?"

Dang it. I summon all my willpower and inner strength. Also, I'm starting to panic a little. Good. I use that too.

"Fffoouurr," I finally say.

"Correct."

Thank God. I can talk. Sort of.

I breathe a sigh of relief. Wait—I just controlled my breathing. I take another breath. On purpose. My mouth is sore. My throat is sore. But it's *my* soreness. I have control.

I'm wearing a breathing mask. It's tight to my face and connected to a hose that goes behind my head.

Can I get up?

No. But I can move my head a little. I look down at my body. I'm naked and connected to more tubes than I can count. There's one in each arm, one in each leg, one in my "gentlemen's equipment," and two that disappear under my thigh. I'm guessing one of them is up where the sun doesn't shine.

That can't be good.

Also, I'm covered with electrodes. The sensor-type stickers like for an EKG, but they're all over the place. Well, at least they're only on my skin instead of jammed into me.

"Wh—" I wheeze. I try again. "Where . . . am . . . I?"

"What's the cube root of eight?" the computer asks.

"Where am I?" I say again. This time it's easier.

"Incorrect. What's the cube root of eight?"

I take a deep breath and speak slowly. "Two times *e* to the two-*i*-pi."

"Incorrect. What's the cube root of eight?"

But I wasn't incorrect. I just wanted to see how smart the computer was. Answer: not very.

"Two," I say.

"Correct."

I listen for follow-up questions, but the computer seems satisfied.

I'm tired. I drift off to sleep again.

I wake up. How long was I out? It must have been a while because I feel rested. I open my eyes without any effort. That's progress.

I try to move my fingers. They wiggle as instructed. All right. Now we're getting somewhere.

"Hand movement detected," says the computer. "Remain still."

"What? Why—"

The robot arms come for me. They move *fast*. Before I know it, they've removed most of the tubes from my body. I didn't feel a thing. Though my skin is kind of numb anyway.

Only three tubes remain: an IV in my arm, a tube up my butt, and a catheter. Those latter two are kind of the signature items I wanted removed, but okay.

I raise my right arm and let it fall back to the bed. I do the same for my left. They feel heavy as heck. I repeat the process a few times. My arms are muscular. That doesn't make sense. I assume I've had some massive medical problem and been in this bed for a while. Otherwise, why would they have me hooked up to all the stuff? Shouldn't there be muscle atrophy?

And shouldn't there be doctors? Or maybe the sounds of a hospital? And what's with this bed? It's not a rectangle, it's an oval and I think it's mounted to the wall instead of the floor.

"Take . . ." I trail off. Still kind of tired. "Take the tubes out. . . ."

The computer doesn't respond.

I do a few more arm lifts. I wiggle my toes. I'm definitely getting better.

I tilt my ankles back and forth. They're working. I raise my knees up. My legs are well toned too. Not bodybuilder thick, but still too healthy for someone on the verge of death. I'm not sure how thick they should be, though.

I press my palms to the bed and push. My torso rises. I'm actually getting up! It takes all my strength but I soldier on. The bed rocks gently as I move. It's not a normal bed, that's for sure. As I raise my head higher up, I see the head and foot of the elliptical bed are attached to strong-looking wall mounts. It's kind of a rigid hammock. Weird.

Soon, I'm sitting on my butt tube. Not the most comfortable sensation, but when is a tube up your butt ever comfortable?

I have a better view of things now. This is no ordinary hospital room. The walls look plastic and the whole room is round. Stark-white light comes from ceiling-mounted LED lights.

There are two more hammock-like beds mounted to the walls, each with their own patient. We are arranged in a triangle and the roof-mounted Arms of Harassment are in the center of the ceiling. I guess they take care of all three of us. I can't see much of my compatriots—they've sunken into their bedding like I had.

There's no door. Just a ladder on the wall leading to . . . a hatch? It's round and has a wheel-handle in the center. Yeah, it's got to be some kind of hatch. Like on a submarine. Maybe the three of us have a contagious disease? Maybe this is an airtight quarantine room? There are small vents here and there on the wall and I feel a little airflow. It could be a controlled environment.

I slide one leg off over the edge of my bed, which makes it wobble. The robot arms rush toward me. I flinch, but they stop short and hover nearby. I think they're ready to grab me if I fall.

"Full-body motion detected," the computer says. "What's your name?"

"Pfft, seriously?" I ask.

"Incorrect. Attempt number two: What's your name?"

I open my mouth to answer.

"Uh . . ."

"Incorrect. Attempt number three: What's your name?"

Only now does it occur to me: I don't know who I am. I don't know what I do. I don't remember anything at all.

"Um," I say.

"Incorrect."

A wave of fatigue grips me. It's kind of pleasant, actually. The computer must have sedated me through the IV line.

". . . waaaait . . ." I mumble.

The robot arms lay me gently back down to the bed.

I wake up again. One of the robot arms is on my face. What is it doing?!

I shudder, more shocked than anything else. The arm retracts back to its home in the ceiling. I feel my face for damage. One side has stubble and the other is smooth.

"You were shaving me?"

"Consciousness detected," the computer says. "What's your name?"

"I still don't know that."

"Incorrect. Attempt number two: What's your name?"

I'm Caucasian, I'm male, and I speak English. Let's play the odds. "J–John?"

"Incorrect. Attempt number three: What's your name?"

I pull the IV out of my arm. "Bite me."

"Incorrect." The robot arms reach for me. I roll off the bed, which is a mistake. The other tubes are still connected.

The butt tube comes right out. Doesn't even hurt. The still-inflated catheter yanks right out of my penis. And that *does* hurt. It's like peeing a golf ball.

I scream and writhe on the floor.

"Physical distress," says the computer. The arms give chase. I crawl along the floor to escape. I get under one of the other beds. The arms stop short, but they don't give up. They wait. They're run by a computer. It's not like they'll run out of patience.

I let my head fall back and gasp for breath. After a while, the pain subsides and I wipe tears from my eyes.

I have no idea what's going on here.

"Hey!" I call out. "One of you, wake up!"

"What's your name?" the computer asks.

"One of you *humans,* wake up, please."

"Incorrect," the computer says.

My crotch hurts so bad I have to laugh. It's just so absurd. Plus, the endorphins are kicking in and making me giddy. I look back at the catheter by my bunk. I shake my head in awe. That thing went through my urethra. Wow.

And it did some damage on the way out. A little streak of blood sits on the ground. It's just a thin red line of—

I sipped my coffee, popped the last fragment of toast into my mouth, and signaled the waitress for my check. I could have saved money by eating breakfast at home instead of going to a diner every morning. Probably would have been a good idea, considering my meager salary. But I hate cooking and I love eggs and bacon.

The waitress nodded and walked over to the cash register to ring me up. But another customer came in to be seated right that moment.

I checked my watch. Just past seven A.M. No rush. I liked to get in to work by seven-twenty so I could have time to prep for the day. But I didn't actually need to be there until eight.

I pulled out my phone and checked my email.

TO: Astronomy Curiosities astrocurious@scilists.org
FROM: (Irina Petrova, PhD) ipetrova@gaoran.ru
SUBJECT: The Thin Red Line

I frowned at the screen. I thought I'd unsubscribed from that list. I left that life a long time ago. It didn't get a lot of volume, and what it did get, if memory served, was usually pretty interesting. Just a bunch of astronomers, astrophysicists, and other domain experts chatting about anything that struck them as odd.

I glanced at the waitress—the customers had a bunch of questions about the menu. Probably asking if Sally's Diner served gluten-free vegan grass clippings or something. The good people of San Francisco could be trying at times.

With nothing better to do, I read the email.

Hello, professionals. My name is Doctor Irina Petrova and I work at the Pulkovo Observatory in St. Petersburg, Russia.

I am writing to you to ask for help.

For the past two years, I have been working on a theory related to infrared emissions from nebulae. As a result, I have made detailed observations in a few specific IR bands of light. And I have found something odd—not in any nebula, but here in our own solar system.

There is a very faint, but detectable line in the solar system that emits infrared light at the 25.984 micron wavelength. It seems to be solely that wavelength with no variance.

Attached are Excel spreadsheets with my data. I have also provided a few renders of the data as a 3-D model.

You will see on the model that the line is a lopsided arc that rises straight up from the sun's North Pole for 37 million kilometers. From there, it angles sharply down and away from the sun, toward Venus. After the arc's apex, the cloud widens like a funnel. At Venus, the arc's cross-section is as wide as the planet itself.

The infrared glow is very faint. I was only able to detect it at all because I was using extremely sensitive detection equipment while searching for IR emissions from nebulae.

But to be certain, I called in a favor from the Atacama observatory in Chile—in my opinion the best IR observatory in the world. They confirmed my findings.

There are many reasons one might see IR light in interplanetary space. It could be space dust or other particles reflecting sunlight. Or some molecular compound could be absorbing energy and re-emitting it in the infrared band. That would even explain why it's all the same wavelength.

The shape of the arc is of particular interest. My first guess was that it is a collection of particles moving along magnetic field lines. But Venus has no magnetic field to speak of. No magnetosphere, no ionosphere, nothing. What forces would make particles arc toward it? And why would they glow?

Any suggestions or theories would be welcome.

What the heck was that?

I remembered it all at once. It just kind of showed up in my head without warning.

I didn't learn much about myself. I live in San Francisco—I remember that. And I like breakfast. Also I used to be into astronomy but now I'm not?

Apparently my brain decided it was critical that I remember that email. Not trivial things like *my own name.*

My subconscious wants to tell me something. Seeing the line of blood must have reminded me of the "Thin Red Line" title of that email. But what's that got to do with me?

I shimmy out from under the bed and sit up against the wall. The arms angle toward me, but still can't reach.

Time to get a look at my fellow patients. I don't know who I am or why I'm here, but at least I'm not alone—aaaand they're dead.

Yes, definitely dead. The one closest to me was a woman, I think. At least, she had long hair. Other than that, she's mostly a mummy. Desiccated skin draped over bones. There's no smell. Nothing is actively rotting. She must have died a long time ago.

The person in the other bed was a man. I think he's been dead even longer. His skin is not only dry and leathery but also crumbling away.

Okay. So I'm here with two dead people. I should be disgusted and horrified, but I'm not. They're so far gone they don't even look human. They look like Halloween decorations. I hope I wasn't close friends with either of them. Or, if I was, I hope I don't remember it.

Dead people is a concern, but I'm more concerned that they've been here so long. Even a quarantine area would remove dead people, wouldn't they? Whatever's wrong must be pretty darn bad.

I get to my feet. It's slow and it takes a lot of effort. I steady myself at the edge of Ms. Mummy's bed. It wobbles and I wobble with it, but I stay upright.

The robot arms make a play for me, but I flatten myself against the wall again.

I'm pretty sure I was in a coma. Yeah. The more I think of it, I was definitely in a coma.

I don't know how long I've been here, but if I was put here at the same time as my roommates it's been a while. I rub my half-shaved face. Those arms are designed to manage long-term unconsciousness. More evidence I was in a coma.

Maybe I can get to that hatch?

I take a step. Then another. Then I sink to the floor. It's just too much for me. I have to rest.

Why am I so weak when I have these well-toned muscles? And if I was in a coma, why do I even have muscles? I should be a withered, spindly mess right now, not beach-bod buff.

I have no idea what my endgame is. What should I do? Am I really sick? I mean, I feel like crud of course, but I don't feel "sick." I'm not nauseated. I don't have a headache. I don't think I have a fever. If I don't have a disease, why was I in a coma? Physical injury?

I feel around my head. No lumps or scars or bandages. The rest of my body seems pretty solid too. Better than solid. I'm ripped.

I want to nod off but I resist it.

Time to take another stab at this. I push myself back up. It's like weightlifting. But it's a little easier this time. I'm recovering more and more (I hope).

I shuffle along the wall, using my back for support as much as my feet. The arms constantly reach for me but I stay out of range.

I pant and wheeze. I feel like I've run a marathon. Maybe I have a lung infection? Maybe I'm in isolation for my own protection?

I finally make it to the ladder. I stumble forward and grab one of the rungs. I'm just so weak. How am I going to climb a 10-foot ladder?

Ten-foot ladder.

I think in imperial units. That's a clue. I'm probably an American. Or English. Or maybe Canadian. Canadians use feet and inches for short distances.

I ask myself: How far is it from L.A. to New York? My gut answer: 3,000 miles. A Canadian would have used kilometers. So I'm English or American. Or I'm from Liberia.

I know Liberia uses imperial units but I don't know my own name. That's irritating.

I take a deep breath. I hang on to the ladder with both hands and put my foot on the bottom rung. I pull myself up. It's a shaky process, but I get it done. Both feet are on the lower rung now. I reach up and grab the next rung. Okay, making progress. I feel like my whole body is made of lead—everything is so much effort. I try to pull myself up, but my hand just isn't strong enough.

I fall backward off the ladder. This is going to hurt.

It doesn't hurt. The robot arms catch me before I hit the ground because I fell into grabbing range. They don't miss a beat. They return me to bed and settle me in like a mother putting her child to sleep.

You know what? This is fine. I'm really tired at this point and lying down kind of works for me. The gentle rocking of the bed is comforting. Something bugs me about how I fell off the ladder. I replay it in my head. I can't put my finger on it, but there's just a . . . "wrongness" to it.

Hmm.

I drift off.

"Eat."

There's a toothpaste tube on my chest.

"Huh?"

"Eat," the computer says again.

I lift the tube. It's white with black text that reads DAY 1—MEAL 1.

"The heck is this?" I say.

"Eat."

I unscrew the cap and smell something savory. My mouth waters at the prospect. Only now do I realize how hungry I am. I squeeze the tube and disgusting-looking brown sludge comes out.

"Eat."

Who am I to question a creepy robot-armed computer overlord? I cautiously lick the substance.

Oh my God it's good! It's so good! It's like thick gravy but not too rich. I squeeze more straight into my mouth and savor it. I swear it's better than sex.

I know what's going on here. They say hunger is the greatest seasoning. When you're starving, your brain rewards you handsomely for finally eating. *Good job,* it says, *we get to not die for a while!*

The pieces fall into place. If I was in a coma for a long time, I must have been getting fed. I didn't have an abdominal tube when I woke up, so it was probably feeding me with an NG tube running down my esophagus. It's the least-intrusive way to feed a patient who can't eat but has no digestion issues. Plus, it keeps the digestive system active and healthy. And it explains why the tube wasn't around when I woke up. If possible, you should remove an NG tube while the patient is still unconscious.

Why do I know that? Am I a doctor?

I squeeze another shot of gravy-goo into my mouth. Still delicious. I gobble it down. Soon the tube is empty. I hold it up. "More of this!"

"Meal complete."

"I'm still hungry! Give me another tube!"

"Food allotment for this meal has been met."

It makes sense. My digestive system is getting used to semi-solid food right now. Best to take it easy. If I eat as much as I want I'll probably get sick. The computer is doing the right thing.

"Give me more food!" No one cares about the right thing when they're hungry.

"Food allotment for this meal has been met."

"Bah."

Still, I feel a ton better than I did before. The food energized me on the spot, plus I've had more rest.

I roll out of bed, ready to make a break for the wall, but the arms don't chase me. I guess I'm allowed out of bed now that I've proven I can eat.

I look down at my naked body. This just doesn't feel right. I know the only other people around are dead, but still.

"Can I have some clothes?"

The computer says nothing.

"Fine. Be that way."

I pull the sheet off the bed and wrap it around my torso a couple of times. I pull one corner over my shoulder from behind my back and tie it to another from the front. Instant toga.

"Self-ambulation detected," says the computer. "What's your name?"

"I am Emperor Comatose. Kneel before me."

"Incorrect."

Time to see what's up that ladder.

I'm a little unsteady, but I start walking across the room. This is a victory in itself—I don't need wobbly beds or walls to cling to. I'm on my own two feet.

I make it to the ladder and grab hold. I don't *need* something to hang on to, but it sure makes life easier. The hatch above looks pretty darn solid. I assume it's airtight. And there's every chance it's locked. But I have to at least try.

I climb up one rung. Tough, but doable. Another rung. Okay, I have the hang of this. Slow and steady.

I make it to the hatch. I hang on to the ladder with one hand and turn the hatch's circular crank with the other. It actually turns!

"Holy moly!" I say.

"Holy moly"? Is that my go-to expression of surprise? I mean, it's okay, I guess. I would have expected something a little less 1950s. What kind of weirdo am I?

I turn the crank three full rotations and hear a click. The hatch tilts downward and I get out of the way. It falls open, suspended by its hefty hinge. I'm free!

Sort of.

Beyond the hatch, there's just darkness. A little intimidating, but at least it's progress.

I reach into the new room and pull myself up to the floor. Lights click on as soon as I enter. Presumably the computer's doing.

The room looks to be the same size and shape as the one I left—another round room.

One large table—a lab table from the look of it—is mounted to the floor. Three lab stools are mounted nearby. All around the walls are pieces of lab equipment. All of it mounted to tables or benches that are bolted to the floor. It's like the room is ready for a catastrophic earthquake.

A ladder along the wall leads to another hatch in the ceiling.

I'm in a well-stocked laboratory. Since when do isolation wards let patients into the lab? And this doesn't look like a medical lab, anyway. What the fudge is going on?!

Fudge? Seriously? Maybe I have young kids. Or I'm deeply religious.

I stand to get a better look at things.

The lab has smaller equipment bolted to the table. I see an 8000x microscope, an autoclave, a bank of test tubes, sets of supply drawers, a sample fridge, a furnace, pipettes—wait a minute. Why do I know all those terms?

I look at the larger equipment along the walls. Scanning electron microscope, sub-millimeter 3-D printer, 11-axis milling machine, laser interferometer, 1-cubic-meter vacuum chamber—I know what everything is. And I know how to use it.

I'm a scientist! Now we're getting somewhere! Time for me to use science. *All right, genius brain: come up with something!*

. . . I'm hungry.

You have failed me, brain.

Okay, well I have no idea why this lab is here or why I'm allowed in. But . . . onward!

The hatch in the ceiling is 10 feet off the ground. It's going to be another ladder adventure. At least I'm stronger now.

I take a few deep breaths and start climbing the ladder. Same as before, this simple act is a massive effort. I may be getting better, but I'm not "well."

Good lord I'm heavy. I make it to the top, but only just.

I situate myself on the uncomfortable bars and push on the hatch's handle. It doesn't budge.

"To unlock hatch, state your name," says the computer.

"But I don't know my name!"

"Incorrect."

I smack the handle with the palm of my hand. The handle doesn't move and now the palm of my hand hurts. So . . . yeah. Not fruitful.

This will have to wait. Maybe I'll remember my name soon. Or find it written somewhere.

I climb back down the ladder. At least, that's my plan. You'd think going down would be easier and safer than going up. But no. No. Instead of gracefully descending the ladder, I put my foot on the next rung down at an awkward angle, lose my grip on the hatch handle, and fall like an idiot.

I flail like an angry cat, reaching out for anything I can grasp. Turns out that's a terrible idea. I fall onto the table and smack a set of supply drawers with my shin. It hurts like a motherfluffer! I cry out, grab my shin in pain, accidentally roll off the table, and fall to the floor.

No robot arms to catch me this time. I land on my back and it knocks the wind out of me. Then, adding insult to injury, the supply-drawer unit falls over, the drawers open, and lab supplies rain down upon me. The cotton swabs aren't a problem. The test tubes just kind of hurt a little (and surprisingly don't shatter). But the tape measure smacks me square in the forehead.

More stuff clatters down, but I'm too busy holding the growing welt on my forehead to notice. How heavy is that tape measure? A 3-foot fall off a table left a bump on my head.

"That. Did not work," I say to no one. That whole experience was just ridiculous. Like something out of a Charlie Chaplin movie.

Actually . . . it really was like that. A little too much like that.

That same feeling of "wrongness" strikes me.

I grab a nearby test tube and toss it into the air. It goes up and comes down like it should. But it annoys me. Something about falling objects ticks me off right now. I want to know why.

What do I have to work with? Well, I have an entire laboratory and I know how to use it. But what's readily at hand? I look around at all the junk that fell to the floor. A bunch of test tubes, sample swabs, Popsicle sticks, a digital stopwatch, pipettes, some Scotch tape, a pen . . .

Okay, I may have what I need here.

I get back to my feet and dust off my toga. There's no dust on it—my whole world seems really clean and sterile, but I do the motions just the same.

I pick up the tape measure and take a look. It's metric. Maybe I'm in Europe? Whatever. Then I grab the stopwatch. It's pretty sturdy, like something you'd take on a hike. It has a solid plastic shell with a hard rubber ring around it. Undoubtedly waterproof. But also dead as a doornail. The LCD screen is completely blank.

I press a few buttons, but nothing happens. I turn it over to get a look at the battery compartment. Maybe I can find a drawer with batteries in it if I know what kind it needs. I spot a little red plastic ribbon coming out of the back. I give it a pull and it comes out entirely. The stopwatch beeps to life.

Kind of like "batteries included" toys. The little plastic tab was there to keep the battery from running down before the owner uses it for the first time. Okay, this is a brand-spanking-new stopwatch. Honestly, everything in this lab looks brand-new. Clean, tidy, no signs of wear. Not sure what to make of that.

I play with the stopwatch for a while until I understand the controls. Pretty simple, really.

I use the tape measure to find out how high the table is. Anyway, the table's underside is 91 centimeters from the floor.

I pick up a test tube. It's not glass. It may be some kind of high-density plastic or something. It certainly didn't break when it fell 3 feet to a hard surface. Anyway, whatever it's made of, it's dense enough for air resistance to be negligible.

I lay it on the table and ready the stopwatch. I push the test tube off the table with one hand and start the stopwatch with the other. I time how long it takes to hit the ground. I get about 0.37 seconds. That's pretty darn fast. I hope my own reaction time isn't skewing the results.

I note the time down on my arm with the pen—I haven't found any paper yet.

I put the test tube back and repeat the test. This time I get 0.33. I do it twenty times total, noting the results, to minimize the effects of my error margin in starting and stopping the timer. Anyway, I end up with an average of 0.348 seconds. My arm looks like a math teacher's chalkboard, but that's okay.

0.348 seconds. Distance equals one-half acceleration times time squared. So acceleration equals two times distance over time squared. These formulas come easily to me. Second nature. I'm definitely skilled at physics. Good to know.

I run the numbers and come up with an answer I don't like. The gravity in this room is too high. It's 15 meters per second per second when it should be 9.8. That's why things falling "feel" wrong to me. They're falling too fast. And that's why I'm so weak despite these muscles. Everything weighs one and a half times as much as it should.

Thing is, nothing affects gravity. You can't increase or decrease it. Earth's gravity is 9.8 meters per second per second. Period. And I'm experiencing more than that. There's only one possible explanation.

I'm not on Earth.

CHAPTER 2

Okay, take a breath. Let's not jump to wild conclusions. Yes, the gravity is too high. Work from there and think of *sensible* answers.

I could be in a centrifuge. It would have to be pretty big. But with Earth's gravity providing 1 g, you could have these rooms at an angle running around a track or on the end of a long solid arm or something. Set that spinning and the aggregate centripetal force plus Earth's gravity could be 15 meters per second per second.

Why would someone make a huge centrifuge with hospital beds and a lab in it? I don't know. Would it even be possible? How big would that radius have to be? And how fast would it go?

I think I know how to find out. I need an accurate accelerometer. Dropping things off a table and timing them is all well and fine for rough estimates, but it's only as accurate as my reaction time on hitting the stopwatch. I need something better. And only one thing will do the job: a small piece of string.

I search the lab drawers.

After a few minutes, I have half the drawers open and have found just about every form of lab supplies except string. I'm about to give up when I finally find a spool of nylon thread.

"Yes!" I pull off a few feet of thread and cut it with my teeth. I tie a loop on one end and tie the other end around the tape measure. The tape measure will be playing the role of "dead weight" in this experiment. Now I just need something to hang it from.

I look above me at the hatch over my head. I climb up the ladder (easier now than ever before) and put the loop over the main latch handle. Then I let the tape measure's weight pull the string taut.

I have a pendulum.

Cool thing about pendulums: The time it takes for one to swing forward and backward—the period—won't change, no matter how wide it swings. If it's got a lot of energy, it'll swing farther and faster, but the period will still be the same. This is what mechanical clocks take advantage of to keep time. That period ends up being driven by two things, and two things only: the length of the pendulum and gravity.

I pull the pendulum to one side. I release it and start the timer. I count cycles as it sways back and forth. It's not exciting. I almost want to fall asleep, but I stay at it.

When I hit the ten-minute mark, the pendulum is barely moving anymore, so I decide that's long enough. Grand total: 346 full cycles in exactly ten minutes.

Onward to phase two.

I measure the distance from the hatch handle to the floor. It's just over two and a half meters. I go back downstairs to the "bedroom." Again, the ladder is no problem. I'm feeling so much better now. That food really did the trick.

"What's your name?" the computer asks.

I look down at my sheet toga. "I am the great philosopher Pendulus!"

"Incorrect."

I hang the pendulum on one of the robot hands near the ceiling. I hope it'll stay still for a while. I eyeball the distance between the robot hand and the ceiling—I'll call it a meter. My pendulum is now four and a half meters lower than it was before.

I repeat the experiment. Ten minutes on the stopwatch, and I count the total cycles. The result: 346 cycles. Same as upstairs.

Golly.

Thing is, in a centrifuge, the farther you get from the center, the higher the centripetal force will be. So if I were in a centrifuge, the "gravity" down here would be higher than it was upstairs. And it isn't. At least, not enough to get a different number of pendulum cycles.

But what if I'm in a *really big* centrifuge? One so huge that the force difference between here and the lab is so small it doesn't change the number of cycles?

Let's see . . . the formula for a pendulum . . . and the formula for the force of a centrifuge . . . wait, I don't have the actual force, just a cycle count, so there's a one-over-*x* factor involved . . . this is actually a very instructive problem!

I have a pen, but no paper. That's okay—I have a wall. After a lot of "crazy prisoner scribbling on a wall"–type stuff, I have my answer.

Let's say I'm on Earth and in a centrifuge. That would mean the centrifuge provides some of the force with the rest being supplied by Earth. According to my math (and I showed all my work!), that centrifuge would need a 700-meter radius (which is almost half a mile) and would be spinning at 88 meters per second—almost 200 miles per hour!

Hmm. I think mostly in metric when doing science stuff. Interesting. Most scientists do, though, right? Even scientists who grew up in America.

Anyway, that would be the largest centrifuge ever built . . . and why would anyone build it? Plus, something like that would be loud as heck. Whizzing through the air at 200 miles per hour? At the very least there'd be some turbulence here and there, not to mention a lot of wind noise. I don't hear or feel anything like that.

This is getting weird. Okay, what if I'm in space? There wouldn't be turbulence or wind resistance, but the centrifuge would have to be bigger and faster because there's no gravity to help out.

More math, more graffiti on the wall. The radius would have to be

1,280 meters—close to a mile. Nothing anywhere near that big has ever been built for space.

So I'm not in a centrifuge. And I'm not on Earth.

Another planet? But there isn't any planet, moon, or asteroid in the solar system that has this much gravity. Earth is the largest solid object in the whole system. Sure, the gas giants are bigger, but unless I'm in a balloon floating around the winds of Jupiter, there's just nowhere I could go to experience this force.

How do I know all that space stuff? I just know it. It feels like second nature—information I use all the time. Maybe I'm an astronomer or a planetary scientist. Maybe I work for NASA or ESA or—

I met Marissa every Thursday night for steak and beer at Murphy's on Gough Street. Always at six P.M., and because the staff knew us, always at the same table.

We'd met almost twenty years ago in grad school. She dated my then-roommate. Their relationship (like most in grad school) was a train wreck and they broke up within three months. But she and I ended up becoming good friends.

When the host saw me, he smiled and jerked his thumb toward the usual table. I made my way through the kitschy décor to Marissa. She had a couple of empty lowball glasses in front of her and a full one in her hand. Apparently, she'd gotten started early.

"Pre-gaming, eh?" I said, sitting down.

She looked down and fidgeted with her glass.

"Hey, what's wrong?"

She took a sip of whiskey. "Rough day at work."

I signaled the waiter. He nodded and didn't even come over. He knew I wanted a rib-eye, medium, mashed potatoes on the side, and a pint of Guinness. Same thing I ordered every week.

"How rough could it be?" I asked. "Cushy government job with the DOE. You probably get, what, twenty days off a year? All you have to do is show up and you get paid, right?"

Again, no laugh. Nothing.

"Oh, come on!" I said. "Who pooped in your Rice Krispies?"

She sighed. "You know about the Petrova line?"

"Sure. Kind of an interesting mystery. My guess is solar radiation. Venus doesn't have a *magnetic* field, but positively charged particles might be drawn there because it's *electrically* neutral—"

"No," she said. "It's something else. We don't know exactly what. But it's something . . . else. But whatever. Let's eat steak."

I snorted. "Come on, Marissa, spill it. What the heck is wrong with you?"

She mulled it over. "Why not? You'll hear it from the president in about twelve hours anyway."

"The president?" I said. "Of the United States?"

She took another gulp of whiskey. "Have you heard of *Amaterasu*? It's a Japanese solar probe."

"Sure," I said. "JAXA has been getting some great data from it. It's really neat, actually. It's in a solar orbit, about halfway between Mercury and Venus. It has twenty different instruments aboard that—"

"Yeah, I know. Whatever," she said. "According to their data, the sun's output is decreasing."

I shrugged. "So? Where are we in the solar cycle?"

She shook her head. "It's not the eleven-year cycle. It's something else. JAXA accounted for the cycle. There's still a downward trend. They say the sun is 0.01 percent less bright than it should be."

"Okay, interesting. But hardly worth three whiskeys before dinner."

She pursed her lips. "That's what I thought. But they're saying that value is increasing. And the *rate* of the increase is increasing. It's some sort of exponential loss that they caught very, very early thanks to their probe's incredibly sensitive instruments."

I leaned back in the booth. "I don't know, Marissa. Spotting an exponential progression that early seems really unlikely. But okay, let's say the JAXA scientists are right. Where's the energy going?"

"The Petrova line."

"Huh?"

"JAXA took a good long look at the Petrova line and they say it's getting brighter at the same rate that the sun is getting dimmer. Somehow or another, whatever it is, the Petrova line is stealing energy from the sun."

She pulled a sheaf of papers from her purse and put them on the table. It looked like a bunch of graphs and charts. She shuffled through them until she found the one she wanted, then pushed it toward me.

The x-axis was labeled "time" and the y-axis was labeled "luminosity loss." The line was exponential, for sure.

"This can't be right," I said.

"It's right," she said. "The sun's output will drop a full percent over the next nine years. In twenty years that figure will be five percent. This is bad. It's really bad."

I stared at the graph. "That would mean an ice age. Like . . . right away. Instant ice age."

"Yeah, at the very least. And crop failures, mass starvation . . . I don't even know what else."

I shook my head. "How can there be a sudden change in the sun? It's a *star*, for cripes' sake. Things just don't happen this fast for stars. Changes take millions of years, not dozens. Come on, you know that."

"No, I don't know that. I used to know that. Now I only know the sun's dying," she said. "I don't know why and I don't know what we could do about it. But I know it's dying."

"How . . ." I furrowed my brow.

She downed the rest of her drink. "President addresses the nation tomorrow morning. I think they're coordinating with other world leaders to all announce at the same time."

The waiter dropped off my Guinness. "Here you go, sir. The steaks should be out shortly."

"I need another whiskey," Marissa said.

"Make it two," I added.

I blink. Another flash of memory.

Was it true? Or is that just a random memory of me talking to someone who got sucked into a bogus doomsday theory?

No. It's real. I'm terrified just thinking about it. And it's not just sudden terror. It's a cozy, comfortable terror with a permanent seat at the table. I've felt it for a long time.

This is real. The sun is dying. And I'm tangled up in it. Not just as a fellow citizen of Earth who will die with everyone else—I'm actively involved. There's a sense of responsibility there.

I still don't remember my own name, but I remember random bits of information about the Petrova problem. They call it the Petrova problem. I just remembered that.

My subconscious has priorities. And it's desperately telling me about this. I think my job is to solve the Petrova problem.

. . . in a small lab, wearing a bedsheet toga, with no idea who I am, and no help other than a mindless computer and two mummified roommates.

My vision blurs. I wipe my eyes. Tears. I can't . . . I can't remember their names. But . . . they were my friends. My comrades.

Only now do I realize I've been facing away from them the whole time. I've done everything I can to keep them out of my line of sight. Scrawling on the wall like a madman with the corpses of people I cared about right behind me.

But now the distraction is over. I turn to look at them.

I sob. It comes without warning. I remember bits and pieces all in a rush. She was funny—always quick with a joke. He was professional and with nerves of steel. I think he was military and he was definitely our leader.

I fall to the floor and put my head in my hands. I can't hold anything back. I cry like a child. We were a lot more than friends. And "team" isn't the right word either. It's stronger than that. It's . . .

It's on the tip of my tongue . . .

Finally, the word slides into my conscious mind. It had to wait until I wasn't looking to sneak in.

Crew. We were a crew. And I'm all that's left.

This is a spacecraft. I know that now. I don't know how it has gravity but it's a spaceship.

Things start to fall into place. We weren't sick. We were in suspended animation.

But these beds aren't magical "freeze chambers" like in the movies. There's no special technology at play here. I think we were in medically induced comas. Feeding tubes, IVs, constant medical care. Everything a body needs. Those arms probably changed sheets, kept us rotated to prevent bedsores, and did all the other things ICU nurses would normally do.

And we were kept fit. Electrodes all over our bodies to stimulate muscle movement. Lots of exercise.

But in the end, comas are dangerous. Extremely dangerous. Only I survived, and my brain is a pile of mush.

I walk over to the woman. I actually feel better, looking at her. Maybe it's a sense of closure, or maybe it's just the calmness that comes after a crying jag.

The mummy has no tubes attached. No monitoring equipment at all. There's a small hole in her leathery wrist. That's where the IV was when she died, I guess. So the hole never healed.

The computer must have removed everything when she died. Waste not, want not, I guess. No point in using resources on dead people. More for the survivors.

More for me, in other words.

I take a deep breath and let it out. I have to be calm. I have to think clearly. I remembered a lot just then—my crew, some aspects of their personalities, that I'm on a spaceship (I'll freak out about that later). The point is I'm getting more memories back, and they're coming sort of when I want them instead of at random intervals. I want to focus on that, but the sadness is just so strong.

"Eat," says the computer.

A panel in the center of the ceiling opens up, and a food tube drops out. One of the robot arms catches it and places it on my bed. The label reads DAY 1—MEAL 2.

I'm not in the mood to eat, but my stomach growls as soon as I see the tube. Whatever my mental state may be, my body has needs.

I open the tube and squirt goop into my mouth.

I have to admit: It's another incredible flavor sensation. I think it's chicken with hints of vegetable. There's no texture, of course—it's basically baby food. And it's a little thicker than my earlier meal. It's all about getting my digestive system used to solid food again.

"Water?" I say between mouthfuls.

The ceiling panel opens again, this time with a metal cylinder. An arm brings it to me. Text on the shiny container reads POTABLE WATER. I unscrew the top and, sure enough, there's water in there.

I take a sip. It's room temperature and tastes flat. It's probably distilled and devoid of minerals. But water's water.

I finish the rest of my meal. I haven't had to use a bathroom yet but I'll need to eventually. I'd rather not go wee on the floor.

"Toilet?" I say.

A wall panel spins around to reveal a metal commode. It's just right there in the wall, like in a prison cell. I take a closer look. It has buttons and stuff on it. I think there's a vacuum pipe in the bowl. And there's no water. I think this might be a zero-g toilet modified for use in gravity. Why do that?

"Okay, uh . . . dismiss toilet."

The wall swivels around again. The toilet is gone.

All right. I'm well fed. I'm feeling a little better about things. Food will do that.

I need to focus on some positives. I'm alive. Whatever killed my friends, it didn't kill me. I'm on a spaceship—I don't know the details, but I know I'm on a ship and it seems to be working correctly.

And my mental state is improving. I'm sure of it.

I sit cross-legged on the floor. It's time for a proactive step. I close my eyes and let my mind wander. I want to remember something—

anything—on purpose. I don't care what. But I want to initiate it. Let's see what I get.

I start with what makes me happy. I like science. I know it. I got a thrill from all the little experiments I've been doing. And I'm in space. So maybe I can think about space and science and see what I get. . . .

I pulled the piping-hot spaghetti TV dinner from the microwave and hustled over to my couch. I peeled the plastic off the top to let the steam escape.

I unmuted the TV and listened to the live feed. Several coworkers and a few friends had invited me to watch this with them, but I didn't want to spend the whole evening answering questions. I just wanted to watch in peace.

It was the most watched event in human history. More than the moon landing. More than any World Cup Final. Every network, streaming service, news website, and local TV affiliate was showing the same thing: NASA's live feed.

A reporter stood with an older man in the gallery of a flight-control room. Beyond them, men and women in blue shirts fixed their attention on their terminals.

"This is Sandra Elias," said the reporter. "I'm here at the Jet Propulsion Laboratory in Pasadena, California. I'm here with Dr. Browne, who is the head of Planetary Sciences for NASA."

She turned to the scientist. "Doctor, what's our status now?"

Browne cleared his throat. "We received confirmation about ninety minutes ago that *ArcLight* successfully inserted into orbit around Venus. Now we're just waiting for that first batch of data."

It had been a heck of a year since the JAXA announcement about the Petrova problem. But study after study confirmed their findings. The clock was ticking and the world needed to find out what was going on. So Project ArcLight was born.

The situation was terrifying, but the project itself was awesome. My inner nerd couldn't help but be excited.

ArcLight was the most expensive unmanned spacecraft ever built. The world needed answers and didn't have time to dillydally. Normally if you asked a space agency to send a probe to Venus in under a year, they'd laugh in your face. But it's amazing what you can do with an unlimited budget. The United States, European Union, Russia, China, India, and Japan all helped cover costs.

"Tell us about going to Venus," the reporter said. "What makes it so hard?"

"The main problem is fuel," said Browne. "There are specific transfer windows when interplanetary travel takes the minimum amount of fuel, but we were nowhere near an Earth-Venus window. So we had to put a lot more fuel in orbit just to get *ArcLight* there in the first place."

"So it's a case of bad timing, then?" the reporter asked.

"I don't think there's ever a good time for the sun to get dimmer."

"Good point. Please go on."

"Venus moves very fast compared to Earth, which means more fuel just to catch up. Even under ideal conditions, it actually takes more fuel to get to Venus than it does to get to Mars."

"Amazing. Amazing. Now, Doctor, some people have asked, 'Why bother with the planet? The Petrova line is huge, spanning an arc from the sun to Venus. Why not somewhere between?'"

"Because the Petrova line is widest there—as wide as the whole planet. And we can use the planet's gravity to help us out. *ArcLight* will actually orbit Venus twelve times while collecting samples of whatever material the Petrova line is made of."

"And what is that material, you think?"

"We have no idea," said Browne. "No idea at all. But we might have answers soon. Once *ArcLight* finishes this first orbit, it should have enough material for its onboard analysis lab."

"And what can we expect to learn tonight?"

"Not much. The onboard lab is pretty basic. Just a high-magnification microscope and an x-ray spectrometer. The real mission here is sample return. It'll be another three months for *ArcLight* to come home with those samples. The lab is a backup to get at least some data in case there's a failure during the return phase."

"Good planning as always, Dr. Browne."

"It's what we do."

A cheer erupted from behind the reporter.

"I'm hearing—" She paused to let the sound die down. "I'm hearing that the first orbit is complete and the data is coming in now. . . ."

The main screen in the control room changed to a black-and-white image. The picture was mostly gray, with black dots scattered here and there.

"What are we looking at, Doctor?" said the reporter's voice.

"This is from the internal microscope," said Browne. "It's magnified ten thousand times. Those black dots are about ten microns across."

"Are those dots what we've been looking for?" she asked.

"We can't be certain," said Browne. "They could just be dust particles. Any major gravity source like a planet will have a cloud of dust surrounding—"

"What the fuck?!" came a voice in the background. Several flight controllers gasped.

The reporter snickered. "High spirits here at JPL. We are coming to you live, so we apologize for any—"

"Oh my God!" said Browne.

On the main screen, more images came through. One after another. All nearly the same.

Nearly.

The reporter looked at the images on-screen. "Are those particles . . . moving?"

The images, playing in succession, showed the black dots deforming and shifting around within their environment.

The reporter cleared her throat and delivered what many would call the understatement of the century: "They look a little like microbes, wouldn't you say?"

"Telemetry!" Dr. Browne called out. "Any shimmy in the probe?"

"Already checked," said someone. "No shimmy."

"Is there a consistent direction of travel?" he asked. "Something that could be explained by an external force? Magnetic, maybe? Static electricity?"

The room fell silent.

"Anyone?!" said Browne.

I dropped my fork right into my spaghetti.

Is this actually alien life? Am I really that lucky?! To be alive when humanity first discovers extraterrestrial life?!

Wow! I mean—the Petrova problem is still terrifying but . . . wow! Aliens! This could be aliens! I couldn't wait to talk about this with the kids tomorrow—

"Angular anomaly," the computer says.

"Darn it!" I say. "I was almost there! I almost remembered myself!"

"Angular anomaly," the computer repeats.

I unfold myself and get to my feet. In my limited interactions with it, the computer seems to have some understanding of what I say. Like Siri or Alexa. So I'll talk to it like I'd talk to one of them.

"Computer, what is an angular anomaly?"

"Angular anomaly: an object or body designated as critical is not at the expected location angle by at least 0.01 radians."

"What body is anomalous?"

"Angular anomaly."

Not much help. I'm on a ship, so it must be a navigational issue. That can't be good. How would I even steer this thing? I don't see anything resembling spaceship controls—not that I really know what those look like. But all I've discovered so far is a "coma room" and a lab.

That other hatch in the lab—the one that leads farther up—that must be important. This is like being in a video game. Explore the area until you find a locked door, then look for the key. But instead of searching bookshelves and garbage cans, I have to search my mind. Because the "key" is my own name.

The computer's not being unreasonable. If I can't remember my own name, I probably shouldn't be allowed into delicate areas of the ship.

I climb onto my bunk and lie on my back. I keep a wary eye on the robot arms above, but they don't move. I guess the computer is satisfied that I'm self-sufficient for now.

I close my eyes and focus on that flash of memory. I can see bits and pieces of it in my mind. Like looking at an old photo that's been damaged.

I'm in my house . . . no . . . apartment. I have an apartment. It's tidy, but small. There's a picture of the San Francisco skyline on one wall. Not useful. I already know I lived in San Francisco.

There's a Lean Cuisine microwave meal on the coffee table in front of me. Spaghetti. The heat still hasn't equalized yet, so there are pockets of nearly frozen noodles next to tongue-melting plasma. But I'm taking bites anyway. I must be hungry.

I'm watching NASA on TV; I see all that stuff from my previous flash of memory. My first thought is . . . I'm elated! Could it be extraterrestrial life? I can't wait to tell the kids!

I have kids? This is a single man's apartment with a single man eating a single man's meal. I don't see anything feminine at all. There's nothing to suggest a woman in my life. Am I divorced? Gay? Either way, there's no sign that children live here. No toys, no pictures of kids on the wall or mantel, nothing. And the place is way too clean. Kids make a mess of everything. Especially when they start chewing gum. They all go through a gum phase—at least, a lot of them do—and they leave it everywhere.

How do I know that?

I like kids. Huh. Just a feeling. But I like them. They're cool. They're fun to hang out with.

So I'm a single man in my thirties, who lives alone in a small apartment, I don't have any kids, but I like kids a lot. I don't like where this is going . . .

A teacher! I'm a schoolteacher! I remember it now!

Oh, thank God. I'm a teacher.

CHAPTER 3

"All right," I said, looking at the clock. "We have one minute until the bell. You know what that means!"

"Lightning round!" yelled my students.

Life had changed surprisingly little since the announcement about the Petrova line.

The situation was dire and deadly, but it was also the norm. Londoners during the Blitz in World War II went about their day as normal, with the understanding that occasionally buildings get blown up. However desperate things were, someone still had to deliver milk. And if Mrs. McCreedy's house got bombed in the night, well, you crossed it off the delivery list.

So it was that with the apocalypse looming—possibly caused by an alien life-form—I stood in front of a bunch of kids and taught them basic science. Because what's the point of even having a world if you're not going to pass it on to the next generation?

The kids sat in neat rows of desks, facing the front. Pretty standard stuff. But the rest of the room was like a mad scientist's lab. I'd spent years perfecting the look. I had a Jacob's ladder in one corner (I kept it unplugged so the kids didn't kill themselves). Along another wall was a bookshelf full of specimen jars of animal parts in formaldehyde. One of the jars was just spaghetti and a boiled egg. The kids speculated on that one a lot.

And gracing the center of the ceiling was my pride and joy—a huge mobile that was a model of the solar system. Jupiter was the size of a basketball, while wee Mercury was as small as a marble.

It had taken me years to cultivate a rep as the "cool" teacher. Kids are smarter than most people think. And they can tell when a teacher actually cares about them as opposed to when they're just going through the motions. Anyway, it was time for the lightning round!

I grabbed a fistful of beanbags off my desk. "What is the actual name of the North Star?"

"Polaris!" said Jeff.

"Correct!" I threw a beanbag to him. Before he even caught it, I fired off the next question. "What are the three basic kinds of rocks?"

"Igneous, sedentary, and metamorphic!" yelled Larry. He was excitable, to say the least.

"So close!" I said.

"Igneous, *sedimentary,* and metamorphic," said Abby with a sneer. Pain in the ass, that one. But smart as a whip.

"Yes!" I threw her a beanbag. "What wave do you feel first during an earthquake?"

"The P-wave," Abby said.

"You again?" I threw her a beanbag. "What's the speed of light?"

"Three times ten to—" Abby began.

"C!" yelled Regina from the back. She rarely spoke up. Good to see her coming out of her shell.

"Sneaky, but correct!" I chucked her a beanbag.

"I was answering first!" Abby complained.

"But she *finished* her answer first," I said. "What's the nearest star to Earth?"

"Alpha Centauri!" Abby said quickly.

"Wrong!" I said.

"No, I'm not!"

"Yes, you are. Anyone else?"

"Oh!" Larry said. "It's the sun!"

"Right!" I said. "Larry gets the beanbag! Careful with your assumptions, Abby."

She folded her arms in a huff.

"Who can tell me the radius of Earth?"

Trang raised his hand. "Three thousand, nine hundre—"

"Trang!" Abby said. "The answer is Trang."

Trang froze in confusion.

"What?" I asked.

Abby preened. "You asked *who could tell you* the radius of Earth. Trang can tell you. I answered correctly."

Outsmarted by a thirteen-year-old. Wasn't the first time. I dropped a beanbag on her desk just as the bell rang.

The kids leapt from their chairs and collected their books and backpacks. Abby, flush with victory, took a little more time than the others.

"Remember to cash in your beanbags at the end of the week for toys and other prizes!" I said to their retreating backs.

Soon, the classroom was empty, and only the echoing sounds of children in the hallway suggested any evidence of life. I collected their homework assignments from my desk and slipped them into my valise. Sixth period was over.

Time to hit the teachers' lounge for a cup of coffee. Maybe I'd correct some papers before I headed home. Anything to avoid the parking lot. A fleet of helicopter moms would be descending on the school to pick up their children. And if one of them saw me, they *always* had some complaint or suggestion. I can't fault someone for loving their kids, and God knows we could do with more parents being engaged in their kids' educations, but there's a limit.

"Ryland Grace?" said a woman's voice.

I looked up with a start. I hadn't heard her come in.

She looked to be in her mid-forties, wearing a well-tailored business suit. She carried a briefcase.

"Uh, yeah," I said. "Can I help you with something?"

"I think you can," she said. She had a slight accent. Something European—I couldn't quite put my finger on it. "My name is Eva Stratt. I'm with the Petrova Taskforce."

"The what?"

"The Petrova Taskforce. It's an international body set up to deal with the Petrova-line situation. I've been tasked with finding a solution. They've given me a certain amount of authority to get things done."

"They? Who's they?"

"Every member nation of the UN."

"Wait, what? How did—"

"Unanimous secret vote. It's complicated. I'd like to talk to you about a scientific paper you wrote."

"Secret vote? Never mind." I shook my head. "My paper-writing days are over. Academia didn't work well for me."

"You're a teacher. You're still in academia."

"Well, yeah," I said. "But I mean, you know, *academia.* With scientists and peer review and—"

"And assholes who get you kicked out of your university?" She raised an eyebrow. "And who got all your funding cut off and ensured you never got published again?"

"Yeah. That."

She pulled a binder out of her briefcase.

She opened it and read the first page. "'An Analysis of Water-Based Assumptions and Recalibration of Expectations for Evolutionary Models.'" She looked up at me. "You wrote this paper, yes?"

"I'm sorry, how did you get—"

"A dull title, but very exciting content, I have to say."

I set my valise on my desk. "Look, I was in a bad place when I wrote that, okay? I'd had enough of the research world and that was sort of a 'kiss-my-butt' goodbye. I'm much happier now as a teacher."

She flipped a few pages. "You spent years combating the assumption that life requires liquid water. You have an entire section here called 'The Goldilocks Zone Is for Idiots.' You call out dozens of eminent scientists by name and berate them for believing a temperature range is a requirement."

"Yeah, but—"

"Your doctorate is in molecular biology, correct? Don't most scientists agree that liquid water is necessary for life to evolve?"

"They're wrong!" I crossed my arms. "There's nothing magical about hydrogen and oxygen! They're required for *Earth* life, sure. But another planet could have completely different conditions. All life needs is a chemical reaction that results in copies of the original catalyst. And you don't need water for that!"

I closed my eyes, took a deep breath, and let it out. "Anyway, I got mad, and I wrote that paper. Then I got a teaching credential, a new career, and started actually enjoying my life. So I'm glad no one believed me. I'm better off."

"I believe you," she said.

"Thanks," I said. "But I have papers to grade. Can you tell me why you're here?"

She put the binder back in her briefcase. "You are aware of the *ArcLight* probe and the Petrova line, I assume."

"I'd be a pretty lame science teacher if I wasn't."

"Do you think those dots are alive?" she asked.

"I don't know—they could just be dust bouncing around in magnetic fields. I guess we'll find out when *ArcLight* gets back to Earth. That's coming up, right? Just a few weeks from now?"

"It returns on the twenty-third," she said. "Roscosmos will recover it from low-Earth orbit with a dedicated Soyuz mission."

I nodded. "Then we'll know soon enough. The most brilliant minds in the world will look at them and find out what they're about. Who's going to do that? Do you know?"

"You," she said. "You're going to do it."

I stared blankly.

She waved her hand in front of my face. "Hello?"

"You want *me* to look at the dots?" I said.

"Yes."

"The whole world put you in charge of solving this problem, and you came directly to a junior high school science teacher?"

"Yes."

I turned and walked out the door. "You're lying, insane, or a combination of the two. I have to get going now."

"This is not optional," she said to my back.

"Seems optional to me!" I waved goodbye.

Yeah. It wasn't optional.

When I got back to my apartment, before I even got to my front door, four well-dressed men surrounded me. They showed me their FBI badges and hustled me into one of three black SUVs parked in the complex parking lot. After a twenty-minute drive where they refused to answer any of my questions or even speak to me at all, they parked and showed me into a generic-looking business-park building.

My feet barely touched the ground as they led me down an empty hallway with unmarked doors every 30 feet or so. Finally, they opened a set of double doors at the end of the hall and gently nudged me inside.

Unlike the rest of the abandoned building, this room was full of furniture and shiny, high-tech devices. It was the most well-stocked biology lab I'd ever seen. And right in the middle of it all was Eva Stratt.

"Hello, Dr. Grace," she said. "This is your new lab."

The FBI agents closed the doors behind me, leaving Stratt and me alone in the lab. I rubbed my shoulder where they had manhandled me a little too hard.

I looked at the door behind me. "So . . . when you say 'a certain amount of authority' . . . "

"I have all of the authority."

"You have an accent. Are you even from America?"

"I'm Dutch. I was an administrator at ESA. But that doesn't matter. Now I'm in charge of this. There is no *time* for slow, international committees. The sun is dying. We need a solution. It's my job to find it."

She pulled up a lab stool and sat down. "These 'dots' are probably a life-form. The exponential progression of solar dimming is consistent with the exponential population growth of a typical life-form."

"You think they're . . . *eating* the sun?"

"They're eating its energy output at least," she said.

"Okay, that's—well, terrifying. But regardless: What the heck do you want from me?"

"The *ArcLight* probe is bringing the samples back to Earth. Some of them might still be alive. I want you to examine them and find out what you can."

"Yeah, you mentioned that earlier," I said. "But I have to believe there are more qualified people to do this than just me."

"Scientists all over the world will be looking at them, but I want you to be the first."

"Why?"

"It lives on or near the surface of the sun. Does that sound like a water-based life-form to you?"

She was right. Water simply can't exist at those temperatures. After about 3,000 degrees Celsius, the hydrogen and oxygen atoms can't stay bound to each other anymore. The surface of the sun was 5,500 degrees Celsius.

She continued. "The field of speculative extraterrestrial biology is small—only five hundred or so people in the world. And everyone I talk to—from Oxford professors to Tokyo University researchers—seems to agree that you could have led it if you hadn't suddenly left."

"Gosh," I said. "I didn't leave on good terms. I'm surprised they said such nice stuff about me."

"Everyone understands the gravity of the situation. There's no time for old grudges. But for what it's worth, you'll be able to show everyone you were right. You don't need water for life. Surely that must be something you want."

"Sure," I said. "I mean . . . yeah. But not like this."

She hopped off her stool and headed to the door. "It is what it is. Be here on the twenty-third at seven P.M. I'll have the sample for you."

"Wha—" I said. "It'll be in Russia, won't it?"

"I told Roscosmos to land their Soyuz in Saskatchewan. The Royal Canadian Air Force will recover the sample and bring it directly here to San Francisco via fighter jet. The U.S. will allow the Canadians use of the airspace."

"Saskatchewan?"

"Soyuz capsules are launched from Baikonur Cosmodrome, which is at a high latitude. The safest landing locations are at that same latitude. Saskatchewan is the closest large, flat area to San Francisco that meets all the requirements."

I held up my hand. "Wait. The Russians, Canadians, and Americans all just do whatever you tell them?"

"Yes. Without question."

"Are you *joshing* me with all this?!"

"Get accommodated with your new lab, Dr. Grace. I have other things to deal with."

She walked out the door without another word.

"Yes!" I pump my fist.

I jump to my feet and climb the ladder to the lab. Once there, I climb that ladder and grab hold of the Mystery Hatch.

Just like last time, as soon as I touch the handle, the computer says, "To unlock hatch, state your name."

"Ryland Grace," I say with a smug smile. "*Dr.* Ryland Grace."

A small click from the hatch is the only response I get. After all the meditation and introspection I did to find out my own name, I wish there'd been something more exciting. Confetti, maybe.

I grab the handle and twist. It turns. My domain is about to grow by at least one new room. I push the hatch upward. Unlike the connector between the bedroom and the lab, this hatch slides to the side. This next room is pretty small, so I guess there wasn't room for the hatch to swing in. And that next room is . . . um . . . ?

LED lights flick on. The room is round, like the other two, but it's not a cylinder. The walls taper inward toward the ceiling. It's a truncated cone.

I've spent the last few days without much information to go on. Now information assaults me from every direction. Every surface is covered with computer monitors and touchscreens. The sheer number of blinking lights and colors is staggering. Some screens have rows of numbers, others have diagrams, and others just look black.

On the edge of the conical walls is another hatch. This one is less mysterious, though. It has the word AIRLOCK stenciled across the top, and the hatch itself has a round window in it. Through the window I can see a tiny chamber—just big enough for one person—with a spacesuit inside. The far wall has another hatch. Yup. That's an airlock.

And in the center of everything is a chair. It's perfectly positioned to be able to reach all screens and touch panels easily.

I climb the rest of the way into the room and settle into the chair. It's comfortable, kind of a bucket seat.

"Pilot detected," the computer says. "Angular anomaly."

Pilot. Okay.

"Where is the anomaly?" I ask.

"Angular anomaly."

HAL 9000 this computer is not. I look around at the many screens for a clue. The chair swivels easily, which is nice in this 360-degree computer pit. I spot one screen with a blinking red border. I lean in to get a better look.

ANGULAR ANOMALY: RELATIVE MOTION ERROR

PREDICTED VELOCITY: 11,423 KPS

MEASURED VELOCITY: 11,872 KPS

STATUS: AUTO-CORRECTING TRAJECTORY. NO ACTION REQUIRED.

Well. That means nothing to me. Except "kps." That might mean "kilometers per second."

Above the text is a picture of the sun. It's jiggling around slightly.

Maybe it's a video? Like a live feed? Or is that just my imagination? On a hunch, I touch the screen with two fingers and drag them apart.

Sure enough, the image zooms in. Just like using a smartphone. There are a couple of sunspots on the left side of the image. I zoom in on those until they fill the screen. The image remains amazingly clear. It's either an extremely high-resolution photo or an extremely high-resolution solar telescope.

I estimate the cluster of sunspots is about 1 percent the width of the disc. Pretty normal for sunspots. That means I'm now looking at half a degree of the sun's circumference (very rough math here). The sun rotates about once per twenty-five days (science teachers know this sort of thing). So it should take an hour for the spots to move off the screen. I'll check back later and see if they have. If so, it's a live image. If not, it's a picture.

Hmm . . . 11,872 kilometers per second.

Velocity is relative. It doesn't make any sense unless you are comparing two objects. A car on the freeway might be going 70 miles per hour compared to the *ground*, but compared to the car next to it, it's moving almost 0. So what is that "measured velocity" measuring the velocity of? I think I know.

I'm in a spaceship, right? I have to be. So that value is probably my velocity. But compared to what? Judging by the big ol' picture of the sun over the text, I'm guessing it's the sun. So I'm going 11,872 kilometers per second with respect to the sun.

I catch a flicker from the text below. Did something change?

ANGULAR ANOMALY: RELATIVE MOTION ERROR

PREDICTED VELOCITY: 11,422 KPS

MEASURED VELOCITY: 11,871 KPS

STATUS: AUTO-CORRECTING TRAJECTORY. NO ACTION REQUIRED.

Those numbers are different! They both went down by one. Oh wow. Hang on. I pull the stopwatch from my toga (the best ancient Greek philosophers always carried stopwatches in their togas). Then

I stare at the screen for what seems like an eternity. Just before I'm about to give up, the numbers both drop by one again. I start the timer.

This time, I'm ready for how long the wait will be. Again, it seems interminable, but I stand firm. Finally, the numbers both drop again and I stop the timer.

Sixty-six seconds.

"Measured velocity" is going down by one every sixty-six seconds. Some quick math tells me that's an acceleration of . . . 15 meters per second per second. That's the same "gravity" acceleration I worked out earlier.

The force I'm feeling isn't gravity. And it's not a centrifuge. I'm in a spaceship that is constantly accelerating in a line. Well, actually it's decelerating—the values are going down.

And that velocity . . . it's a lot of velocity. Yes, it's going down, but wow! To reach Earth orbit you only need to go 8 kps. I'm going over 11,000. That's faster than anything in the solar system. Anything that fast will escape the sun's gravity and go flying off into interstellar space.

The readout doesn't have anything to indicate what direction I'm going. Just a relative velocity. So now my question is: Am I barreling *toward* the sun, or *away* from it?

It's almost academic. I'm either on a collision course with the sun or on my way out to deep space with no hope of returning. Or, I might be headed in the sun's general direction, but not on a collision course. If that's the case, I'll miss the sun . . . and *then* fly off into deep space with no hope of returning.

Well, if the image of the sun is real-time, then the sunspot will get larger or smaller on-screen as I travel. So I just have to wait until I know if it's real-time. That'll take about an hour. I start the stopwatch.

I acquaint myself with the million other screens in the little room. Most of them have something to say, but one of them just shows an image of a circular crest. I think it's probably an idle screen or something. If I touch it, that computer will wake up. But that idle screen might be the most informative thing in here.

It's a mission crest. I've seen enough NASA documentaries to know one when I see one. The circular crest has an outer ring of blue with white text. The text reads HAIL MARY across the top and EARTH across the bottom. The name and "port of call" for this vessel.

I didn't think the ship came from somewhere *other* than Earth, but okay. Anyway, I guess I finally know the name of this ship I'm on.

I'm aboard the *Hail Mary*.

Not sure what to do with that information.

But that's not all the crest has to tell me. Inside the blue band, there's a black circle with weird symbols inside: a yellow circle with a dot in the middle, a blue circle with a white cross, and a smaller yellow circle with a lowercase *t*. No idea what any of that is supposed to mean. Around the edge of the black area it says: "姚," "ИЛЮХИНА," and "GRACE."

The crew.

I'm "Grace," so those other two must be the names of the mummies in the bunks downstairs. A Chinese person and a Russian person. The memory of them is almost at the surface, but I can't quite pull it up. I think some internal defense mechanism is suppressing it. When I remember them, it's going to hurt, so my brain refuses to remember them. Maybe. I don't know—I'm a science teacher, not a trauma psychologist.

I wipe my eyes clear. Maybe I won't push too hard for that memory just yet.

I have an hour to kill. I let my mind wander to see what else I can remember. It's getting easier and easier.

"I'm not one hundred percent comfortable with all this," I said. My voice was muffled by the full hazmat suit I wore. My breath fogged up the clear vinyl face-window thingy.

"You'll be fine," said Stratt's voice over the intercom. She watched from the other side of double-paned, very thick glass.

They'd made a few upgrades to the lab. Oh, the equipment was all the same, but now the entire room was air-sealed. The walls were lined with thick plastic sheets, all held together with some kind of special tape. I saw CDC logos everywhere. Quarantine protocols. Not at all comforting.

The only entry now was through a big plastic airlock. And they made me put on the hazmat suit before going in. An air line led to my suit from a spool in the ceiling.

All the top-of-the-line equipment was ready for whatever I wanted to do. I'd never seen a lab so well stocked. And in the middle was a wheeled cart holding a cylindrical container. Stenciled writing on the cylinder read образец. Not deeply useful.

Stratt wasn't alone in the observation room. About twenty people in military uniforms stood with her, all looking on with interest. There were definitely some Americans, some Russians, a few Chinese officers, plus many more unique uniforms I didn't even recognize. A large international group. None of them said a word, and by some silent agreement, they all stayed a few feet behind Stratt.

I grabbed the air hose with my gloved hand and gestured to Stratt with it. "Is this really necessary?"

She pressed the intercom button. "There's a very good chance the sample in that cylinder is an alien life-form. We're not taking any chances."

"Wait . . . *you're* not taking any chances. But I am!"

"It's not like that."

"How is it not like that?"

She paused. "Okay, it's exactly like that."

I walked to the cylinder. "Did everyone else have to go through all this?"

She looked at the military people and they shrugged at her. "What do you mean by 'everyone else'?"

"You know," I said. "The people who transferred it to this container."

"That's the sample container from the capsule. It's three centimeters of lead surrounding a shell of centimeter-thick steel. It's been sealed since it left Venus. It has fourteen latches you'll need to open to get to the sample itself."

I looked at the cylinder, back to her, back to the cylinder, and back to her. "This is some bull-puckey."

"Look at the bright side," she said. "You'll be forever known as the man who made first contact with extraterrestrial life."

"If it even is life," I mumbled.

I got the fourteen latches open with some effort. Those things were tight. I vaguely wondered about how the *ArcLight* probe closed them in the first place. Must have been some kind of cool actuated system.

The inside wasn't impressive. I didn't expect it to be. Just a small, clear, plastic ball that appeared to be empty. The mysterious dots were microscopic and there weren't very many of them.

"No radiation detected," Stratt said through the intercom.

I shot a glance over at her. She watched her tablet intensely.

I took a good long look at the ball. "Is this under vacuum?"

"No," she said. "It's full of argon gas at one atmosphere of pressure. The dots have been moving around the whole time the probe was returning from Venus. So it looks like the argon doesn't affect them."

I looked all around the lab. "There's no glove box here. I can't just expose unknown samples to normal air."

"The entire room is full of argon," she said. "Make sure you don't kink your air line or rip your suit. If you breathe argon—"

"I'll suffocate and won't even know it's happening. Yeah, okay."

I took the ball to a tray and carefully twisted it until it came apart in two halves. I placed one half in a sealed plastic container and mopped the other half with a dry cotton swab. I scraped the swab against a slide and took it to a microscope.

I thought they'd be harder to find, but there they were. Dozens of little black dots. And they were indeed wriggling around.

"You recording all this?"

"From thirty-six different angles," she said.

"Sample consists of many round objects," I said. "Almost no variance in size—each appears to be approximately ten microns in diameter . . ."

I adjusted the focus and tried various intensities of backlighting. "Samples are opaque . . . I can't see inside, even at the highest available light setting. . . ."

"Are they alive?" Stratt asked.

I glared at her. "I can't just tell that at a glance. What do you expect to happen here?"

"I want you to find out if they're alive. And if so, find out how they work."

"That's a tall order."

"Why? Biologists worked out how bacteria works. Just do the same thing they did."

"That took thousands of scientists two centuries to work out!"

"Well . . . do it faster than that."

"Tell you what"—I pointed back to the microscope—"I'm going to get back to work now. I'll tell you anything I work out when I work it out. Until then, you can all enjoy some quiet study time."

I spent the next six hours doing incremental tests. Over that time, the military people wandered out, eventually leaving only Stratt by herself. I had to admire her patience. She sat in the back of the observation room and worked on her tablet, sometimes looking up to see what I was doing.

She perked up as I cycled my way through the airlock and into the observation room. "Got something?" she asked.

I unzipped the suit and stepped out of it. "Yeah, a full bladder."

She typed on her tablet. "I hadn't accounted for that. I'll get a bathroom installed inside the quarantine area tonight. It'll have to be a chemical toilet. We can't have plumbing going in and out."

"Fine, whatever," I said. I hustled off to the facilities to do my business.

When I returned, Stratt had pulled a small table and two chairs to the center of the observation room. She sat in one of the chairs and gestured to the other. "Have a seat."

"I'm in the middle of—"

"Have a seat."

I took a seat. She had a commanding presence, that's for sure. Something about her tone of voice or her general confidence level, maybe? One way or another, when she spoke you just kind of assumed you should do what she said.

"What have you found so far?" she asked.

"It's only been one afternoon," I said.

"I didn't ask how long it's been. I asked what you've found out so far."

I scratched my head. After hours in that suit, I was sweaty and presumably smelled bad. "It's . . . weird. I don't know what those dots are made of. And I'd really like to know."

"Is there some equipment you need that you don't have?" she asked.

"No, no. There's everything a guy could hope for in there. It just . . . doesn't work on these dots." I settled back into the chair. I'd been on my feet most of the day and it was nice to relax for a moment. "First thing I tried was the x-ray spectrometer. It sends x-rays into a sample, making it emit photons and you can tell from the wavelengths of the photons what elements are present."

"And what did that tell you?"

"Nothing. As far as I can tell, these dots just absorb x-rays. The x-rays go in and they never come out. Nothing comes out. That's very odd. I can't think of anything that does that."

"Okay." She took some notes on her tablet. "What else can you tell me?"

"Next I tried gas chromatography. That's where you vaporize the sample and then identify the elements or compounds in the resulting gas. That didn't work either."

"Why not?"

I threw up my hands. "Because the darn things just won't vaporize. That led me down a rabbit hole of burners, ovens, and crucible furnaces that turned up nothing. The dots are unaffected at temperatures up to two thousand degrees Celsius. Nothing."

"And that's odd?"

"It's crazy odd," I said. "But these things live on the sun. At least some of the time. So I guess having a high resistance to heat makes sense."

"They *live* on the sun?" she said. "So they're a life-form?"

"I'm pretty sure they are, yeah."

"Elaborate."

"Well, they move around. It's plainly visible through the microscope. That alone doesn't prove they're alive—inert stuff moves all the time from static charge or magnetic fields or whatever. But there is something else I noticed. Something weird. And it made the pieces fall into place."

"Okay."

"I put a few dots under a vacuum and ran a spectrograph. Just a simple test to see if they emit light. And they do, of course. They give off infrared light at the 25.984 micron wavelength. That's the Petrova frequency—the light that makes the Petrova line. I expected that. But then I noticed they only emit light when they're moving. And boy, do they emit a lot of it. I mean, not a lot from our point of view, but for a tiny single-celled organism it's a ton."

"And how is that relevant?"

"I did some back-of-the napkin math. And I'm pretty sure that light is how they move around."

Stratt raised an eyebrow. "I don't follow."

"Believe it or not, light has momentum," I said. "It exerts a force. If you were out in space and you turned on a flashlight, you'd get a teeny, tiny amount of thrust from it."

"I didn't know that."

"Now you do. And a teeny-tiny thrust on a teeny-tiny mass can be an effective form of propulsion. I measured the dots' average mass at about twenty picograms. That took a long time, by the way, but that lab equipment is awesome. Anyway, the movement I see is consistent with the momentum of the emitted light."

She set her tablet down. I had, apparently, accomplished the rare feat of getting her undivided attention. "Is that something that happens in nature?"

I shook my head. "No way. Nothing in nature has that kind of energy storage. You don't understand how much energy these dots are emitting. It's like . . . getting to the scales of mass conversion. $E = mc^2$ kind of stuff. These tiny dots have more energy stored up in them than remotely makes sense."

"Well," she said. "They did just come from the sun. And the sun is losing energy."

"Yeah. That's why I think it's a life-form," I said. "It consumes energy, stores it in some way we don't understand, then uses it for propulsion. That's not a simple physical or chemical process. That's complex and directed. Something that must have evolved."

"So the Petrova line is . . . tiny little rocket flares?"

"Probably. And I bet we're only seeing a small percentage of the total light coming off that area. They use it to propel themselves to Venus or to the sun. Or both. I don't know. Point is, the light will go away from their direction of travel. Earth isn't in that line, so we only see the light that reflects off nearby space dust."

"Why do they go to Venus?" she asked. "And how do they reproduce?"

"Good questions. Ones I don't have answers for. But if they're single-celled stimulus/response organisms, they probably reproduce through mitosis." I paused. "That's when the cell splits in half to become two new cells—"

"Yes, I know that much, thank you." She looked to the ceiling. "People always assumed our first contact with alien life—if any existed—would be little green men in UFOs. We never considered the idea of a simple, unintelligent species."

"Yeah," I said. "This isn't Vulcans dropping by to say hi. This is . . . space algae."

"An invasive species. Like cane toads in Australia."

"Good analogy." I nodded. "And the population is growing. Fast. The more of them there are, the more solar energy gets consumed."

She pinched her chin. "What would you call an organism that exists on a diet of stars?"

I struggled to remember my Greek and Latin root words. "I think you'd call it 'Astrophage.'"

"Astrophage," she said. She typed it into her tablet. "Okay. Get back to work. Find out how they breed."

Astrophage!

The word alone makes all my muscles clinch up. A chilling terror that hits like a lead weight.

That's the name. The thing that threatens all life on Earth. Astrophage.

I glance at the monitor with my zoomed-in image of the sun. The sunspots have moved noticeably. Okay, it's a real-time image. Good to know.

Waaaaait . . . I don't think they're moving at the right speed. I check the stopwatch. I was only daydreaming for ten minutes or so. The sunspots should have moved a fraction of a degree. But they're halfway off the screen. Way more than they should have moved.

I pull the tape measure from my toga. I zoom out the image and actually measure the widths of the sun and sunspot cluster on the screen. No more rough estimates. I want real math here.

The solar disc is 27 centimeters on-screen and the sunspots are 3 millimeters. And they moved half their width (1.5 millimeters) in ten minutes. Actually, it was 517 seconds, according to my stopwatch. I scribble some math on my arm.

At this resolution, they're moving 1 millimeter every 344.66 seconds. To cross the entire 27 centimeters it would take (scribble, scribble) just over 93,000 seconds. So it'll take that long for the cluster to cross the near side of the sun. It'll take twice that long to get all the way around. So 186,000 seconds. That's a little over two days.

Over ten times faster than the rotation should be.

This star I'm looking at . . . it's not the sun.

I'm in a different solar system.

CHAPTER 4

Okay.

I think it's time I took a *long gosh-darned look* at these screens!

How am I in another solar system?! That doesn't even make sense! What star is that, anyway?! Oh my God, I am so going to die!

I hyperventilate for a while.

I remember what I tell my students: If you're upset, take a deep breath, let it out, and count to ten. It dramatically reduced the number of tantrums in my classroom.

I take a breath. "One . . . two . . . thr—this isn't working! I'm going to die!"

I hold my head in my hands. "Oh God. Where the heck am I?"

I scour the monitors for anything I can make sense of. There's no lack of information—there's too much. Each screen has a handy label on the top. "Life Support," "Airlock Status," "Engines," "Robotics," "Astrophage," "Generators," "Centrifuge"—wait a minute. Astrophage?

I check the Astrophage panel closely.

REMAINING: 20,906 KG

CONSUMPTION RATE: 6.045 G/S

Far more interesting than those numbers is the diagram below them. It shows what I assume is the *Hail Mary*. My first real overview of what this ship looks like.

The top of the ship is a cylinder with a nose cone at the front. That's a rocket shape if ever I saw one. Judging by the tapered, conical walls of the control room, this must be the very front of the ship. Beneath me is the lab. On the diagram that room is labeled "Lab." Below that is the room I woke up in.

The one with my dead friends.

I sniffle and wipe away a tear. No time for that right now. I put it out of my head and keep looking at the diagram. That room is named "Dormitory." Okay, so this whole diagram lines up with my experiences. And it's nice to know the official names of things. Underneath the dormitory is a much shorter room, maybe about 1 meter high, named "Storage." Aha! There must be a panel in the floor that I missed. I make a mental note to check that out later.

But there's more. A lot more. Under the storage area, there's an area labeled "Cable Faring." No idea what that is or why it exists. Beneath that, the ship fans out and there appear to be three cylinders the same width as my little area. They're all side by side. My guess is they assembled this ship in space and the largest diameter they could launch was about 4 meters.

The trio of cylinders—I'd estimate they're 75 percent of the total ship's volume—are labeled "Fuel."

The fuel area is broken up into nine subcylinders. I tap one of them out of curiosity, and it brings up a screen for that one fuel bay. It says ASTROPHAGE: 0.000 KG. It also has a button labeled "Jettison."

Well, I'm not sure why I'm here or what these things are all about, but I definitely don't want to hit any button labeled Jettison.

It's probably not as dramatic as it seems. These are fuel tanks. If the fuel has been spent, the ship can ditch the tank to reduce its mass and make the remaining fuel last longer. It's the same reason rockets lifting off from Earth have multiple stages.

Interesting that the ship didn't automatically eject them as they became empty. I dismiss the window and return to the main ship map.

Under each of those large fuel zones is a trapezoidal area labeled "Spin Drive." I've never heard that term before, but since it's in the back of the ship and has the word "drive" in its name, I assume it's the propulsion system.

Spin drive . . . spin drive . . . I close my eyes and try to think about it. . . .

Nothing happens. I can't call up memories at will. I'm not quite there yet.

I peer at the diagram more closely. Why is there 20,000 kilograms of Astrophage on this ship? I've got a strong suspicion. It's the fuel.

And why not? Astrophage can propel itself with light and has absurd energy-storage capability. It's had God-knows-how-many billion years of evolution to get good at it. Just like a horse is more energy efficient than a truck, Astrophage is more energy efficient than a spaceship.

Okay, that explains why there's a buttload of Astrophage on the ship. It's fuel. But why put a diagram of the ship on this screen? That's like putting a blueprint of a car on its gas gauge.

Interestingly, the diagram doesn't really care about the rooms. It doesn't even show what's inside them—just a label for each one and that's it. However, the diagram is *very* focused on the hull and the rear part of the ship.

I see red pipes leading from the fuel areas to the spin drives. Probably how fuel gets to the engines. But I also see the pipes all along the hull of the ship. And they cut across the Cable Faring area. So the Astrophage fuel is mostly in the fuel tank, but also kept in a shell all around the hull.

Why do that?

Oh, and there are temperature readings all over the place. I guess temperature is important because the readings are every few meters along the hull. And every single one of them reads 96.415°C.

Hey, I know that temperature. I know that exact temperature! What do I know it from? Come on, brain . . . *come on* . . .

96.415°C, read the display.

"Huh," I said.

"What is it?" Stratt said immediately.

It was my second day in the lab. Stratt still insisted I be the only person to look at Astrophage—at least for the time being. She dropped her tablet on the table and came to the observation-room window. "Something new?"

"Kind of. The ambient temperature of an Astrophage is 96.415 degrees Celsius."

"That's pretty hot, isn't it?"

"Yeah, almost the boiling point of water," I said. "For anything living on Earth it would be deadly. But for a thing that's comfortable near the sun, who knows?"

"So what's significant about it?"

"I can't get them hotter or colder." I pointed to the experiment I'd set up in the fume hood. "I put some Astrophage in ice-cold water for an hour. When I pulled them out, they were 96.415 degrees Celsius. Then I put some in a lab furnace at one thousand degrees. Again, after I pulled them out: 96.415 degrees."

Stratt paced next to the window. "Maybe they have extremely good insulation?"

"I thought of that, so I did another experiment. I took an extremely small droplet of water and put a few Astrophage in it. After a few hours, the whole droplet was 96.415 degrees. The Astrophage heated up the water, so that means heat energy can move out of it."

"What conclusion can you draw?" she asked.

I tried to scratch my head, but the vinyl suit got in the way. "Well, we know they have a huge amount of energy stored inside. I'm guessing they use it to maintain body temperature. Same way you and I do."

"A warm-blooded microorganism?" she said.

I shrugged. "Looks that way. Hey, how much longer am I going to be the only person working on this?"

"Until you stop discovering new stuff."

"One guy alone in a lab? That's not how science works," I said. "There should be hundreds of people all over the world working on this."

"You're not alone in that thought," she said. "I've had three different heads of state call me today."

"Then let other scientists in on it!"

"No."

"Why not?"

She looked away for a moment, then back through the window at me. "Astrophage is an alien microbe. What if it can infect humans? What if it's deadly? What if hazmat suits and neoprene gloves aren't enough protection?"

I gasped. "Wait a minute! Am I a guinea pig? I'm a guinea pig!"

"No, it's not like that," she said.

I stared at her.

She stared at me.

I stared at her.

"Okay, it's exactly like that," she said.

"Dang it!" I said. "That's just not cool!"

"Don't be dramatic," she said. "I'm just playing it safe. Imagine what would happen if I sent Astrophage to the most brilliant minds on the planet and it killed them all. In an instant we'd lose the very people we need the most right now. I can't risk it."

I scowled. "This isn't some cheesy movie, Stratt. Pathogens evolve slowly over time to attack specific hosts. Astrophage has never even been on Earth before. There's just no way it can 'infect' humans. Besides, it's been a couple of days and I'm not dead. So send it out to the real scientists."

"You *are* a real scientist. And you're making progress as fast as anyone else would. There's no point in me risking other lives while you're getting it done on your own."

"Are you kidding?" I said. "With a couple hundred minds working on this, we'd make a lot more progress on—"

"Also, most deadly diseases have a minimum of least three days of incubation time."

"Ah, there it is."

She walked back to her table and picked up her tablet. "The rest of the world will have their turn in time. But for now it's just you. At least tell me what the hell those things are made of. Then we can talk about giving it to other scientists."

She resumed reading her tablet. The conversation was over. And she'd ended it by laying down what my students would call a "sick burn." Despite my best efforts, I still had no idea what the heck Astrophage was made of.

They were opaque to every wavelength of light I threw at them. Visible, infrared, ultraviolet, x-ray, microwaves . . . I even put a few Astrophage in a radiation-containment vessel and exposed it to the gamma rays emitted by Cesium-137 (this lab has *everything*). I called it the "Bruce Banner Test." Felt good about that name. Anyway, even gamma couldn't penetrate the little bastards. Which is like shooting a .50-caliber round at a sheet of paper and having it bounce off. It just doesn't make any sense.

I sulked back to the microscope. The little dots hung out on the slide where they'd been for hours. This was my control set. The ones I hadn't battered with various light sources. "Maybe I'm overthinking this . . ." I muttered.

I poked around the lab supplies until I found what I needed: nanosyringes. They were rare and expensive, but the lab had them. Basically, they were teeny, tiny needles. Small enough and sharp enough to be used for poking microorganisms. You could pull mitochondria out of a living cell with one of those babies.

Back to the microscope. "Okay, you little reprobates. You're radiation-proof, I'll grant you that. But how about I stab you in the face?"

Normally a nanosyringe would be controlled by finely tuned equipment. But I just wanted some stabby time and didn't care about the tool's integrity. I grabbed the collet (where it would normally mount to the control machinery) and brought the needle into view in the microscope. They're called nanosyringes, but they're actually about 50 nanometers wide. Still, the needle was tiny compared to the hulking 10-micron Astrophage—only about one two-thousandth the width.

I poked an Astrophage with the needle and what happened next was nothing I could have expected.

First off, the needle penetrated. No doubt on that front. For all its resistance to light and heat, apparently, Astrophage was no better at dealing with sharp things than any other cell.

The instant I poked a hole in it, the whole cell became translucent. No longer a featureless black dot, but a cell with organelles and everything else a microbiologist like me wants to see. Just like that. It was like flicking a switch.

And then it died. The ruptured cell wall simply gave up the ghost and completely unraveled. The Astrophage went from being a cohesive roundish object to a slowly widening puddle with no outer boundary. I grabbed a normal needle from a nearby shelf and sucked up the goop.

"Yes!" I said. "I killed one!"

"Good for you," Stratt said without looking up from her tablet. "First human to kill an alien. Just like Arnold Schwarzenegger in *Predator.*"

"Okay, I know you're trying to be funny, but that Predator died by deliberately setting off a bomb. The first human to actually kill a Predator was Michael Harrigan—played by Danny Glover—in *Predator 2.*"

She stared at me through the window for a moment, then shook her head and rolled her eyes.

"Point is, I can finally find out what Astrophage is made of!"

"Really?" She set the tablet down. "Killing it did the trick?"

"I think so. It's not black anymore. Light is getting through. Whatever weird effect was blocking it isn't anymore."

"How did you do it? What killed it?"

"I penetrated the outer cell membrane with a nanosyringe."

"You poked it with a stick?"

"No!" I said. "Well. Yes. But it was a scientific poke with a very scientific stick."

"It took you two days to think of poking it with a stick."

"You . . . be quiet."

I took the needle to the spectroscope and ejected the Astrophage goop onto the platform. Then I sealed the chamber and fired up the analysis. I bounced from one foot to the other like a little kid while I waited for the results.

Stratt craned her neck to watch me. "So what's this you're doing now?"

"It's the atomic-emission spectroscope," I said. "I told you about it earlier—it sends x-rays into a sample to excite the atoms, then watches the wavelengths that come back. Didn't work at all when I tried it on the live Astrophage, but now that the magic light-stopping properties are gone, things should work like normal."

The machine beeped.

"All right! Here we go! Time to find out what chemicals are in a life-form that doesn't use water!" I read the LCD screen. It showed all the peaks and the elements they represented. I stared at the screen silently.

"Well?" Stratt said. "Well?!"

"Um. There's carbon and nitrogen . . . but the vast majority of the sample is hydrogen and oxygen." I sighed and plopped down in the chair next to the machine. "The ratio of hydrogen to oxygen is two to one."

"What's wrong?" she asked. "What does that mean?"

"It's water. Astrophage is mostly water."

Her mouth fell open. "How? How can something that exists on the surface of the sun have water?"

I shrugged. "Probably because it maintains its internal temperature at 96.415 degrees Celsius no matter what's going on outside."

"What does this all mean?" she asked.

I put my head in my hands. "It means every scientific paper I ever wrote is wrong."

Well. That's a kick in the pants.

But I wasn't happy in that lab anyway. And they must have brought in smarter people than me, because here I am: at another star in a ship powered by Astrophage.

So why am I the one out here? All I did was prove that my lifelong belief was wrong.

I guess I'll remember that part later. For now, I want to know what star that is. And why we built a ship to bring people here.

All important things, to be sure. But right now, there's a whole area of the ship that I haven't explored yet.

Storage.

Maybe I can find something other than a makeshift toga to wear.

I climb down the ladder to the lab, and then farther downward into the dormitory.

My friends are still there. Still dead. I try not to look at them.

I scan the floor for any hint of an access panel. Nothing. So I get down on my hands and knees and crawl around. Finally, I spot it—a very thin seam marking a square directly under my male crewmate's bunk. I can't even wedge my fingernail into the seam it's so thin.

There were all manner of tools in the lab. I'm sure there's a flathead screwdriver I could use to pry this open. Or . . .

"Hey computer! Open this access panel."

"Specify aperture to open."

I point to the panel. "This. This thing. Open it."

"Specify aperture to open."

"Uh . . . open aperture to supply room."

"Unsealing supply room," says the computer.

There's a click and the panel raises a couple of inches. A rubber gasket around the seam gets torn apart in the process. I couldn't see it when the panel was closed, things were that tight. I'm glad I didn't try to pry it open. It would have been a pain in the butt.

I pull the remnants of the seal off the panel and the panel becomes loose in the opening. I jiggle it a bit before figuring out I have to rotate it. Once I rotate it 90 degrees it detaches and I set it aside. I poke my head into the room below and see a bunch of soft-sided white cubes. I guess that makes sense. Packing stuff in soft containers lets you cram more things into the room.

Just as the diagram in the control room said, the storage area is about a meter high. And completely full of those soft containers. I would have to remove a bunch just to get in there—if I wanted to get in there. I guess I'll have to eventually. It looks a bit claustrophobic, to be honest. Like the crawlspace under a house.

I grab the nearest package and pull it up through the opening.

The package is held together by Velcro straps. I pull them apart and the container unfolds like a Chinese takeout box. Inside are a bunch of uniforms.

Jackpot! Though not really a coincidence. Whoever packed this probably did it with careful planning. And they knew the crew would want uniforms as soon as they woke up. So they're in the first bag. There are at least a dozen uniforms in the package. They're each in vacuum-sealed plastic bags. I open one at random.

It's a light-blue, one-piece jumpsuit. Astronaut clothes. The fabric is thin but feels comfortable. On the left shoulder is the *Hail Mary* mission patch. Same design I saw in the control room. Beneath that is the Chinese flag. The right shoulder has a white patch with a blue chevron triangle surrounded by a wreath design and the letters "CNSA." I recognize it immediately, nerd that I am. It's the Chinese National Space Agency logo.

There's a name tag over the left breast pocket. It reads 姚—the same character I saw in the *Hail Mary* mission crest. It's pronounced Yáo.

How do I know—? Of course I know. Commander Yáo. He was

our leader. I can see his face now. Young and striking, eyes full of determination. He understood the severity of the mission and the weight on his shoulders. He was ready for the task. He was stern but reasonable. And you knew—you just knew—he would give up his life in a second for the mission or his crew.

I pull out another uniform. Much smaller than the commander's. The mission patch is the same, but there's a Russian flag beneath it. And the right shoulder has a tilted red chevron surrounded by a ring. It's the symbol of Roscosmos—the Russian space agency. The name patch reads ИЛЮХИНА, another name from the crest. This was Ilyukhina's uniform.

Olesya Ilyukhina. She was hilarious. She could have you laughing your butt off within thirty seconds of meeting you. She just had one of those infectious and jovial personalities. As serious as Yáo was, Ilyukhina was casual. They butted heads about it from time to time, but even Yáo couldn't resist her charms. I remember when he finally broke down and laughed at one of her jokes. You can't be a hundred percent serious forever.

I stand up and look to the bodies. No longer a stern commander; no longer a cheerful friend. Just two empty husks that once held souls but now barely looked human. They deserve more than this. They deserve a burial.

The container holds multiple outfits for each crewmember. I eventually find the ones for me. They are exactly as I assumed they would be. *Hail Mary* mission patch with a U.S. flag underneath, a NASA logo on the right shoulder, and a name tag that says GRACE.

I put on my jumpsuit. After more digging in the storage area I find footwear. They're not shoes, really. Just thick socks with rubber soles—booties with some grip. I guess that's all we'd need for the mission. I put them on as well.

Then I go about the grim task of dressing my departed comrades. The jumpsuits don't remotely look the right size on their thin, desiccated bodies. I even put the booties on. Why not? This is our uniform. And a traveler deserves to be buried in uniform.

I start with Ilyukhina. She weighs almost nothing. I carry her over my shoulder as I climb the ladders all the way to the control room. Once there, I set her on the floor and open the airlock. The spacesuit inside is bulky and in the way. I move it, piece by piece, into the control room and set it on the pilot's chair. Then I put Olesya into the airlock.

The airlock controls are self-explanatory. The air pressure inside the airlock and even the outer door are controllable by the panel in the control room. There's even a Jettison button. I close the door and activate the jettison process.

It starts with a buzzing alarm, blinking lights inside the airlock, and a verbal countdown. There are three different blinking Abort switches inside the airlock. Anyone who finds themselves in there during a jettison can easily cancel it.

Once the countdown finishes, the airlock decompresses to 10 percent of an atmosphere (according to the readouts). Then it releases the outer door. With a whoosh, Olesya is gone. And, with the constantly accelerating ship, the body simply falls away.

"Olesya Ilyukhina," I say. I don't remember her religion or if she even had one. I don't know what she would have wanted said. But at least I will remember her name. "I commend your body to the stars." It seems appropriate. Maybe corny, but it makes me feel better.

Next I carry Commander Yáo to the airlock. I set him inside, seal it, and jettison his remains in the same way.

"Yáo Li-Jie," I say. I don't know how I remembered his given name. It just came to me in the moment. "I commend your body to the stars."

The airlock cycles and I am alone. I was alone all along, but now I am truly alone. The sole living human within several light-years, at least.

What do I do now?

"Welcome back, Mr. Grace!" said Theresa.

The kids all sat in their desks, primed for science class.

"Thanks, Theresa," I said.

Michael piped in. "The substitute teacher was booooring."

"Well, I'm not," I said. I picked up four plastic bins from the corner. "Today we're going to look at rocks! Okay, maybe that is a little boring."

A chuckle from the kids.

"You're going to divide into four teams and each team will get a bin. You have to separate the rocks into igneous, sedimentary, and metamorphic. First team to finish—and get every rock correctly categorized—gets beanbags."

"Can we pick our own teams?" Trang asked excitedly.

"No. That just leads to a bunch of drama. Because children are animals. Horrible, horrible animals."

Everyone laughed.

"Teams will be alphabetical. So the first team is—"

Abby raised her hand. "Mr. Grace, can I ask a question?"

"Sure."

"What's happening to the sun?"

The whole class suddenly grew much more attentive.

"My dad says it's not a big deal," Michael said.

"*My* dad says it's a government conspiracy," said Tamora.

"Okay . . ." I set the bins down and sat on the edge of my desk. "So . . . basically, you know how there's algae in the ocean, right? Well, there's sort of a space algae growing in the sun."

"Astrophage?" said Harrison.

I almost slipped off the desk. "Wh-Where did you hear that word?"

"That's what they're calling it now," said Harrison. "The president called it that in a speech last night."

I'd been so isolated in that lab I didn't even know the president had given a speech. And holy cow. I invented that word for Stratt the *day before*. In that time it got from her to the president to the media.

Wow.

"Okay, yes. Astrophage. And it's growing on the sun. Or near it. People aren't sure."

"So what's the problem?" Michael asked. "Algae in the ocean doesn't hurt us. Why would algae on the sun?"

I pointed to him. "Good question. Thing is, Astrophage is starting to absorb a lot of the sun's energy. Well, not a lot. Just a tiny percentage. But that means Earth gets a tiny bit less sunlight. And that can cause real problems."

"So it'll be a little colder? Like a degree or two?" Abby asked. "What's the big deal?"

"You guys know about climate change, right? How our CO_2 emissions have caused a lot of problems in the environment?"

"My dad says that's not real," said Tamora.

"Well, it is," I said. "Anyway. All the environmental problems we have from climate change? They happened because the world's average temperature went up one and a half degrees. That's it. Just one and a half degrees."

"How much will this Astrophage stuff change Earth's temperature?" asked Luther.

I stood and paced slowly in front of the class. "We don't know. But if it breeds like algae does, at about that same speed, climatologists are saying Earth's temperature could drop ten to fifteen degrees."

"What'll happen?" Luther asked.

"It'll be bad. Very bad. A lot of animals—entire species—will die out because their habitats are too cold. The ocean water will cool down, too, and it might cause an entire food-chain collapse. So even things that could survive the lower temperature will starve to death because the things they eat all die off."

The kids stared at me, awestruck. Why had their parents not explained this to them? Probably because they didn't understand it themselves.

Besides, if I had a nickel for every time I wanted to smack a kid's parents for not teaching them even the most basic things . . . well . . . I'd have enough nickels to put in a sock and smack those parents with it.

"Animals are going to die too?!" Abby asked, horrified.

Abby rode horses competitively and spent most of her time at her grandfather's dairy farm. Human suffering is often an abstract concept to kids. But animal suffering is something else entirely.

"Yes, I'm sorry, but a lot of livestock will die. And it's worse than that. On land, crops will fail. The food we eat will become scarce. When that happens, the social order often breaks down and—" I stopped myself there. These were kids. Why was I going this far?

"How—" Abby began. I'd never seen her at a loss for words. "How long before this happens?"

"Climatologists think it'll happen within the next thirty years," I said.

Just like that, all the kids relaxed.

"Thirty years?" Trang laughed. "That's forever!"

"It's not that long . . ." I said. But to a bunch of twelve- and thirteen-year-olds, thirty years may as well be a million.

"Can I be on Tracy's team for the rock-sorting assignment?" asked Michael.

Thirty years. I looked out at their little faces. In thirty years they'd all be in their early forties. They would bear the brunt of it all. And it wouldn't be easy. These kids were going to grow up in an idyllic world and be thrown into an apocalyptic nightmare.

They were the generation that would experience the Sixth Extinction Event.

I felt a cramp in the pit of my stomach. I was looking out at a room full of children. Happy children. And there was a good chance some of them would literally die of starvation.

"I . . ." I stammered. "I have to go do a thing. Forget the rock assignment."

"What?" asked Luther.

"Do . . . study hall. This is study hall for the rest of the hour. Just do homework from other classes. Stay in your seats and work quietly until the bell rings."

I left the room without another word. I almost collapsed in the hall from the shakes. I went to a nearby drinking fountain and splashed water on my face. Then I took a deep breath, got some self-control back, and jogged to the parking lot.

I drove fast. Way too fast. I ran red lights. I cut people off. I never do any of that, but that day was different. That day was . . . I don't even know.

I screeched into the lab parking lot and left my car parked at an odd angle.

Two U.S. Army soldiers were at the doors to the complex. Just as they had been the previous two days while I'd been working there. I stormed past them.

"Should we have stopped him?" I heard one ask the other. I didn't care what the response was.

I stomped into the observation room. Stratt was there, of course, reading her tablet. She looked up and I caught a glimpse of genuine surprise on her face.

"Dr. Grace? What are you doing here?"

Past her, through the windows, I spotted four people in containment suits working in the lab.

"Who are they?" I said, pointing at the window. "And what are they doing in my lab?"

"Can't say I like your tone—" she said.

"I don't care."

"And it's not your lab. It's my lab. Those technicians are collecting the Astrophage."

"What are you going to do with it?"

She held her tablet under her arm. "Your dream is coming true. I'm dividing up the Astrophage and sending it to thirty different labs around the world. Everything from CERN to a CIA bioweapons facility."

"The CIA has a biowea—?" I began. "Never mind. I want to do more work on this."

She shook her head. "You've done your part. We thought it was anhydrous life. Turns out it wasn't. You proved that. And since no alien exploded out of your chest, we can consider the guinea-pig phase over too. So you're done."

"No, I'm not done. There's a lot more to learn."

"Of course there is," she said. "And I have thirty labs all eagerly waiting to get started on it."

I stepped forward. "Leave some Astrophage here. Let me work it some more."

She stepped forward as well. "No."

"Why not?!"

"According to your notes, there were one hundred and seventy-four living Astrophage cells in the sample. And you killed one yesterday, so we're down to a hundred and seventy-three."

She pointed to her tablet. "Each of these labs—huge, national labs—will get five or six cells each. That's it. We're down to that level of scarcity. Those cells are the one hundred and seventy-three most important things on Earth right now. Our analysis of them will determine if humanity survives."

She paused and spoke a little more softly. "I get it. You spent your whole life trying to prove that life doesn't require water. Then, unbelievably, you get some actual extraterrestrial life and it turns out to need water. That's rough. Shake it off and get back to your life. I've got it from here."

"I'm still a microbiologist who spent his career working up theoretical models for alien life. I'm a useful resource with a skill set almost no one else has."

"Dr. Grace, I don't have the luxury of leaving samples here just to stroke your bruised ego."

"Ego?! This isn't about my *ego*! It's about my *children*!"

"You don't have children."

"Yes, I do! Dozens of them. They come to my class every day. And they're all going to end up in a *Mad Max* nightmare world if we don't solve this problem. Yeah, I was wrong about the water. I don't care about that. I care about those kids. So *give me some gosh-darned Astrophage!*"

She stepped back and pursed her lips. She looked to the side, thinking it over. Then she turned back to me. "Three. You can have three Astrophage."

I unclenched my muscles. "Okay." I breathed a little. I didn't realize how tense I'd been. "Okay. Three. I can work with that."

She typed on her tablet. "I'll keep this lab open. It's all yours. Come back in a few hours and my guys will be gone."

I was already halfway into a containment suit. "I'm getting back to work now. Tell your guys to stay out of my way."

She glared at me but didn't say anything further.

I have to do this for my kids.

I mean . . . they're not *my* kids. But they're my kids.

I look at the screens arrayed before me. I need to think about this.

My memory is spotty. Seems reliable enough, but incomplete. Instead of waiting for an epiphany where I remember everything, what can I work out right now?

Earth is in trouble. The sun is infected with Astrophage. I'm in a spaceship in another solar system. This ship wasn't easy to build and it had an international crew. We're talking about an interstellar mission—something that should be impossible with our technology. Okay, so humanity put a lot of time and effort into this mission, and Astrophage was the missing link that enabled it.

There's only one explanation: There's a solution to the Astrophage problem here. Or a potential solution. Something promising enough to dedicate a huge amount of resources.

I scour the screens for more info. Mostly they seem to be the kinds of things you'd expect on a spaceship. Life support, navigation, that sort of thing. One screen is labeled "Beetles." The next screen over says—

Wait, beetles?

Okay, I don't know if it has anything to do with anything, but I need to find out if there are a bunch of beetles on this ship. That's the sort of thing a guy needs to know.

The screen is broken into four quadrants, each one showing nearly the same thing. A little schematic and a bunch of text information. The schematics each show a bulbous, oblong shape with a pointed head and a trapezoid on the back. If you tilt your head just right and squint, I suppose it kind of looks like a beetle. Each beetle also has a name up top: "John," "Paul," "George," and "Ringo."

Yeah, I get it. I'm not laughing, but I get it.

I arbitrarily pick one beetle, John, and give it a good look.

John is no insect. I'm pretty sure he's a spaceship. The trapezoid in the rear is labeled "Spin Drive," and the entire bulbous part is labeled "Fuel." The little head has a "Computer" label and a "Radio" label.

I look a little closer. The Fuel info box says ASTROPHAGE: 120KG—TEMP: 96.415°C. The Computer box says LAST MEMORY CHECK: 3 DAYS AGO. 5 TB FUNCTIONING CORRECTLY. And the Radio info just says STATUS: 100%.

It's an unmanned probe. Something small, I guess. The entire mass of the fuel is just 120 kilograms. That's not a lot. But a little Astrophage goes a long way. There aren't any scientific instruments labeled. What's the point of an unmanned ship with nothing on board?

Wait . . . what if the 5 terabytes of storage is the point of the ship?

A realization dawns on me.

"Oh. Shucks," I say.

I'm out in space. I'm in another star system. I don't know how much Astrophage it took to get here, but it was probably a lot. Sending a ship to another star probably took an absurd amount of fuel. Sending that ship to another star *and bringing it back* would take ten times as much fuel.

I check the Astrophage panel to refresh my memory.

REMAINING: 20,862 KG

CONSUMPTION RATE: 6.043 G/S

The consumption rate was 6.045 grams per second before. So it's gone down a little bit. And the fuel amount went down too. Basically, as the fuel gets consumed, the total mass of the ship goes down, so it needs less fuel per second to maintain the constant acceleration. Okay, that all makes sense.

I have no idea what the *Hail Mary*'s mass is, but to be able to shove it along at 1.5 g's of acceleration on a few grams of fuel per second . . . Astrophage is amazing stuff.

Anyway, I don't know exactly how the consumption rate will change over time (I mean, I could work it out, but it's complicated). So for now I'll just approximate it to 6 grams per second. How long will that fuel last?

It's nice to have a jumpsuit on. It's got pockets for all sorts of knickknacks. I still haven't found a calculator, so I do the math with a pen and paper. Grand total, I'll run out of fuel in about forty days.

I don't know what star that is, but it's not the sun. And there's just no way to get from any other star to Earth with just forty days of accelerating at 1.5 g's. It probably took *years* to get here from Earth—which might be why I was in a coma. Interesting.

Anyway, all this can only mean one thing: The *Hail Mary* isn't going home. This is a one-way ticket. And I'm pretty sure these beetles are how I'm supposed to send information back to Earth.

There's no way I have a radio transmitter powerful enough to broadcast several light-years. I don't know if that would even be possible to build. So instead, I have these little "beetle" ships with 5 terabytes of information each. They'll fly back to Earth and broadcast their data. There's four of them for redundancy. I'm probably supposed to put copies of my findings in each one and send them all home. If at least one survives the journey, Earth is saved.

I'm on a suicide mission. John, Paul, George, and Ringo get to go home, but my long and winding road ends here. I must have known all this when I volunteered. But to my amnesia-riddled brain this is new information. I'm going to die out here. And I'm going to die alone.

CHAPTER 5

I glared at the Astrophage. "Why the heck do you go to Venus?"

The microscope view was displayed on the big wall-mounted monitor. Each of the three little cells were a foot across at this magnification. I watched for any clues to their motivations, but Larry, Curly, and Moe offered no answer.

I'd named them, of course. It's a teacher thing.

"What's so special about Venus? And how do you even find it?" I crossed my arms. If Astrophage understood body language, they'd know I wasn't messing around. "It takes a room full of really smart people at NASA to work out how to get to Venus. And you do it as a single-celled organism with no brain."

It had been two days since Stratt left me alone with the lab. The army guys were still at the doors. One was named Steve. Friendly guy. The other never spoke to me.

I ran my hands through my greasy hair (I'd neglected to shower that morning). At least I didn't have to wear the hazmat suit anymore. Scientists in Nairobi had taken a chance with one of their Astrophage and exposed it to Earth atmosphere to see what happened. It was unaffected. So, thanks to them, labs all over the world could breathe a sigh of relief and stop working in argon-filled rooms.

I glanced at the pile of papers on a desk. The scientific community had moved into overdrive in a very unscientific way. Gone were the days of careful peer review and published articles. Astrophage research was a free-for-all where researchers posted their findings immediately and without proof. It led to misunderstandings and mistakes, but we just didn't have time to do things the right way.

Stratt kept me in the loop on most stuff. Not everything, I was sure. Who knows what other weird things she was up to. She seemed to have authority everywhere.

A Belgian research team was able to prove that Astrophage reacts to magnetic fields, but only sometimes. Other times, it seems to ignore magnetic fields entirely, no matter how powerful. Still, the Belgians were able to (very inconsistently) steer Astrophage around by putting it in a magnetic field and changing the field's orientation. Was that useful? No idea. At this point the world was just collecting data.

A researcher in Paraguay showed that ants will get disoriented when they're within a few centimeters of Astrophage. Was that useful? Okay, that one probably wasn't useful. But it was interesting.

Most notably, a group in Perth sacrificed one of their Astrophage and did a detailed analysis on all the organelles inside. They found DNA and mitochondria. In any other situation, this would have been the most important discovery of the century. Alien life—indisputably alien—had DNA and mitochondria!

And . . . grumble . . . a bunch of water . . .

Point is: The inside of an Astrophage wasn't much different from the inside of any single-celled organism you'd find on Earth. It used ATP, RNA transcription, and a whole host of other extremely familiar things. Some researchers speculated that it *originated* on Earth. Others postulated this specific set of molecules was the only way for life to occur and Astrophage evolved it independently. And a smaller, vocal faction suggested life might not have evolved on Earth at all, and that Astrophage and terrestrial life have a common ancestor.

"You know," I told the Astrophage, "if you boys weren't threatening all life on my planet, you'd be pretty awesome. You have mysteries within mysteries."

I leaned against a table. "You have mitochondria. Okay, so that means you use ATP as your energy storage, just like we do. But the light you use to move around requires waaaay more energy than your ATP can hold. So you have another energy-storage pathway. One we don't understand."

One of the Astrophage on-screen darted slightly to the left. It was pretty common. Once in a while, for no real reason, they'd just wiggle.

"What makes you move? Why move? And how does this random jerky motion get you from the sun to Venus? And why do you go to Venus at all?!"

Lots of people were working on the internals of Astrophage. Trying to figure out what made it tick. Analyzing its DNA. Good for them. I wanted to know the basic life-cycle. That was my goal.

Single-celled organisms don't just store buttloads of energy and fly through space for no reason. There had to be something Astrophage needed from Venus or it would just stay on the sun. And it needed something from the sun, too, or it would stay on Venus.

The sun part was pretty easy: It was there for the energy. Same reason plants grew leaves. Got to get that sweet, sweet energy if you're going to be a life-form. Makes perfect sense. So what about Venus?

I picked up a pen and fidgeted with it as I thought.

"According to the Indian Space Research Organization, you guys get going up to 0.92 times the speed of light." I pointed at them. "Didn't know we could do that, did ya? Figure out your velocity? They used Doppler-shift analysis of the light you emit to work it out. And because of that, they also know you're going both directions: *to* and *from* Venus."

I frowned. "But if you hit an atmosphere at that speed you should die. So why don't you?"

I rapped my forehead with a knuckle. "Because you can handle any amount of heat. Right. So you blast into the atmosphere, but you don't get any hotter. Okay, but you'd have to at least slow down. So you'd just be in the upper atmosphere of Venus. Then you . . . what? Turn around and go back to the sun? Why?"

I stared at the screen for a solid ten minutes, lost in thought.

"All right, enough of this. I want to know how you find Venus."

I went to the local hardware store and bought a bunch of two-by-fours, three-quarter-inch plywood, power tools, and other stuff I'd need. Steve the army guy helped me carry a lot of it in. Jerk army guy did nothing.

Over the next six hours, I built a lightproof closet with a shelf in it. It was just big enough for me to get in and out. I set the microscope on the shelf. The "door" was a plywood panel that I could remove with screws.

I ran power and video lines into the closet through a little hole that I plugged up with putty to make sure no light could get in through there either. I set my IR camera up on the microscope and sealed up the closet.

Out in the lab, the monitor showed the infrared light the camera saw. It was basically a frequency shift. Very low bands of IR would show up as red. Higher-energy bands would be orange, yellow, and so on up the rainbow. I could see the Astrophage cells as little red blobs, which was expected. At their constant temperature of 96.415 degrees Celsius they would naturally emit an IR wavelength of 7.8 microns or so—the low end of what I'd set the camera to look for. It was good confirmation that the setup was working.

But I didn't care about that dark-red color. I wanted to see a bright-yellow flash. That would be the Petrova frequency that Astrophage spit out to move around. If any of my Astrophages moved even the tiniest amount, I'd see a very obvious yellow flash.

But it never came. Nothing happened. Nothing at all. Usually, I'd see a jerky motion from at least one of them every few seconds. But now there was nothing.

"So," I said. "You little brats have settled down, eh?"

Light. Whatever their navigation system was, it was based on light. I suspected that would be the case. What else could you use in space? There's no sound. No smell. It would have to be light, gravity, or electromagnetism. And light's the easiest of those three to detect. At least, as far as evolution is concerned.

For my next experiment, I taped a little white LED and a watch battery together. Of course, I wired it backward at first and the LED didn't light up. That's pretty much a rule in electronics: You never get diodes right on the first try. Anyway, I rewired it correctly and the LED lit up. I taped the whole contraption to the inside wall of the closet. I made sure to position it so the Astrophage on the sample slide would have a direct line of sight on it. Then I sealed everything up again.

Now, from the Astrophage's point of view, there was a lot of black nothingness and one shining spot of white. That's kind of what Venus might look like if you were out in space and looking directly away from the sun.

They didn't budge. No hint of motion at all.

"Hmph," I said.

To be fair, it wasn't likely to work. If you were at the sun, looking away from it for the brightest splotch of light you could see, you'd probably zero in on Mercury, not Venus. Mercury is smaller than Venus, but it's a lot closer so you'd see more light.

"Why Venus?" I mused. But then I thought of a better question. "How do you guys *identify* Venus?"

Why did they move randomly? My theory: By pure chance, every few seconds or so, an Astrophage thought it had spotted Venus. So it thrusted in that direction. But then the moment passed, so it stopped thrusting.

The key had to be frequencies of light. My boys didn't wiggle at all in darkness. But it wasn't just about the sheer volume of light, or they would have gone for the LED. It had to be something about the *frequency* of the light.

Planets don't just reflect light. They also *emit* it. Everything emits light. The temperature of the object defines the wavelength of light emitted. Planets are no exception. So maybe Astrophage looked for Venus's IR signature. It wouldn't be as bright as Mercury's, but it would be distinct—a different "color."

A little googling told me Venus's average temperature was 462 degrees Celsius.

I had a whole drawer full of replacement bulbs for microscopes and other lab stuff. I grabbed one and hooked it up to a variable power supply. Incandescent bulbs work by getting the filament so hot it emits visible light. That happens around 2,500 degrees Celsius. I didn't need anything so dramatic. I just needed a measly 462 degrees. I adjusted power going through the bulb up and down, watching with an IR camera, until I got exactly the light frequency I wanted.

I moved the whole contraption into my test closet, watched the monitor with my boys on it, and turned on the artificial Venus.

Nothing. Absolutely no movement from the little jerks.

"What do you want from me?!" I demanded.

I pulled my goggles off and threw them to the ground. I drummed my fingers on the table. "If I were an astronomer, and someone showed me a blob of light, how would I know if it's Venus?"

I answered myself. "I'd look for that IR signature! But that's not what Astrophage does. Okay, someone shows me a blob of light and says I'm not allowed to use emitted IR to work out the temperature of the body. How *else* could I find out if it's Venus?"

Spectroscopy. Look for carbon dioxide.

I raised an eyebrow as the idea came to me.

When light hits gas molecules, the electrons get all worked up. Then they calm down and re-emit the energy as light. But the frequency of the photons they emit is very specific to the molecules involved. Astronomers used this for decades to know what gases are out there far, far away. That's what spectroscopy is all about.

Venus's atmosphere is ninety times Earth's pressure and almost entirely carbon dioxide. Its spectroscopy signature of CO_2 would be overwhelmingly strong. Mercury had no carbon dioxide at all, so the nearest competitor would be Earth. But we had a minuscule CO_2 signature compared to Venus. Maybe Astrophage used emission spectra to find Venus?

New plan!

The lab had a seemingly infinite supply of light filters. Pick a frequency, and there's a filter for it. I looked up the spectral signature of carbon dioxide—the peak wavelengths were 4.26 microns and 18.31 microns.

I found the appropriate filters and built a little box for them. Inside I put a small white lightbulb. Now I had a box that would emit the spectral signature of carbon dioxide.

I put it in the test closet and went out to watch the monitor. Larry, Curly, and Moe hung out on their slide, just like they had all day long.

I flicked on the light box and watched for any reaction.

The Astrophage left. They didn't just meander toward the light. They were gone. Absolutely gone.

"Um . . ."

I had been recording the camera input, of course. I ran it back to watch frame by frame. Between two frames they simply disappeared.

"Um!"

Good news: Astrophage were attracted to carbon dioxide's spectral signature!

Bad news: My three irreplaceable, 10-micron-wide Astrophage had launched off somewhere—maybe at velocities approaching the speed of light—and I had no idea where they went.

"Craaaaaap."

Midnight. Darkness everywhere. The army guys changed shift to two guys I didn't know. I missed Steve.

I had aluminum foil and duct tape up over every window of the lab. I sealed the cracks around the entrances and exits with electrical tape. I turned off every piece of equipment that had a readout or LED of any kind. I put my watch in a drawer because it had glow-in-the-dark paint on the hands.

I let my eyes adjust to the total darkness. If I saw so much as a single shape that wasn't my imagination, I sought out the light leak and put tape over it. Finally, I reached a level of darkness so intense I couldn't see anything. Opening or closing my eyes had no effect at all.

The next step was my newly invented IR goggles.

The lab had many things, but infrared goggles were not among them. I'd considered asking Steve the army guy if he could score some. I probably could have called Stratt and she would have had the president of Peru personally deliver them or something. But this was faster.

The "goggles" were just the LCD output screen of my IR camera with a bunch of tape around them. I pressed them to my face and added more tape. Then more and more and more. I'm sure I looked ridiculous. But whatever.

I fired up the camera and looked around the lab. Plenty of heat signatures. The walls were still warm from sunlight earlier that day, everything electrical had a glow, and my body shined like a beacon. I adjusted the frequency range to look for much hotter things. Specifically, things over 90 degrees Celsius.

I crawled into my makeshift microscope closet and looked at the light box I'd used for the CO_2 spectral emission.

Astrophage are only 10 microns across. No chance I'd see something so small with the camera (or with my eyes, for that matter). But my little aliens are very hot, and they stay hot. So, if they're not moving, they will have spent the last six hours or so slowly heating up their surroundings. That was the hope.

It panned out. I immediately saw a circle of light on one of the plastic light filters.

"Oh thank God," I gasped.

It was very faint but it was there. The spot was about 3 millimeters across and grew fainter and colder away from the center. The little fella had been heating up the plastic for hours. I scanned back and forth across the two plastic squares. I quickly found a second spot.

My experiment worked way better than I expected. They saw what they thought was Venus and beelined for it. When they hit the light filters, they couldn't go any farther. They probably kept pushing until I turned off the light.

Anyway, if I could just confirm that all three Astrophage were present, I could bag the filters, then spend however long I needed to find and harvest the boys from them with a microscope and pipette.

And there it was. The third Astrophage.

"The gang's all here!" I said. I reached into my pocket for a sample bag and got ready to *very carefully* pull the filter off the light box. That's when I saw the fourth Astrophage.

Just . . . minding its own business. A fourth cell. It was right in the same general cluster as the first three, on the filters.

"Holy . . ."

I'd been staring at these guys for a week. There's no way I would have missed one. There could only be one explanation: One of the Astrophage divided. I'd accidentally made the Astrophage reproduce.

I stared at that fourth spot of light for a full minute, taking in the magnitude of what had just happened. Breeding Astrophage meant we would have an unlimited supply for study. Kill them, poke them, take them apart, do whatever we wanted. This was a game changer.

"Hello, Shemp," I said.

I spent the next two days obsessively studying this new behavior. I didn't even go home—I just slept in the lab.

Steve the army guy brought me breakfast. Great guy.

I should have shared all my findings with the rest of the science community, but I wanted to be sure. Peer review may have fallen by the wayside, but at least I could self-review. Better than nothing.

The first thing that bothered me: CO_2 spectral emissions are 4.26 and 18.31 microns. But Astrophage are only 10 microns across, so it couldn't really interact with light that had a larger wavelength. How could it even see the 18.31 micron band?

I repeated my earlier spectral experiment with just the 18.31 micron filter and got a result I didn't expect. Strange things happened.

First off, two of the Astrophage whipped over to the filter. They saw the light and went right for it. But how? It should be impossible for Astrophage to interact with a wavelength that big. I mean . . . literally *impossible*!

Light is a funny thing. Its wavelength defines what it can and can't interact with. Anything smaller than the wavelength is functionally nonexistent to that photon. That's why there's a mesh over the window of a microwave. The holes in the mesh are too small for microwaves to pass through. But visible light, with a much shorter wavelength, can go through freely. So you get to watch your food cook without melting your face off.

Astrophage is smaller than 18.31 microns but somehow still absorbs light at that frequency. How?

But that's not even the strangest thing that happened. Yes, two of them took off for the filter, but the other two stayed put. They didn't seem to care. They just hung out on the slide. Maybe they didn't interact with the larger wavelength?

So I did one more experiment. I shined the 4.26 micron light at them again. And I got the same results. The same two went right for the filter as before, and the other two just didn't care.

And there it was. I couldn't be 100 percent certain, but I was pretty sure I'd just discovered the whole Astrophage life-cycle. It clicked in my mind like puzzle pieces finally fitting together.

The two holdouts didn't want to go to Venus anymore. They wanted to go back to the sun. Why? Because one of them just divided and created the other.

Astrophage hang out on the surface of the sun gathering energy via heat. They store it internally in some way no one understands.

Then, when they have enough, they migrate to Venus to breed, using that stored energy to fly through space using infrared light as a propellant. Lots of species migrate to breed. Why would Astrophage be any different?

The Aussies already worked out that the inside of Astrophage wasn't much different from Earth life. It needed carbon and oxygen to make the complex proteins required for DNA, mitochondria, and all the other fun stuff found in cells. There's plenty of hydrogen on the sun. But the other elements just aren't present. So Astrophage migrates to the nearest supply of carbon dioxide: Venus.

First, it follows magnetic field lines and goes straight away from the sun's North Pole. It has to do that, or the light from the sun would be too blinding to find Venus. And going straight up from the pole means the Astrophage will have a full view of Venus's entire orbital path—no portion of it occluded by the sun.

Ah, and that's why Astrophage is so inconsistent on reacting to magnetic fields. It only cares about them at the very beginning of its journey and at no other time.

Then it looks for Venus's massive carbon dioxide spectral signature. Well, not really "looks for." It's probably more a simple stimulus-response thing initiated by the 4.26 and 18.31 micron light bands. Anyway, once it "sees" Venus, it goes straight to it. The path it takes—straight away from the solar pole, then sharply turning toward Venus—that's the Petrova line.

Our heroic Astrophage reaches the upper atmosphere of Venus, collects the CO_2 it needs, and can finally reproduce. After that, both parent and child return to the sun and the cycle begins anew.

It's simple, really. Get energy, get resources, and make copies. It's the same thing all life on Earth does.

And that was why two of my little Stooges didn't walk toward the light.

So how does Astrophage find the sun? My guess: Look for the extremely bright thing and head that way.

I separated Moe and Shemp (the sun-seekers) from Larry and Curly (the Venus-seekers). I put Larry and Curly on a different slide and put it in a light-sealed sample container. Then I set up an experiment in the dark closet for Moe and Shemp. This time, I put a bright incandescent bulb in there and turned it on. I expected them to head right toward it, but no dice. They didn't budge. Probably not bright enough.

I went to a photography store downtown (San Francisco has a lot of photography enthusiasts) and bought the largest, brightest, most powerful flash I could find. I replaced the lightbulb with the flash and did the experiment again.

Moe and Shemp took the bait!

I had to sit down and take a breath. I should have taken a nap—I hadn't slept in thirty-six hours. But this was too exciting. I pulled out my cell phone and dialed Stratt's number. She answered halfway through the first ring.

"Dr. Grace," she said. "Find something?"

"Yeah," I said. "I figured out how Astrophage reproduce and managed to make it happen."

Silence for a second. "You successfully bred Astrophage?"

"Yes."

"Nondestructively?" she asked.

"I had three cells. I now have four. They're all alive and well."

Silence for another second. "Stay there."

She hung up.

"Huh," I said. I put the phone back in my lab coat. "Guess she's on her way."

Steve the army guy burst into the lab. "Dr. Grace?!"

"Wha . . . uh, yeah?"

"Please come with me."

"Okay," I said. "Let me just get my Astrophage samples put away—"

"There are lab techs on the way to deal with all that. You have to come with me now."

"O-Okay . . ."

The next twelve hours were . . . unique.

Steve the army guy drove me to a high school football field where a U.S. Marine Corps helicopter had already landed. Without words, they hustled me into the chopper and up we went into the sky. I tried not to look down.

The chopper took me to Travis Air Force Base, about 60 miles north of the city. Did the marines often land at air force bases? I don't know much about the military, but that seemed odd. It also seemed a bit extreme to send in the marines just to keep me from driving through a couple of hours of traffic, but okay.

There was a jeep waiting for me on the tarmac where the helicopter landed, with an air force guy standing next to it. He introduced himself, I swear he did, but I don't remember his name.

He drove me across the tarmac to a waiting jet. No, not a passenger jet. And not a Learjet or anything like that. This was a fighter jet. I don't know what kind. Like I said, I don't know military stuff.

My guide hustled me up a ladder and into the seat behind the pilot. He gave me a pill and a little paper cup of water. "Take this."

"What is it?"

"It'll keep you from puking all over our nice, clean cockpit."

"Okay."

I swallowed the pill.

"And it'll help you sleep."

"What?"

Away he went, and the ground crew pulled away the ladder. The pilot didn't say a word to me. Ten minutes later, we took off like a bat out of hell. I'd never felt acceleration like that in my life. The pill did its job. I *definitely* would have puked.

"Where are we going?" I asked through the headset.

"I'm sorry, sir. I'm not allowed to speak to you."

"This is going to be a boring trip, then."

"They usually are," he said.

I don't know exactly when I fell asleep but it was within minutes of taking off. Thirty-six hours of mad science plus whatever was in that pill put me right into dreamland regardless of the ridiculous jet-engine noise surrounding me.

I awoke in darkness to a jolt. We'd landed.

"Welcome to Hawaii, sir," said the pilot.

"Hawaii? Why am I in Hawaii?"

"I wasn't given that information."

The jet taxied onto some side runway or whatever and a ground crew brought a ladder. I hadn't gotten halfway down the ladder yet when I heard "Dr. Grace? This way, please!"

It was a man in a U.S. Navy uniform.

"Where the hell am I?!" I demanded.

"Naval Station Pearl Harbor," said the officer. "But not for long. Please follow me."

"Sure. Why not?"

They put me in *another* jet with *another* non-talkative pilot. The only difference was that this time it was a navy jet instead of an air force jet.

We flew for a *long* time. I lost track of the hours. Keeping track was meaningless anyway. I didn't know how long we'd be in the air. Finally, I kid you not, we landed on an honest-to-God aircraft carrier.

Next thing I knew, I was on the flight deck looking like an idiot. They gave me earmuffs and a coat and shuffled me over to a helipad. A navy chopper was waiting for me.

"Will this trip . . . end? Like . . . ever?!" I asked.

They ignored me and got me strapped in. The chopper took off immediately. This time, the flight wasn't nearly so long. Just an hour or so.

"This should be interesting," said the pilot. It was the only thing he'd said the whole flight.

We descended and the landing gear deployed. Below us was another aircraft carrier. I squinted at it. Something looked different. What was it . . . oh, right. It had a big Chinese flag flying over it.

"Is that a Chinese aircraft carrier?!" I asked.

"Yes, sir."

"Are we, a U.S. Navy helicopter, going to land on that Chinese aircraft carrier?"

"Yes, sir."

"I see."

We landed on the carrier's helipad and a bunch of Chinese Navy guys watched us with interest. There would be no post-flight servicing of this chopper. My pilot leered through the windows at them and they leered right back.

As soon as I stepped out, he took off again. I was in China's hands now.

A navy man came forward and gestured for me to follow him. I don't think anyone spoke English, but I got the general idea. He led me to a door in the tower structure and we went inside. We wound through passageways, stairwells, and rooms I didn't even understand the purpose of. All the while, Chinese sailors watched me with curiosity.

Finally, he stopped at a door with Chinese characters on it. He opened the door and pointed inside. I walked in and he slammed the door behind me. So much for my guide.

I think it was an officer's conference room. At least, that was my assumption based on the big table with fifteen people sitting at it. They all turned their heads to look up at me. Some were white, some were black, some were Asian. Some wore lab coats. Others wore suits.

Stratt, of course, sat at the head of the table. "Dr. Grace. How was your trip?"

"How was my trip?" I said. "I got dragged across the gosh-darned world without any notice—"

She held up her hand. "It was just a pleasantry, Dr. Grace. I don't actually care how your trip was." She stood and addressed the room. "Ladies and gentlemen, this is Dr. Ryland Grace from the United States. He figured out how to breed Astrophage."

Gasps came from around the table. One man shot to his feet and spoke with a thick German accent. "Are you serious? *Stratt, warum haben sie—?*"

"*Nur Englisch,*" Stratt interrupted.

"Why are we only hearing of this now?" the German demanded.

"I wanted to confirm it first. While Dr. Grace was en route, I had technicians pack up his lab. They collected four live Astrophage from his lab. I only left him three."

An elderly man in a lab coat spoke Japanese in a calm, soothing voice. Next to him, a younger Japanese man in a charcoal suit translated. "Dr. Matsuka would like to respectfully request a detailed description of the process."

Stratt stepped aside and gestured to her chair. "Doctor, have a seat and lay it out for us."

"Hold on," I said. "Who are these people? Why am I on a Chinese aircraft carrier? And have you ever heard of Skype?!"

"This is an international body of high-level scientists and political operatives that I have assembled to spearhead Project Hail Mary."

"What's that?"

"That would take a while to explain. Everyone here is eager to hear about your Astrophage findings. Let's start with that."

I shuffled to the front of the room and sat awkwardly at the head of the table. All eyes turned to me.

So I told them. I told them all about the wooden closet experiments. I explained all my tests, what I did for each one, and how I did them. Then I explained my conclusions: I told them my hypothesis about the Astrophage life-cycle, how it works, and why. There were a few questions from the assembled scientists and politicos, but mostly they just listened and took notes. Several had translators whispering in their ear during the process.

"So . . . yeah," I said. "That's pretty much everything. I mean—it's not rigorously tested yet but it seems pretty simple."

German Guy raised his hand. "Would it be possible to breed Astrophage on a large scale?"

Everyone leaned forward a little. Apparently this was a pretty important question and it was on everyone's mind. I was taken aback by the sudden intensity of the room.

Even Stratt seemed unusually interested. "Well?" she said. "Please answer Minister Voigt."

"Sure," I said. "I mean . . . why not?"

"How would you do it?" asked Stratt.

"I guess I'd make a big elbow-shaped ceramic pipe and fill it with carbon dioxide. Make one end of it as hot as you can get it and have a bright light there. Wrap a magnetic coil around it to simulate the magnetic field of the sun. Put an IR light emitter at the other end of the elbow and have it emit light at 4.26 and 18.31 microns. Make the inside of the pipe as black as you can. That should do it."

"How does that 'do it'?" she said.

I shrugged. "The Astrophage will gather energy at the 'sun' side and when they're ready to breed, they'll follow that magnetic field to the pipe's elbow. They'll see the IR light at the other end and head toward it. Seeing that light and being exposed to carbon dioxide makes them breed. Then the parent and daughter cells will go back to the sun side. Simple enough."

A political-looking man raised his hand and spoke with some kind of African accent. "How much Astrophage could be made this way? How fast is the process?"

"It would have a doubling time," I said. "Like algae or bacteria. I don't know how long it is, but considering the sun is getting dim it must be pretty quick."

A woman in a lab coat had been on her phone. She set it down, then spoke with a thick Chinese accent. "Our scientists have reproduced your results."

Minister Voigt scowled at her. "How did you even know his process? He *just* told us!"

"Spies, presumably," said Stratt.

The German huffed. "How *dare* you circumvent us with—"

"Shush," said Stratt. "We're past all that. Ms. Xi, do you have any additional information to share?"

"Yes," she said. "We estimate the doubling time to be just over eight days, under optimal conditions."

“What does that mean?” the African diplomat said. “How much can we make?”

“Well.” I launched my phone’s calculator app and tapped a few buttons. “If you started with the one hundred and fifty Astrophage we have, and bred them for a year, at the end of it you’d have . . . about 173,000 kilograms of Astrophage.”

“And would this Astrophage be at maximum energy density? Would it all be ready to reproduce?”

“So you want . . . I guess you’d call it ‘enriched’ Astrophage?”

“Yes,” he said. “That’s a perfect word for it. We want Astrophage that is holding as much energy as it can.”

“Uh . . . I guess that could be arranged,” I said. “First, breed up the number of Astrophage you want, then expose them to lots of heat energy but don’t let them see any carbon dioxide spectral lines. They’ll collect energy and just sort of sit there waiting until they can see somewhere to get CO_2.”

“What if we needed two million kilograms of enriched Astrophage?” said the diplomat.

“It’s doubling every eight days,” I said. “Two million kilos would be another four doublings or so. So, one month longer.”

A woman leaned forward on the table, her fingers steepled. “We might just have a chance.” She had an American accent.

“An outside chance,” said Voigt.

“There is hope,” said the Japanese translator—presumably speaking for Dr. Matsuka.

“We need to talk amongst ourselves,” said Stratt. “Go get some rest. The sailor outside will show you to a bunk.”

“But I want to know about Project Hail Mary!”

“Oh, you will. Believe me.”

I slept for fourteen hours.

Aircraft carriers are awesome in many ways, but they aren’t five-star hotels. The Chinese had given me a clean, comfy cot in an officer's bunkroom. I had no complaints. I could have slept on the flight deck I was so tired.

I felt something weird on my forehead when I woke up. I reached up and it was a Post-it note. Someone put a Post-it on my head while I slept. I pulled it off and read it:

> *Clean clothes and toiletries in the duffel under your bunk. Show this note to any sailor when you've cleaned up:* 请带我去甲板7的官员会议室
>
> *—Stratt*

"She is such a pain in my butt . . ." I mumbled.

I stumbled out of my cot. A few officers gave me passing glances but otherwise ignored me. I found the duffel and, as promised, there were clothes and dental-hygiene stuff and soap. I glanced around the bunkroom and saw through a doorway into a locker room.

I used the bathroom (or "head" I guess, because I was on a ship). Then I took a shower with three other guys. I dried off and put on the jumpsuit onesie Stratt had left me. It was bright yellow, had Chinese writing along the back, and a big red stripe down the left leg of the pants. My guess was to make sure everyone knew I was a foreign civilian and not allowed in certain places.

I flagged down a passing sailor and showed him the note. He nodded and gestured for me to follow. He led me through a maze of twisty little passages, all alike, until we arrived back at the room I'd been in the previous day.

I stepped in to see Stratt and some of her . . . teammates? A subset of the previous day's gang. Just Minister Voigt, the Chinese scientist—I think her name was Xi—and a guy in a Russian military uniform. The Russian had been there the previous day but hadn't said anything. They all looked deep in concentration and the table was littered with paper. They mumbled to one another here and there. I didn't know the exact relationships going on, but Stratt was definitely at the head of the table.

She looked up as I entered.

"Ah. Dr. Grace. You look refreshed." She gestured to her left. "There's food on the credenza."

And there was! Rice, steamed buns, deep-fried dough sticks, and an urn of coffee. I rushed over and helped myself. I was hungry as heck.

I sat at the conference table with a full plate and cup of coffee.

"So," I said with a mouth full of rice. "You gonna tell me why we're on a Chinese aircraft carrier?"

"I needed an aircraft carrier. The Chinese gave me one. Well, they lent it to me."

I slurped my coffee. "There was a time when something like that would surprise me. But . . . you know . . . not anymore."

"Commercial air travel takes too long and is prone to delays," she said. "Military aircraft work on whatever schedule they want and travel supersonically. I need to be able to get experts from anywhere on Earth in the same room with no delays."

"Ms. Stratt can be extremely persuasive," said Minister Voigt.

I shoveled more food into my mouth. "Blame whoever gave her all that authority," I said.

Voigt chuckled. "I was part of that decision, actually. I am Germany's minister of foreign affairs. The equivalent of your country's secretary of state."

I paused my chewing. "Wow," I managed to say. I gulped down the mouthful. "You're the most high-ranking person I've ever met."

"No, I'm not." He pointed to Stratt.

She put a piece of paper in front of me. "This is what led to the Hail Mary Project."

"You're showing him?" Voigt said. "Now? Without getting him a clearance—"

Stratt put her hand on my shoulder. "Dr. Ryland Grace, I hereby grant you top-secret clearance to all information pertaining to Project Hail Mary."

"That's not what I meant," Voigt said. "There are processes and background checks to—"

"No time," Stratt said. "No time for any of that stuff. That's why you put me in charge. Speed."

She turned toward me and tapped the paper: "These are readings from amateur astronomers all over the world. They show something very important."

The page had columns of numbers. I noticed the column titles: "Alpha Centauri," "Sirius," "Luyten 726-8," and so on.

"Stars?" I said. "These are all stars in our local cluster. And wait—did you say *amateur* astronomers? If you can tell the German minister of foreign affairs what to do, why don't you have professional astronomers working for you?"

"I do," Stratt said. "But this is historical data collected over the past several years. Professional astronomers don't study local stars. They look at faraway things. It's the amateurs who log data on local stuff. Like train spotters. Hobbyists in their backyards. Some of them with tens of thousands of dollars' worth of equipment."

I picked up the paper. "Okay, so what am I looking at?"

"Luminosity readings. Normalized across thousands of amateur-generated data sets and corrected for known weather and visibility conditions. Supercomputers were involved. The point is this: Our sun is not the only star that's getting dimmer."

"Really?" I said. "Ohhh! That makes perfect sense! Astrophage can travel at 0.92 times the speed of light. If it can go dormant and stay alive long enough, it could infect nearby stars. It spores! Just like mold! It spreads from star to star."

"That's our theory, yes," said Stratt. "This data goes back decades. It's not deeply reliable but the trends are there. The NSA back-calculated that—"

"Wait. NSA? The U.S. National Security Agency?"

"They have some of the best supercomputers in the world. I needed their supercomputers and engineers to try all kinds of scenarios and propagation models for how Astrophage could get around in the galaxy. Back to the point: These local stars have been dimming for decades. And the rate of dimming increases exponentially—just like we're seeing with the sun."

She handed me another piece of paper. It had a bunch of dots connected by lines. Above each dot was a star name. "Owing to the speed of light, our observations of the dimming had to be adjusted for the distances of the stars and whatnot, but there's a clear pattern of 'infection' from star to star. We know when each star was infected and by which infected star. Our sun was infected by a star called WISE 0855–0714. That star was infected by Sirius, which was infected by Epsilon Eridani. From there, the trail goes cold."

I peered at the chart. "Huh. WISE 0855–0714 also infected Wolf 359, Lalande 21185, and Ross 128."

"Yes, every star eventually infects all of its neighbors. Judging from our data, we think Astrophage has a maximum range of just under eight light-years. Any star within that range of an infected star will eventually be infected."

I looked at the data. "Why eight light-years? Why not more? Or less?"

"Our best guess is the Astrophage can only survive so long without a star and it can coast about eight light-years in that time."

"That's sensible, from an evolution point of view," I said. "Most stars have another star within eight light-years, so that's as far as Astrophage had to evolve to travel while sporing."

"Probably," Stratt said.

"Nobody noticed those stars getting dimmer?" I said.

"They only get to about ten percent dimmer before they stop dimming. We don't know why. It's not obvious to the naked eye, but—"

"But if our sun dims by ten percent, we're all dead," I said.

"Pretty much."

Xi leaned forward on the table. Her posture was extremely proper. "Ms. Stratt has not told you the most important part yet."

The Russian nodded. It was the first time I'd seen him move at all.

Xi continued. "Do you know what Tau Ceti is?"

"Do I know?" I said. "I mean—I know it's a star. It's about twelve light-years away, I think."

"Eleven point nine," said Xi. "Very good. Most would not know that."

"I teach junior high school science," I said. "These things come up."

Xi and the Russian shot each other surprised looks. Then they both looked at Stratt.

Stratt stared them down. "There's more to him than that."

Xi regained her composure (not that she'd lost much of it anyway). "Ahem. In any event, Tau Ceti is very much inside the cluster of infected stars. In fact, it is near the center."

"Okay," I said. "I'm sensing there's something special about it?"

"It is not infected," Xi said. "Every star around it is. There are two very infected stars well within eight light-years of Tau Ceti, yet it remains unaffected."

"Why?"

Stratt shuffled through her papers. "That's what we want to find out. So we're going to make a ship and send it there."

I snorted. "You can't just 'make' an interstellar ship. We don't have the technology. We don't have anything *close* to the technology."

The Russian spoke for the first time. "Actually, my friend, we do."

Stratt gestured to the Russian. "Dr. Komorov is—"

"Please call me Dimitri," he said.

"*Dimitri* heads up the Russian Federation's research into Astrophage," she said.

"It is pleasure to meet you," he said. "I am happy to report that we can actually make interstellar voyage."

"No, we can't," I said. "Unless you've got an alien spaceship you never told anyone about."

"In a way, we do," he said. "We have many alien spaceships. We call them Astrophage. You see? My group has studied the energy management of Astrophage. It is *very* interesting."

I suddenly forgot everything else going on in the room. "Oh God, please tell me you understand where the heat goes. I can't figure out what the heck it's doing with the heat energy!"

"We have figured this out, yes," said Dimitri. "With lasers. It was very illuminating experiment."

"Was that a pun?"

"It was!"

"Good one!"

We both laughed. Stratt glared at us.

Dimitri cleared his throat. "Er . . . yes. We pointed tight-focus one-kilowatt laser at a single Astrophage cell. As usual, it did not get hotter. But after twenty-five minutes, light starts to bounce off. Our little Astrophage is full. Good meal. It consumed 1.5 megajoules of light energy. Does not want more. But this is very much energy! Where does it put all this energy?"

I'm leaning way too far forward over the table, but I can't help myself. "Where?!"

"We measure Astrophage cell before and after experiment, of course."

"Of course."

"Astrophage cell is now seventeen nanograms heavier. You can see where this goes, yes?"

"No, it can't be. It must have gained that weight from reactions with the air or something."

"No, it was in a vacuum for the test, of course."

"Oh my God." I was giddy. "Seventeen nanograms . . . times nine times ten to the sixteenth . . . 1.5 megajoules!"

I flopped back into my chair. "Holy . . . I mean just . . . wow!"

"This was how I felt, yes."

Mass conversion. As the great Albert Einstein once said: $E = mc^2$. There's an absurd amount of energy in mass. A modern nuclear plant can power an entire city for a year with the energy stored in just one kilogram of Uranium. Yes. That's it. The entire output of a nuclear reactor for a year comes from a single kilogram of mass.

Astrophage can, apparently, do this in either direction. It takes heat energy and somehow turns it into mass. Then when it wants the energy back, it turns that mass back into energy—in the form of

Petrova-frequency light. And it uses that to propel itself along in space. So not only is it a perfect energy-storage medium, it's a perfect spaceship engine.

Evolution can be insanely effective when you leave it alone for a few billion years.

I rub my head. "This is just crazy. In a good way, though. Is it internally producing antimatter, you think? Something like that?"

"We do not know. But it definitely increases in mass. And then, after using light as thrust, it loses mass appropriate to energy released."

"That's . . . ! Dimitri, I want to hang out with you. Like—can we hang out? I'll buy you a beer. Or vodka. Or anything. I bet there's an officers' club on this boat, right?"

"It would be my pleasure."

"Glad you're making friends," said Stratt. "But you've got a lot of work to do before you start hitting the bars."

"Me? What do I have to do?"

"You need to design and create an Astrophage-breeding facility."

I blinked. Then I shot to my feet. "You're going to make an Astrophage-powered ship!"

They all nodded.

"Holy cow! It's the most efficient rocket fuel ever! How much would we need to—oh. Two million kilograms, right? That's why you wanted to know how long it would take to make that much?"

"Yes," said Xi. "For a one hundred thousand kilogram ship, we would need two million kilograms of Astrophage to get it to Tau Ceti. And, thanks to you, we now know how to activate the Astrophage and make it generate thrust at will."

I sat back down, pulled out my phone, and launched the calculator app. "This would take, like . . . a *lot* of energy. Like, more energy than the world has. It would be around ten to the twenty-third Joules. The largest nuclear reactor on Earth makes about eight gigawatts. It would take that reactor *two million years* to create that much energy."

"We have ideas for finding the energy," said Stratt. "Your job is to make the breeder. Start small and get a prototype going."

"Okay, sure," I said. "But I didn't exactly love the 'militaries of the world' grand tour on the way here. Can I take a passenger jet home? Coach is fine."

"You are home," said Stratt. "The flight hangar is empty. Just tell me what you need—including staff—and I'll make it happen."

I looked at the others in the conference room. Xi, Voigt, and Dimitri all nodded. Yes, this was real. No, Stratt wasn't kidding.

"Why?!" I demanded. "Why the heck can't you just be normal, Stratt?! If you want fast military transport, well, okay, but why not just work at an air base or something sane people would do?!"

"Because we'll be experimenting with a bunch of Astrophage once we breed it up. And if we accidentally activate even a couple of kilograms of that stuff, the resulting explosion will be bigger than the largest nuclear bomb ever made."

"Tsar Bomba," said Dimitri. "Made by my country. Fifty megatons. Boom."

Stratt continued. "So we'd rather be out in the middle of the ocean where we won't eradicate any cities."

"Oh," I said.

"And as we get more and more Astrophage, we'll go further and further out to sea. Anyway. Head down to the hangar deck. I have carpenters building accommodations and offices as we speak. Pick some you like and lay claim."

"This is our life now," said Dimitri. "Welcome."

CHAPTER 6

Okay, if I'm going to die, it's going to have meaning. I'm going to figure out what can be done to stop Astrophage. And then I'll send my answers off to Earth. And then . . . I'll die. There are lots of avenues for painless suicide here—from overdosing on meds to reducing the oxygen until I fall asleep and die.

Cheerful thought.

I eat a delicious tube of "Day 4—Meal 2." I think it's beef-flavored. The food is getting chunkier now. There are actually some solids in there. I think I'm chewing on a little cube of carrot. It's nice to feel some texture in the food for a change.

"More water!" I say.

The NannyBot (as I've come to call it) quickly takes my plastic cup away and replaces it with a full one. It's funny. Three days ago those ceiling-mounted arms were a mechanical monster that haunted me. Now they're just . . . there. Part of life.

I've found the dormitory to be a good place for thinking. Now that the dead bodies are gone, anyway. The lab doesn't have anywhere comfortable to relax. The control room has a nice chair, but it's cramped and has blinking lights everywhere. But the dormitory has my nice, comfortable bed I can lie back on while I think about what to do next. Plus, the bedroom is where all the food comes from.

I remembered a lot over the past couple of days. Looks like Project Hail Mary was a success, because here I am, in another star system. Tau Ceti, I assume. It makes sense that I'd mistake it for the sun. Tau Ceti is very similar to the sun as stars go. Same spectral type, color, and so on.

And I know why I'm here! Not just in vague terms like "Oh hey, the world's ending. Make that not happen." But very specifically: Find out why Tau Ceti wasn't affected by Astrophage.

Easy to say. Hard to do. Hopefully I remember more details later.

A million questions run through my mind. Some of the most important are:

1. How do I scour an *entire solar system* for information about Astrophage?
2. What am I supposed to do? Throw some of my Astrophage fuel at Tau Ceti to see what happens?
3. How do I steer this ship anyway?
4. If I do find useful information, how do I tell Earth about it? I think that's what the beetles are for, but how do I upload data to them? How do I aim them? How do I launch them?
5. Why would I, of all people, be part of this mission? Yes, I worked out a bunch of stuff about Astrophage, but so what? I'm a lab coat, not an astronaut. It's not like they sent Wernher von Braun into space. Surely there were more qualified people.

I decide to start small. First I have to work out what this ship can do and how to control it. They put the crew in comas. They must have known it might mess with our minds. There has to be an instruction manual somewhere.

"Flight manual," I say out loud.

"Ship information can be found in the control room," says the NannyBot.

"Where?"

"Ship information can be found in the control room."

"No. Where in the control room can ship information be found?"

"Ship information can be found in the control room."

"You kind of suck," I say.

I make my way up to the control room and take a good long look at every screen. I spend an hour in there cataloging what each area seems to say, and make guesses as to what the functions are. What I'm really looking for is something like "Information" or "Here to save humanity? Press this button to learn more!"

No such luck. After hours of poking at screens, I've found nothing. I guess they figured if the crew are so brain-mushy that they don't remember how to use the ship, they're probably not useful as scientists anyway.

I did find out that any screen can show any instrument panel. They're pretty much interchangeable. Just tap the upper-left corner and a menu shows up. Pick whatever panel you like.

That's nice. You can customize what you're looking at. And the screen directly in front of the pilot's seat is the largest.

I decide on a more tactile approach: I'm gonna start pushing buttons!

Hopefully there's no "Blow Up the Ship" button. I think Stratt would have kept that from happening.

Stratt. I wonder what she's doing right now. Probably in a control room somewhere with the pope making her a cup of coffee. She was (is?) a really domineering person. But gosh darn it, I'm glad she was in charge of making this ship happen. Now that I'm aboard it and all. Her attention to detail and insistence on perfection are nice to have all around me.

Anyway, I bring up the "Scientific Instrumentation" panel on the main screen. It's the same panel I spent a lot of quality time with earlier—the one that currently shows an image of Tau Ceti. It has the word "Helioscope" in the upper-left corner. I hadn't noticed that before. The left side of the screen has a bunch of icons. Other equipment, I assume. I press one at random.

Tau Ceti disappears. The top-left corner changes to read "External Collection Unit." The screen shows a diagram of a featureless rectangle. There are some controls here and there to change the angle and to "open bow side" and "open stern side." Okay. Noted. Not sure what to do with that information. I press another icon at random.

This time it changes to "Petrovascope." Beyond that, there's just a black screen with an error message: PETROVASCOPE CANNOT BE USED WHILE SPIN DRIVE IS ACTIVE.

"Hmph," I say.

Okay, what's a Petrovascope? Best guess: a telescope and/or camera that looks specifically for the IR light that Astrophage emit. It looks for the Petrova line via the Petrova wavelength so it's a Petrovascope and we really need to stop putting "Petrova" in front of everything.

Why can't I use it when the spin drive is active?

I don't know how a spin drive works, or why it's called a spin drive, but I do know I have one in the back of the ship and it's consuming Astrophage as fuel. So it's my engine. It probably activates enriched Astrophage to use them as thrust.

Ah . . . that would mean there's a *ridiculous* amount of IR light coming out the back of the ship right now. Like . . . enough to vaporize a battleship or something. I'd have to do the math to know for sure but—I can't help it, I want to do the math right now.

The engines consume 6 grams of Astrophage per second. Astrophage stores energy as mass. So basically, the spin drive converts 6 grams of mass into pure energy every second and spits it out the back. Well, it's the Astrophage doing the work, but whatever.

I bring up the "Utility" panel on a smaller screen to my right. It has a bunch of familiar applications, all ready to go. One of them is a calculator. I use it to calculate the mass-conversion energy of that 6 grams . . . good Lord. It's 540 *trillion* Joules. And the ship is emitting that much energy every second. So it's 540 trillion watts. I can't even fathom that amount of energy. It's considerably more than the surface of the sun. Literally. Like . . . you would get hit by less energy if you were on the *surface of the sun* than if you were standing behind the *Hail Mary* at full thrust.

I'm decelerating right now. Have to be. The plan is to come to rest in the Tau Ceti system. So I'm probably pointed away from the star and slowing down—having spent a really long time at near light speed during the trip.

Okay, so all that light energy will hit dust particles, ions, and anything else between me and Tau Ceti as I plug along. Those poor little particles will be brutally vaporized. And that'll scatter some IR light back at the ship. Not much compared to the engine output, but it would be blinding to the Petrovascope, which is finely tuned to look for trace amounts of that exact frequency.

So no using the Petrovascope with the engine on.

But man. I would *love* to know if Tau Ceti has a Petrova line.

Theoretically, any star infected with Astrophage should have one, right? The little blighters need carbon dioxide to breed. Can't get that from the star (unless you go way into the core, and I don't know if even Astrophage could survive those temperatures).

If I see a Petrova line, it means that Tau Ceti has an active Astrophage population that, for some reason, hasn't grown out of control like it has everywhere else. And that line will lead to a planet that has carbon dioxide. Maybe there's some other chemical in that atmosphere that impedes the Astrophage? Maybe the planet has a weird magnetic field that messes with their ability to navigate? Maybe the planet has a bunch of moons that the Astrophage physically collides with?

Maybe Tau Ceti just doesn't have any planets with carbon dioxide in their atmospheres. That would suck. It would mean this whole trip was for nothing and Earth is doomed.

I could speculate all day. Without data, it's just pure guesswork. And without the Petrovascope, I don't have data. At least, not the data I want.

I turn my attention to the Navigation screen. Should I mess with it?

I mean—I don't know how to fly this ship. The ship does, but I don't. If I push the wrong button, I'll be dead in space.

Actually, it would be worse than that. I'd be hurtling toward Tau Ceti at—I check the info on-screen—7,595 kilometers per second. Wow! A couple days ago, that was over 11,000. That's what constantly accelerating at 1.5 g's will do for you. Or "decelerating," I guess. From a physics standpoint it's all the same. Point is, I'm slowing down with respect to the star.

There's a button on-screen that just says "Course." That seems reasonable to tap, right? Famous last words. Really I should just wait until the computer feels like the trip is done. But I can't help myself.

I tap the button. The screen changes to show the Tau Ceti solar system. Tau Ceti itself sits at the center, denoted with the Greek letter tau.

Ohhhh . . . that's what the lowercase *t* is on the *Hail Mary* crest. It's a tau, for "Tau Ceti." Okay.

Anyway, four planetary orbits are shown as thin white ellipses around the star. The locations of the planets themselves are shown as circles with error bars. We don't have super-accurate information on exoplanets. If I could figure out how to get the science instruments working, I could probably get much better info on those planet locations. I'm twelve light-years closer to them than astronomers on Earth.

A yellow line runs almost directly into the system from off-screen. It bends toward the star somewhere between the third and fourth planets and into a circle. There's a yellow triangle on the line, way far away from the four planets. Pretty sure that's me. And the yellow line is my course. Above the map is the text:

TIME TO ENGINE CUTOFF: 0005:20:39:06

The final digit decrements once per second. Okay, I learned a couple of things here. First off, I have about five days left (closer to six) before the engine cuts off. Second off, the readout has four digits for days. That means this journey took at least one thousand days. Over three years. Well, it takes light *twelve* years to make this trip, so it should take me a long time too.

Oh, right. Relativity.

I have no idea how much time it took. Or, rather, I have no idea how much time I experienced. When you get going near the speed of light, you experience time dilation. More time will have gone by on Earth than I have experienced since I left Earth.

Relativity is weird.

Time is of the essence here. And unfortunately, while I slept, Earth experienced at least thirteen years. And even if I find a solution to the Astrophage problem right now, it would take at least thirteen years for that information to get back to Earth. So that means there'll be an absolute minimum of twenty-six years of Astrophage misery on Earth. I can only hope they are coming up with ways to deal with it. Or at least ameliorate the damage. I mean, they wouldn't have sent the *Hail Mary* out at all if they didn't think they could survive at least twenty-six years, right?

In any event, the trip took at least three years (from my point of view). Is that why we were put in comas? Was there a problem with us just being awake for the duration?

I only notice the tears when the first of them drops off my face. That decision to put us in comas killed two close friends of mine. They're gone. I don't remember a single moment with either of them, but the feeling of loss is overwhelming. I'll be joining them soon. There's no way home. I'll die out here too. But unlike them, I'll die alone.

I wipe my eyes and try to think of other things. My whole species is at stake here.

Judging by the path on the map, the ship will automatically put me in a stable orbit around Tau Ceti, between the third and fourth planets. If I had to guess, I would say that's probably 1 AU. The distance that Earth is from the sun. A nice, safe distance from the star. A slow orbit that takes about a year to complete. Probably longer, because

Tau Ceti is smaller than the sun, so it probably has less mass. Less mass means less gravity and a slower orbital period at a given distance.

Okay, I have five days to kill until engine cutoff. Rather than mess around with stuff, I'll just wait it out. Once the engines are off, I'll fire up the Petrovascope and see what's out there. Until then, I'll try to learn as much about the ship as I can.

I'll do just about anything right now to keep from thinking about Yáo and Ilyukhina.

Technically the carrier was named the *People's Liberation Army Navy Gansu*. Why their navy has "Army" in its name I'll never know. Regardless, people stopped calling it that and started calling it *Stratt's Vat*. Despite objections from the sailors aboard, the name stuck. We wandered around the South China Sea, never getting too close to land.

I'd spent a blissful week doing nothing but science.

No meetings. No distractions. Just experimentation and engineering. I'd forgotten how much fun it was to get immersed in a task.

My first breeder prototype had demonstrated another successful run. It wasn't much to look at—mostly a 30-foot-long metal pipe with a bunch of ugly control equipment welded on here and there. But it did the trick. It could only generate a few micrograms of Astrophage per hour, but the concept was solid.

I had a staff of twelve people—engineers from all over the world. A couple of Mongolian brothers were my best engineers. When I got a call from Stratt to meet her in the conference room, I left them in charge.

I found her alone in the meeting room. The table was strewn with papers and charts, like always. Graphs and diagrams adorned all the walls—some new, some old.

Stratt sat at one end of the long table, with a bottle of Dutch gin and a lowball glass. I'd never seen her drink before.

"You wanted to see me?" I said.

She looked up. Her eyes had bags. She hadn't slept. "Yeah. Have a seat."

I sat in the chair next to her. "You look terrible. What's going on?"

"I have to make a decision. And it's not easy."

"How can I help?"

She offered me the gin. I shook my head. She topped off her own glass. "The *Hail Mary* is going to have a very small crew compartment—about 125 cubic meters."

I cocked my head. "That's actually kind of big as spaceships go, right?"

She wiggled her hand back and forth. "Big for a capsule like Soyuz or Orion. But tiny for a space station. It's about one-tenth as big as the International Space Station's crew compartment."

"Okay," I said. "What's the problem?"

"The problem"—she picked up a manila folder and dropped it in front of me—"is that the crew will kill each other."

"Huh?" I opened the folder. Inside were lots of typewritten pages. Actually, they were scans of typed pages. Some were in English, some in Russian. "What is all this?"

"During the Space Race, the Soviets briefly set their sights on Mars. They figured if they put people on Mars, the U.S. moon landing would be trivial in comparison."

I closed the folder. The Cyrillic writing was nonsense to me. But my guess was Stratt could read it. She always seemed to know whatever language was being used.

She rested her chin on her hands. "Getting to Mars with 1970s technology would mean using a Hohmann transfer trajectory, which means the crew would have to spend just over eight months aboard a ship. So the Soviets tested out what happens when you put people together in a cramped, isolated environment for several months."

"And?"

"After seventy-one days, the men inside were getting in fistfights every day. They stopped the experiment on day ninety-four because one of the subjects tried to stab another one to death with broken glass."

"How big will the crew be for the mission?"

"The current plan is three," she said.

"Okay," I said. "So you're worried what happens when we send three astronauts on a four-year trip in a 125-cubic-meter compartment?"

"It's not just about them getting along. Each crew member would spend the whole trip knowing that they're going to die in a few years. And that the few rooms on that ship are the only world they will know for the rest of their short lives. The psychiatrists I've talked to say that crushing depression is likely. And suicide is a real risk."

"Yeah, that is some rough psychology," I said. "But what else can we do?"

She picked up a stapled sheaf of papers and slid it toward me. I picked it up and read the title: "A Study of Long-Term Primate and Human Coma Patients and Detrimental Aftereffects—Srisuk et al."

"Okay. What am I looking at here?"

"That's a study by a failed company in Thailand." She swirled the gin in her glass. "Their idea was to put cancer patients into induced comas for their chemotherapy treatments. The patient gets the chemo, but doesn't have to be awake to suffer through the process. Wake them up when the cancer goes into remission. Or when it's no longer treatable and it's time for hospice. Either way, they skip a lot of misery."

"That . . . sounds like a great idea," I said.

She nodded. "It would be, if it wasn't so lethal. Turns out the human body just isn't supposed to be in a coma for a long time. Chemo lasts months, and often needs additional rounds after that. They tried various means for medically induced comas on primates, and the primates either died during the coma or came out of it with mush for brains."

"So why are we talking about it?"

"Because they did more studies—this time on historical human coma patient data. They looked at humans who had come through long comas relatively unscathed and tried to see what they had in common. They found it."

Old Russian space-agency documents were a mystery to me, but scientific papers were my forte for a long time. I flipped through the paper and skimmed to the findings. "Gene markers?" I said.

"Yes," she said. "They found a collection of genes that give a human 'coma resistance.' That's what they're calling it. The sequences are in what scientists used to think was junk DNA. But apparently it's something we evolved a long time ago for some unknown reason and still lurks in some people's genetic code."

"Are they sure these genes *cause* coma resistance?" I said. "They correlate, but do they *cause* it?"

"Yes, they're sure. The genes are found in lower primates too. Whatever it is, it goes way back in the evolutionary tree. There's speculation it might go all the way back to our aquatic ancestors that used to hibernate. In any event, they ran tests on primates with those genes and they survived long comas with no side effects. Every single one of them."

"Okay. I see where you're going with this." I put the paper down. "Do DNA tests on all applicants, and use only the people who have those coma-resistance genes. During the trip, put the crew in comas. They don't have to experience four years of getting on each other's nerves or introspection about their deaths."

She raised her glass to me. "It gets better. Having the crew in comas makes the food situation much easier. Powdered, nutritionally balanced slurry pumped right into their stomachs. No need for a thousand kilograms of diverse meals. Just powder and a self-contained water-recycling system."

I smiled. "This seems like a dream come true. Like suspended animation in sci-fi novels. Why are you drinking and stressed-out?"

"There are a couple of catches," she said. "First off, we'd have to develop a completely automated monitoring and action system to take care of the coma patients. If it broke down, everyone would die. There's more to it than just monitoring vitals and pushing the right drugs through an IV. It would have to physically move and clean the patients, deal with bedsores, diagnose and treat secondary issues like inflammation and infection around the various IV and probe entry points. Stuff like that."

"Okay, but that seems like something the global medical community could work out for us," I said. "Use your Stratt magic to boss them around or something."

She took another sip. "That's not the main problem. The main problem is this: On average, only one in every seven thousand humans has that genetic sequence."

I sat back in my chair. "Whoa."

"Yeah. We wouldn't be able to send the most qualified people. We'd be sending the seven-thousandth most qualified people."

"Three-thousand-five-hundredth most qualified people on average," I said.

She rolled her eyes.

"Still," I said. "One seven-thousandth of the world's population is a million people. Think of it that way. You'd have a pool of one million people to look through for candidates. All you need are three."

"Six," she said. "We need a primary crew and a backup crew. Can't have the mission fail because some guy gets hit by a car crossing the street the day before launch."

"Okay, then six."

"Yeah. Six people of astronaut caliber, who have the scientific skills necessary to work out what's going on with Astrophage at Tau Ceti, and who are willing to go on a suicide mission."

"Out of a population of a million," I said. "A *million*."

She fell silent and took another sip of gin.

I cleared my throat. "So you either take your chances with picking the best possible candidates and maybe they kill each other, or you take your chances on yet-to-be-developed medical technology to automatically care for a lower tier of talent."

"More or less. Either way, it's a terrible risk. It's the hardest decision I've ever had to make."

"Good thing you already made up your mind, then," I said.

She raised an eyebrow. "Huh?"

"Sure," I said. "You just wanted someone to tell you what you already know. If you leave the crew awake, there's nothing you can do about the psychosis risk. But we've got years to perfect the automated-coma-bed technology."

She scowled a bit but didn't speak.

I softened my voice. "Besides. We're already asking these people to die. We shouldn't ask them to suffer emotional torment for four years too. Science and morality both give the same answer here, and you know it."

She nodded, almost imperceptibly. Then, she downed the rest of her gin. "All right. You can go." She slid her laptop over and began typing.

I left without another word. She had her stuff to deal with and I had mine.

The memories are coming back more smoothly now. I still can't remember everything, but it's no longer an epiphany when they happen. It's just sort of . . . "Oh hey, I know that. Always knew it, really."

I guess I'm one of those people with coma resistance. That explains why I'm here instead of any of the far more qualified candidates that should have been sent.

But Yáo and Ilyukhina probably had those genes, too, and they didn't make it. My guess is the medical robot wasn't perfect. They must have had some medical situation arise it couldn't figure out.

I shake off their memory.

The next several days are an exercise in patience. I learn more about the ship to distract myself.

I catalog the entire lab. One of the first things I find is a touchscreen computer in a pull-out drawer in the center table. It's actually a fantastic find, because it has a bunch of research-related screens. As opposed to the panels in the control room, which are all about the ship or its instruments.

I see a bunch of math and science apps—most of which are off-the-shelf that I'm familiar with. But the real boon is the library!

As far as I can tell, this panel can bring up literally any scientific textbook ever written, every scientific paper ever published on any topic, and a whole lot more. There's one directory just called "Library of Congress," and it appears to be the entire digital catalog of everything that's ever been copyrighted in the United States. No books about the *Hail Mary,* unfortunately.

And the reference manuals. So many reference manuals. Data on top of data with data in between. I guess they figured solid-state hard drives are light, so there was no reason to be stingy with information. Heck, they may have just burned the data into ROMs.

They gave me reference material on stuff that can't possibly be useful. But hey, it's nice to know that if I need the average rectal temperature of a healthy goat, I can find that out! (It's 103.4°F / 39.7°C.)

Playing with the panel leads to my next discovery: I know how I'll report back to Earth with the beetles.

I knew they'd be involved, but now I know specifics. In addition to the absurd data storage array aboard the ship, the panel also has four comparatively small external drives mounted: John, Paul, George, and Ringo. Each one of those shows 5 terabytes free. It's not a huge leap to assume that's the beetle's data.

So how do I launch them when the time comes? To find out, I head to the control room.

I have to dig through a few layers of UI on the Beetles panel to find the launch command, but I find it. As far as I can tell, it's just a button labeled "Launch." I guess they orient themselves based on stars and head toward Earth on their own. The *Hail Mary* did the same thing to get here, so they know how to do it. No reason to introduce human error in the course selection.

While I'm here, I poke around the Scientific Instrumentation screen. The first few subwindows are the helioscope, the Petrovascope, and a telescope that can see in the visible spectrum, IR spectrum, and a bunch of other bands.

I play with the visible-light telescope. It's kind of fun. I can look at the stars. I mean, there's nothing else out there. Even Tau Ceti's planets would just be little dots from where I am. But it's still nice to see the outside from my confined little world.

I also found a dedicated EVA screen. It has more or less what I would have expected. There are a bunch of controls for the EVA suit itself, so an operator in the control room can manage any issue with the suit during an EVA. That way, the person in the suit doesn't have to deal with it. Plus, it looks like the ship has a complicated tethering system on the hull. Basically a bunch of tracks that the tether hook can run along. They really figured an EVA would be important. Probably to collect local Astrophage.

If there is any.

If Tau Ceti has a Petrova line, then there's Astrophage to be collected. Getting ahold of some would be step one. Getting that down to the lab, and seeing if it differs from the Astrophage on Earth. Maybe it's a less virulent strain?

The next two days are, basically, me worrying about what happens next. Oh, I know what happens next—I'm just worrying about it anyway.

I fidget in the control room and watch the seconds tick away.

"You're going to be in zero g," I say. "You are not going to be falling. You will not be in danger. The acceleration of the ship will stop. But that's okay."

I don't like roller coasters or water slides. That dropping sensation scares the pants off me. And in a few seconds I'm going to feel that exact sensation because the "gravity" I've been experiencing will stop altogether.

The seconds tick off. "Four . . . three . . . two . . ."

"Here we go," I said.

"One . . . zero."

Right on schedule, the engines shut off. The 1.5 g's I've been feeling all this time vanishes. Gravity is gone.

I panic. No amount of mental preparation would have worked. I straight-up panic.

I scream and flail around. I force myself to curl into a fetal position—it's comforting and keeps me from hitting any controls or screens.

I shiver and shake as I float around the control room. I should have strapped myself to the chair, but I didn't think to. Dummy.

"I'm not falling!" I scream. "I'm not falling! This is just space! Everything is fine!"

It's not fine. I feel my stomach in my throat. I'm going to puke. Puke in zero g is not okay. I don't have a bag. I severely underprepared for this. I was stupid to think I could just talk myself out of a primal fear.

I pull the collar of my jumpsuit open and tilt my head down. I'm just in the nick of time. I puke out the entirety of "Day 9—Meal 3" into my shirt. I hold the collar tight to my chest afterward. It's disgusting, but contained. Better than letting it float around the control room and becoming a choking hazard.

"Oh gosh . . ." I whimper. "Gosh . . . this is . . ."

Can I do this? Will I be rendered completely worthless from this point on? Will humanity die because I can't handle zero g?

No.

I clench my teeth. I clench my fists. I clench my butt. I clench every part of me that I know how to clench. It gives me a feeling of control. I'm doing something by aggressively doing nothing.

After an eternity, the panic begins to ebb away. Human brains are amazing things. We can get used to just about anything. I'm making the adjustment.

The slight reduction of fear has a feedback effect. I know I will get less afraid now. And knowing that makes the fear subside even faster. Soon, the panic dies down to fear, which diffuses into general anxiousness.

I look around the control room and nothing seems right. Nothing changed, but now there's no down. I still feel sick to my stomach. I grab my collar in case I need to puke again but it isn't necessary. I hold it in.

The feeling of warm vomit squishing between my chest and jumpsuit is disgusting. I need to change.

I aim myself at the hatchway leading to the lab and kick off the bulkhead behind me. I float down and into the lab. The whole room is cluttered with random floating debris. I left things out on the table when I cataloged them. Now all that stuff is wandering around freely, wafted along by currents from the life-support air vents.

"Dummy," I say to myself. I really should have seen that coming.

I continue onward to the bedroom. Not surprisingly, it's also got junk floating everywhere. I opened most of the bins in the storage area to see what was inside. Now the bins and their contents drift to and fro.

"Clean me!" I say to the arms.

The arms don't do anything.

I strip down and use the jumpsuit to wipe gross stuff from my body. I found the sponge-bath zone a few days ago—just a sink with sponges that comes out of the wall. No room for a shower, I guess. Anyway, I clean up with that stuff.

I'm not sure what to do with the gross, dirty stuff.

"Laundry?" I say.

The arms reach down and take the dirty jumpsuit from my hands. A panel in the ceiling opens and they put it in there somewhere. What happens when that fills up? No idea.

I find a replacement jumpsuit in the flotsam and put it on. Putting on clothes in zero g is interesting. I wouldn't say it's harder, but it's different. I do manage to get the new jumpsuit on. It's a little tight. I check the name patch. It says 姚. It's one of Yáo's jumpsuits. Well, it's not too tight. And I don't want to bounce around the bedroom all day looking for one of mine. I'll organize it all later.

For now, I'm too excited to see what's out there. I mean, come on! I'm the first human to explore another star system! And I'm here!

I launch off the floor toward the hatchway . . . and miss. I crash into the ceiling. At least I get my arms up in time to protect my face. I bounce off the ceiling and back to the floor.

"Ow," I mumble. I try again, this time a little more slowly, and I'm successful. I coast up through the lab, and into the control room. Getting around sure is a lot easier when there's no gravity. I still feel queasy but I have to admit: This is pretty fun.

I pull myself into the pilot's chair and strap myself in to keep from floating away.

The Navigation screen reads PRIMARY TRANSIT COMPLETE. The Spin Drive screen says THRUST: 0. But most important, the Petrovascope screen says READY.

I rub my hands together, then reach for the screen. The interface is simple enough. The corner has an icon that is a toggle switch with two states: "Visible" and "Petrova." It's currently set to "Visible." The rest of the screen shows a visible-light view from the ship. Seems like an ordinary camera. I poke at the screen and quickly realize I can pan, zoom in or out, rotate, and so on.

All I see is stars in the distance. I guess I should pan around until I find Tau Ceti. I swipe my finger left, left, left . . . just generally trying to see where the star is. I don't have a frame of reference to work with. Every few left swipes I throw in a down swipe. Just to cover all angles over time. I do finally find Tau Ceti, but it doesn't look like it should.

A few days ago, when I looked at it with the helioscope, it looked like any other star. But now it's a solid black circle with a hazy ring of light around it. I realize why immediately.

The Petrovascope is a pretty sensitive piece of equipment. It's fine-tuned to spot even the smallest amounts of the Petrova wavelength. A star will give off absolutely *obscene* amounts of light at all wavelengths. It'd be like staring at the sun with binoculars. The equipment has to protect itself from the star. It probably has a physical metal plate that it keeps between its sensors and the star at all times. So I'm looking at the back of that plate.

Good design.

I reach up to the toggle switch. This is it. If there's no Petrova line here, I don't know what to do. I mean, I'll try to figure out something. But I'll be kind of lost.

I flip the toggle.

The stars disappear. The hazy ring surrounding Tau Ceti remains. That's to be expected. It's the star's corona, which will be emitting plenty of light, so some of it's bound to be the Petrova wavelength.

I search the image desperately. Nothing at first, but then I see it. A beautiful dark-red arch coming out of the bottom-left portion of Tau Ceti.

I clap my hands. "Yes!"

The shape is unmistakable. It's a Petrova line! Tau Ceti has a Petrova line! I do a wiggly little dance in my chair. It's not easy in zero g but I give it my all. Now we're getting somewhere!

There are so many experiments I'll need to do, I don't even know where to begin. I should see where the line leads, for starters. One of the planets, obviously, but which one and what's interesting about it? And I should get a sample of local Astrophage to see if it's the same as what we have back on Earth. I could do that by flying into the Petrova line itself and then scraping the dust off the hull with an EVA.

I could spend a week just writing up a list of experiments I want to do!

I spot a flash on the screen. Just a quick blip of light.

"What's that?" I say. "Another clue?"

The flash happens again. I pan and zoom in on that portion of space. It's nowhere near the Petrova line or Tau Ceti. Maybe a reflection from a planet or asteroid?

I can see how that might happen. A highly reflective asteroid could be bouncing enough light from Tau Ceti around that I see it on the Petrovascope, but it's intermittent, so maybe it's an irregular shape that's rotating and—

The flash becomes a solid light source. It's just . . . "on" now. Non-stop.

I peer at the screen. "What . . . what's going on here? . . ."

The light source becomes brighter. Not instantly. Just gradually over time. I watch for a minute. It seems to get brighter faster now.

Is it an object headed toward me?

An instant hypothesis pops into my mind: Maybe Astrophage are somehow attracted to other Astrophage? Maybe some subset of them saw the flare from my engines, which would be the wavelength they use, and they headed toward me. Maybe this is how they find the main migration group? So this could be a clump of Astrophage headed my way, thinking I can lead them to the planet with the carbon dioxide?

Interesting theory. Nothing to back it up, though.

The steady light grows brighter, brighter, brighter, and then finally disappears.

"Huh," I say. I wait a few minutes, but the light does not return.

"Hmm. . . ." I make a mental note of the anomaly. But for now there's nothing I can do about it. Whatever it was, it's gone now.

Back to the Petrova line. The first thing I want to do is find out which planet the line leads to. I guess I'll have to work out how to navigate the ship, but that's another challenge.

I pan back to look at the Petrova line. Something's wrong now. Half of it is just . . . gone.

It's coming out of Tau Ceti, just like it was a few minutes ago, but then it stops abruptly at a seemingly arbitrary point in space.

"What is going on?"

Did I mess up their migration pattern, maybe? If it's that easy, wouldn't we have worked that out when the *Hail Mary* was wandering around our own solar system?

I zoom in on the cutoff point. It's just a straight line. Like someone took an X-Acto knife to the whole Petrova line and threw away the scrap.

A giant line of migrating Astrophage doesn't just disappear. I have a simpler explanation: There's something on the camera lens. Some blob of debris. Maybe a wad of overexcitable Astrophage. That would be nice. I'd have a sample to look at right away!

Maybe a visible-light view will give me a better idea of what's going on. I press the toggle button.

And that's when I see it.

There is an object blocking my view of the Petrova line. It's right next to my ship. Maybe a few hundred meters away. It's roughly triangle-shaped and it has gable-like protrusions along its hull.

Yes. I said hull. It's not an asteroid—the lines are too smooth; too straight. This object was made. Fabricated. Constructed. Shapes like that don't occur in nature.

It's a ship.

Another ship.

There's another ship in this system with me. Those flashes of light—those were its engines. It's Astrophage-powered. Just like the *Hail Mary*. But the design, the shape—it's nothing like any spacecraft I've ever seen. The whole thing is made of huge, flat surfaces—the worst possible way to make a pressure vessel. No one in their right mind would make a ship that shape.

No one on Earth would, anyway.

I blink a few times at what I'm seeing. I gulp.

This . . . this is an alien spacecraft. Made by aliens. Aliens intelligent enough to make a spacecraft.

Humanity isn't alone in the universe. And I've just met our neighbors.

"Holy fucking shit!"

CHAPTER 7

A flood of thoughts hit me all at the same time: We're not alone. This is an alien. That ship is weird, how does the engineering of that work? Do they live here? Is this their star? Am I starting an interplanetary incident by wandering into alien territory?!

"Breathe," I tell myself.

Okay, one thing at a time. What if this is another ship from Earth? One I don't remember? Heck, it took me a few days to remember my name. Maybe Earth sent multiple ships with different designs? Like, for redundancy or to increase the odds that at least one of them works. Maybe that ship is the *Praise Allah* or the *Blessings of Vishnu* or something.

I look all around the control room. There are screens and controls for everything, but there's nothing for a radio. The EVA panel has some radio controls, but that's obviously just for talking to crewmates when they're outside.

If they'd sent multiple ships, surely they would have had some radio system so we could talk to each other.

Also, that ship . . . it's insane.

I cycle through the navigation console screens until I find the Radar panel. I'd noticed it earlier, but didn't think much of it. I assume it's there so I can get near asteroids or other objects and not collide with them.

After a few halting attempts, I manage to turn it on. It immediately spots the other ship and sounds an alarm. The shrill noise hurts my ears.

"Whoa, whoa, whoa!" I say. I frantically scan the panel until I see a button labeled "Mute Proximity Alert." I press it and the noise stops.

I scan the rest of the screen. There's a lot of data here, all in a window titled "BLIP-A." I guess if there were multiple contacts I'd get multiple windows. Whatever. It's all just raw numbers about the reading. Nothing useful like an isometric *Star Trek* scan or anything.

"Velocity" is zero. They have matched my velocity exactly. That can't be a coincidence.

"Range" is 217 meters. I'm assuming that's the distance to the closest part of the other ship. Or maybe the average. No, it would be the closest part. The point of this system is probably to avoid collisions.

Speaking of collisions—217 meters is a ridiculously small distance compared to the size of a solar system. There's no way this is a coincidence. That ship positioned itself here on purpose because I'm here.

Another reading, "Angular width," is 35.44 degrees. Okay, some basic math should handle this.

I bring up the Utility panel on the main screen and launch the calculator app. Something 217 meters away is occupying 35.44 degrees of the view. Presuming the radar can see in all 360 degrees (it would be a pretty cruddy radar if it couldn't) . . . I type some numbers into the calculator to do an ARCTAN operation, and:

The ship is 139 meters long. Roughly.

I bring the Astrophage panel up on another screen. The little map there shows that the *Hail Mary* is just 47 meters long. So yeah. The alien ship is three times the size of mine. There's just no way Earth sent something that big.

And the shape. What is up with that shape? I turn my attention back to the Petrovascope (which is now just acting as a camera).

The center of the ship is diamond-shaped—a rhombus. Well, I guess it's an octahedron, really. Looks like it has eight faces, each triangular. That part alone is about the size of my ship.

The diamond is connected by three thick rods (I don't know what else to call them) to a wide trapezoidal base. That looks like it might be the rear. And in front of the diamond is a narrow stalk (just making up terms at this point) that has four flat panels attached parallel to the main ship axis. Maybe solar panels? The stalk continues forward to a pyramid-shaped nose cone. Nose pyramid, I guess.

Every part of the hull is flat. Even the "rods" have flat faces.

Why would anyone do that? Flat panels are a terrible idea. I don't know anything about who made this, but presumably they need some kind of atmosphere inside, right? Huge, flat panels are *awful* at that.

Maybe this is just a *probe* and not an actual ship. Maybe there's no atmosphere inside because there's nothing alive inside. I might be looking at an alien artifact instead of a ship.

Still the most exciting moment in human history.

So it's Astrophage-powered. That was the steady Petrova-frequency glow I saw earlier. Interesting that they have the same propulsion tech as we do. But considering it's the best energy-storage medium possible, that's not a surprise. When European mariners first came across Asian mariners, no one was surprised they both used sails.

But the "why." That's what gets me. Some entity aboard (either a computer or a crew) decided to come to my ship. How did they even know I was here?

Same way I saw them, I guess. The massive IR light coming off my engines. And since the rear of my ship was pointed at Tau Ceti, that means I was shining a 540-trillion-watt flashlight in their direction. Depending on where they were at the time, I might have appeared even brighter than Tau Ceti itself. At least, in the Petrova frequency.

So they can see the Petrova frequency. And so can I.

I flip through the Spin Drive console screens until I find one labeled "Manual Control." When I select it, a warning dialog pops up:

MANUAL CONTROL IS RECOMMENDED ONLY FOR EMERGENCIES. ARE YOU SURE YOU WANT TO ENTER MANUAL CONTROL MODE?

I tap "Yes."

It brings up another dialog.

SECOND CONFIRMATION: TYPE "Y-E-S" TO ENTER MANUAL CONTROL MODE.

I groan and type Y-E-S.

The panel finally takes me to the Manual Control screen. It's a bit scary. Not because it's complex, but because it's so simple.

There are three sliders labeled "Drive 1," "Drive 2," and "Drive 3," each presently at zero. The top of each slider is labeled "10^7 N." The N must mean "Newtons"—a unit of force. I guess if I threw all three drives to maximum, it would give me 30 million Newtons. That's about sixty times the thrust a jumbo jet's engines produce during takeoff.

Science teachers know a lot of random facts.

There are a bunch more little sliders. In groups labeled "Yaw," "Pitch," and "Roll." There must be little spin drives on the sides of the ship to adjust its orientation. I can definitely see why it's a bad idea to mess with this panel. One screw-up and I'll put the ship into a spin that tears it apart.

But at least they thought of that. There's a button in the middle of the screen labeled "Zero All Rotation." Good.

I check the Petrovascope again. Blip-A hasn't moved. It's on my port side, and slightly forward.

I flick the Petrovascope back to Petrova-frequency mode, and the screen turns mostly black. As before, I can see the Petrova line in the background, occluded by Blip-A.

"Let's see if you have anything to say . . ." I mumble. Spin drive 2 is in the center of the ship. Its thrust will be along my central axis and hopefully won't introduce attitude change. We'll see.

I set it to 0.1% power for one second, then back to 0.

Even with just one engine, at one one-thousandth power, for one second, the ship drifts a bit. The "Velocity" value for Blip-A on the Radar panel shows 0.086 m/s. That tiny thrust set my ship moving about 8 centimeters per second.

But I don't care about that. I care about the other ship.

I watch the Petrovascope. A bead of sweat separates from my forehead and floats away. I feel like my heart is going to beat out of my chest.

Then, the rear of the ship lights up in the Petrova frequency for one second. Just like I did.

"Wow!"

I flick the drive on and off several times: three short bursts, a long one, and one more short one. There's no message there. I just want to see what they do with it.

They were more prepared this time. Within seconds, the other ship repeats the pattern.

I gasp. And I smile. Then I wince. Then I smile again. This is a lot to take in.

That was too fast for any probe to respond. If it had remote control or something, the controllers would have to be at least a few light-minutes away—there's just nothing around here that could be housing them.

There is an intelligent life-form aboard that ship. I am about 200 meters away from an honest-to-God alien!

I mean . . . my ship is powered by aliens. But this new one is intelligent!

Oh my gosh! This is it! First Contact! I'm the guy! I'm the guy who meets aliens for the first time!

The *Blip-A* (that's what I'm calling their ship for now) fires up its engines again briefly. I watch closely to memorize the sequence, but it's just a single low-intensity light. They're not signaling. They're maneuvering.

I check the Radar panel. Sure enough, the *Blip-A* brings itself alongside the *Hail Mary* and holds position at 217 meters.

I flick through the Scientific panel to bring the normal telescopic cameras back up. The Petrovascope's normal-light camera is just to orient things for the main scope itself. The telescope has much better resolution and clarity. I guess I'm too excited to think clearly because it took me until now to think of it.

The image is far clearer through the main telescope. I guess it's just an insanely high-resolution camera, because I can still zoom in and out with no loss of clarity. I have a very good view of the *Blip-A* now.

The ship's hull is a mottled gray and tan. The pattern seems random and smooth, like someone started mixing paint but stopped way too early.

I spot motion in the corner of the screen. An irregular-shaped object slides along a track in the hull. It's a stalk sticking up with five articulated "arms" coming out of the top. Each arm has a clamp-like "hand" on the end.

It's only now that I notice a network of the tracks all along the hull.

It's a robot. Something controlled from the inside. At least, I assume it is. It doesn't look like a little green man, and it certainly doesn't look like an alien EVA suit.

Not that I have any idea what either of those things would look like.

Yeah, I'm pretty sure that's a hull-mounted robot. Space stations back at Earth have them. They're a nice way to do stuff outside your ship without having to suit up.

The robot works its way along the hull until it reaches the spot closest to the *Hail Mary*. One of its little clamp hands holds a cylindrical object. I don't really have a sense of scale, but the robot is tiny compared to the ship. I feel like it's about my size or maybe smaller, but that's a wild guess.

The robot stops, reaches toward my ship, and gently releases the cylinder into space.

The cylinder moves slowly toward me. It has a slight rotation, end-over-end. Not perfect, but still a very smooth release.

I check the Radar panel. The *Blip-A* is at velocity zero. And there's a "Blip-B" screen now. It shows the much smaller cylinder approaching at 8.6 centimeters per second.

Interesting. That's the *exact* same velocity I moved the *Hail Mary* a moment ago while flashing the engine to say hi. That can't be a coincidence. They want me to have that cylinder, and they want to deliver it to me at a velocity they know I'm comfortable working with.

"Very considerate of you . . ." I say.

These are smart aliens.

I have to assume friendly intent at this point. I mean, they're going out of their way to say hi and be accommodating. Besides, if there is hostile intent, what would I do about it? Die. That's what I'd do. I'm a scientist, not Buck Rogers.

Well, I mean, I guess I could point the spin drives at their ship, fire them up to full, which would vaporize—you know what? I'm just not going to think along those lines right now.

Some quick math tells me the cylinder will take over forty minutes to reach me. I have that long to get in an EVA suit, go outside, and position myself on the hull for humanity's first touchdown-pass reception with an alien quarterback.

I learned a lot about the airlock when I was giving my crewmates a burial in space and—

Ilyukhina would have loved this moment. She would have been absolutely bouncing around the cabin with excitement. Yáo would have been stoic and steady, but he would have cracked a smile when he thought we weren't looking.

The tears ruin my vision. Lacking gravity, they coat my eyes. It's like trying to see underwater. I wipe them off and fling them across the control room. They splatter onto the opposite wall. I don't have time for this. I have an alien thingy to catch.

I unhook the belt on the chair and float over to the airlock. My mind is awhirl with ideas and questions. And I'm jumping to wild, unfounded conclusions left and right. Maybe this intelligent alien species invented Astrophage. Maybe they genetically engineered it specifically to "grow" spaceship fuel. The ultimate in solar power.

Maybe once I explain what's happening to Earth, they'll have a solution.

Or maybe they'll board my ship and lay eggs in my brain. You can never be sure.

I open the inner airlock door and pull out the EVA suit. So, do I have any idea how to get into this thing? Or how to safely use it?

I disable the chrysalis-lock of the Orlan-MKS2 EVA suit and open the rear hatch. I activate main power by flicking a switch on the belt. The suit boots up almost immediately and the status panel attached to the chest component reads ALL SYSTEMS FUNCTIONAL—what the heck? I know everything that's going on in here.

We were probably trained on this thing extensively. I know it the same way I know physics. It's there in my mind, but I don't remember learning it.

The Russian-made suit is a single-pressure vessel. Unlike American models where you put the top and bottom on, then a bunch of complex stuff for the helmet and gloves, the Orlan series is basically a onesie with a hatch in the back. You step into it, close the hatch, and you're done. It's like an insect molting in reverse.

I open the back and wriggle into the suit. Zero g is a real boon here. I don't have to fight with the suit nearly as much as I normally would. Weird. I know this is easier than other times I've done it, but don't remember any other times I've done it. I think I have brain damage from that coma.

I'm functional enough for now. I press on.

I get my arms and legs into their respective holes. The jumpsuit is uncomfortable in the Orlan. I'm supposed to be wearing a special undergarment. I even know what it looks like, but it's just for temperature regulation and bio-monitoring. I don't have time to find it in the storage area. I have a date with a cylinder.

Now in the suit, I push steadily against the airlock wall with my legs to push the open rear flap to the wall. Once it gets to within a few inches (centimeters, I should say. This is Russian-made after all), a light turns green on the chest-mounted status panel. I reach up to the panel with my thickly gloved hand and press the Autoseal button.

The suit ratchets the opening closed with a series of loud clicks. With a final "clunk" the outer seal locks into place. My status board reads green and I have seven hours of life support available. Internal pressure is 400 hectopascals—about 40 percent of Earth's atmosphere at sea level. That's normal for spacesuits.

The whole process took only five minutes. I'm ready to go outside.

Interesting. I didn't have to go through a decompression step. On space stations back home, astronauts have to spend hours in an airlock slowly acclimating to the low pressure needed for the EVA suit before they can go out. I don't have that problem. Apparently, the entire *Hail Mary* is at that 40 percent pressure.

Good design. The only reason space stations around Earth have a full atmosphere of pressure is in case the astronauts have to abort and return to Earth in a hurry. But for the *Hail Mary* crew . . . where would we go? May as well use the low pressure all the time. Makes things easier on the hull and lets you do rapid EVAs.

I take a deep breath and let it out. A soft whir comes from somewhere behind me and cool air flows along my back and shoulders. Air conditioning. It feels nice.

I grab a handhold and spin myself around. I pull the inner airlock door closed and then rotate the primary lever to begin the cycling sequence. A pump fires up. It's louder than I would have thought. It sounds like an idling motorcycle. I keep my hand on the lever. Pushing it back to the original position will cancel the cycle and repressurize. If I see even a *hint* of a red light on my suit panel, I'm going to throw that lever so fast it'll make my head spin.

After a minute, the pump grows quieter. Then quieter still. It's probably as loud as it ever was. But with the air leaving the chamber, there's no way for the noise to get to me other than through my feet touching the Velcro pads on the floor.

Finally, the pump stops. I'm in total silence aside from the fans inside the suit. The airlock controls show that the pressure inside is zero, and a yellow light turns green. I'm clear to open the outer door.

I grab the hatch crank, then hesitate.

"What am I doing?" I say.

Is this really a good idea? I want that cylinder so badly I'm just plowing ahead without any sort of plan. Is this worth risking my life over?

Yes. Unequivocally.

Okay, but is it worth risking the lives of everyone on Earth over? Because if I mess up and die out there, then the whole Hail Mary Project will have been in vain.

Hmm.

Yes. It's still worth it. I don't know what these aliens are like, what they want, or what they're planning to say. But they will have information. Any information, even stuff I'd rather not know, is better than none.

I spin the handle and open the door. The empty blackness of space lies beyond. The light of Tau Ceti glistens off the door. I peek my head out and see Tau Ceti with my own eyes. At this distance, it's a little less bright than the sun as seen from Earth.

I double-check my tether to make darn sure I'm attached, then I step out into space.

I'm good at this.

I must have practiced a lot. Maybe in a neutral-buoyancy tank or something. But it comes as second nature to me.

I exit the airlock and clamp one of my tethers to a rail on the outside hull. Always have two tethers. And always have at least one attached. That way you're never at risk of floating away from the ship. The Orlan-MKS2 is possibly the best EVA suit ever made, but it doesn't have a SAFER unit like NASA's EMU suit. At least with a

SAFER unit you have minimal thrust capability to return to the ship if you fall adrift.

All that information floods into my mind at once. I guess I've put a lot of time and thought into spacesuits. Maybe I'm our crew's EVA specialist? I don't know.

I flip up the sun visor and peer toward the *Blip-A*. I wish I could glean some special insight by seeing it in person, but it's pretty far away. The *Hail Mary*'s telescope gave me a much better view. Still, there's something . . . unique about staring directly at an alien spacecraft.

I catch a glint of the cylinder. Every now and then the flat ends of the gently tumbling cylinder reflect Taulight.

I've decided "Taulight" is a word, by the way. Light from Tau Ceti. It's not "sunlight." Tau Ceti isn't the sun. So . . . Taulight.

I still have a good twenty minutes before the cylinder reaches the ship. I watch it for a while to guess where it'll hit. It'd be nice to have a crewmate inside at the radar station.

It'd be nice to have a crewmate at all.

After five minutes, I have a good bead on the cylinder. It's headed for roughly the center of the ship. It's as good a place as any for aliens to aim for.

I make my way across the hull. The *Hail Mary* is pretty big. My little pressurized area is only half its length and the back half flares out to be three times as wide. Most of that will be empty now, I guess. It used to be full of Astrophage for my one-way trip here.

The hull is crisscrossed with rails and latch points for EVA tethering. Tether by tether, rail by rail, I make my way toward the center of the ship.

I have to step over a thick ring. It circles the crew compartment area of the ship. It's a good 2 feet thick. I don't know what it is, but it must be pretty heavy. Mass is everything when it comes to spaceship design, so it must be important. I'll speculate about that later.

I continue along, one hull latch point at a time, until I'm roughly in the center of the hull. The cylinder creeps closer. I adjust my position a tad to keep up with it. After an excruciatingly long wait, it's almost within reach.

I wait. No need to get greedy. If I paw at it too early, I might knock it off course and into space. I'd have no way of recovering it. I don't want to look dumb in front of the aliens.

Because they're surely watching me right now. Probably counting my limbs, noting my size, figuring out what part they should eat first, whatever.

I let the cylinder get closer and closer. It's moving less than 1 mile per hour. Not exactly a bullet pass.

Now that it's so close, I can estimate its size. It's not big at all. About the size and shape of a coffee can. It's a dull gray color with splotches of slightly darker gray randomly here and there. Similar to the *Blip-A*'s hull, kind of. Different color but same blotchiness. Maybe it's a stylistic thing. Random splotches are "in" this season or something.

The cylinder floats into my arms and I grab it with both hands.

It has less mass than I expected. It's probably hollow. It's a container. There's something inside they want me to see.

I hold the cylinder under one arm and use the other to deal with tethers. I hurry back to the airlock. It's a stupid thing to do. There's no reason to hurry and it literally endangers my life. One slip-up and I'd be off in space. But I just can't wait.

I get back into the ship, cycle the airlock, and float into the control room with my prize in hand. I open the Orlan suit, already thinking about what tests I'll run on the cylinder. I have a whole lab to work with!

The smell hits me immediately. I gasp and cough. The cylinder is bad!

No, not bad. But it *smells* bad. I can barely breathe. The chemical smell is familiar. What is it? Cat pee?

Ammonia. It's ammonia.

"Okay," I wheeze. "Okay. Think."

My gut instinct is to close the suit again. But that would just trap me in a small volume with the ammonia that's already in here. Better to let the cylinder air out in the larger volume of the ship.

Ammonia isn't toxic—at least, not in small quantities. And the fact that I can still breathe at all tells me it's a small quantity. If it weren't, my lungs would have caustic burns and I'd be unconscious or dead now.

As it is, there's just a bad smell. I can handle a bad smell.

I climb out the back of the suit while the cylinder floats in the middle of the console room. Now that it's not a shock anymore, I can handle the ammonia. It's no worse than using a bunch of Windex in a small room. Unpleasant but not dangerous.

I grab the cylinder—and it's hot as heck!

I yelp and pull my hands away. I blow on them for a moment and check for burns. It wasn't too bad. Not stovetop hot. But hot.

Grabbing it with my bare hands was stupid. Flawed logic. I assumed that since I'd been holding it earlier it was okay to do now. But earlier I had very thick spacesuit gloves protecting my hands.

"You've been a bad alien cylinder," I say to it. "You need a time-out."

I pull my arm into my sleeve and wrap my hand in the cuff. I use my now-protected knuckles to nudge the cylinder into the airlock. Once it's in, I close the door.

I'll let it be for now. It'll cool down to ambient air temperature eventually. And while it does, I don't want it floating randomly around my ship. I don't think there's anything in the airlock that can get hurt by some heat.

How hot was it?

Well, I had both hands on it (like an idiot) for a fraction of a second. My own reaction time was enough to keep me from getting burned. So it's probably less than 100 degrees Celsius.

I open and close my hands a few times. They don't hurt anymore, but the memory of the pain lingers.

"Where'd the heat come from?" I mumbled.

The cylinder was out in space for a good forty minutes. Over that time it should have radiated heat via blackbody radiation. It should be *cold,* not hot. I'm about 1 AU from Tau Ceti, and Tau Ceti has half the luminosity of the sun. So I don't think the Taulight could have heated the cylinder up much. Definitely not more than blackbody radiation would cool it down.

So either it has a heater inside or it was extremely hot when it started its trip. I guess I'll find out soon enough. It's not very heavy, so it's probably thin. If there's no internal heat source, it'll cool off very fast in the air here.

The room still smells like ammonia. Yuck.

I float down to the lab. I don't know where to begin. So many things I want to do. Maybe I should start by just identifying the material the cylinder is made of? Something harmless to the *Blip-A*'s crew might be incredibly toxic to me and neither of us would know it.

Maybe I should check for radiation.

I drift down to the lab table and put out a hand to steady myself. I'm getting better at the zero-g thing. I think I remember seeing an astronaut documentary saying some people handle it fine, while others really struggle. Looks like I'm one of the lucky ones.

I'm using "lucky" loosely here. I'm on a suicide mission. So . . . yeah.

The lab is a mystery. It has been for a while. It's clearly set up with the idea that there'll be gravity. It has tables, chairs, test-tube trays, et cetera. There's none of the usual stuff you would expect to see in a weightless environment. No Velcro on the walls, no computer screens at all angles. No efficient use of space. Everything assumes there will be a "floor."

The ship can accelerate just fine. For a good long time too. It had me at 1.5 g's for probably a few years. But they can't expect me to just leave the engines on and fly in circles to keep gravity in the lab, right?

I look around at each piece of lab equipment and try to relax my mind. There has to be a reason for this. And it's in my memory somewhere. The trick is to think about what I want to know, but not stress about it too much. It's like falling asleep. You can't really do it if you concentrate on it too hard.

So many top-of-the-line pieces of equipment. I let my mind wander as I scan across them all. . . .

CHAPTER 8

By the time we reached Geneva, I'd completely lost track of what day it was.

The computer models for the Astrophage breeder weren't lining up with the real-world performance. Though I had managed to breed up almost six grams of Astrophage so far. When all was said and done, the aircraft carrier's reactor just couldn't generate enough heat to speed up the reaction any further. Stratt kept vaguely saying they were going to provide a heat source capable of keeping up, but nothing had come of it yet.

I typed away on my computer even as the luxury private jet came to a halt at the gate. Stratt had to nudge me to make me stop working at all.

Three hours later, we waited in a conference room.

Always a conference room. My life was a collection of conference rooms these days. This one was nicer than most, at least. With fancy wood paneling and a stylish mahogany table. It was really something.

Stratt and I didn't talk. I worked on heat-transfer-rate coefficients while she typed away on her laptop doing gosh-knows-what. We spent enough time together as it was.

Finally, a dour-looking woman entered the room and sat across from Stratt.

"Thank you for seeing me, Ms. Stratt," she said with a Norwegian accent.

"No need to thank me, Dr. Lokken," she said. "I'm here against my will."

I looked up from my laptop. "You are? I thought you scheduled this."

She didn't take her eyes off the Norwegian. "I scheduled it because I had six different world leaders on the phone at the same time nagging me to do it. I finally relented."

"And you are . . . ?" Lokken asked me.

"Ryland Grace."

She actually backed away. "*The* Ryland Grace? Author of 'An Analysis of Water-Based Assumptions and Recalibration of Expectations for Evolutionary Models'?"

"Yeah, got a problem with that?" I said.

Stratt half smiled at me. "You're famous."

"Infamous," said Lokken. "His childish paper was a slap in the face to the entire scientific community. This man works for you? Absurd. All his assumptions about alien life were proven wrong."

I scowled. "Hey. My claim is life doesn't *need* water to evolve. Just because we found some life that does use water, that doesn't mean I'm wrong."

"Of course it does. Two life-forms independently evolved to require water—"

"Independently?!" I snorted. "Are you out of your mind? Do you honestly think something as complicated as mitochondria would evolve the same way *twice*? This is obviously a panspermia event."

She waved off my statement as if it were an annoying insect. "Astrophage mitochondria is very different from Earth mitochondria. They clearly evolved separately."

"They're ninety-eight percent identical!"

"Ahem," said Stratt. "I don't really get what you're fighting about, but can we—"

I pointed at Lokken. "This idiot thinks Astrophage evolved independently, but it's obvious Astrophage and Earth life are related!"

"That's fascinating, but—"

Lokken slapped the table. "How could a common ancestor have gotten across interstellar space?"

"The same way Astrophage does it!"

She leaned toward me. "Then why haven't we seen interstellar life all along?"

I leaned toward her. "No idea. Maybe it was a fluke."

"How do you explain the differences in mitochondria?"

"Four billion years of divergent evolution."

"Stop," Stratt said calmly. "I don't know what this is . . . some sort of science-related pissing contest? That's not what we're here for. Dr. Grace, Dr. Lokken, please sit down."

I plopped into my seat and folded my arms. Lokken sat as well.

Stratt fiddled with a pen. "Dr. Lokken, you've been hassling governments to hassle me. Over and over. Day in and day out. I know you want to be involved in Project Hail Mary, but I won't make it a huge international mess. We don't have time for the politicking and kingdom-building that always happens on big projects."

"I'm not happy to be here either," Lokken said. "I'm here, at great inconvenience to me as well as you, because this was the only way to tell you a critical design flaw in the *Hail Mary*."

Stratt sighed. "We sent out those preliminary designs for general feedback. Not command appearances in Geneva."

"Then file this under 'general feedback.' "

"Could have been an email."

"You would have deleted it. You have to listen to me, Stratt. This is important."

Stratt twirled the pen around a few more times. "Well, I'm here. Go ahead."

Lokken cleared her throat. "Correct me if I'm wrong, but the entire purpose of the *Hail Mary* is to be a laboratory. One we can send to Tau Ceti to see why that star—and that star alone—is immune to Astrophage."

"That's right."

She nodded. "Then would you also agree that the lab aboard the ship itself is the most important component?"

"Yes," Stratt said. "Without it, the mission is meaningless."

"Then we have a serious problem." Lokken pulled several sheets of paper from her purse. "I have a list of the lab equipment you want aboard. Spectrometers, DNA sequencers, microscopes, chemistry lab glassware—"

"I'm aware of the list," Stratt said. "I was the one who signed off on it."

Lokken dropped the papers on the table. "Most of this stuff won't work in zero g."

Stratt rolled her eyes. "We've thought of that, of course. Companies all over the world are working on zero-g-rated versions of this equipment as we speak."

Lokken shook her head. "Do you have any idea how much research and development went into making electron microscopes? Gas chromatographs? Everything else on this list? A century of scientific advances brought about by failure after failure. You want to just *assume* that making these things zero-g functional is going to work on the first try?"

"I don't see any way around it, unless you invented artificial gravity."

"We *have* invented artificial gravity," Lokken insisted. "A long time ago."

Stratt shot me a look. Obviously that had caught her off guard.

"I think she means a centrifuge," I said.

"I know she means a centrifuge," Stratt said. "What do you think?"

"I hadn't thought of it before. I guess . . . it could work. . . ."

Stratt shook her head. "No. That won't fly. We have to keep things simple. As simple as possible. Big, solid ship, minimal moving parts. The more complications we have the more points of failure we risk."

"It's worth the risk," said Lokken.

"We'd have to add a huge counterweight to the *Hail Mary* to even make that work." Stratt pursed her lips. "I'm sorry, but we barely have enough energy to make the Astrophage for the current mass limit. We can't just double it."

"Wait. We have enough energy to make all the fuel? When did that happen—?" I said.

"You don't need to add mass," Lokken said. She pulled another paper from her purse and slapped it down on the table. "If you take the current design, cut it in half between the crew compartment and the fuel tanks, the two sides will have a good mass ratio for a centrifuge."

Stratt peered at the diagram. "You put all the fuel on the same side. That's two million kilograms."

"No." I shook my head. "The fuel would be gone."

They both looked at me.

"It's a suicide mission," I said. "The fuel will be gone when they get to Tau Ceti. Lokken picked a split point where the back of the ship will weigh three times as much as the front. It's a good mass ratio for a centrifuge. It could work."

"Thank you," said Lokken.

"How do you cut a ship in half?" asked Stratt. "How does it become a centrifuge?"

Lokken flipped the diagram over to reveal a detailed image showing a faring between the two ship halves. "Spools of Zylon cabling between the crew compartment and the rest of the ship. We could simulate one g of gravity with a hundred meters of separation."

Stratt pinched her chin. Had someone actually changed her mind on something?

"I don't like complexity . . ." she said. "I don't like risk."

"This *removes* complexity and risk," Lokken said. "The ship, the crew, the Astrophage . . . it's all just a support system for the lab equipment. You *need* reliable equipment. Stuff that's been in use for years with millions of man-hours of commercial use. Every imaginable kink has been worked out of those systems. If you have one g of gravity—to make sure they'll be in the environment they were perfected for—you get the benefit of all that reliability."

"Hmm," said Stratt. "Grace? Your thoughts?"

"I . . . I think it's a good idea."

"Really?"

"Yeah," I said. "I mean, we already have to design the ship to withstand four years of constant acceleration at one and a half g's or so. It's going to be pretty solid."

She took a longer look at Lokken's diagram. "Wouldn't this make the artificial gravity in the crew area upside down?"

And she was right. The *Hail Mary* was designed so that "down" was "toward the engines." As the ship accelerates, the crew is pushed "down" to the floor. But inside a centrifuge, "down" is always "away from the center of rotation." So the crew would all be pushed toward the nose of the ship.

"Yes, that would be a problem." Lokken pointed to the diagram. The cables didn't attach directly to the crew compartment. They attached to two large discs on either side. "The cabling attaches to these big hinges. The whole front half of the ship can rotate 180 degrees. So when they're in centrifuge mode, the nose will face inward toward the other half of the ship. Inside the crew compartment, the force of gravity will be away from the nose—same as when the engines are thrusting."

Stratt took it in. "This is a fairly complicated piece of machinery and you'll be breaking the ship into two parts. You honestly think this is less of a risk?"

"Less risk than using brand-new, insufficiently tested equipment. Trust me, I've used sensitive equipment most of my career," I said. "It's finicky and delicate even in ideal conditions."

Stratt picked up her pen and tapped it on the table several times. "Okay. We'll do it."

Lokken smiled. "Excellent. I'll write up a paper and send it along to the UN. We can form a committee—"

"No, I said we'll do it." Stratt stood up. "You're with us now, Dr. Lokken. Pack a bag and meet us at Genève Aéroport. Terminal 3, private plane called *Stratt*."

"What? I work for ESA. I can't just—"

"Yeah, don't bother," I said. "She's going to call your boss or your boss's boss or whatever and have you assigned to her. You just got drafted."

"I . . . I wasn't volunteering to *design* it personally," Lokken protested. "I only meant to point out—"

"I never said you volunteered," Stratt said. "It's not voluntary at all."

"You can't just force me to work for you."

But Stratt was already walking out of the room. "Meet us at the airport in one hour or I'll have the Swiss Gendarmerie drag you there in two hours. Your call."

Lokken stared at the door, flabbergasted, then back to me.

"You get used to it," I said.

The ship is a centrifuge! I remember it all now!

That's why there's a mysterious area called "Cable Faring." That's where the spools and Zylon cables are. The ship can break in half, turn the crew compartment around, and spin.

That turning-around part—that's the weird ring I saw on the hull during my EVA! I remember the design now. It has two big hinges on it, allowing the crew compartment to turn around before the centrifuge is activated.

It's strangely reminiscent of Apollo spacecraft. The lunar lander was attached below the command module at launch, but they'd separate, turn the command module around, and reconnect with the lander during their trip to the moon. It's one of those things that looks ridiculous but ends up being the most effective way to solve a problem.

I float back up to the cockpit and flip through screens on various consoles. As each one fails to be what I want, I move to the next. Finally, I find it. The "Centrifuge" screen. It was hiding out as a subpanel in the Life Support screen.

It looks simple enough. There are yaw, pitch, and roll readouts, showing the current state of the ship, just like the Navigation panel has. A separate readout is labeled "Crew Compartment Angle"—that must be the turning-around bit. Each one reads "0° per second."

Below those is a button labeled "Engage Centrifuge Sequence." Underneath that are a bunch of numbers related to rotational acceleration rate, final speed, spooling rate, estimated g-force at the floor of the lab, four different screens for spool status (I guess there are four spools, two on each side), which emergency protocols to follow if there's a problem, and a lot more stuff I won't pretend to understand. The important thing is all those readouts have values already in them.

Got to love computers. They do all the thinking for you so you don't have to.

I do take a closer look at the emergency protocol mode. It just reads "Spin Down." I tap the readout and a dropdown appears. Looks like my options are: "Spin Down," "Halt All Spools," and one in red labeled "Separate." I'm pretty sure I don't want to do that. I suspect "Spin Down" will slowly decelerate the ship's spin if there's a problem. Sounds good, so I'll leave it set to that.

I'm about to engage the centrifuge, but then I pause. Is everything tied down? Is it safe to suddenly have a bunch of force acting on the ship? I shake it off. The ship was accelerating constantly for several years. It has to be comfortable with a little centrifuge action, right?

Right?

As hundreds of astronauts have done before, I place my faith and my life in the hands of the engineers who designed the system. Dr. Lokken, I guess. Hope she did her job.

I push the button.

First, nothing happens. I wonder if I even pressed it right, or if I just fumbled at the screen like I have so many times on my phone in the past.

But then the alert chimes throughout the ship. The piercing triple beep repeats every few seconds. There is no way for any crewmember to miss a signal like that. A final warning, I guess, in case the crew had a failure to communicate.

Over my head, the Petrovascope screen changes to lock-out mode. That confirms my earlier suspicion that the ship's maneuvering engines are Astrophage-based. I mean, it's kind of obvious when you think about it. But I wasn't sure until now.

The beeping stops and nothing really happens. Then I notice that I'm closer to the Nav panel than I was before. I drifted to the edge of the room. I put my arm out to steady myself and get back to normal. And then I drift toward the Nav panel again.

"Ohhh," I say.

It's begun. I'm not drifting toward the Nav panel. The whole cockpit is drifting toward me. The ship is starting to spin.

Everything veers off and changes direction. That'll be because as the ship spins, the crew compartment is also turning around. This could get complicated.

"Uh . . . right!" I kick off the wall and into the pilot seat.

I tilt. Or, rather, the room tilts. No, that doesn't make sense. Nothing tilts. The ship is spinning around faster and faster. It's also accelerating the acceleration. Also, the front half of the ship has detached from the rear, and it's rotating around those two big hinges. When it's done, the nose will be pointed in toward the rear half of the ship. All of this is going on at the same time, so the forces I'm feeling are really weird. Extremely complicated stuff, but also not my problem. It's up to the computer to deal with.

I watch the Centrifuge panel. The pitch rate reads 0.17° per second. Another readout labeled "Component Separation" reads 2.4 meters. There's a little beep and the "Crew Compartment Angle" readout blinks. It shows as 180°. I assume this whole sequence was worked out well in advance to minimize shock to the system and/or crew.

I feel a slight pressure on my butt as the seat pushes up against me. The transition is very smooth. I just . . . experience more and more gravity in what feels like a tilting room. It's a weird sensation.

I know, logically, that I'm in a ship spinning around. But there are no windows to see out of. Only screens. I check the telescope screen that's still pointed at the *Blip*-A. The stars in the background do not move. It's accounting for my rotation somehow and canceling it. That bit of software was probably tricky, considering the camera probably isn't at the exact center of rotation.

My arms grow heavy, so I put them on the armrests. I have to start using my neck muscles again for the first time in a while.

Five minutes after the sequence began, I experience a little less than normal Earth gravity. A quadruple beep announces the end of the sequence.

I check the Centrifuge screen. It shows a pitch rate of 20.71° per second, a total separation of 104 meters, and a "Lab Gravity" of 1.00 g.

The diagram of the ship shows the *Hail Mary* split in two pieces, the nose of the crew compartment pointed inward toward the other half. The two halves are comically far apart, and the entire system spins slowly. Well, actually pretty fast, but it looks slow at that scale.

I unstrap from the chair, walk to the airlock, and open the hatch. The smell of ammonia drifts into the cockpit again, but not nearly as bad as before. The alien artifact lies on the floor. I give it a quick touch with my finger to gauge temperature. It's still pretty warm, but no longer scalding hot. Good. There's no internal heater or weird stuff like that. It just started out really hot.

I pick it up. Time to see what this thing is made of. And what's inside.

Before leaving the cockpit, I take one last look at the Telescope screen. I don't know why—I guess I just like to keep track of what extraterrestrial ships in my vicinity are up to.

The *Blip*-A spins in space. It rotates end-over-end, probably at the exact same rate as the *Hail Mary*. I guess they saw me spin up the centrifuge and figured it was another communication thing.

Humanity's first miscommunication with an intelligent alien race. Glad I could be a part of it.

I set the cylinder on the lab table. Where do I begin? Everywhere!

I check to see if it's radioactive with a Geiger counter. It's not. That's nice.

I poke it with various things to get a feel for its hardness. It's hard.

It looks like metal but doesn't feel quite like metal. I use a multimeter to see if it's conductive. It isn't. Interesting.

I get a hammer and chisel. I want a small chip of the cylinder material for the gas chromatograph—that way I'll know what elements it's made of. After a few smacks with the hammer, the chisel chips. The cylinder isn't even dented.

"Hm."

The cylinder is too big to put in the gas chromatograph. But I find a handheld x-ray spectrometer. It looks like a UPC scanner gun. Easy enough to use, and it'll give me some idea of what this thing is made of. It's not as accurate as the chromatograph, but better than nothing.

After a quick scan, it tells me the cylinder is made of xenon.

"What . . . ?"

I use the spectrometer on the steel lab table to make sure it's working correctly. It reports iron, nickel, chromium, and so on. Just what it should say. So I check the cylinder again and get the same wacky results as with my first test. I test it four more times but keep getting the same answer.

Why did I run the test so many times? Because those results make no sense at all. Xenon is a noble gas. It doesn't react with anything. It doesn't form bonds with anything. And it's a gas at room temperature. But somehow it's part of this solid material?

And no, it's not a cylinder filled with xenon or anything like that. A spectrometer is not a deep, penetrating scan. It can only tell you what's on the surface. If I pointed it at gold-plated nickel, it would say "100% gold," because that's all it can see. It can only tell me what the molecules on the surface of the cylinder are made of. Apparently, they're made of xenon.

This handheld spectrometer can't detect elements lower than aluminum. So there could be carbon, hydrogen, nitrogen, whatever is lurking in there too. But as for elements within the detector's range . . . I'm looking at pure xenon.

"How?!"

I plop down onto a stool and stare at the cylinder. What a strange artifact. What do I even call noble gases that react with things? Ignobles?

But being flummoxed has one good side effect. It makes me stop my frenzied attack on the cylinder and just look at it. For the first time, I see that there is a thin line running around the circumference about an inch from the top. I feel it with my fingernail. It's definitely an indentation of some kind. Is that a lid? Maybe it just opens.

I pick up the cylinder and try to pull off the top. It doesn't budge. On a whim, I try to unscrew it. It also doesn't budge.

But there's no reason aliens would follow the righty-tighty-lefty-loosey rule, is there?

I turn the lid to the right and it rotates. My heart skips a beat!

I keep turning. After 90 degrees I feel it release. I pull the two chunks apart.

Both halves have complicated stuff going on inside. They look like . . . models of some kind? They both feature whisker-thin poles sticking up from their bases, leading to spheres of various sizes. I don't see any moving parts, and everything appears to be made out of the same weird material as the case.

I check out the bottom half first. Have to start somewhere.

A single whisker holds up . . . an abstract sculpture? It's a marble-sized sphere and a BB-sized sphere each held in place by thinner whiskers branching off the main vertical "trunk." There's also an oddly parabolic shape connecting the tops of the two spheres. This whole thing looks familiar to me . . . why . . . ?

"Petrova line!" I blurt out.

I've seen that arc shape enough times to know it by heart. My heart races.

I point to the large sphere. "So you must be a star. And the little guy must be a planet."

These aliens are aware of Astrophage. Or, at least, they're aware of the Petrova line. But that doesn't really tell me anything. They're in an Astrophage-powered ship, so of course they know about Astrophage. And we're chatting in a solar system that has a Petrova line, so that's not surprising either. This might be their home system for all I know.

This is a good start, though. We were "talking" by flashing our engines. So they know I use Astrophage and that I can "see" (with help from the ship) the Petrova frequency. From that, they concluded I must be able to see the Petrova line. They're smart.

I look at the other half of the doohickey. Dozens of whiskers rise from the base. They're all different lengths and each one ends in a sphere less than a millimeter across. I poke a whisker with my finger and it doesn't bend. I press harder and harder. Eventually the whole doohickey slides on the table. Those whiskers are stronger than anything that thin should be.

I guess xenon makes pretty strong material when you get it to react with things. It infuriates my tender scientist's heart! I try to put it out of my head and get back to the task at hand.

I count thirty-one whiskers, each with its little sphere at the end. While counting, I spot something special. There's one whisker sticking up from the exact center of the disc, but unlike the others, it's not connected to a sphere. I squint to get a good look.

Instead of a single sphere, it's two spheres of different sizes and an arc—okay, I see. It's a very small replica of the Petrova-line model on the other half of the doohickey. Maybe one-twentieth the scale.

And that little Petrova-line model has an even *thinner* whisker connecting it to another sphere at the tip of a different whisker. No, not quite a sphere. It's another Petrova-line model. I scour the rest of the doohickey for any more of them, but I don't see any. Just the one in the middle and the one off to the side.

"Wait a minute . . . waaaaait a minute . . ."

I pull out the drawer that has the lab computer panel in it. Time to make use of that virtually infinite reference material. I find a huge spreadsheet with the information I need, bring it into Excel (Stratt loves well-tested, off-the-shelf products), and do a bunch of operations on it. Soon, I have the data plot I wanted. And it matches.

Stars. The little spheres on the end of the whiskers are stars. Of course they are. What else would have a Petrova line?

But they're not just any old stars. These are specific stars. They're all in the correct relative positions to one another, with Tau Ceti right in the center. The map's point of view is kind of odd. To make the spheres match my data plot of star locations, I have to hold the doohickey at a 30-degree angle and kind of rotate it around a bit.

But of course, all of Earth's data is based on Earth's orbital plane being the reference point. People from a different planet would have a different coordinate system. But no matter how you look at it, the end result is the same: The doohickey is a map of the local stars.

Then I'm suddenly *very* interested in that little filament connecting the center sphere (Tau Ceti) to another sphere. I check the corresponding star in my catalog: It's called 40 Eridani. But I bet the crew of the *Blip-A* call it home.

That's the message. "We're from the 40 Eridani system. And now we're here at Tau Ceti."

But there's even more to it than that. They're also saying "40 Eridani has a Petrova line, just like Tau Ceti."

I stop to let that sink in.

"Are you in the same boat?!" I say.

Of course they are! Astrophage is getting at all the local stars. These people are from a planet orbiting 40 Eridani, and 40 Eridani is infected just like Earth's sun! They have some pretty good science going on, so they did the same thing we did. Make a ship, and go to Tau Ceti to see why it's not dying!

"Holy cow!" I say.

Yes, I'm jumping to a conclusion there. Maybe they harvest Astrophage from their Petrova line and consider it a boon. Maybe they *in-*

vented Astrophage. Maybe they just think Petrova lines are pretty. There are a bunch of different things this could mean. But the most likely, in my admittedly biased opinion, is that they're here to find a solution.

Aliens.

Actual aliens.

Aliens from the 40 Eridani system. So I guess that makes them Eridanians? Hard to say, even harder to remember. Eridans? No. How about Eridians? Sounds kind of like "iridium," which is one of the cooler-sounding elements on the periodic table. Yeah, I'm going to call them Eridians.

And I think it's pretty obvious how I should respond.

I thoroughly searched the lab a few days ago. There's an electronics kit in one of the drawers. The trick is remembering which one.

I don't remember, of course. It takes me a while of searching and not-quite swearing while I do, but I eventually find it.

I don't have any xenonite (that's what I'm calling this weird alien compound, and no one can stop me). But I do have solder and a soldering iron. I break off a little piece of solder, melt one end, and stick it to the Tau Ceti sphere. It sticks pretty well, which is a relief. You never know with xenonite.

I check, double-check, and triple-check to make sure I correctly identify which one of the little stars in the model is Sol (Earth's sun). I solder the other side of the wire to Sol.

I search the lab until I find some hard paraffin. With some poking, open flames, and mild swearing, I'm able to make a really poor approximation of the Petrova-line icon they sent me. I smush it onto Sol in the model. It looks all right. At least, good enough that they should get the idea.

I take a look. The sleek, thin lines of the xenonite whiskers are ruined by my crooked, blob-ended solder addition and crappy wax model. It's like someone added a crayon drawing into the corner of a Da Vinci, but it will have to do.

I try to screw the top and bottom of the doohickey back together.

They refuse to mate. I try again. It still doesn't work. I remember that Eridians use left-handed threading in their screws. So I do what, to me, is an unscrewing motion. The two pieces connect perfectly.

Time to throw it back to them. Politely.

Except I can't. Not with the ship spinning around like this. If I tried to step out of the airlock, I'd go flying off into space.

I grab the doohickey and climb up to the control room. I strap myself into the chair and order the ship to spin down.

Like last time, I feel the room tilt, though this time it tilts the other way. And again, I know it's not actually tilting, it's my perception of the lateral acceleration being applied, but whatever.

I feel the gravity decrease and the tilt of the room reduce until I'm back in zero g again. This time there's no disorientation. I guess my lizard brain has made its peace with the fact that gravity comes and goes. The operation ends with a final "clunk" as the reoriented crew compartment seats into the rear half of the ship.

I get back in the EVA suit, grab the doohickey, and head out into space once again. I don't need to work my way across the hull with tethers this time. I just clip my tether in the airlock.

The *Blip-A* has stopped spinning—probably did it when the *Hail Mary* stopped. And it's still 217 meters away.

I don't have to be Joe Montana to make this pass. I just need to set the doohickey in motion toward the *Blip-A*. It's over a hundred meters across. I should be able to hit it.

I give the doohickey a shove. It floats away from me at a reasonable speed. Maybe 2 meters per second—roughly a jogging pace. This is communication of a sort too. I'm telling my new friends that I can handle slightly faster deliveries.

The doohickey floats off toward the Eridian ship and I head back into mine.

"Okay, guys," I say. "The enemy of my enemy is my friend. If Astrophage is your enemy, I'm your friend."

I watch the Telescope screen. Occasionally I look away. Sometimes I play Klondike solitaire on the Nav panel. But I never go more than a few seconds without checking the telescope. A thick pair of gloves, harvested from the lab earlier, tries to float away. I grab them and wedge them behind the pilot's seat.

It's been two hours and my alien friends haven't had anything to say. Are they waiting for me to say something else? I just told them what star I was from. It's their turn to say something, right?

Do they even have a concept of taking turns? Or is that a purely human thing?

What if Eridians have a life-span of 2 million years and waiting a century to reply is considered polite?

How am I going to get rid of this red 7 on the rightmost pile? I don't have any black 8s in my deck and—

Movement!

I spin to the Telescope screen so fast my legs float out into the middle of the control room. There's another cylinder coming my way. I guess the many-armed hull-robot thing threw it just a moment ago. I check the Radar screen. Blip-B is plugging along at over a meter per second. I only have a few minutes to suit up!

I get back into the EVA suit and cycle the airlock. Once I open the outer door, I spot the cylinder tumbling end-over-end. Might be the same one as before, might be new. And this time, it's headed straight for the airlock. I guess they saw that's where I exited and reentered the ship and decided to make things easier for me.

Very considerate of them.

They're accurate too. A minute later, the cylinder floats right through the center of the open hatchway. I catch it. I wave to the *Blip-A* and close the hatch. They probably don't know what a wave is, but I felt compelled to do it.

I return to the control room and wriggle out of the EVA suit, leaving the cylinder to float near the airlock. The ammonia smell is powerful, but this time I'm ready for it.

I put the thick lab gloves on and grab the cylinder. Even through the fireproof gloves, I can feel the warmth. I know I should wait for it to cool down but I don't want to.

It looks the same as before. I unscrew it the same left-handed way. This time, there's no star map. Instead, it's a model. What am I looking at here?

A single post from the base holds up an irregular shape. No, *two* irregular shapes connected by a tube. Hey, wait. One of the shapes is the *Hail Mary*. Oh, and the other one is the *Blip-A*.

The models have no detail or texture. But they're good enough for me to recognize what they represent, so they did their job. The *Hail Mary* is only 3 inches long, while the *Blip-A* is closer to 8 inches. Man, that ship is huge.

And that tube connecting them? It connects to the *Hail Mary*'s airlock and leads to the center of the *Blip-A*'s diamond-shaped segment. The tunnel is just wide enough to cover my airlock door.

They want to meet.

CHAPTER 9

I let the model float in the middle of the room. The xenonite is nearly indestructible, so I don't need to worry about it bumping into anything.

Is this a good idea? I have a planet to save. As awesome as it is to meet up with intelligent aliens, is this risk worth it?

The Eridians clearly understand Astrophage. At least well enough to make engines out of it. And—I think—they're trying to tell me they're here for the same reason I am. They might have information I don't know. They might even have the solution I'm looking for. And they seem friendly enough.

But this is the interstellar equivalent of a stranger offering me candy. I want the candy (information), but I don't know the stranger.

What's my alternative? Ignore them?

I could carry on with my mission as if I never saw them at all. They're probably as spooked to see me as I am to see them. They might continue trying to talk, but they wouldn't get hostile, I don't think.

Or would they? I have no way of knowing.

No, this is a no-brainer. I've got to at least have a conversation with them. If they have any information about Astrophage at all, no matter how minor, I have to talk to them. It's a risk, yes, but this whole mission is a risk.

Okay. So what would I do if I were them?

I'm an Eridian. I want to build a tunnel that connects to the weird human ship. But I don't know what the human ship's material is made of. How can I guarantee any kind of attachment or seal? My xenonite knowledge is beyond dispute, but how do I connect it to "humanium" or whatever that ship is made of? I've sent the human xenonite models. So he knows what I have. But I still don't know what he has.

They'll need a sample of my hull. And they'll need to *know* it's a sample of my hull.

"Right," I say to no one.

I don't know if this is a good idea or a terrible idea. But I'm going to knock a chunk of my hull off.

I grab a set of EVA tools. They live in the lab in Drawer 17E. I found them a while ago. They're on a tool belt that can clip onto the EVA suit and everything. Stratt and the gang made sure we had all the equipment we would need for hull repairs if needed. Normally it would be Ilyukhina's job to fix stuff, but she's gone.

Huh. Random memory. Ilyukhina was our engineer—our fix-it gal. Okay. Well, now it's me.

I get back in the EVA suit, and back outside. Again. Bouncing in and out is getting kind of annoying. I hope this tunnel thing works.

I make my way along the hull, one tether adjustment at a time. And I get to thinking . . .

What good is a tunnel, exactly? I doubt we have compatible environments. We can't just connect the ships with a tunnel and shake hands. I think there's a lot of ammonia over there.

And then there's the temperature. Those cylinders are hot when I get them.

Some back-of-the-napkin math tells me that first cylinder they sent should have lost 100 degrees Celsius or more during that forty-minute trip (depending on what temperature it started at). And it was still hot when I got it. So it was *really* hot when it left their ship. Like . . . way higher than the boiling point of water.

I try not to speculate too wildly, but come on. I'm a scientist and these are aliens. I'm going to speculate.

Do Eridians live in an environment hotter than the boiling point of water? If so, it proves I was right! The goldilocks zone is bull-puckey! You don't need liquid water for life!

I should be more focused on the "first contact with intelligent aliens" thing or the "save all of humanity" thing, but gosh darn it, I can spend a moment to be happy about being right when everyone said I was wrong!

I finally reach a spot of hull that seems right for the job. I'm aft of the entire pressurized portion of the ship, well past the part where it widens out. If I'm right, I'm standing on a big empty tank that used to be full of Astrophage. If I breach the hull here, it shouldn't matter.

I pull out a hammer and chisel. Not the most elegant way to do this, but I can't think of anything better. I start by putting one corner of the chisel on the hull and giving it a little tap. There's a notable dent. It doesn't take much to get through this outermost layer.

I use the hammer and chisel to separate a 6-inch circle of hull material. There's a layer of something underneath. I can feel it with the chisel. Probably insulation.

I have to pry the circle out with the chisel. The underlayer holds strong, but then gives way suddenly. The hull sample flies off into space.

"Shoot!"

I leap off the ship. I get a hand on the circle right before my tether snaps tight. I breathe for a second, thinking about how dumb I am, then pull myself back along the tether to the ship. Looking at the circle it seems like there's a light, foam substance attached to the underside. Styrofoam, maybe. Probably something more complicated than that.

"I hope you guys watched all that," I say. "Because I'm not doing it again."

I throw the hull chunk at the *Blip-A*.

By doing this right in front of them, they'll know for sure I'm sending them a sample of the hull. I hope it's enough for what they want to do. I don't even know if they wanted it or needed it. They might be looking at their screens right now and saying, "What is this idiot doing? Is he poking a hole in his own ship? Why?"

I stay on the hull and watch as the chunk tumbles in the Taulight. The multi-armed robot on the *Blip-A*'s hull slides along its rails for the reception. Once positioned, it waits for the hull chunk to arrive and makes a perfect catch.

And then, I swear to God, it waves at me! One of its little arms waves at me!

I wave back.

It waves again.

Okay, this could go on all day. I head back toward the airlock.

Your move, guys.

Their move is taking a long time and I'm getting bored.

Wow. I'm sitting here in a spaceship in the Tau Ceti system waiting for the intelligent aliens I just met to continue our conversation . . . and I'm bored. Human beings have a remarkable ability to accept the abnormal and make it normal.

I look through the controls of the Radar panel to see what other features it has. After some digging through preference dialogs, I find what I'm looking for: the proximity-warning parameters. Currently set to 100 kilometers. Fairly reasonable. You would expect things to be millions of kilometers away. Tens of thousands at the very least. So if some rock is within 100 kilometers of you, that's a major problem.

I change the setting to 0.26 kilometers. I worry it'll reject the setting as too low, but it doesn't.

I stretch my back and float out of the pilot seat. The *Blip-A* is 271 meters away. If they get closer than 260 meters, or if they send another present that gets within that range, the proximity alert will go off. I don't have to sit here and stare at the screen anymore. The control room will blare a warning when the *Blip-A* does anything interesting.

I float down to the dormitory.

"Food," I say.

The arms pull a box out of their little stash in the ceiling and stick it to my bunk. Someday I should look around in there and see what's available. For now I kick off the ceiling and float down to the food. The box, labeled DAY 10—MEAL 1, has a Velcro-like strip on the bottom that helps it stay in place on the bedsheet. I open it up and see a burrito.

Not sure what I expected, but okay. Burrito it is.

Turns out it's a room-temperature burrito. Beans, cheese, some red sauce . . . all pretty tasty, really. But room temperature. Either the crew doesn't get hot meals around here or the machine doesn't trust a recent coma patient not to burn himself on hot food. Probably the latter.

I float up to the lab and put the burrito in the sample furnace. I leave it in there for a few minutes before pulling it out with tongs. The cheese bubbles and a cloud of steam slowly emanates out in all directions.

I leave the burrito to float in the air and cool.

I snicker. If I *really* wanted a hot burrito, I'd turn on the spin drives, do an EVA, and hold the burrito in the light emitted from it. That'd get it hot really quick. As in: It would get vaporized along with my arm and whatever else was in the blast range, because—

"Welcome to Little Russia!" said Dimitri. He gave a theatrical wave at the aircraft carrier's lower hangar deck. The whole space had been repurposed into a bunch of labs full of high-tech equipment. Dozens of lab-coated scientists toiled away at their tasks, occasionally speaking Russian to one another. Dimitri's Denizens, we called them.

We probably put more effort into naming stuff than we should have.

I clutched my little sample container like Scrooge with a bag of coins. "I'm not happy with this."

"Oh, hush," said Stratt.

"I've only made eight grams of Astrophage so far, and I'm supposed to just give away two grams of it? Two grams may not seem like much, but it's ninety-five billion Astrophage cells."

"It is for a good cause, my friend!" said Dimitri. "I promise you will like it. Come, come!"

He led Stratt and me through to the main lab. The center was dominated by a huge cylindrical vacuum chamber. The chamber was open and three technicians mounted something to a table inside.

Dimitri said something in Russian to them. They said something back. He said some other thing and pointed to me. They smiled and made happy Russian sounds.

Then Stratt said something stern in Russian.

"Sorry," said Dimitri. "English only for now, my friends! For the American!"

"Hello, American!" said one of the technicians. "I am speak of English for you! You have fuel?"

I gripped my sample container tighter. "I have *some* fuel. . . ."

Stratt looked at me the way I look at stubborn students in my class. "Hand it over, Dr. Grace."

"You know, my breeder doubles Astrophage population over time, right? Taking away two grams now is like taking away four grams next month."

She pulled the container out of my hands and handed it to Dimitri.

He held the small metal vial up and admired it. "This is a good day. I have looked forward to this day. Dr. Grace, please let me show you my spin drive!"

He gestured for me to follow and bounced up the stairs into the vacuum chamber. The technicians exited one at a time to make room for us.

"All is attached," said one of them. "Checklist is done. Ready for test."

"Good, good," Dimitri said. "Dr. Grace, Ms. Stratt. Come, come!"

He led Stratt and me into the vacuum chamber. A thick, shiny metal plate leaned against one wall. The middle of the chamber had a round table with some kind of device resting on it.

"This is spin drive." Dimitri beamed.

It wasn't much to look at. It was a couple of feet across, mostly circular, but with one side of it cut flat. Sensors and wires came out from apertures all over the place.

Dimitri lifted the top casing off to reveal the innards. Things got more complicated. Inside was a clear triangle on a rotor. Dimitri gave it a little spin. "See? Spin. Spin drive."

"How's it work?" I asked.

He pointed to the triangle. "This is the revolver—high-tensile-strength transparent polycarbonate. And this"—he pointed to a nook between the revolver and the outer casing—"is where fuel comes in. IR emitter inside that part of revolver emits small amount of light with 4.26 and 18.31 microns wavelength—that is wavelengths which attract Astrophage. Astrophage go to that revolver face. But not too hard. Astrophage thrust is based on strength of IR light. Dim light make weak thrust. But enough to make Astrophage stick to surface."

He rotated the triangle and aligned an edge with the flat part of the casing. "Rotate 120 degrees, this face of revolver with Astrophage stuck to it now points out the back of the ship. Increase strength of IR light inside. Astrophage now *very* excited, push *very* hard toward IR light! Their thrust—Petrova-frequency light—leaves back of ship. This pushes ship forward. Millions of little Astrophages pushing on back of ship make it go, yes?"

I bent down for a look. "I see . . . this way no part of the ship has to be in the blast area of the light."

"Yes, yes!" said Dimitri. "Astrophage force limited only by the brightness of IR light attracting it. I did very much math and decided best is to make Astrophage exhaust all energy in four seconds. Any faster and force will break revolver."

He rotated the revolver another 120 degrees and pointed to the remaining third of the casing. "This is cleaning area. Squeegee wipes dead Astrophage off revolver."

He pointed to the cleaning area, then the fueling area, and then the open face. "All three areas active at same time. So while this area cleans dead Astrophage off this face, fueling area adds Astrophage to that face, and other face is pointed out back of ship, providing thrust. This pipelining means the part of triangle pointed out back of ship is always thrusting."

Dimitri opened my vial of Astrophage and set it in the fueling chamber. I guess since the Astrophage will find their way to the triangle face, no special handling was required. He could just . . . let the fuel see the IR.

"Come, come," he said. "Experiment time!"

We left the vacuum chamber and Dimitri sealed it off. He yelled something in Russian, and all the Russians started repeating it. Everyone made their way to the far side of the hangar deck, including us.

They'd set up a folding table. It had a laptop on it with Cyrillic writing on the screen.

"Ms. Stratt. How far is carrier from closest land?" Dimitri asked.

"About three hundred kilometers," she said.

"This is good."

"Wait, why?" I said. "Why is that good?"

Dimitri pursed his lips. "It is . . . good. Time for science!"

He pushed a button. There was a muffled *whump* from the far side of the bay, followed by a hum, and then nothing.

"Experiment done." He leaned forward to read the screen. "Sixty thousand Newtons of force!"

He turned to the other Russians. "60,000 ньютонов!"

They all cheered.

Stratt turned to me. "That's a lot, right?"

I was too busy staring slack-jawed at Dimitri to answer her. "Did you say sixty *thousand* Newtons?"

He pumped his fist in the air. "Yes! Sixty thousand Newtons! Maintained for one hundred microseconds!"

"Oh my God. From that little thing?!" I started to walk forward. I had to see this for myself.

Dimitri grabbed my arm. "No. You stay here, friend. We all stay here. One point eight billion Joules of light energy was released. This is why we needed vacuum chamber and one thousand kilograms of silicon. No air to ionize. Light goes directly to silicon block. Energy is absorbed by melting the metal. See?"

He turned the laptop toward me. A camera feed from inside the vacuum chamber showed the glowing blob that was once a thick plate of metal.

"Whoa . . ." I said.

"Yes, yes," Dimitri said. "That Mr. Einstein with his $E = mc^2$. Very powerful stuff. We let the cooling system work on it for a few hours. Uses seawater. Will be fine."

I just shook my head in awe. In just 100 microseconds—that's one ten-thousandth of a second—Dimitri's spin drive melted a metric ton of metal. All that energy had been stored up in my little Astrophages. Slowly harvested from the carrier's nuclear reactor heat over time by my breeder. I mean, the math all checked out, but to see it actually demonstrated like that was another thing entirely.

"Wait . . . how much Astrophage did you use there?"

Dimitri smiled. "I can only estimate based on thrust generated. But was close to twenty micrograms."

"I gave you two entire *grams*! Can I have the rest back, please?"

"Don't be greedy," Stratt said. "Dimitri needs it for further experimentation."

She turned to him. "Good work. How big will the real drive be?"

Dimitri pointed to the video feed. "That big. That is real drive."

"No, I mean the one on the ship."

"That," he said, pointing again. "You want redundancy, safety, reliability, yes? So we don't make just one big engine. We make thousand little ones. One thousand and nine, actually. Enough for all thrust needed and much to spare. Some malfunction during trip? Not a problem. More thrust from the others to compensate."

"Ah." Stratt nodded. "Tons of little spin drives. I like it. Keep up the good work."

She headed to the stairwell.

I stared at Dimitri. "If you'd set off all two grams of that sample at once . . ."

He shrugged. "Fwoosh! We are vapor. All of us. Carrier too. Explosion would make small tsunami. But three hundred kilometers away from land, so is okay."

He slapped me on the back. "And I would owe you drink in afterlife, yes?! Ha-ha-ha-ha!"

"Huh," I say to myself. "So that's how the spin drive works."

I munch on my burrito.

So I guess I have a thousand of those ("A thousand and nine!" I hear Dimitri's voice in my head). At least—that's how many I started with. Some probably went kaput during the trip. There's probably a panel on the Spin Drive console that'll tell me the status of each little one.

The proximity alert interrupts my thoughts.

"Finally!"

I "drop" the burrito (it floats where I leave it) and launch myself up to the control room. The hatch from the dormitory to the lab doesn't line up with the hatch from the lab to the control room, but there's a diagonal line of travel that will send me through both if I do it just right.

I don't get it right this time. I have to push off a lab wall en route. Still, I'm getting better at it.

I check the Radar panel and, sure enough, the *Blip-A* is approaching! Not a cylinder this time. The whole ship is coming my way. Nice and slow. Maybe they're going for a nonthreatening kind of approach? In any event, it's almost here.

Looks like its hull has a new addition. In that diamond part that's as big as the whole *Hail Mary*, there's a cylindrical tube sticking straight up. The hull robot is sitting next to it, looking proud of itself. I may be anthropomorphizing a tad.

The tube looks like xenonite. Patchy gray and tan with grainlike lines running its length. Hard to tell from this angle, but it also looks to be hollow.

I think I know what comes next. If they follow the plan they indicated with the model, they'll be putting the other end of it against my airlock.

How will they attach their tunnel? My airlock does have docking capability—probably for whatever ship brought me and my crewmates to the *Hail Mary*—but I can't expect Eridians to know the intricacies of a universal airlock.

The *Blip-A* edges ever closer. What if there's a mistake? What if they miscalculate? What if they accidentally poke a hole in my hull? I'm all that stands between humanity and extinction. Will an alien math error doom my entire species?

I hustle to the airlock and pull on the EVA suit. I'm in there in record time. Better safe than sorry.

The *Blip-A* is so close now, the Telescope screen just shows a patch of mottled hull. I switch to the external cameras. My hull is littered with them. They're all controlled from a window on the EVA panel. Always good to know where your astronaut is when giving them EVA instructions, I guess.

The tunnel is about 20 feet long. Or 7 meters. Man, being an American scientist sucks sometimes. You think in random, unpredictable units based on what situation you're in.

The hull robot reaches out with some seriously telescoping arms. I had no idea it could do that. It extends well beyond the tunnel toward my airlock. Not creepy at all. Five ever-growing alien robot arms reaching for my front door. No cause for alarm.

Each arm's three-fingered "hand" is holding . . . something. A curved bar with a flat plate attached on the ends. Like a coffee-mug handle. Three of the arms reach the *Hail Mary* and stick the flat parts of their devices to the hull. Shortly after, the other two arms do the same. Then, all five retract, pulling the *Hail Mary* toward the tunnel.

Okay. So those flat things are handles. How are they attached? Good question! My hull is smooth and made of nonmagnetic aluminum (why do I remember that all of a sudden?). The handles certainly aren't connected by any mechanical means. Must be an adhesive.

And it all starts to make sense.

Of course they aren't going to work out how the docking mechanism works. They're going to glue one end of the tunnel to my ship. Why not? Much simpler.

My ship groans. It's a 100,000-kilogram piece of equipment that was definitely not designed to be pulled along by its airlock. Will the hull put up with this?

I double-check the seals on my EVA suit.

The control room moves around me. It's not fast—just a few centimeters per second. Hey, for small spaceship velocities I think in metric! Much better than "cubits per fortnight" or whatever.

I let the wall catch up to me. At some lizard-brain level, I like being a little farther from the airlock. Some scary stuff is going on over there.

Clunk.

The Eridian tunnel has hit the hull. Clicks and scrapes follow. I watch the hull camera feeds.

The mouth of the tunnel, now firmly held to the airlock aperture, is larger than the entire airlock door. I guess that's that. Presuming the glue will hold pressure. They don't even know what my atmospheric pressure is. What's the glue made of? So many questions.

I can't operate the control-room panels with my EVA suit gloves. I wish I could zoom in or something. I squint at one of the feeds showing the tunnel. It sure looks tight against the hull to me. There's some curvature to the hull around that spot. Kind of a complicated shape to make, but the Eridians duplicated it perfectly.

After another minute, the robot arms let go of their handles, leaving them on the hull.

A muffled sound comes from the airlock. It's a whooshing sound. Is that airflow? They're pressurizing the tunnel!

My heart races. Can my hull handle this? What if their air dissolves aluminum? What if aluminum is highly toxic to Eridians and one whiff of it kills them instantly? This is a terrible idea!

The whooshing stops.

I gulp.

They're done. Nothing dissolved yet. I float over to the airlock for a look-see.

I had both airlock doors sealed, of course. More protection in case of a breach. I open the inner door and float inside. I peek out the porthole window.

The blackness of space gone, replaced with the blackness of a dark tunnel. I turn on the helmet lamps and angle my head to shine light through the porthole.

The end of the tunnel is too close. I don't mean I'm bothered by it. I mean the end of it is not 20 feet away. It's more like 10 feet. And while the rest of the tunnel is made of gray and tan blotchy xenonite, the wall at the end is a hexagonal pattern of random colors.

They didn't just connect a tunnel. They connected my airlock to theirs, with a wall in the middle.

Clever.

I close the inner airlock door with me inside and depressurize it. I spin the outer door's hatch handle and push. It opens without resistance. The tunnel is a vacuum—at least, it is on my side of the divider.

I think I see. This is a test. They had all the same concerns I had. Attach it, let me pressurize my half with my air, and see what happens. Either it works or it doesn't. If it works, great! If not, they'll try something else. Or maybe ask me to try something.

Okay. Let's see.

I tell the airlock to repressurize. It refuses—the outer door is open. Nice to know that safety interlock is there, but I'll have to work around it.

It's not hard—there's a manual relief valve that will just let air from the ship into the airlock. It bypasses all computer controls. You don't want someone to die because of a software malfunction, right?

I open the relief valve. Air rushes in from the *Hail Mary* and, with the airlock wide open, into the tunnel. Within three minutes, the airflow slows and then stops. My suit readings tell me there's 400 hectopascals of pressure outside. The *Hail Mary* has equalized with my part of the tunnel.

I close the relief valve and wait. I watch the external pressure gauge on my EVA suit. The pressure stays put at 400 hectopascals. We have a good seal.

Eridians know how to glue xenonite to aluminum. Of course they do. Aluminum's an element, and any species that could invent xenonite in the first place must know their way around the periodic table a thousand times better than we do.

Time for a leap of faith. I pop the seals of the EVA suit and climb out the back. The strong smell of ammonia permeates the air but it's otherwise breathable. It's my own air supply, after all. I push the EVA suit back toward the airlock. The helmet lamps are my only source of light, so I finagle the suit so the lights stay pointed down the tunnel.

I float over to the mystery wall and reach out to touch it, but stop short. I can feel the heat even from a few inches away. Eridians like it hot.

In fact, I'm starting to sweat. The tunnel walls are heating up my air. It's uncomfortable, but not too bad. I can open the *Hail Mary*'s inner airlock door if I want my climate control to take over. Then our life-support systems can fight it out. They'll keep the hot side hot and I'll keep the cold side cold.

Even with the sweat forming on my brow and the strong ammonia odor making my eyes water, I press on. I'm just too curious not to. Could anyone blame me?

There are at least twenty little hexagons on this wall. They're all different colors and textures and I think a couple of them might be translucent. I should catalog each one and figure out if I can identify what they're made of. Looking closer, I see there's a definite seam running along the edges of the hexes.

That's when I hear a sound come from the other side:

Knock, knock, knock.

CHAPTER 10

They knocked, so it's only polite for me to knock back. I know that wall is going to be hot, so I rap my knuckles on it as fast as I can.

I knock three times, just like they did.

There's no immediate response. I take a good long look at the hex wall. There are forty hexes, I'd say, and each one seems to be unique. Different materials, maybe? I feel like I'm supposed to do something here, but what?

Are they watching me? I don't see anything that looks like a camera.

I hold up my finger and point back to my airlock. I don't know if they can see me or if they have any idea what that hand gesture means. I kick off the hex wall and back to the airlock, and then I open the inner door. Why not? The pressure is the same on both sides. It's okay to leave the airlock open. If there's a pressure loss in that tunnel, the air leaving the ship will slam the inner airlock door shut and I'll get to stay alive.

I go to the lab and pack a bag with a few choice items, then return to the tunnel.

First I tape LED lamps to various spots along the tunnel and aim them at the hex wall. Now I can see what I'm doing, at least. I pull out my trusty handheld x-ray spectrometer and scan one of the hexes. It's xenonite. Almost the same composition as the cylinders they sent me earlier.

Almost.

There are a few differences in the trace elements. Interesting. Maybe xenonite is like steel—lots of different recipes? I check the next hex over. Another slightly unique combination.

Best guess: Different types of xenonite are optimal for different situations. They had no idea what my air was like. So they want to test various compounds against it. When I leave the tunnel, they'll inspect the hexes to decide which one fares best.

That means I should leave the tunnel. Should I depressurize my side for them? Seems polite. I could easily do it—I'd just tell the airlock to cycle. It would think, "Golly, there sure is a lot of air in me today!" but would just keep pumping until there was a vacuum.

But then again, maybe they have a way of sampling the air on this side. If so, I should leave it here, right?

I decide to leave it be. They probably have a sampling technique. If I were making this tunnel, that's what I'd do, and they seem pretty bright.

I turn back toward the airlock, but something catches my eye. Movement!

I shoot my attention back to the hex wall. Nothing's changed. But I could swear I saw something move. Some of the hexes are shiny—I probably caught a glimpse of my reflection.

Wait . . .

One hex stands out. Why?

It's near the tunnel wall. Not very obvious. I float over to take a closer look.

"Holy cow!" I say.

This hex is clear! All the others are opaque, but this one is like glass! I pull one of the lamps off the wall and hold it up to the hex. I press my head against the hot wall to get a closer look.

Light gets through into the other side. I can see the tunnel walls beyond. Either their side is a vacuum or their air is clear. Either way, there's nothing blocking or dulling my view.

Suddenly, a rock hits the other side of the hex. It stays there. It's just a few inches away from me. It's roughly triangular, kind of a dark brown, and has rough, jagged edges. Like you might see on the tip of a spear from a caveman.

Have I met spacefaring cavemen?

Stop being stupid, Ryland.

Why did they put a rock there? And is it sticky? Are they trying to block my view? If so, they're doing a terrible job. The little triangle is only a couple of inches wide at the thickest point and the hex is a good 8 inches across.

And it gets sillier. Now the rock is bending at articulated joints, and there are two similar rocks that do the same thing, and there's a longer rock attached to them that—

That's not a rock. It's a claw! It's a claw with three fingers!

I'm desperate to see more! I press my face against the hex. It burns, but I resist the urge to pull away. There's pain, yes, and it's probably going to leave a mark. I should go back to the lab and find a camera, but come on. No one would have that presence of mind at a time like this.

I groan as my face aches, but I'm rewarded with a better view.

The alien's claw—er . . . I'll call it a hand. That's less scary. The alien's *hand* has three triangular fingers, each one with articulation points. Knuckles, I guess. They can close up into a raindrop shape or widen out to a sort of three-legged starfish.

The skin is weird. It looks like brownish-black rock. It's irregular and bumpy, like someone carved the hand out of granite and hasn't gotten around to smoothing it out yet. Natural armor, maybe? Like a turtle shell but less organized?

There's an arm too. I can barely see it from this angle, no matter how hard I stupidly press my face into the Hot Wall of Pain. But there's definitely an arm leading away from the hand. I mean, there'd have to be, right? Not just a magic floating hand.

I can't take the pain anymore. I pull my head away. I feel my face. It's pretty raw, but there aren't any blisters.

Tap-tap-tap.

The alien is tapping the clear hex with a finger. So I flick it with my finger three times.

It taps the hex again, three times. So I tap again as well.

Then comes something creepy. The cla—*hand*—retreats and returns with an object and holds it against the clear hexagon. Whatever it is, it's small. I let myself drift closer to the wall for a better look. The heat warms my face.

The object is xenonite, of course. It's about a half-inch high and finely detailed. It looks like a doll. But it has an oversized head and really thick arms and legs—

"Oh!"

It's me. It's a teeny, tiny Russian Orlan-MKS2 EVA suit. That's all they've seen of me so far.

Another hand shows up. Hey, I have two hands, so I shouldn't be surprised that they do too. The second hand holds a model of the *Hail Mary*. It looks to be at the same scale as the figurine of me. The hands then push the little me into the little *Hail Mary*'s airlock.

Pretty clear. It's saying, *Go back into your ship.*

I give a thumbs-up. The alien releases Mini-Me and the *Hail Mary* model to float away. Then it contorts a hand into something resembling a thumbs-up. It's just two fingers curled into a ball with the third pointed up. At least it's not the middle one that's pointed up.

I return to the *Hail Mary* and close the airlock door behind me.

I pant and wheeze with excitement. I can't believe that just happened.

That's an alien. I just saw an alien. Not just an alien ship. An *alien being*. I mean—just his claw—er . . . hand. But yeah.

Well, I say "his hand," but maybe it's *her* hand. Or some other pronoun I don't have a word for. They might have seventeen biological sexes, for all I know. Or none. No one ever talks about the really *hard* parts of first contact with intelligent alien life: pronouns. I'm going to go with "he" for now, because it just seems rude to call a thinking being "it."

Also, until I hear otherwise, his name is Rocky.

Okay, now what? Rocky told me to go back into my ship. So I did.

I feel kind of stupid. There's a whole bunch of science I should be doing, right?

I peek through the airlock porthole. My lamps are still taped to the walls in the tunnel and I can see there have been some . . . changes.

The hex wall is gone. Just plain gone. I can see all the way to the *Blip-A*'s hull. And there's a hull robot attached to it reaching out and doing stuff with its little robot hands.

And yeah, its hands look like Rocky's hands, broadly speaking. Three fingers. About the same size as Rocky's hands. Probably controlled with a Nintendo Power Glove kind of thing inside the ship.

Man, I'm old.

The robot takes a particular interest in my lamps. Heck, I'd take an interest too. Those are alien artifacts with alien technology. Sure, they're just lights, but they're *alien* lights to my Eridian friends over there. Probably the most exciting scientific find of their history. The robot arm puts them in a little cubby on the *Blip*-A hull and a latch closes. I bet those are going to be the most heavily studied lamps in the history of lamps.

I'm glad they got to have that moment of discovery and all, but they took my light source away. I can hear the occasional clunk but it's pitch-dark in there.

That's interesting in and of itself. I'm not an alien from 40 Eridani, but if I were working with a remote-controlled robot, I'd have a camera on it somewhere and a light source to see what I was doing. But they don't need that. They don't need light.

Well, hold on. Their visible spectrum might be completely different from ours. Humans only see a tiny fraction of all the wavelengths of light out there. We evolved to see the wavelengths that are most plentiful on Earth. Maybe Eridians evolved to see different wavelengths. The room could be well illuminated with infrared or ultraviolet light and I wouldn't see a thing.

Hmm. A robot. Why a robot? They had a living being there a few minutes ago—my boy Rocky. Why replace him with a robot?

Vacuum.

They probably took all the air out of the tunnel. They have a sample of my hull—they know it's made of aluminum and roughly how thick it is. Maybe they aren't sure if my ship can handle outside pressure. Or maybe their atmosphere reacts badly with aluminum.

So they keep the tunnel a vacuum, which means they have to do work with a robot.

I feel like Sherlock Holmes. All I saw was "nothing," and I drew a bunch of conclusions! Conclusions that are wildly speculative and with nothing to prove them, but conclusions!

I could get another lamp—the lab has a few more. I could shine it in there to see what Robo-Rocky is doing. But I'll know soon enough. And I don't want to be in some other part of the ship if something interesting happens.

Just as I'm thinking that, something interesting happens.

Knock-knock-knock.

No, that's not creepy at all. Being in a spaceship twelve light-years from home and having someone knock on the door is totally normal.

Okay, now I *need* another lamp. I pinball down to the lab to grab another one, then back up to the control room. I cycle the airlock without bothering to put on the EVA suit. I turn the manual vent valves on both doors of the airlock to repressurize the tunnel. It works just like I expect. There's still a good seal out there.

I open the outer door and float in, lamp in hand.

The hex wall is gone—it's been replaced by a solid wall of clear material. And on the other side of that wall is Rocky.

He's a spider. A big-assed spider.

I turn to flee. But my rational brain takes over.

"Easy . . . easy . . . they're friendly," I say to myself. I turn back and take in the scene.

Rocky is smaller than a human. He's about the size of a Labrador. He has five legs radiating out from a central carapace-looking thing. The carapace, which is roughly a pentagon, is 18 inches across and half as thick. I don't see eyes or a face anywhere.

Each leg has a joint in the middle—I'll call it an elbow. Each leg (or should I say arm?) ends in a hand. So he's got five hands. Each hand has those triangular fingers I got a good look at last time. Looks like all five hands are the same. I don't see any "front" or "back" to him. He appears to be pentagonally symmetrical.

He wears clothing. The legs are bare, showing the rocklike skin, but there's cloth on the carapace. Sort of like a shirt with five armholes. I don't know what the shirt is made of but it looks thicker than typical human clothing. It's a dull greenish-brown, and inconsistently shaded.

The top of the shirt has a large open hole. Like where the neck goes on a human's T-shirt. That hole is smaller than the carapace. So he must have to put that shirt on by pulling it downward and sliding the arms through their respective holes. Again, like a human's shirt.

But there's no neck or head to go through that hole on top. Just a hard-looking rocky pentagon that sticks up a little bit from the crusty skin.

On his side of the tunnel, he has handles and latticework on the walls. He casually hangs on to a couple of bars with two of his hands. I guess when you have five hands, zero g isn't that big a deal. Just allocate a hand or two for keeping in one place and use the other three to do stuff.

For me, the tunnel is kind of small. But for him it's absolutely spacious.

He waves to me with a free arm. He knows one human greeting and by golly he plans to use it.

I wave back. He waves again. I shake my head. No more waving.

He pivots his "shoulders" to rotate his carapace back and forth. He "shook his head" inasmuch as he could. I wonder how we're going to break out of this game of "Eridian See Eridian Do," but he takes care of that for me.

He taps the clear wall three times with a finger, then keeps the finger extended. Is he . . . pointing?

I follow the line and wow, there's stuff in the tunnel with me! They left me a present!

I can be forgiven for not noticing. Seeing an alien kind of distracted me from the small collection of objects on the tunnel wall.

"All right," I say. "Let's see what you left me."

"♩♫♪♪♫," says Rocky.

My jaw drops. Yes, I'm in zero g. It still drops.

There was no pronunciation or inflection of the sounds. Just notes. Like whale song. Except not quite like whale song, because there were several at once. Whale chords, I guess. And he was responding to me. That means he can hear too.

And notably, the sounds were in my range of hearing. Some of the notes were low, some of them high. But definitely audible. That alone is amazing when I think about it. He's from a different planet, and totally different evolutionary line, but we ended up with compatible sound ranges.

On top of all that, he decided my noises warranted a response.

"You have a language!" I say. "How do you have a language?! You don't have a mouth!"

"♫♫♩," Rocky explains.

Thinking rationally, you can't make spaceships without a civilization and you can't have civilization without being able to communicate. So of course they have language. It's interesting that communication is done with sound, like humans do. Coincidence? Maybe not. Maybe that's just the easiest way to evolve that trait.

"♪." Rocky points to the objects they left me.

"Right, right," I say. The whole language thing is way more interesting to me, and I'd rather explore that. But for now, Rocky wants to know what I think of his presents.

I float over to the objects. They're attached to the wall with my own tape.

The objects are a pair of spheres. Each one has a raised image embossed on it. One has the *Hail Mary* and the other has the *Blip-A*.

I pull the *Hail Mary* ball off the tape. It's not warm. In fact, the tunnel isn't warm anymore. Interesting. Maybe they noticed I like things cooler and they did something to make it more comfortable for me.

There's a rattle from inside the ball. I shake it and listen. More rattling.

I find a seam. I rotate the top and bottom of the ball against each other and sure enough, they rotate. Left-handed screw, of course.

I look to Rocky for approval. He has no face and thus no facial expressions. He just floats there, watching me. Well, not watching . . . no eyes. Actually, wait. How does he know what I'm doing? He clearly knows—he waved and stuff. He must have eyes somewhere. I probably just don't recognize them.

I turn my attention back to the sphere. I pull the two halves apart and inside is . . . a bunch more little spheres.

I sigh. This raises more questions than it answers.

The little beads float out and drift across my field of view. They're not individual items. They're connected to one another by little strings. Like a complicated necklace. I spread it out as best I can.

They look like—for lack of a better term—beaded handcuffs. Two circles of threaded beads connected to each other by a little bridge of thread. Each circle has eight beads on it. The connecting thread has none. This seems very deliberate. But I have no idea what it means.

Maybe the other ball—the one with the *Blip-A* picture on it—will shed more light. I let the handcuffs float and pull the *Blip-A* ball off the wall. I shake it and hear lots of rattling from inside. I unscrew the two halves and another set of beads comes out.

Unlike the handcuffs, there's only one ring in this construction. And it has seven beads, not eight. Also, it has three connector strings sticking out of the circle and leading to a single bead each. Kind of like a necklace with some ornamentation hanging off of it.

There's more stuff inside. I shake the model and another necklace floats out. I take a look and it's identical to the one I just inspected. I keep shaking and more and more necklaces come out. Each one the same. I collect them all and stuff them in my pockets.

"This reminds me of something . . ." I thump my forehead. "What does this remind me of . . . ?"

Rocky taps his carapace with a claw. I know he's just mimicking my movements but it feels like he's saying, *Think, dummy!*

What would I tell my students at a time like this?

Why did I suddenly think of my students? I got an image of my classroom. A flash of memory. I'm holding a model of a molecule and explaining—

"Molecules!" I grab the handcuffs and hold them out to Rocky. "These are molecules! You're trying to tell me something about chemistry!"

"♫♪♫♫♪."

But wait. These are some weird molecules. They make no sense. I look at the handcuffs. Nothing forms a molecule like this. Eight atoms on one side, eight on the other, and connected by . . . what? Nothing? The connector string isn't even coming off a bead. It's just teeing off strings from the two circles.

"Atoms!" I say. "The beads are *protons.* So the circles of beads are atoms. And the little connectors are chemical bonds!"

"Okay, if that's the case . . ." I hold up the handcuffs and count everything again. "Then this is two atoms, each with eight protons, connected to each other. Element number eight is oxygen. Two oxygens. O_2! And it was in the *Hail Mary* ball."

I hold it toward Rocky. "You clever fellow, this is my atmosphere!"

I grab the other set of beads. "So your atmosphere is . . . seven protons connected to three individual atoms with one proton each. A nitrogen attached to three hydrogens. Ammonia! Of course it's ammonia! You breathe ammonia!"

That explains the pervasive smell on all of the little presents they left me. Residual traces of their air.

My smile fades. "Yikes. You breathe ammonia?"

I count all the little ammonia necklaces they gave me. I only got one O_2 molecule, but he gave me twenty-nine ammonias.

I think about it for a moment.

"Oh," I say. "I get it. I see what you're saying."

I look to my alien counterpart. "You have twenty-nine times as much atmosphere as I do."

Wow. Two things come immediately to mind: First, Eridians live in *immense* pressure. Like—similar to being a thousand feet deep in the ocean back on Earth. Secondly, xenonite is some amazing stuff. I don't know how thick that wall is—half an inch, maybe? Less? But it's holding back a relative pressure of 28 atmospheres. All while being a big, un-reinforced flat panel (the absolute worst way to make a pressure vessel). Heck, their whole ship is made of big flat panels. The tensile strength of that stuff must be off the charts. No wonder I couldn't bend or break the things they sent earlier.

We don't have *remotely* compatible environments. I'd die in seconds if I were on his side of the tunnel. And my guess is he wouldn't do well in one twenty-ninth his normal atmospheric pressure and with no ammonia at all.

Okay, not a problem. We have sound and we can pantomime. That's a good start for communication.

I take a moment to let this all sink in. This is amazing stuff. I have an alien buddy here, and we're chatting! I can barely contain myself! The problem is—I haven't contained myself. Fatigue washes over me so hard I can barely concentrate. It's been two days since I slept. There's just always been something monumental going on. I can't just stay up forever. I need to sleep.

I hold up a finger. The "hang on a sec" motion. Hopefully he remembers it from last time. He holds up a finger on one of his hands to match.

I rush back into the ship and careen down to the lab. There's an analog clock on the wall. Because every lab needs an analog clock. It takes some doing, but I pull it off the wall and put it under my arm. I also grab a dry-erase marker from the workstation.

Back I go, through the control room and into the Tunnel of Aliens. Rocky is still there. He seems to perk up when I return. How could I know that? I don't know. He just kind of repositioned himself and seems more attentive.

I show him the clock. I spin the time-set dial in the back. I just want him to see how the hands move around. He makes a circular motion with a hand. He gets it!

I set the clock to 12:00. Then I use the dry-erase marker to draw a long line from the center toward the twelve and a short line from the center to the two. I'd rather sleep a solid eight hours, but I don't want to keep Rocky waiting too long. I'll settle for a two-hour nap. "I'll come back when the clock matches this," I say. As if that would help him understand.

"♩♪♫." He makes a gesture. He reaches forward with two of his hands and grabs . . . nothing. And then he pulls the nothing toward him.

"What?"

He taps the wall and points to the clock, then repeats the gesture. Does he want the clock to be closer to the wall?

I push the clock closer. This seems to excite him. He makes the gesture more rapidly. I move it further forward. The clock is almost touching the wall now. He does the gesture one more time, but this time a little slower.

At this point, I have no idea what he wants. So I just push the clock up against the wall. It's touching now. He raises his hands and kind of shakes them. Alien jazz hands. Is that a good thing?

Okay, I hope he understands I'll be back in two hours. I turn to leave but immediately hear *tap-tap-tap*.

"Whaaat?" I say.

"♪♪♫♪," he says, pointing to the clock. It drifted a little bit away from the wall. He doesn't like that.

"Um, okay," I say. I pull a loop of tape off the wall, unloop it, and rip it in half. I use the two halves to tape the left and right sides of the clock to the clear wall.

Rocky gives me the jazz hands signal again. I think it means "yes" or "I approve of this." Like nodding.

I turn to leave again, but *tap-tap-tap*!

I spin around once more. "Dude, I just want a darn nap!"

He holds up a finger. Using my own sign language against me. Now I have to wait! I guess that's fair. I hold up my finger to acknowledge it.

He opens a circular door leading into his ship. It's the right size for an Eridian—I would have a hard time squeezing through if that ever became a plan. He disappears inside, leaving the door open. I'd love to know what's beyond the door, but I can't see anything. It's pitch-black in there.

Hmm. Interesting. It is completely dark in his ship. That door probably leads to an airlock. But even an airlock would have some lights in it, wouldn't it?

Rocky didn't have any problem getting around. But I know he can see—he responds to my gestures. This lends strength to my earlier theory about Eridian vision: I think they see a different part of the spectrum than humans do. Maybe they see entirely in infrared or entirely in ultraviolet. That airlock might be perfectly lit up as far as Rocky's concerned and I can't see a thing. Conversely, my lights are completely useless to him.

I wonder if we have any wavelengths in common. Maybe red (the color with the lowest wavelength that humans can see) is "♪♫♩," the highest wavelength they can see. Or something. Might be worth looking into. I should bring a rainbow of lights in and find out if he can—oh, he's back.

Rocky bounces into the tunnel and spider-walks along the rails to the dividing wall. He's incredibly graceful at it. Either he's very seasoned at being in zero g or Eridians are just really good at climbing around. They have five hands with opposable fingers, and he's an interstellar traveler, so it's probably a little bit of both.

With one of his hands, he holds a device up for me to see. It's . . . I don't know what it is.

It's a cylinder (man, these people like cylinders), a foot long and maybe 6 inches wide. I can see that his grip deforms the casing a little bit. It's made of a soft material, like foam rubber. The cylinder has five horizontally aligned square windows. Inside each window is a shape. I think they might be letters. But they're not just ink on paper. They're on a flat surface, but the symbols themselves are raised an eighth of an inch or so.

"Huh," I say.

The symbol on the right rotates away to be replaced by a new symbol. After a couple of seconds it happens again. Then again.

"It's a clock!" I say. "I showed you a clock, so you showed me a clock!"

I point to my clock, still taped to the wall, and then to his. He does the jazz hands with two of the hands he's not using at the moment. I do jazz hands back.

I watch the Eridian clock for a while. Rocky just holds it in place for me to see. The symbols—numbers, probably—cycle through on the rightmost window. They're on a rotor. Like an old-school digital clock back home. After a while, the rotor one step to the left of it changes one position. Aha!

As far as I can tell, the right rotor changes once every two seconds. A little more than two seconds, I think. It cycles through six unique symbols before repeating: "ℓ," "I," "V," "λ," "+," and "∀," in that order. Whenever it reaches "ℓ," the next rotor to the left advances one step. Eventually, after about a minute of this, that second-from-the-right rotor works its way through all the symbols, and when it reaches "ℓ," the third rotor from the right advances.

Looks like they read information from left to right—same as English. Neat coincidence. Though not incredibly unlikely. I mean, there's really only four options: left to right, right to left, top to bottom, or bottom to top. So there was a 1 in 4 chance we'd be the same.

So his clock is intuitive for me to read. And it works like an odometer. "ℓ" is clearly their 0. From that, I know that "I" is 1, "V" is 2, "λ" is 3, "+" is 4, and "Ɐ" is 5. What about 6 through 9? They don't exist. After "Ɐ" we go back to "ℓ." Eridians use base six.

Of all the things I teach my students, numerical bases are the hardest to make them truly understand. There's nothing special about the number 10. We have ten unique digits because we have ten fingers. Simple as that. Rockies have three fingers per hand and I guess they only like to use two hands when counting (they probably keep the other three feet/hands on the ground to stay steady). So they have six fingers to work with.

"I like you, Rocky! You're a genius!"

And he is! With this simple act, Rocky showed me:

- How Eridian numbers work (base six)
- How Eridian numbers are written (ℓ, I, V, λ,+, Ɐ)
- How Eridians read information (left to right)
- How long an Eridian second is

I hold up a finger and rush back into the ship to get my stopwatch. I come back and time Rocky's clock. I start the timer just as the *third* rotor changes state. The right rotor continues clicking over every two seconds or so, and every six steps, the next rotor advances one. This is going to take a while, but I want as accurate a count as possible. It takes around a minute and a half for the third rotor to move just one step. I can expect to be at this for ten minutes or so. But I plan to watch the whole time.

Rocky gets bored. At least, I think that's what happens. He starts fidgeting, and then lets the clock float in place near the divider wall. Then he wanders around his side of the tunnel. I'm not sure if he's doing anything in particular. He opens a door leading into his ship, begins to climb through, and then stops. He seems to think it over, then changes his mind. He closes the door. He doesn't want to leave while I'm still here. After all, I might do or say something interesting.

"♪♪♩," he says.

"I know, I know," I say. I hold up a finger.

He holds up his finger, then returns to slowly bouncing from wall to wall. Zero-g pacing.

Finally, the third rotor completes a full lap and I stop my timer. Total time: 511.0 seconds. I don't have a calculator, and I'm too excited to go back into the ship to get one. I pull out a pen and do long division on the palm of my other hand. One Eridian second is 2.366 Earth seconds.

I circle the answer on my palm and stare at it. I add a few exclamation points nearby because I feel like they're warranted.

I know it doesn't seem like much, but this is a huge deal. Rocky and I are astronauts. If we're going to talk, we're going to talk science. And just like that, Rocky and I have established a fundamental unit of time. Next up: length and mass!

No, actually. Next up—a nap. I'm so tired. I pull my clock off the wall, circle the "2" with my dry-erase marker—just to be as clear as possible, then tape it back in place. I wave. He waves back. Then I go back for a nap.

This is ridiculous. How can I expect to sleep? How could anyone under these circumstances? I'm still wrapping my head around what's happening. There's an alien out there.

And it's killing me that I can't find out what he knows about Astrophage. But you can't talk about complex scientific concepts with someone via pantomime. We need a shared language, however rudimentary.

I just need to keep doing what I'm doing. Work on science communication. The verbs and nouns of physics. It's the one set of concepts we're guaranteed to share—physical laws are the same everywhere. And once we have enough words to actually talk about science, we'll start talking about Astrophage.

And in "VVℓλI" Eridian seconds I'll be talking to him again. How the heck can a guy sleep at a time like this? There's no way I can just—

CHAPTER 11

My timer beeps at me. I'd set it for a two-hour countdown. It just reached zero. I blink a couple of times. I'm floating in a fetal position in the control room. I didn't even make it to the dormitory.

I am not rested at all. Every pore of my being yells at me to go back to sleep, but I told Rocky I'd be back in two hours and I wouldn't want him to think humans are untrustworthy.

I mean . . . we're pretty untrustworthy, but I don't want him to know that.

I trudge (can you trudge in zero g? I say yes) through the airlock. Rocky is there waiting for me in the tunnel. He's been busy in my absence. There's all sorts of stuff in there now.

The Eridian clock is still ticking away—now mounted to one of the lattice poles. But more interesting to me is the box that's been added to the dividing wall. It's a 1-foot cube and it juts out into my half of the tunnel. It's made of the same transparent xenonite that the rest of the wall is made of.

On Rocky's side, the box has a flat panel door with an opaque xenonite border. Also, there's a square hole with a perfectly fitted square pipe leading away.

There are some . . . controls? . . . on the pipe near the box. Buttons, maybe? A wire coming from the control box snakes along the pipe, disappearing into the hull where the pipe does.

Meanwhile, on my side of the cube is a crank, roughly the same shape as my own airlock door's crank. And that's attached to a square panel like the one on Rocky's side and—

"It's an airlock!" I said. "You made an airlock in our airlock tunnel!"

Brilliant. Simply brilliant. Rocky and I can both access it. He can control the air in that little chamber by means of the mystery pipe, which presumably leads back to some pumps or something in the *Blip-A*. And those buttons or whatever are the controls. Just like that, we have a way to transfer stuff back and forth.

I do jazz hands. He does them back.

Hmm. Again with the square, flat panels. Who makes a square airlock? Especially one designed to handle Eridian atmospheric pressure. Even the pipe that runs the mini-airlock is square. I know they can make round xenonite—the cylinders he sent me when we first met were round. This tunnel is round.

Maybe I'm overthinking this. Xenonite is so strong you don't have to carefully shape it into pressure vessels. Flat panels are probably easier to make.

This is awesome. I hold up a finger—he returns the gesture. I fly down to the lab and grab a tape measure. He showed me a unit of time, so I'll show him a unit of length. The tape measure is metric, thank God. It's going to be confusing enough using base-6 Eridian seconds. The last thing I want to throw in there is imperial units—even if they are natural to me.

Back in the tunnel, I hold up the tape measure. I pull it out a bit, then release it to let it retract. I repeat the process a few times. He does jazz hands. I point to the "squarelock" (well, what else should I call it?) and he does jazz hands again.

I hope that means there isn't 29 atmospheres of ammonia in there at the moment. I guess we'll see. . . .

I turn the crank and open my door. It swings outward toward me easily.

Nothing explodes. In fact, I don't even smell ammonia. And it wasn't a vacuum in there either. I wouldn't have been able to pull the door open at all if it had been. Rocky set that up to be exactly my atmosphere. Considerate of him.

I put the tape measure in the approximate center of the box and let it float there. I close the door and turn the crank.

Rocky presses a button on the controls and I hear a muffled *fwump* followed by a steady hiss. A foggy gas rushes in from the pipe. Ammonia, presumably. The tape measure bounces inside—pushed around like a leaf in the wind. Soon, the hiss dulls to a trickle.

And then I realize my mistake.

The tape measure is one of those solid, construction-site kinds that are made of metal with tool-grade rubber grip pads. Thing is, Eridians like it hot. How hot? I can't say for sure, but I now know it's hotter than the melting point of the rubber on the tape measure.

The blob of liquid rubber undulates on the tape measure, sticking to the tool via surface tension. Rocky opens his door and carefully grabs my faulty present by the metal. At least that's still solid. I think it's made of aluminum. It's nice to know Eridian air isn't hot enough to melt that too.

As Rocky pulls the tape measure toward him, the rubber blob separates from it and floats off in his side of the tube.

He pokes the rubber blob and it sticks to his claw. He shakes it off without much trouble. Obviously the temperature doesn't bother him. I guess it's no different from a human shaking water off his hand.

In my atmosphere, rubber that hot would burn. There'd be all these nasty, noxious gases coming off of it too. But there's no oxygen on Rocky's side of the wall. So the rubber just kind of . . . stays a liquid. It floats off to the tunnel wall and sticks there.

I shrug at him. Maybe he'll know that means "I'm sorry."

He sort of shrugs back. But he does it with all five shoulders. Looks weird and I don't know if he caught my meaning.

He pulls the tape out a bit, then lets it snap back. He's clearly surprised, even though he must have known it was coming. He releases it entirely and lets it spin in front of him. He grabs it and does it again. Then again.

And again.

"Yeah, it's fun," I say. "But look at the markings. Those are centimeters. CEN-TI-ME-TERS."

The next time he pulls the tape out, I point to the tape. "Look!"

He just keeps pulling it out and back again. I don't see any indication that he cares about what's written there.

"Ugh!" I hold up a finger. I go back to the lab and get another tape measure. It's a well-stocked lab and no space mission would be complete without redundancy. I come back to the tunnel.

Rocky is still playing with the tape measure. Now he's really having a ball. He pulls the tape out as far as he can, which is about a meter, then releases both the tape and the tape measure at the same time. The resulting recoil and snap-back makes the tape measure spin wildly in front of him.

"♩♪♫♪!!!" he says. I'm pretty sure that was a squeal of glee.

"Look. Look," I say. "Rocky. Rocky! Yo!"

He finally stops playing with the unintentional toy.

I pull some tape out on my tape measure, then point to the markings. "Look! Here! See these?"

He pulls his own out to approximately the same distance. I can see the markings on his are still there—they didn't get baked off in the blistering Eridian heat or anything. What is the problem?

I point at the 1-centimeter line. "Look. One centimeter. This line. Here." I tap the line repeatedly.

He holds the tape out with two hands and taps it with a third. He matches my tempo, but he's nowhere near the 1-centimeter mark.

"Here!" I tap the mark harder. "Are you blind?!"

I pause.

"Wait. Are you blind?"

Rocky taps the tape some more.

I've always assumed he had eyes somewhere and I didn't recognize them. But what if he doesn't have eyes at all?

The airlock of the *Blip*-A was dark, and Rocky didn't have any problem with it. So I figured he saw in frequencies of light I can't see. But the tape measure has white tape with black markings on it. *Any* vision in *any* spectrum should be able to discern black on white. Black is the absence of light and white is all frequencies equally reflected.

Wait—this doesn't make sense. He knows what I'm doing. He mimics my gestures. If he doesn't have vision, how can he read my clock? How can he read *his own* clock?

Hmm . . . his clock has thick numbers. Like an eighth of an inch. And, thinking back, he actually did have some trouble with my clock. He needed me to tape it to the divider wall. When it floated an inch away he got upset. Just being close to the divider wasn't enough. The clock had to be *touching* it.

"Sound?" I say. "Do you 'see' with sound?"

It would make sense. Humans use electromagnetic waves to understand our three-dimensional environment. So why couldn't a different species use sound waves? Same principle—and we even have it on Earth. Bats and dolphins use echolocation to "see" with sound. Maybe Eridians have that ability, but on steroids. Unlike bats and dolphins, Eridians have *passive* sonar. They use ambient sound waves to resolve their environment instead of making a specific noise to track prey.

Just a theory. But it fits the data.

That's why his clock numbers are thick. Because his sonar can't perceive things that are too thin. My clock was a challenge to him. He can't "see" the ink, but the hands are solid objects. So he knew about them. But the whole thing is encased in plastic. . . .

I slapped my forehead. "That's why you needed the clock pressed against the wall. You needed the sound waves bouncing around in it to get to you more easily. And the tape measure I just handed you is useless. You can't see the ink at all!"

He plays with the tape measure some more.

I hold up a finger. He's more focused on the tape measure toy, but he absently returns the gesture with one of his spare hands.

I fly back into the ship, through the control room, and into the lab. I grab a screwdriver and head farther down to the dormitory. I detach a storage panel from the floor. Simple aluminum sheet stock. Maybe one-sixteenth of an inch thick, with the edges rounded so we don't cut ourselves. Strong, durable, and light. Perfect for space travel. I fly back to the tunnel.

Rocky has wrapped one end of the tape around one of his tunnel's grab-handles and tied it in a somewhat crude knot. He hangs on to the dispenser with one hand and uses the other four to climb backward along the bars.

"Hey," I say. I hold up my hand. "Hey!"

He stops playing with the tape measure for a moment. "♩♪♩?"

I hold up two fingers.

Rocky holds up two fingers.

"Yeah. Okay. We're in mimic mode again." I hold up one finger, then switch to two, then back to one, and then finally three.

Rocky repeats the sequence, just as I hoped he would.

Now I put the aluminum panel between my hand and Rocky. Behind the panel, I hold up two fingers, then one, then three, then five.

Rocky holds up two fingers, then one, then all three. He brings in a second hand to hold up two more fingers for a total of five.

"Wow!" I say.

One-sixteenth-inch aluminum will stop pretty much all light. Some absurdly high frequencies can get through, but those frequencies would also pass right through me. So he wouldn't see my hands. But sound travels through metals just fine.

That's proof. He's not using light to perceive what's going on. It has to be sound. To Rocky, that metal plate is like a glass window.

Maybe it muddles the image a little, but not much. Heck, he probably knows what the *Hail Mary*'s control room looks like. Why not? The hull is just more aluminum.

How did he see me out in space? No air in space. So no sound.

Wait. No. That's a dumb question. He's not a caveman wandering around in space. He's an advanced interstellar traveler. He has technology. He probably has cameras and radar and stuff that translate data into something he can understand. No different from my Petrovascope. I can't see IR light, but it can and then it shows it to me on a monitor with light frequencies I can see.

The *Blip*-A control room probably has awesome-looking Braille-like readouts. Well, I'm sure it's way more advanced than that.

"Wow . . ." I stare at him. "Humans spent thousands of years looking up at the stars and wondering what was out there. You guys never saw stars at all but you still worked space travel. What an amazing people you Eridians must be. Scientific geniuses."

The knot in the tape comes loose, recoils wildly, and smacks Rocky's hand. He shakes the affected hand in pain for a moment, then continues messing with the tape measure.

"Yeah. You're definitely a scientist."

"All rise," said the bailiff, "the United States District Court for the Western District of Washington is now in session. The Honorable Justice Meredith Spencer presiding."

The entire courtroom stood as the judge took her seat.

"Be seated," the bailiff said. He handed the justice a folder. "Your Honor, today's case is *Intellectual Property Alliance v. Project Hail Mary*."

The judge nodded. "Plaintiff, are you ready for trial?"

The plaintiff's table was crowded with well-dressed men and women. The eldest of them, a man in his sixties, stood to answer. "We are, Your Honor."

"Defense, are you ready for trial?"

Stratt sat alone at the defense table, typing away on her tablet.

The justice cleared her throat. "Defense?"

Stratt finished typing and stood. "I'm ready."

Justice Spencer gestured to Stratt's table. "Counselor, where is the rest of your team?"

"Just me," she said. "And I'm not a counselor—I'm the defendant."

"Ms. Stratt." Spencer took off her glasses and glared. "The defendant in this case is a rather famous intergovernmental consortium of scientists."

"Led by me," said Stratt. "I move to dismiss."

"You can't make motions yet, Ms. Stratt," said Spencer. "Just tell me if you're ready to proceed."

"I'm ready,"

"All right. Plaintiff, you may begin your opening statement."

The man stood. "May it please the court and ladies and gentlemen of the jury, my name is Theodore Canton, counsel for the Intellectual Property Alliance in this action.

"During this trial, we will show that Project Hail Mary has overstepped its authority in the matter of digital data acquisition and licensing. They have, in their possession, a gigantic solid-state-drive array upon which they have copied literally *every single piece* of software that has ever been copyrighted, as well as *every single book and literary work* that has ever been available in any digital format. All of this was done without payment or licensing to the proper copyright holders or intellectual property owners. Furthermore, many of their technological designs violate patents held by—"

"Your Honor," Stratt interrupted. "Can I make motions now?"

"Technically," said the justice, "but it's irregul—"

"I move to dismiss."

"Your Honor!" Canton protested.

"On what grounds, Ms. Stratt?" said the justice.

"Because I don't have time for this bullshit," she said. "We are building a ship to literally save our species. And we have very little time to get it done. It will have three astronauts—just three—to do experiments we can't even conceive of now. We need them to be prepared for any possible line of study they deem necessary. So we are giving them everything. The collected knowledge of humankind, along with all software. Some of it is stupid. They probably won't need Minesweeper for Windows 3.1, and they probably don't need an unabridged Sanskrit-to-English dictionary, but they're going to have them."

Canton shook his head. "Your Honor, my clients don't dispute the noble nature of the Hail Mary Project. The complaint is in the illegal use of copyrighted material and patented mechanisms."

Stratt shook her head. "It would take a ridiculous amount of time and energy to work out licensing agreements with every company. So we're not doing it."

"I assure you, Ms. Stratt, you will comply with the law," said the justice.

"Only when I want to." Stratt held up a sheet of paper. "According to this international treaty, I am personally immune from prosecution for any crime anywhere on Earth. The United States Senate ratified that treaty two months ago."

She held up a second piece of paper. "And to streamline situations like this, I also have a preemptive pardon from the president of the United States for any and all crimes I am accused of within U.S. jurisdictions."

The bailiff took the papers and handed them to the justice.

"This . . ." said the justice, "this is exactly what you say it is."

"I'm only here as a courtesy," said Stratt. "I didn't have to come at all. But since the software industry, patent trolls, and everyone else related to intellectual property banded together in one lawsuit, I figured it would be fastest to nip this in the bud all at once."

She grabbed her satchel and put the tablet inside. "I'll be on my way."

"Hold on, Ms. Stratt," said Justice Spencer. "This is still a court of law, and you will remain for the duration of these proceedings!"

"No, I won't," said Stratt.

The bailiff walked forward. "Ma'am. I'll have to restrain you if you don't comply."

"You and what army?" Stratt asked.

Five armed men in military fatigues entered the courtroom and took up station around her. "Because I have the U.S. Army," she said. "And that's a damn fine army."

I browse through my available software while munching on a peanut-butter tortilla. I know that doesn't sound tasty, but it is.

I've learned how to grip the lab chair with my legs so I don't float off as I use the laptop. Turns out I have a bunch of laptops. At least six that I've found in the storage area so far. And they're all connected to a shipwide Wi-Fi network. Handy.

If memory serves, I should have pretty much all the software lurking around somewhere on the ship. The trick is finding the one I need. I wouldn't even know what it's called. Fortunately, one of the books in the digital library is a list of software applications. So that helped.

Ultimately I find something that will work: "Tympanum Labs Waveform Analyzer." There are all sorts of waveform-analysis software packages in my library. This one just has the highest reviews according to a 2017 computer magazine that reviewed waveform analyzers.

I install the software on one of the laptops. It's pretty simple to use and has a plethora of features. But the one I'm most interested in is the Fourier transform. It's the most basic tool in sound-wave analysis and arguably the most important. There's a lot of complicated math on how to make it happen, but the end result is this: if you run a sound wave through a Fourier transform, it will give you a list of the individual notes being played at the same time. So if I played a C-major chord and let this app listen to it, the app would tell me there's a C, an E, and a G. It's incredibly useful.

No more pantomime. It's time to learn Eridianese. Yes, I just made up that word. No, I don't feel bad about it. I'm doing a lot of things for the first time in human history out here and there's a lot of stuff that needs naming. Just be glad I don't name stuff after myself.

I launch Microsoft Excel on another laptop and tape the two laptops together back to back. Yes, I could just run both applications on one laptop, but I don't want to switch back and forth.

I fly up through the ship and back into the tunnel. Rocky isn't there.

Hmph.

Rocky can't just spend all day waiting around for me, but why don't they have someone in the tunnel at all times? If my crewmates were still around, we would definitely rotate a watch or something. Heck, Ilyukhina would probably be camped out here nonstop and only leave when she had to sleep.

What if they *are* having different people in the tunnel? How do I know Rocky is just one person? I don't know how to tell Eridians apart. Maybe I've been talking to six different people. That's an unsettling thought.

No . . . that's not it. I'm pretty sure Rocky is just Rocky. The ridges on his carapace and rocky protrusions on his hands are unique. I remember there's an irregular craggy bit sticking up out of one of his fingers . . . yeah. It's the same guy.

If you looked at a rock for several hours, and someone replaced it with a very similar, but slightly different rock, you would know.

Okay, so where is the rest of the crew? I'm alone because my crewmates didn't make it. But Eridians have better technology, space-wise. Bigger ship, nigh-indestructible hull material. There has to be a crew in there.

Ah! I bet Rocky's the captain! He puts himself at risk by talking to the scary alien. Everyone else stays back on the ship. That's what Captain Kirk would do. So why not Captain Rocky?

Anyway, I have cool stuff I want to do and I'm impatient.

"Yo! Rocky!" I yell. "Come here!"

I listen for any sounds of movement. "Come on, man! Your entire ranged sensory input is sound—I bet you can hear a pin drop a mile away! You know I'm calling you! Move your . . . whatever serves as your butt! I want to talk!"

I wait and wait, but no Rocky.

My guess is I'm a pretty high priority to him. So whatever he's doing must be really important. After all, he's got a ship to deal with. He probably needs to eat and sleep. Well, he has to eat, anyway—all biological organisms need to get energy somehow. I don't know if Eridians sleep.

Come to think of it . . . sleep might not be such a bad idea. Out of the past forty-eight hours I've had a two-hour nap and nothing else. Rocky's clock is still there, wedged between a grab bar and the divider wall. It's ticking away as normal. It's interesting that his clock only has five digits. By my math, it'll roll over back to ℓℓℓℓℓ every five hours or so. Maybe that's the length of an Eridian day?

Speculate later. Sleep is the priority. I set up a spreadsheet on my Excel laptop to convert from Rocky time to mine and vice versa. I want to sleep for eight hours. I enter the current time on Rocky's clock, which is IℓIVλ, and have the spreadsheet tell me what that clock will say eight hours from now. The answer: Iλ+V̶V̶λ.

I hurry back to the lab to pick up a bunch of Popsicle sticks and tape. Rocky can't see ink, so I have to improvise.

I tape the sticks to the divider wall to let Rocky know when I'll return: Iλ+V̶V̶λ. Fortunately, the symbols are mostly made of straight lines, so my little craft project should be good enough for him to read.

Interestingly, my return time has six digits. One more digit than Rocky's clock shows. But I'm sure he'll figure it out. If Rocky said "I'll be back at thirty-seven o'clock," I'd understand what he meant.

Before I hit the hay, I harvest a mini-camera from the lab's vacuum chamber. It's just a small wireless camera that talks to a portable LCD clipped to the chamber. I tape the camera up in the tunnel, pointed at the divider wall. I bring the readout screen with me to my bunk.

There. Now I have a baby-monitor setup in the tunnel. There's no audio—the camera is for watching experiments, not chatting with people. But it's better than nothing.

I tuck the bunk's sheets and blankets in tight all around the oval mattress pad. I shimmy in between the tight bedding. This way I won't just float around while I sleep.

My grand plans for communicating with Rocky will have to wait. I'm a little frustrated, but not for long. I conk out almost immediately.

CHAPTER 12

Tap-tap-tap.

The sound barely penetrates my consciousness. It's far away.

Tap-tap-tap.

I wake from a dreamless sleep. "Huh?"

Tap-tap-tap.

"Breakfast," I mumble.

The mechanical arms reach into a compartment and pull out a packaged meal. It's like Christmas every morning around here. I pull the top off and steam wafts out in all directions. There's a breakfast burrito inside.

"Nice," I say. "Coffee?"

"Preparing . . ."

I take a bite of the breakfast burrito. It's good. All the food is good. I guess they figured if we're going to die, we may as well eat good stuff.

"Coffee," says the computer. A mechanical arm hands me a pouch with a pinch-straw in it. Like a Capri Sun for adults. Zero-g accommodations.

I let the burrito float nearby and take a sip of coffee. It's delicious, of course. It even has just the right amount of cream and sugar. That's a very personal preference that varies wildly from person to person.

Tap-tap-tap.

What is that, anyway?

I check the LCD screen taped near my bunk. Rocky is in the tunnel tapping on the divider wall.

"Computer! How long was I asleep?"

"Patient was unconscious for ten hours and seventeen minutes."

"Oh crud!"

I wriggle out of my bedding and bounce up through the ship toward the control room. I carry the burrito and coffee with me because I'm starving.

I bounce into the tunnel. "Sorry! Sorry!"

Rocky taps the divider louder than before now that I'm here. He points to the Popsicle-stick numbers I taped to the divider and then to his clock. He balls one of his hands into a fist.

"I'm sorry!" I clasp my hands together as if praying. I don't know what else to do. There's no interplanetary symbol for supplication. I don't know if he understands, but he unclenches his fist.

Maybe it was a mild admonishment. I mean, he could have made five fists, but he only made one.

Anyway, I kept him waiting over two hours. He's understandably upset. Hopefully this next trick will make up for it.

I hold up a finger. He returns the gesture.

I grab my duct-taped laptops and launch the waveform-analysis software on one and Excel on the other. I press them against the tunnel wall and secure them there with tape.

I pull the Popsicle-stick numbers off the divider wall. They're as good a place to start as any. I hold up the "I" and point to it. "One," I say. "One."

I point to my mouth, then back to the Eridian number. "One." Then I point to Rocky.

He points to the "I" and says "♪."

I pause the waveform analyzer and scroll back a few seconds.

"There we go . . ." Rocky's word for "one" is just two notes played at the same time. There are a bunch of harmonics and resonances in there, too, but the main frequency peaks are just two notes.

I type "one" into the spreadsheet on the other computer and note the relevant frequencies.

"Okay . . ." I return to the divider and hold up the "V" symbol. "Two," I say.

"♪," he says. Another one-syllable word. The oldest words in a language are usually the shortest.

This time, it's a chord made of four distinct notes. I enter "two" and record the frequencies for that word.

He starts to get excited. I think he knows what I'm up to and it's got him happy.

I hold up the "λ" and before I can even speak, he points to it and says, "♫♪."

Excellent. Our first two-syllable word. I have to scroll back and forth a bit in the waveform data to get the chords right. The first syllable has just two notes and the second has five! Rocky can make at least five different notes at the same time. He must have multiple sets of vocal cords or something. Well, he has five arms and five hands. So why not five sets of vocal cords?

I don't see a mouth anywhere. The notes are just coming from somewhere inside him. When I first heard him speak, I thought it sounded like whale song. That may have been more accurate than I thought. Whales sound like they do because they move air back and forth across their vocal cords without expelling it. Rocky may be doing the same thing.

Tap-tap-tap-tap!

"What?" I look back at him.

He points to the "λ" symbol still in my hand and then to me. Then back to the "λ" and back to me. He's almost frantic about it.

"Oh, sorry," I say. I hold the digit up properly and say, "Three."

He does jazz hands. I throw some jazz hands back.

Huh. While we're on the subject . . .

I stand still for a moment so he'll know there was a break in the conversation. Then I do jazz hands and say, "Yes."

I repeat the gesture. "Yes."

He does it back to me and says, "♫♩."

I note and record the frequencies in my laptop.

"Okay, we have 'yes' in our vocabulary now," I say.

Tap-tap-tap.

I look over. Once he knows he has my attention, he does jazz hands again and says, "♫♩." Same chord as before.

"Yes," I say. "We covered this."

He holds up a finger for a moment. Then he balls two of his fists and taps them together. "♪♪."

. . . What?

"Ohhh," I say. I'm a teacher. What would I teach someone who just learned the word 'yes'?

"That's 'no.'"

At least I hope so.

I ball my fists and tap them together. "No."

"♫♩," he says. I check the laptop. He just said yes.

Wait. Does that mean it's not no? Is that another yes? Now I'm confused.

"No?" I ask

"*No,*" he says in Eridian.

"So, 'yes'?"

"*No, yes.*"

"Yes?"

"*No. No.*"

"Yes, yes?"

"*No!*" He balls a fist at me, clearly frustrated.

Enough of this interspecies Abbott and Costello routine. I hold up a finger.

He unballs his fist and returns the gesture.

I enter the frequencies for what I think is "no" into my spreadsheet. If I'm wrong, I'm wrong and we'll work it out later.

I hold up the "+" symbol. "Four."

He holds up three fingers on one hand, and one finger on another. "♩♩."

I make note of the frequencies.

For the next several hours, we expand our shared vocabulary to several thousand words. Language is kind of an exponential system. The more words you know, the easier it is to describe new ones.

Communication is hampered by my slow and clumsy system for listening to Rocky. I check the frequencies he emits with one laptop, then look them up in my spreadsheet on the other laptop. It's not a great system. I've had enough.

I excuse myself for an hour to write some software. I'm not a computer expert, but I know some rudimentary programming. I write a program to take the audio-analysis software's output and look up the words in my table. It's barely even a program—more of a script. It's not efficient at all, but computers are fast.

Fortunately, Rocky speaks with musical chords. While it's very difficult to make a computer turn human speech into text, it's very easy to make a computer identify musical notes and find them in a table.

From that point on, my laptop screen shows me the English translation of what Rocky is saying in real-time. When a new word comes up, I enter it into my database and the computer knows it from then on.

Rocky, meanwhile, doesn't use any system to record what I'm saying or doing. No computer, no writing implement, no microphone. Nothing. He just pays attention. And as far as I can tell, he remembers everything I told him. Every word. Even if I only told it to him once several hours earlier. If only my students were that attentive!

I suspect Eridians have much better memory than humans.

Broadly speaking, the human brain is a collection of software hacks compiled into a single, somehow-functional unit. Each "feature" was added as a random mutation that solved some specific problem to increase our odds of survival.

In short, the human brain is a mess. Everything about evolution is messy. So, I assume Eridians are also a mess of random mutations. But whatever led to their brains being how they are, it gave them what we humans would call "photographic memory."

It's probably even more complicated than that. Humans have a whole chunk of our brains dedicated to sight, and it even has its own memory cache. Maybe Eridians are just really good at remembering sounds. After all, it's their primary sense.

I know it's too early, but I can't wait any longer. I get a vial of Astrophage from the lab supplies and bring it to the tunnel. I hold it up. "Astrophage," I say.

Rocky's entire posture changes. He hunkers his carapace a little lower. He tightens his claws a bit on the bars he uses to keep in place. "♫♪♫," he says, his voice more quiet than usual.

I check the computer. It's not a word I've recorded yet. It must be his word for Astrophage. I note it in the database.

I point to the vial. "Astrophage on my star. Bad."

"♫♩♪♫ ♫♪♫♩ ♫♪♫," Rocky says.

The computer translates: *Astrophage on me star. Bad bad bad.*

Okay! Theory confirmed. He's here for the same reason I am. I want to ask so many more questions. But we just don't have the words. It's infuriating!

"♫♫ ♫♩♪♪♫ ♫♪♫," Rocky says.

My computer pops up the text: *You come from where, question?*

Rocky has picked up the basic word ordering of English. I think he realized early on that I can't automatically remember stuff, so he works with my system rather than trying to teach me his. I probably seem pretty stupid, honestly. But some of his own grammar sneaks in once in a while. He always ends a question with the word "question."

"No understand," I say.

"You star is what name, question?"

"Oh!" I say. He wants the *name* of my star. "Sol. My star is called 'Sol.'"

"Understand. Eridian name for you star is ♫♪♫♪♩♩."

I note down the new word. That's Rocky's word for "Sol." Unlike two humans fumbling to communicate, Rocky and I can't even pronounce each other's proper nouns.

"My name for your star is 'Eridani,'" I say. Technically we call it "40 Eridani," but I decide to keep it simple.

"Eridian name for my star is ♫♩♩♪♪♪."

I add the word to the dictionary. "Understand."

"Good."

I don't have to read the computer screen for that particular translation. I've started to recognize some of the more frequent words like "you," "me," "good," "bad," et cetera. I've never been artistic and I'm about as far from having a musical ear as anyone can be. But after you hear a chord a hundred times, you tend to remember it.

I check my watch—yes, I have a watch now. The stopwatch has a clock feature. It took me a while to notice. I had other things on my mind.

We've been at it all day and I'm exhausted. Do Eridians even know what sleep is? I guess it's time to find out.

"Human bodies must sleep. Sleep is this." I curl up into a ball and close my eyes in an overdramatic representation of sleep. I make a fake snoring sound because I'm a bad actor.

I return to normal and point to his clock. "Humans sleep for twenty-nine thousand seconds."

Along with perfect memory, Eridians are extremely good at math. At least, Rocky is. As we worked our way through scientific units, it became immediately apparent that he can convert from his units to mine in the blink of an eye. And he has no problem understanding base ten.

"Many seconds . . ." he says. *"Why be still so many seconds, question . . . Understand!"*

He relaxes his limbs and they go limp. He curls up like a dead bug and remains motionless for a while. *"Eridians same! ♪♫♫♪!"*

Oh thank God. I can't imagine explaining "sleep" to someone who had never heard of it. *Hey, I'm going to fall unconscious and hallucinate for a while. By the way, I spend a third of my time doing this. And if I can't do it for a while, I go insane and eventually die. No need for concern.*

I add his word for "sleep" to the dictionary.

I turn to leave. "I'm going to sleep now. I'll come back in twenty-nine thousand seconds."

"I observe," he says.

"You observe?"

"I observe."

"Uh . . ."

He wants to watch me sleep? In any other context that would be creepy, but when you're studying a new life-form it's appropriate, I guess.

"I will be still for twenty-nine thousand seconds," I warn him. "Many seconds. I will not do anything."

"I observe. Wait."

He returns to his ship. Is he finally going to get something to take notes with? After a few minutes, he comes back with a device in one of his hands and a satchel held in two more.

"I observe."

I point to the device. "What is that?"

"*♫♪♩♫*." He pulls some kind of tool out of the satchel. "*♫♪♩♫ not function.*" He pokes the device with the tool a few times. "*I change. ♫♪♩♫ function.*"

I don't bother to note down the new word. What would I enter it as? "Thing Rocky was holding that one time"? Whatever it is, it has a couple of wires sticking out and an opening that reveals some complex internals.

The object itself is irrelevant. The point is he's repairing it. New word for us.

"Fix." I say. "You fix."

"♫♪♫♪," he says.

I add "fix" to the dictionary. I suspect it'll come up a lot.

He wants to watch me sleep. He knows it's not going to be exciting, but he wants to do it anyway. So he brought some work with him to keep busy.

Okay. Whatever floats his boat.

"Wait," I say.

I return to the ship and head to the dormitory.

I pull the mattress pad, sheets, and blanket from my bunk. I could use one of the other two bunks but . . . they had my dead friends in them so I don't want to.

I bring the pad and sheets through the lab, awkwardly through the control room, and into the tunnel. I use a copious amount of duct tape to affix the mattress pad to the wall, then cinch up the sheets and blanket.

"I sleep now," I say.

"Sleep."

I turn off the lights in the tunnel. Total darkness for me, no effect for Rocky, who wants to watch me. Best of both worlds.

I shimmy into bed and resist the urge to say good night. It would just lead to more questions.

I drift off to the occasional *clink* and *scrape* of Rocky working on his device.

The next several days are repetitive, but far from boring. We greatly increase our shared vocabulary and a decent amount of grammar. Tenses, plurals, conditionals . . . language is tricky. But we're getting it piece by piece.

And slow though the process is, I'm memorizing more of his language. I don't need the computer as often. Though I still can't go without it completely—that'll take a long time.

I spend an hour every day studying Eridian vocabulary. I made a little script to pick random words from my Excel spreadsheet and play the notes with a MIDI app. Again, a rudimentary program, inefficiently written but computers are fast. I want to be free of the spreadsheet as soon as I can. For now, I still need it all the time. But once in a while I'll understand an entire sentence without resorting to the computer. Baby steps.

Every night, I sleep in the tunnel. He watches. I don't know why. We haven't talked about it yet. We've been too busy with other stuff. But he really doesn't want me to sleep without him watching. Even if I just want to catch a quick nap.

Today I want to work on an extremely important scientific unit that's been eluding us. Mainly because we live in zero g.

"We need to talk about mass."

"Yes. Kilogram."

"Right. How do I tell you about a kilogram?" I ask.

Rocky produces a small ball from his satchel. It's about the size of a ping-pong ball. *"I know mass of this ball. You measure. You tell me how many kilograms ball is. Then I know kilogram."*

He thought it through!

"Yes! Give me the ball."

He hangs on to several support poles with various hands and puts it in the mini-airlock. After a few minutes of waiting for it to cool, I have it in my hands. It's smooth and made of a metal. Fairly dense, I think.

"How will I measure this?" I mumble.

"Twenty-six," Rocky says out of nowhere.

"What about twenty-six?"

He points to the ball in my hand. *"Ball is twenty-six."*

Oh, I get it. The ball weighs twenty-six of something. Whatever his unit is. Okay. All I have to do is work out the mass of this ball, divide by twenty-six, and tell him the answer.

"I understand. The ball is a mass of twenty-six."

"No. Is not."

I pause. "It isn't?"

"Is not. Ball is twenty-six."

"I don't understand."

He thinks for a moment, then says, "*Wait.*"

He disappears into his ship.

While he's gone, I speculate on how to weigh something in zero g. It still has mass, of course. But I can't just put it on a scale. There's no gravity. And I can't spin up the *Hail Mary*'s centrifugal gravity. The tunnel is connected to her nose.

I could make a small centrifuge. Something big enough for the smallest lab scale I have. Rotate at some constant rate with the scale inside. Measure something I know the mass of and then measure the ball. I could calculate the mass of the ball from the ratio of the two measurements.

But I'd have to build a consistent centrifuge. How would I do that? I can spin something in the zero-g environment of the lab easily enough, but how do I spin it at a constant rate across multiple experiments?

Oooh! I don't need a constant rate! I just need a string with a mark in the center!

I fly into the *Hail Mary*. Rocky will forgive me for running off. Heck, he can probably "observe" me from wherever he is on his ship anyway.

I bring the ball down to the lab. I get a piece of nylon string and tie each end around a plastic sample canister. I now have a string with little buckets at each end. I put the canisters next to each other and pull the now-folded string taut. I use a pen to mark the farthest point. That's the exact center of this contraption.

I wave the ball back and forth with my hand to get a feel for its mass. Probably less than a pound. Less than half a kilogram.

I leave everything floating in the lab and kick my way down to the dormitory.

"Water," I say.

"Water requested," says the computer. The metal arms hand me a zero-g "sipper" of water. Just a plastic pouch with a straw on it that only lets water through if you unlatch a little clip. And inside is 1 liter of water. The arms always give me water a liter at a time. You have to stay hydrated if you want to save the world.

I return to the lab. I squirt about half of the water into a sample box and seal it. I put the half-depleted sipper into one of the buckets and the metal ball into the other. I set the whole thing spinning in the air.

The two masses clearly aren't equal. The lopsided rotation of the two connected containers shows the water side is much heavier. Good. That's what I wanted.

I pluck it out of the air and take a sip of water. I start it spinning again. Still off-center but not as bad.

I take more sips, do more spins, take more sips, and so on until my little device rotates perfectly around the marked center point.

That means the mass of the water is equal to the mass of the ball.

I pull out the sippy. I know the density of water—it's 1 kilogram per liter. So all I need to know is the volume of this water to know its mass and therefore the mass of the metal ball.

I get a large plastic syringe from the supplies. It can pull a maximum of 100 cc of volume.

I attach the syringe to the sippy and unclip the straw. I draw out 100 cc of water, then squirt it into my "wastewater box." I repeat this a few more times. The last syringe is only about a quarter full when I empty the bag.

Result: 325 ccs of water, which weighs 325 grams! Therefore Rocky's ball also weighs 325 grams.

I return to the tunnel to tell Rocky all about how smart I am.

He balls a fist at me as I enter. *"You left! Bad!"*

"I measured the mass! I made a very smart experiment."

He holds up a string with beads on it. *"Twenty-six."*

The beaded string is just like the ones he sent me back when we talked about our atmospheres—

"Oh," I say. It's an atom. That's how he talks about atoms. I count the beads. There are twenty-six in all.

He's talking about element 26—one of the most common elements on Earth. "Iron," I say. I point at the necklace. "Iron."

He points at the necklace and says, "♫♩♪♫♫." I record the word in my dictionary.

"Iron," he says again, pointing at the necklace.

"Iron."

He points to the ball in my hand. *"Iron."*

It takes a second to sink in. Then I slap my forehead.

"You are bad."

It was a fun experiment, but a total waste of time. Rocky was giving me all the information I needed. Or trying to, at least. I know how dense iron is, and I know how to calculate the volume of a sphere. Getting to mass from there is just a little arithmetic.

I pull a pair of calipers out of the toolkit I keep in the tunnel and measure the sphere's diameter. It's 4.3 centimeters. From that I work out the volume, multiply by the density of iron, and get a much more precise and accurate mass of 328.25 grams.

"I was only off by one percent," I grumble.

"You talk to you, question?"

"Yes! I'm talking to me."

"Humans are unusual."

"Yes," I say.

Rocky stretches his legs. *"I sleep now."*

"Wow," I say. This is the first time he's had to sleep since we met. Good. This will provide me some time for some lab work. But how much time?

"How long do Eridians sleep?"

"I not know."

"You don't know? You're Eridian. How can you not know how long Eridians sleep?"

"Eridians not know how long sleep last. Maybe short time. Maybe long time."

They sleep unpredictable amounts of time. I guess there's no rule saying sleep has to evolve as a regular pattern. Does he at least know a range of times it might be?

"Is there a minimum time? A maximum time?"

"Minimum is 12,265 seconds. Maximum is 42,928 seconds."

I often get strangely specific numbers from Rocky on things that should be rough estimates. It took me a while to figure out, but I finally did. He actually is coming up with rough, round numbers. But they're in his units and in base six. It's actually easier for him to convert those values to base-ten Earth seconds than it is for him to think directly in Earth seconds.

If I converted those values back to Eridian seconds and looked at the numbers in base six, I bet they'd be some round number. But I'm too lazy. Why un-convert data he already converted? I've never seen him be wrong on arithmetic.

Meanwhile, I have to divide by 60 twice on a calculator just to convert from one of my own planet's units to another of my own planet's units. He'll sleep for a minimum of three and a half hours and a maximum of almost twelve hours.

"I understand," I say. I head back toward the airlock.

"You observe, question?" Rocky asks.

He watched me sleep, so it's only fair he offer to let me watch him. I'm sure Earth scientists would jump all over the place to learn anything about what an Eridian sleeping looks like. But I finally have time to do some deep analysis of xenonite and I'm just *dying* to know how xenon bonds with other elements. If I can get any of my lab equipment to work in zero g, that is.

"Not necessary."

"You observe, question?" he asks again.

"No."

"Observe."

"You want me to observe you sleep?"

"Yes. Want want want."

Through unspoken agreement, a tripled word means extreme emphasis.

"Why?"

"I sleep better if you observe."

"Why?"

He waves a few arms, trying to find a way to phrase it. *"Eridians do that."*

Eridians watch one another sleep. It's a thing. I should be more culturally sensitive, but he threw shade when I talked to myself. "Eridians are unusual."

"Observe. I sleep better."

I don't want to watch a dog-sized spider not move for several hours. There's a crew in there, right? Have one of them do it. I point to his ship. "Have some other Eridian observe you."

"No."

"Why not?"

"I am only Eridian here."

My mouth hangs open. "You're the *only* person on that huge ship?!"

He's quiet for a moment, then says, "♫♩♪♫♩♪♫ ♫♪ ♩♪♫ ♫♪♫♪♩ ♫♪♩♪ ♫♩ ♪ ♫♩♪ ♫ ♩♪♫♩♪ ♫♩♪ ♫."

Complete nonsense. Did my kludged-together translation software fail? I check it out. No, it's working fine. I examine the waveforms. They seem similar to the ones I'd seen before. But they're lower. Come to think of it, that whole sentence seemed lower in pitch than anything Rocky has ever said before. I select the whole segment in the software's recording history and bump it up an octave. The octave is a universal thing, not specific to humans. It means doubling the frequency of every note.

The computer immediately translates the result. *"Original crew was twenty-three. Now is only me."*

That octave-drop . . . I think it's emotion.

"They . . . did they die?"

"Yes."

I rub my eyes. Wow. The *Blip-A* had a crew of twenty-three. Rocky is the sole survivor and he's understandably upset about it.

"Wh . . . er . . ." I stammer. "Bad."

"Bad bad bad."

I sigh. "My original crew was three. Now it's just me." I put my hand up against the divider.

Rocky puts a claw on the divider opposite my hand. *"Bad."*

"Bad bad bad," I say.

We stay like that for a moment. "I'll watch you sleep."

"Good. Me sleep," he says.

His arms relax and he looks for all the world like a dead bug. He floats free in his side of the tunnel, no longer hanging on to any support bars.

"Well, you're not alone anymore, buddy," I say. "Neither of us are."

CHAPTER 13

"Mr. Easton, I don't think we need to be searched," said Stratt.

"I think you do," said the head prison guard. His thick New Zealand accent sounded friendly, but there was an edge to it. This man had made a whole career out of not putting up with people's crap.

"We're exempt from all—"

"Stop," Easton said. "No one gets in or out of Pare without a full search."

Auckland Prison, which the locals called "Pare" for some reason, was New Zealand's only maximum-security prison unit. The sole point of entry was awash with security cameras and a micro-scanner for all guests. Even the guards passed through the detector on their way in.

Easton's assistant and I stood off to the side while our bosses had their dispute. He and I looked at each other and mutually shrugged. A small fraternity of underlings with stubborn bosses.

"I'm not turning over my Taser. I can call your prime minister if you like," Stratt said.

"Sure," said Easton. "She'll tell you the same thing I'm about to tell you now: We don't let weapons anywhere near those animals in there. Even my own guards only have batons. There are some rules we don't change. I'm fully aware of your authority, but it has limits. You're not magical."

"Mr. E—"

"Torch!" Easton said, holding out his hand.

His assistant handed over a small flashlight. He clicked it on. "Please open your mouth wide, Ms. Stratt. I need to check for contraband."

Whoa boy. I stepped forward before this got any worse. "I'll go first!" I opened my mouth wide.

Easton shined the light into my mouth and looked this way and that. "You're clear."

Stratt just glared at him.

He held the flashlight at the ready. "I can get a female guard in here and order a much more thorough search if you like."

For a few seconds, she did nothing. Then she pulled her Taser from its holster and handed it over.

She must have been tired. I'd never seen her give up on a power trip before. Though, I also hadn't seen her get into a useless peeing contest before either. She had a lot of authority and wasn't afraid to flex when needed, but she usually wasn't one to argue when a simple solution was present.

Soon, guards escorted Stratt and me through the cold, gray walls of the prison.

"What the heck is wrong with you?" I said.

"I don't like little dictators in their little kingdoms," she said. "Drives me crazy."

"You can bend a little once in a while."

"I'm out of patience and the world is out of time."

I held up a finger. "No, no, no! You can't just use 'I'm saving the world' as an excuse every time you're a jerk."

She thought it over. "Yeah, okay. You may have a point."

We followed the guards down a long corridor to the Maximum Security Unit.

"Maximum security seems like overkill," she said.

"Seven people died," I reminded her. "Because of him."

"It was accidental."

"It was criminal negligence. He deserves what he got."

The guards led us around a corner. We followed along. The whole place was a maze.

"Why bring me here at all?"

"Science."

"As always." I sighed. "Can't say I like this."

"Noted."

We entered a stark room containing a single metal table. On one side sat a prisoner in a bright-orange jumpsuit. A balding man in his late forties, maybe early fifties. He was handcuffed to the table. He didn't look anything like a threat.

Stratt and I sat down opposite him. The guards closed the door behind us.

The man looked at us. He tilted his head slightly, waiting for someone to speak.

"Dr. Robert Redell," Stratt said.

"Call me Bob," he said.

"I'll call you Dr. Redell." She pulled a file out of her briefcase and looked it over. "You're currently serving a life sentence for seven counts of culpable homicide."

"That's their excuse for me being here, yes," he said.

I piped up. "Seven people died on your rig. Because of your negligence. Seems like a pretty good 'excuse' for you to be here."

He shook his head. "Seven people died because the control room didn't follow procedure and activated a primary pumping station while workers were still in the reflector tower. It was a horrible accident, but it was an accident."

"Enlighten us, then," I said. "If the deaths at your solar farm weren't your fault, why are you here?"

"Because the government thinks I embezzled millions of dollars."

"And why do they think that?" I asked.

"Because I embezzled millions of dollars." He adjusted his shackled wrists into a more comfortable position. "But that had nothing to do with the deaths. Nothing!"

"Tell me about your blackpanel power idea," Stratt said.

"Blackpanel?" He drew back. "It was just an idea. I emailed that anonymously."

Stratt rolled her eyes. "Do you really think email sent from a prison computer lab is anonymous?"

He looked away. "I'm not a computer guy. I'm an engineer."

"I want to hear more about blackpanel," she said. "And if I like what I hear, it could reduce your jail time. So start talking."

He perked up. "Well . . . I mean . . . okay. What do you know about solar thermal power?"

Stratt looked at me.

"Uh," I said. "It's when you have a whole bunch of mirrors set up to reflect sunlight to the top of a tower. If you get a few hundred square meters of mirror focusing all that sunlight onto a single point, you can heat up water, make it boil, and run a turbine."

I turned to Stratt. "But that's not new. Heck, there's a fully functional solar thermal power plant in Spain right now. If you want to know about it, talk to them."

She silenced me with a hand motion. "And that's what you were making for New Zealand?"

"Well," he said. "It was *funded* by New Zealand. But the idea was to provide power for Africa."

"Why would New Zealand pay a bunch of money to help Africa?" I asked.

"Because we're nice," Redell said.

"Wow," I said. "I know New Zealand is pretty cool but—"

"And it was going to be a New Zealand–owned company that charged for the power," Redell said.

"There it is."

He leaned forward. "Africa needs infrastructure. To do that, they need power. And they have nine million square kilometers of useless land that gets some of the most intense continuous sunlight on Earth. The Sahara Desert is just *sitting there,* waiting to give them everything they need. All we needed to do was build the damn power plants!"

He flopped back in his chair. "But every local government wanted a piece of the pie. Graft, bribes, payoffs, you name it. You think I embezzled a lot? Shit, that's nothing compared to what I had to pay in bribes just to build a solar plant in the middle of fucking nowhere."

"And then?" Stratt said.

He looked at his shoes. "We built a pilot plant—one square kilometer of mirror area. All of it focused on a large metal drum full of water on top of a tower. Boil the water, run a turbine, you know the drill. I had a crew checking the drum for leaks. When anyone's in the tower, the mirrors are supposed to be angled away. But someone in the control room fired up the whole system when they thought they were starting a virtual test."

He sighed. "Seven people. All dead in an instant. At least they didn't suffer. Much. Someone had to pay. The victims were all New Zealanders, and so am I. So the government came after me. It was a farce of a trial."

"And the embezzlement?" I said.

He nodded. "Yeah, that came up in the trial too. But I would have gotten away with it if the project had been successful. I'm not to blame here. I mean, yeah, stealing money, okay, I'm guilty of that. But I didn't kill those people. Not through negligence or any other means."

"Where were you when the accident happened?" Stratt said.

He paused.

"Where were you?" she repeated.

"I was in Monaco. On a vacation."

"You'd been there for three months on that vacation. Gambling away your embezzled money."

"I . . . have a gambling problem," he said. "I admit that. I mean, it was gambling debt that made me embezzle in the first place. It's a sickness."

"And what if you had been doing your job instead of going on a bender for three months? What if you'd been there the day the accident happened? Would the accident still have happened?"

His expression was answer enough.

"Okay," Stratt said. "Now we're past the excuses and bullshit. You're not going to convince me you're an innocent scapegoat. And now you know that. So let's move on: Tell me about blackpanels."

"Yeah, okay." He composed himself. "I've spent my whole life in the energy sector, so obviously Astrophage is really interesting to me. A storage medium like that—man, if it weren't for what it's doing to the sun, it would be the greatest stroke of luck for humanity in history."

He shifted in his seat. "Nuclear reactors, coal plants, solar thermal plants . . . in the end they all do the same thing: Use heat to boil water, use the steam to drive a turbine. But with Astrophage, we don't need any of that crap. It turns heat *directly* into stored energy. And it doesn't even need a big heat differential. Just anything above 96.415 degrees."

"We know that," I said. "I've been using a nuclear reactor's heat to breed up Astrophage for the last several months."

"What'd you get? Maybe a few grams? My idea can get you a thousand kilograms per day. In a few years you'll have enough for the whole *Hail Mary* mission. It'll take you longer than that to build the ship anyway."

"All right, you have my attention," I said. Of course, Stratt hadn't told me anything about whatever "blackpanel" was.

"Get a square of metal foil. Pretty much any metal will do. Anodize it until it's black. Don't paint it—anodize it. Put clear glass over it and leave a one-centimeter gap between the glass and the foil. Seal the edges with brick, foam, or some other good insulator. Then set it out in the sun."

"Okay, what good will that do?"

"The black foil will absorb sunlight and get hot. The glass will insulate it from outside air—any heat loss has to pass through the glass, and that's slow. It'll reach an equilibrium temperature well over one hundred degrees Celsius."

I nod. "And at that temperature you can enrich Astrophage."

"Yes."

"But it would be ridiculously slow," I said. "If you had a one-square-meter box and ideal weather conditions . . . say, one thousand watts per square meter of solar energy . . ."

"It's about half a microgram per day," he said. "Give or take."

"That's a far cry from 'a thousand kilograms' per day."

He smiled. "It's just a matter of how many square meters you make of it."

"You'd need two trillion square meters to get a thousand kilograms per day."

"The Sahara Desert is *nine* trillion square meters."

My jaw dropped open.

"That went by fast," said Stratt. "Explain."

"Well," I said. "He wants to pave a chunk of the Sahara Desert with blackpanels. Like . . . a *quarter* of the entire Sahara Desert!"

"It'd be the biggest thing ever made by humanity," he said. "It'd be starkly visible from space."

I glared at him. "And it would destroy the ecology of Africa and probably Europe."

"Not as much as the coming ice age will."

Stratt held up her hand. "Dr. Grace. Would it work?"

I fidgeted. "Well, I mean . . . it's a sound concept. But I don't know if it's even possible to implement. This isn't like making a building or a road. We're talking about literally trillions of these things."

Redell leaned in. "That's why I designed the blackpanels to be made entirely out of foil, glass, and ceramics. All materials we have plenty of here on Earth."

"Wait," I said. "How do the Astrophage breed in this scenario? Your blackpanels will enrich them, sure, and they'll be breed-ready. But there are a bunch of steps they need to go through when they breed."

"Oh, I know." He smirked. "We'll have a static magnet in there to give them a magnetic field to follow—they need that to kick off their migration response. Then we'll have a small IR filter on one part of the glass. It'll only let the CO_2 IR spectral signature wavelengths through. The Astrophage will go there to breed. Then, after dividing, they'll head toward the glass because that's the direction of the sun. We'll have a small pinhole somewhere in the side of the panel for air exchange with the outside. It'll be slow enough that it doesn't cool down the panel, but fast enough to replenish the CO_2 used by Astrophage while breeding."

I opened my mouth to protest, but I couldn't find anything wrong with it. He'd thought it all through.

"Well?" said Stratt.

"As a breeder system it's horrible," I said. "Way less efficient and far lower yield than my system on the carrier's reactor. But he didn't design it for efficiency. He designed it for scalability."

"That's right," he said. He pointed to Stratt. "I hear you have godlike authority over pretty much the whole world right now."

"That's an exaggeration," she said.

"Not much of one, though," I said.

Redell continued. "Can you get China to orient their industrial base around making blackpanels? Not just them but pretty much every industrial nation on Earth? That's what it would take."

She pursed her lips. After a moment, she said, "Yes."

"And can you tell the goddamned corrupt government officials in North Africa to stay out of the way?"

"That part will be easy," she said. "When this is all over, those governments will keep the blackpanels. They'll be the industrial-energy powerhouse of the world."

"See, there we go," he said. "Save the world and permanently lift Africa out of poverty while we're at it. Of course, this is all just a theory. I have to develop the blackpanel and make sure we can mass-produce it. I'd need to be in a lab instead of prison."

Stratt mulled it over. Then she stood.

"Okay. You're with us."

He pumped his fist.

I wake up in my bed, which is mounted to the tunnel wall. That first night was a kludge with duct tape. Since then, I learned that epoxy glue works well on xenonite, so I was able to attach a couple of anchor points and mount the mattress properly.

I sleep in the tunnel every night now. Rocky insists. And, once every eighty-six hours or so, Rocky sleeps in the tunnel and wants me to watch. Well, he's only slept three times so far, so my data on his waking period is a bit sparse. But he's been kind of consistent on it.

I stretch out my arms and yawn.

"Good Morning," Rocky says.

It's pitch-dark. I turn on the lamp mounted next to the bed.

Rocky has an entire workshop set up on his side of the tunnel. He's always making modifications or repairs to something or other. Seems like his ship is constantly in need of repair. Right this moment he holds an oblong metal device with two of his hands and uses another two to poke at the innards with needle-like tools. The remaining hand grasps a handle on the wall.

"Mornin'," I say. "I'm going to eat. I'll be back."

Rocky waves absently. *"Eat."*

I float down to the dormitory for my morning ritual. I eat a prepackaged breakfast (scrambled eggs with pork sausage) and a bag of hot coffee.

It's been a few days since I last cleaned up, and I can smell my own body odor. Not a good sign. So I sponge off at the sponge-bath station and get a clean jumpsuit. All this technology and I haven't seen any means of cleaning clothing. So I've taken to soaking it in water and putting it in the lab freezer for a while. Kills off all the germs, and those are what cause the smell. Fresh, not-clean clothes.

I pull the jumpsuit on. I've decided today is the day. After a week of honing our language skills, Rocky and I are ready to start having real conversations. I can even understand him without having to look at the translation about a third of the time now.

I float back to the tunnel, sipping the last of my coffee.

Okay. *Finally* I think we have the words needed for this discussion. Here goes.

I clear my throat. "Rocky. I am here because Astrophage makes Sol sick but doesn't make Tau Ceti sick. Are you here for the same reason?"

Rocky puts the device and his tools on his bandoleer and climbs along the support rails to the divider. Good. He understands this is a serious conversation.

"Yes. No understand why Tau not sick but Eridani is sick. If Astrophage no leave Eridani, my people die."

"Same!" I say. "Same same same! If Astrophage continues to infect Sol, all the humans will die."

"Good. Same. You and me will save Eridani and Sol."

"Yes yes yes!"

"Why did other humans on you ship die, question?" Rocky asks.

Oh. So we're going to talk about that?

I rub the back of my head. "We, uh . . . we slept all the way here. Not a normal sleep. A special sleep. A dangerous sleep, but necessary. My crewmates died, but I didn't. Random luck."

"Bad," he says.

"Bad. Why did the other Eridians die?"

"I not know. Everyone get sick. Then everyone die." His voice quavers. *"I not sick. I not know why."*

"Bad," I say with a sigh. "What kind of sick?"

He thinks for a moment. *"I need word. Small life. Single thing. Like Astrophage. Eridian body made of many many of these."*

"Cell," I say. "My body is many many cells also."

He says the Eridian word for "cell," and I add the tones to my ever-growing dictionary.

"Cell," he says. "My crew have problem with cells. Many many cells die. Not infection. Not injury. No reason. But not me. Never me. Why, question? I not know."

Each individual cell in the affected Eridians died? That sounds horrible. It also sounds like radiation sickness. How am I going to describe that? I shouldn't have to. If they're a spacefaring people, they should already understand radiation. We don't have a word for it between us yet, though. Let's work on that.

"I need a word: fast-moving hydrogen atoms. Very very fast."

"Hot gas."

"No. Faster than that. Very very very fast."

He wiggles his carapace. He's confused.

I try another approach. "Space has very very very fast hydrogen atoms. They move almost the speed of light. They were created by stars long long long ago."

"No. No mass in space. Space is empty."

Oh boy. "No, that's wrong. There are hydrogen atoms in space. Very very fast hydrogen atoms."

"Understand."

"You didn't know that?"

"No."

I stare in shock.

How can a civilization develop space travel without ever discovering radiation?

"Dr. Grace," she said.

"Dr. Lokken," I said.

We sat across from each other at a small steel table. It was a tiny room, but spacious by aircraft-carrier standards. I didn't quite understand its original purpose and its name was written in Chinese characters. But I think it was a place for the navigator to look at charts . . . ?

"Thank you for making time to see me," she said.

"Not a problem."

As a rule, we tried to avoid each other. Our relationship had matured from "annoyed with each other" to "very annoyed with each other." I was as much a part of the problem as she was. But we got off on the wrong foot all those months ago back in Geneva and never really improved.

"Of course, I don't think this is necessary."

"Neither do I," I said. "But Stratt insisted you run this stuff by me. So here we are."

"I have an idea. But I want your opinion." She pulled out a file and handed it to me. "CERN is going to release this paper next week. This is a rough draft. But I know everyone there, so they let me see an advance copy."

I opened the folder. "Okay, what's it about?"

"They figured out how Astrophage stores energy."

"Really?!" I gasped. Then I cleared my throat. "Really?"

"Yes, and frankly it's amazing." She pointed to a graph on the first page. "Long story short: It's neutrinos."

"Neutrinos?" I shook my head. "How the heck . . ."

"I know. It's very counterintuitive. But there's a large neutrino burst every time they kill an Astrophage. They even took samples to the IceCube Neutrino Observatory and punctured them in the main detector pool. They got a massive number of hits. Astrophage can only contain neutrinos if it's alive, and there's a lot of them in there."

"How does it make neutrinos?"

She flipped a few pages in the paper and pointed to another chart. "This is more your area than mine, but microbiologists have confirmed Astrophage has a lot of free hydrogen ions—raw protons with no electron—zipping around just inside the cell membrane."

"Yeah, I remember reading about that. It was a group in Russia that found that out."

She nodded. "CERN is pretty sure that, through a mechanism we don't understand, when those protons collide at a high enough velocity, their kinetic energy is converted into two neutrinos with opposite momentum vectors."

I leaned back, confused. "That is really odd. Mass usually doesn't just 'happen' like that."

She wiggled her hand. "Not quite true. Sometimes gamma rays, when they pass close to an atomic nucleus, will spontaneously become an electron and a positron. It's called 'pair production.' So it's not unheard-of. But we've never seen neutrinos created that way."

"That's kind of neat. I never got too deep into atomic physics. I've never heard of pair production before."

"It's a thing."

"Okay."

"Anyway," she said, "there's a lot of complicated stuff about neutrinos I won't get into—there are different kinds and they can even change what kind they are. But the upshot is this: They're an extremely small particle. Their mass is something like one twenty-billionth the mass of a proton."

"Waaaaaait," I said. "We know Astrophage is always 96.415 degrees Celsius. Temperature is just the velocity of particles inside. So we should be able to calcu—"

"Calculate the velocity of the particles inside," she said. "Yes. We know the average velocity of the protons. And we know their mass, which means we know their kinetic energy. I know where you're going with this and the answer is yes. It balances."

"Wow!" I put my hand on my forehead. "That's amazing!"

"Yes. It is."

That was the answer to the long-asked question: Why is Astrophage's critical temperature what it is? Why not hotter? Why not colder?

Astrophage makes neutrinos in pairs by slamming protons together. For the reaction to work, the protons need to collide with a higher kinetic energy than the mass energy of two neutrinos. If you work backward from the mass of a neutrino, you know the velocity those protons have to collide at. And when you know the velocity of particles in an object, you know its temperature. To have enough kinetic energy to make neutrinos, the protons have to be 96.415 degrees Celsius.

"Oh man," I said. "So any heat energy above the critical temperature will just make the protons collide harder."

"Yes. They'll make neutrinos and have leftover energy. Then they bump into other protons, et cetera. Any heat energy above the critical temperature gets quickly converted into neutrinos. But if it drops below critical temperature, the protons are going too slow and neutrino production stops. End result: You can't get it hotter than 96.415 degrees. Not for long, anyway. And if it gets too cold, the Astrophage uses stored energy to heat back up to that temperature—just like any other warm-blooded life-form."

She gave me a moment to let that all sink in. CERN really came through. But a couple of things still bothered me.

"Okay, so it makes neutrinos," I said. "How does it turn them back into energy?"

"That's the easy part," she said. "Neutrinos are what's called Majorana particles. It means the neutrino is its own antiparticle. Basically, every time two neutrinos collide, it's a matter-antimatter interaction. They annihilate and become photons. Two photons, actually, with the same wavelength and going opposite directions. And since the wavelength of a photon is based on the energy in the photon . . ."

"The Petrova wavelength!" I yelped.

She nodded. "Yes. The mass energy of a neutrino is exactly the same as the energy found in one photon of Petrova-wavelength light. This paper is truly groundbreaking."

I rested my chin on my hands. "Wow . . . just wow. I guess the only remaining question is how does an Astrophage keep neutrinos inside?"

"We don't know. Neutrinos routinely pass through the entire planet Earth without hitting a single atom—they're just that small.

Well, it's more about quantum wavelengths and probabilities of collision. But suffice it to say, neutrinos are famously hard to interact with. But for some reason, Astrophage has what we call 'super cross-sectionality.' That's just a fancy term meaning nothing can quantum-tunnel through it. It goes against every law of particle physics we thought we knew, but it's been proven over and over."

"Yeah." I tapped my finger on the table. "It absorbs all wavelengths of light—even wavelengths that should be too large to interact with it."

"Yes," she said. "Turns out it also collides with all matter that tries to get by, no matter how unlikely that collision should be. Anyway, as long as an Astrophage is alive, it exhibits this super cross-sectionality. And that brings us nicely to what I wanted to talk to you about."

"Oh?" I said. "There's more?"

"Yes." She pulled a diagram of the *Hail Mary* hull out of her bag. "This is what I need you for: I'm working on radiation protection for the *Hail Mary*."

I perked up. "Of course! Astrophage will block it all!"

"Maybe," she said. "But I need to know how space radiation works to be sure. I know the broad strokes, but not the details. Please enlighten me."

I folded my arms. "Well, there's two kinds, really. High-energy particles emitted by the sun, and GCRs that are just kind of everywhere."

"Start with the solar particles," she said.

"Sure. Solar particles are just hydrogen atoms emitted by the sun. Sometimes a magnetic storm on the sun can cause it to spit out a whole bunch of them. Other times it's relatively quiet. And lately, the Astrophage infection has been robbing so much energy from the sun that magnetic storms are less common."

"Horrifying," she said.

"I know. Did you hear that global warming has been almost undone?"

She nodded. "Humanity's recklessness with our environment accidentally bought us an extra month of time by pre-heating the planet."

"We fell in poop and came out smelling like roses," I said.

She laughed. "I have not heard that one. We don't have that expression in Norwegian."

"You do now." I smiled.

She looked down at the hull plan—a little faster than I think was necessary, but whatever.

"How fast do these solar particles travel?" she asked.

"About four hundred kilometers per second."

"Good. We can ignore them." She scribbled a note to herself on the paper. "The *Hail Mary* will be going away faster than that within eight hours. They won't be able to catch up, let alone do any damage."

I whistled. "It's really amazing what we're doing. I mean . . . jeez. Astrophage would be the best thing ever if it weren't, you know, destroying the sun."

"I know," she said. "Now, tell me about GCRs."

"Those are trickier," I said. "It stands for—"

"Galactic cosmic rays," she said. "And they're not cosmic rays, right?"

"Right. They're just hydrogen ions—protons. But they're going a *lot* faster. They're going near the speed of light."

"Why are they called cosmic rays if they're not even electromagnetic emissions?"

"People used to think they were. The name stuck."

"Do they come from some common source?"

"No, they're omnidirectional. They're made by supernovas, which have happened all over the place. We're just kind of constantly awash with GCRs in all directions. And they're a huge problem for space travel. But not anymore!"

I leaned forward to look at her schematic again. It was a cross-section of a hull. There was a 1-millimeter void between two walls. "Are you going to fill that area with Astrophage?"

"That's the plan."

I pondered the schematic. "You want to fill the hull with fuel? Isn't that dangerous?"

"Only if we let it see CO_2-band light. If it doesn't see CO_2, it won't do anything. And it'll be in the dark between the hulls. Dimitri plans to make a fuel slurry out of Astrophage and low-viscosity oil to make it easier to transport to the engines. I want to line the hull with that stuff."

I pinched my chin. "It could work. But Astrophage can die from physical trauma. You can kill one by poking it with a sharp nano-stick."

"Yes, that's why I asked CERN to do some off-the-books experiments for me as a favor."

"Wow. CERN will just do whatever you want? Are you, like, mini-Stratt or something?"

She chuckled. "Old friends and contacts. Anyway, they found that even particles moving near light speed can't get past Astrophage. And none of them seem to kill it either."

"That actually makes a lot of sense," I said. "It evolved to live on the surface of stars. They must get bombarded by energy and very fast-moving particles all the time."

She pointed to a zoomed-in schematic of Astrophage canals. "The entire radiation load will be halted. All we need is a layer of Astrophage slurry thick enough to guarantee there's always an Astrophage cell in the way of any incoming particles. One millimeter should be more than enough. Plus, we don't waste any mass. We'll be using the fuel itself as insulation. And if the crew need that last little bit of Astrophage, well, consider it a reserve."

"Hmm . . . a 'reserve' that could power New York City for twenty thousand years."

She looked at the diagram, then back to me. "You did all that math in your head?"

"Eh, I had some shortcuts. We're dealing with such absurd scales of energy here, I tend to think in 'New York City years' of energy, which is about one-half of one gram of Astrophage."

She rubbed her temples. "And we need to make two million kilograms of it. If we make a mistake along the way . . ."

"We'll save Astrophage the trouble of destroying humanity by doing it ourselves," I say. "Yeah. I think about that a lot."

"So, what do you think?" she said. "Is this a terrible idea, or could it work?"

"I think it's genius."

She smiled and looked away.

CHAPTER 14

Another day, another staff meeting. Who would have thought saving the world could be so boring?

The science team sat around the meeting-room table. Me, Dimitri, and Lokken. For all her talk about cutting out bureaucracy, Stratt ended up with a bunch of de facto department heads and daily staff meetings.

Sometimes, the stuff we all hate ends up being the only way to do things.

Stratt sat at the head of the table, of course. And next to her was a man I'd never seen before.

"Everyone," Stratt said. "I want you to meet Dr. François Leclerc."

The Frenchman to her left waved halfheartedly. "Hello."

"Leclerc is a world-renowned climatologist from Paris. I've put him in charge of tracking, understanding, and—if possible—ameliorating the climate effects of Astrophage."

"Oh, is that all?" I said.

Leclerc smiled, but it faded quickly.

"So, Dr. Leclerc," Stratt said. "We've been getting a lot of conflicting reports on exactly what to expect from the reduction of solar energy. It's hard to find any two climatologists who agree."

He shrugged. "It's hard to find two climatologists who agree on the color of an orange. It is, unfortunately, an inexact field. There is a lot of uncertainty and—if I'm being honest—a lot of guesswork. Climate science is in its infancy."

"You're not giving yourself enough credit. Out of all the experts, you're the only one I could find whose climate-prediction models were proven true over and over again for the last twenty years."

He nodded.

She gestured to a disorderly mass of papers on the meeting table. "I've been sent every kind of prediction from minor crop failures to global biosphere collapse. I want to hear what you have to say. You've seen the predicted solar-output numbers. What's your take?"

"Disaster, of course," he said. "We're looking at extinction of many species, complete upheaval of biomes all over the world, major changes in weather patterns—"

"Humans," Stratt said. "I want to know how this affects humans, and when. I don't care about the mating grounds of the three-anused mud sloth or any other random biome."

"We're part of the ecology, Ms. Stratt. We're not outside it. The plants we eat, the animals we ranch, the air we breathe—it's all part of the tapestry. It's all connected. As the biomes collapse, it'll have a direct impact on humanity."

"Okay, then: numbers," Stratt said. "I want numbers. Tangible things, not vague predictions."

He scowled at her. "Okay. Nineteen years."

"Nineteen years?"

"You wanted a number," he said. "There's a number. Nineteen years."

"Okay, what's nineteen years?"

"That's my estimate for when half the people currently alive will be dead. Nineteen years from now."

The silence that followed was unlike anything I'd ever experienced. Even Stratt was taken aback. Lokken and I looked to each other. I don't know why but we did. Dimitri's mouth fell agape.

"Half?" Stratt said. "Three point five billion people? Dead?"

"Yes," he said. "Is that tangible enough for you?"

"How can you possibly know that?" she said.

He pursed his lips. "And just like that another climate denier is born. See how easy it is? All I have to do is tell you something you don't want to hear."

"Don't patronize me, Dr. Leclerc. Just answer my questions."

He crossed his arms. "We're already seeing major weather-pattern disruptions."

Lokken cleared her throat. "I heard there were tornadoes in Europe?"

"Yes," he said. "And they're happening more and more often. European languages didn't even have a *word* for tornado until Spanish conquistadors saw them in North America. Now they're happening in Italy, Spain, and Greece."

He tilted his head. "Partially, it's because of shifting weather patterns. And partially it's because some lunatic decided to *pave the Sahara Desert* with black rectangles. As if a massive disruption of heat distribution near the Mediterranean Sea wouldn't have any effects."

Stratt rolled her eyes. "I knew there'd be weather effects. We just don't have any other choice."

He pressed on. "Your abuse of the Sahara aside, we're seeing bizarre phenomena all over the world. The cyclone season is off by two months. It snowed in Vietnam last week. The jet stream is a convoluted mess changing day by day. Arctic air is being brought to places it's never been before, and tropical air is going well north and south. It's a maelstrom."

"Get back to the three and a half billion dead people," Stratt said.

"Sure," he said. "The math of famine is actually pretty easy. Take all the calories the world creates with farming and agriculture per day, and divide by about fifteen hundred. The human population cannot be greater than that number. Not for long, anyway."

He fiddled with a pen on the table. "I've run the best models I have. Crops are going to fail. The global staple crops are wheat, barley, millet, potatoes, soy, and most important: rice. All of them are pretty sensitive about temperature ranges. If your rice paddy freezes over, the rice dies. If your potato farm floods, the potatoes die. And if your wheat farm experiences ten times normal humidity, it gets fungal parasites and dies."

He looked at Stratt again. "If only we had a stable supply of three-anused mud sloths, maybe we'd survive."

Stratt pinched her chin. "Nineteen years isn't enough time. It'll take thirteen years for the *Hail Mary* to get to Tau Ceti, and another thirteen for any results or data to come back. We need at least twenty-six years. Twenty-seven would be better."

He looked at her as if she'd grown another head. "What are you saying? This isn't some optional outcome. This is happening. And there's nothing we can do about it."

"Nonsense," she said. "Humanity has been accidentally causing global warming for a century. Let's see what we can do when we really set our minds to it."

He drew back. "What? Are you kidding?"

"A nice blanket of greenhouse gases would buy us some time, right? It would insulate Earth like a parka and make the energy we are getting last longer. Am I wrong?"

"Wha—" he stammered. "You aren't wrong, but the scale . . . and the morality of *deliberately* causing greenhouse-gas emissions . . ."

"I don't care about morality," Stratt said.

"She really doesn't," I said.

"I care about saving humanity. So get me some greenhouse effect. You're a climatologist. Come up with something to make us last at least twenty-seven years. I'm not willing to lose half of humanity."

Leclerc gulped.

She made a shooing motion. "Get to work!"

It takes three hours and the addition of fifty words to our shared vocabulary, but I am finally able to explain radiation—and its effects on biology—to Rocky.

"Thank," he says in unusually low tones. Sad tones. *"Now I know how my friends died."*

"Bad bad bad," I say.

"Yes," he chimes.

During the conversation, I learned the *Blip*-A has no radiation protection at all. And I know why Eridians never discovered radiation. It took a while to assemble all of this information, but here is what I know:

The Eridian homeworld is the first planet in the 40 Eridani system. Humans actually spotted it a while ago, obviously not knowing there was a whole civilization there. The catalog name for it is "40 Eridani A b." That's a mouthful. The planet's actual name, from the Eridians, is a collection of chords like any other Eridian word. So I'll just call it "Erid."

Erid is extremely close to its star—about one-fifth as far as Earth is from our sun. Their "year" is a little over forty-two Earth days long.

It's what we call a "super-Earth," weighing in at eight and a half times Earth's mass. It's about twice Earth's diameter, and a little over double the surface gravity. Also, it spins *very* fast. Absurdly fast. Their day is only 5.1 hours long.

That's when things started to fall into place.

Planets get magnetic fields if the conditions are right. You have to have a molten-iron core, you have to be in the magnetic field of a star, and you have to be spinning. If all three of these things are true, you get a magnetic field. Earth has one—that's why compasses work.

Erid has all of those features *on steroids*. They are larger than Earth, with a larger iron core. They are close to their star, so they have a much stronger magnetic field powering their own field, and they spin extremely fast. All told, Erid's magnetic field is at least twenty-five times as strong as Earth's.

Plus, their atmosphere is extremely thick. Twenty-nine times as thick.

You know what strong magnetic fields and thick atmospheres are really good at? Radiation protection.

All life on Earth evolved to deal with radiation. Our DNA has error-correction built in because we're constantly bombarded with radiation from the sun and from space in general. Our magnetic field and atmosphere protect us somewhat, but not 100 percent.

For Erid, it's 100 percent. Radiation just doesn't get to the ground. Light doesn't even get to the ground—that's why they never evolved eyes. The surface is pitch-dark. How does a biosphere exist in total darkness? I haven't asked Rocky how that works yet, but there is plenty of life deep in Earth's oceans where the sun doesn't shine. So it's definitely doable.

Eridians are extremely susceptible to radiation, and they never even knew it existed.

The next conversation took another hour and added a few dozen more words to the vocabulary.

Eridians invented space travel quite a while ago. And with their unparalleled materials technology (xenonite) they actually made a space elevator. Basically a cable leading from Erid's equator up to the synchronous orbit with a counterweight. They literally take elevators to get into orbit. We could do that on Earth if we knew how to make xenonite.

Thing is, they never left orbit. There was no reason to. Erid has no moon. Planets that close to a star rarely do. The gravitation tidal forces tend to rip would-be moons out of orbit. Rocky and his crew were the first Eridians to leave orbit at all.

So they never found out that Erid's magnetic field, which extends well beyond its synchronous orbit, had been protecting them all that time.

One mystery remained.

"Why did I not die, question?" Rocky asks.

"I don't know," I say. "What's different? What do you do that the rest of your crew didn't do?"

"I fix things. My job is to repair broken things, create needed things, and keep engines running."

Sounds like an engineer to me. "Where were you most of the time?"

"I have room in ship. Workshop."

I'm getting an idea. "Where is workshop?"

"In back of ship near engines."

That's a sensible place to put your ship's engineer. Near the engines, where things are most likely to need maintenance or repairs.

"Where does your ship store Astrophage fuel?"

He waves a hand generally around the rear of the ship. *"Many many containers of Astrophage. All in back of ship. Close to engines. Easy to refuel."*

And there's the answer.

I sigh. He's not going to like this. The solution was so simple. They just didn't know it. They didn't even know the problem until it was too late.

"Astrophage stops radiation," I say. "You were surrounded by Astrophage most of the time. Your crewmates weren't. So the radiation got to them."

He doesn't respond. He needs a moment to let that sink in.

"Understand," he says in low notes. *"Thank. I now know why I not die."*

I try to imagine the desperation of his people. With a space program far behind Earth's, no knowledge of what's outside, and still making an interstellar ship in a bid to save their race.

No different from my situation, I guess. I just have a little more technology.

"Radiation is here too," I say. "Stay in your workshop as much as you can."

"Yes."

"Bring Astrophage to this tunnel and put it on the wall."

"Yes. You do same."

"I don't need to."

"Why not, question?"

Because it doesn't matter if I get cancer. I'm going to die here anyway. But I don't want to explain that I'm on a suicide mission right now. The conversation's been pretty heavy already. So I'll tell him a half-truth.

"Earth's atmosphere is thin and our magnetic field is weak. Radiation gets to the surface. So Earth life evolved to survive radiation."

"Understand," he says.

He continues working on his repairs while I float in the tunnel. A random thought occurs to me. "Hey, I have a question."

"Ask."

"Why is Eridian science and human science so similar? Billions of years, but almost the same progress."

It's been bugging me for a while. Humans and Eridians evolved separately in separate star systems. We had no contact with each other until now. So why is it that we have almost identical technology? I mean, Eridians are a *little* behind us in space technology, but not a ton. Why aren't they in their stone age? Or some superfuturistic age that makes modern Earth look antiquated?

"Has to be, or you and I would not meet," Rocky says. *"If planet has less science, it no can make spaceship. If planet has more science it can understand and destroy Astrophage without leaving their system. Eridian and human science both in special range: Can make ship, but can't solve Astrophage problem."*

Huh. I hadn't thought of that. But it's obvious now that Rocky says it. If this happened when Earth was in the Stone Age, we would have just died. And if it happened a thousand years from now, we'd probably work out how to deal with Astrophage without breaking a sweat. There is a fairly narrow band of technological advancement that would cause a species to send a ship to Tau Ceti to look for answers. Eridians and humans both fall into that band.

"Understand. Good observation." But it nags at me. "Still unusual. Humans and Eridians are close in space. Earth and Erid are only sixteen light-years apart. The galaxy is one hundred thousand light-years wide! Life must be rare. But we are so close together."

"Possible we are family."

We're related? How could—

"Oh! You mean . . . whoa!" I have to wrap my head around this one.

"I not certain. Theory."

"It's a darn good theory!" I say.

The panspermia theory. I argued with Lokken about it all the time.

Earth life and Astrophage are way too similar for it to be coincidence. I suspected Earth was "seeded" by some ancestor of Astrophage. Some interstellar progenitor species that infected my planet. But it never occurred to me until now that the same thing might have happened to Erid.

There could be life all over the place! Anywhere it can possibly evolve from an Astrophage-like ancestor into the cells I have today. I don't know what this "pre-Astrophage" organism would be like, but Astrophage is pretty darn tough. So any planet that can possibly support life of any kind would be likely to get it.

Rocky might be a long-lost relative. *Very* long. The trees outside my house back home are closer relatives to me than Rocky. But still.

Wow.

"Very good theory!" I say again.

"Thank," Rocky says. I guess he'd worked that all out a while ago. But I still had to let it sink in.

For once, an aircraft carrier was the perfect place to be.

The Chinese Navy didn't even question Stratt's orders anymore. The higher-ups got sick of approving every action and finally just issued a general order to do whatever she said as long as it didn't involve firing weapons.

We anchored off the coast of western Antarctica in the dead of night. The coastline sat in the extreme distance, visible only by moonlight. The entire continent had been evacuated of humans. Probably an overreaction—the Amundsen–Scott South Pole Station was 1,500 kilometers away. The people there would have been just fine. Still, no reason to take chances.

It was the largest naval exclusion zone in history. So big, even the U.S. Navy had to stretch itself thin to make sure no commercial ships entered the area.

Stratt spoke into a walkie-talkie. "Destroyer One, confirm observation status."

"Ready," came an American accent.

"Destroyer Two, confirm observation status."

"Ready," came a different American's voice.

The scientific team stood together on the carrier's flight deck, staring toward land. Dimitri and Lokken hung back away from the edge. Redell was off in Africa running the blackpanel farm.

And of course Stratt stood slightly ahead of everyone else.

Leclerc looked for all the world like a man being led to the gallows. "We're almost ready," he said with a sigh.

Stratt clicked on her walkie-talkie again. "Submarine One, confirm observation status."

"Ready," came the response.

Leclerc checked his tablet. "Three minutes . . . mark."

"All ships: We are at Condition Yellow," Stratt said into her radio. "Repeat: Condition Yellow. Submarine Two, confirm observation status."

"Ready."

I stood next to Leclerc. "This is unbelievable," I said.

He shook his head. "I wish to God this wasn't on my shoulders." He fiddled with his tablet. "You know, Dr. Grace, I have spent my entire life as an unapologetic hippie. From my childhood in Lyon to my university days in Paris. I am a tree-hugging antiwar throwback to a bygone era of protest politics."

I didn't say anything. He was having the worst day of his life. If I could help by just listening, I'd do it.

"I became a climatologist to help save the world. To stop the nightmarish environmental catastrophe we were sinking ourselves into. And now . . . this. It's necessary, but horrible. As a scientist yourself, I'm sure you understand."

"Not really," I said. "I spent my whole scientific career looking away from Earth, not toward it. I'm embarrassingly weak on climate science."

"Mm," he said. "Western Antarctica is a roiling mass of ice and snow. This whole region is a giant glacier, slowly marching to the sea. There are hundreds of thousands of square kilometers of ice here."

"And we're going to melt it?"

"The sea will melt it for us, but yes. Thing is, Antarctica used to be a jungle. For millions of years it was as lush as Africa. But continental drift and natural climate change froze it over. All those plants died and decomposed. The gases from that decomposition—most notably methane—got trapped in the ice."

"And methane's a pretty powerful greenhouse gas," I said.

He nodded. "Far more powerful than carbon dioxide."

He checked his tablet again. "Two minutes!" he called out.

"All ships: Condition Red," Stratt radioed. "Repeat: Condition Red."

He turned back to me. "So here I am. Environmental activist. Climatologist. Antiwar crusader." He looked out to sea. "And I'm ordering a nuclear strike on Antarctica. Two hundred and forty-one nuclear weapons, courtesy of the United States, buried fifty meters deep along a fissure at three-kilometer intervals. All going off at the same time."

I nodded slowly.

"They tell me the radiation will be minimal," he said.

"Yeah. If it's any consolation, they're fusion bombs." I pulled my jacket tighter. "There's a small fission reaction with uranium and stuff that sets off the much larger fusion reaction. And the big explosion is just hydrogen and helium. No radiation from that."

"Well, that's something."

"And this was the only option?" I asked. "Why can't we have factories mass-produce sulfur hexafluoride, or some other greenhouse gas?"

He shook his head. "We'd need thousands of times the production that we could possibly do. Remember, it took us a century of burning coal and oil on a global scale to even notice it was affecting the climate at all."

He checked his tablet. "The shelf will cleave at the line of explosions and slowly work its way into the sea and melt. Sea levels will rise about a centimeter over the next month, the ocean temperature will drop a degree—which is a disaster of its own but never mind that for now. Enormous quantities of methane will be released into the atmosphere. And now, methane is our friend. Methane is our *best* friend. And not just because it'll keep us warm for a while."

"Oh?"

"Methane breaks down in the atmosphere after ten years. We can knock chunks of Antarctica into the sea every few years to moderate the methane levels. And if *Hail Mary* finds a solution, we just have to wait ten years for the methane to go away. You can't do that with carbon dioxide."

Stratt approached us. "Time?"

"Sixty seconds," he said.

She nodded.

"So this solves everything?" I asked. "Can we just keep poking Antarctica for more methane to keep Earth's temperature right?"

"No," he said. "It's a stopgap at best. Dumping this crap into our atmosphere will keep the warmth in the air, but the disruption to our ecosystem will still be massive. We'll still have horrific and unpredictable weather, crop failures, and biome annihilation. But maybe, just maybe, it won't be quite as bad as it would have been without the methane."

I looked at Stratt and Leclerc standing side by side. Never in human history had so much raw authority and power been invested into so few people. These two people—just these two—were going to literally change the face of the world.

"I'm curious," I say to Stratt. "Once we launch *Hail Mary*. What will you do then?"

"Me?" she said. "Doesn't matter. Once the *Hail Mary* launches, my authority ends. I'll probably be put on trial by a bunch of pissed-off governments for abuse of power. Might spend the rest of my life in jail."

"I'll be in the cell next to you," said Leclerc.

"Are you at all concerned about that?"

She shrugged. "We all have to make sacrifices. If I have to be the world's whipping boy to secure our salvation, then that's my sacrifice to make."

"You have a strange logic to you," I said.

"Not really. When the alternative is death to your entire species, things are very easy. No moral dilemmas, no weighing what's best for whom. Just a single-minded focus on getting this project working."

"That's what I tell myself," Leclerc said. "Three . . . two . . . one . . . detonation."

Nothing happened. The coastline remained as it was. No explosion. No flash. Not even a pop.

He looked at his tablet. "The nukes have detonated. The shockwave should be here in ten minutes or so. It'll just sound like distant thunder, though."

He looked down at the carrier deck.

Stratt put her hand on his shoulder. "You did what you had to do. We're all doing what we have to do."

He buried his face in his hands and cried.

Rocky and I talk about biology for hours. Both of us are intensely interested in how the other's body works. We'd be pretty lame scientists if we weren't.

Eridian physiology is, frankly, amazing.

Erid is so close to its star, the sheer amount of energy entering the biosphere is ridiculous. And Eridians, being at the top of the food chain, have a heck of a lot more energy to work with than human bodies do. How much more? They have sacs in their body that just hold ATP—the main energy-storage medium of DNA-based life. Usually it lives in cells, but they have so much they have to evolve more efficient storage for it.

We're talking *absurd* amounts of energy here. They pull oxygen off minerals to get metals. Eridians are, in effect, biological smelters.

Humans have hair, fingernails, tooth enamel, and other "dead" stuff on our bodies that serve critical purposes. Eridians take that concept to the ultimate extreme. Rocky's carapace is made of oxidized minerals. His bones are honeycombed metallic alloys. His blood is mostly liquid mercury. Even his nerves are inorganic silicates transmitting light-based impulses.

All told, Rocky only has a few kilograms of biological material. Single-celled organisms travel through the bloodstream, building up or repairing the body as needed. They also manage digestion and service the brain, which sits safely in the center of his carapace.

If bees evolved to make hives that could walk, and the queen was as intelligent as a human, that life-form would be similar to an Eridian. Except the Eridian's "bees" are single-celled organisms.

Eridian muscles are inorganic. They're made of porous, sponge-like material sealed in flexible sacs. The majority of the body's water is tied up in those sacs. And the atmospheric pressure is so high, the 210°C water is still a liquid.

They have two separate circulatory systems: the "ambient" system and the "hot" system. The ambient blood is 210 degrees Celsius. But the hot blood is kept at 305 degrees, which is hot enough to boil water even at Erid's air pressure. Both circulatory systems have blood vessels that expand or contract around the muscles as needed to set their temperature. Want to expand? Make it hot. Want to contract? Make it cold.

In short: Eridians are steam-powered.

Because of this, the ambient circulatory system ends up as the heat sinks when muscles are cooled. It constantly needs to be cooled back down to normal temperature, hence the radiator. Rocky "breathes" in a sense, but only to pass outside ammonia across capillaries in a radiator-like organ in the top of his carapace. Five slits at the top allow the air in and out, but at no point does any of it enter his bloodstream.

While Eridians don't "breathe," they do still use oxygen. They're just much more self-contained than a human body. They have plant-like cells and animal-like cells inside. Oxygen to CO_2, CO_2 to oxygen, back and forth, always kept in balance. Rocky's body is a little biosphere. All it needs is energy via food and airflow to dump heat.

Meanwhile, the hot blood is too hot for any biological material to survive inside—it boils the water inside. This is handy for sterilizing incoming food of pathogens, by the way.

But in order for his worker cells to service any part of the hot-blood system, the system has to be cooled to ambient levels. And when that happens, the Eridian can't use muscles at all. And that's why Eridians sleep.

They don't "sleep" like a human does. They're legitimately paralyzed. And the brain, also being maintained, has no conscious function during that period. A sleeping Eridian *can't* wake up.

That's why they keep an eye on each other when they sleep. Someone has to keep you safe. Probably dates back to caveman (cave-Eridian?) days, and now it's just a social norm.

As amazed as I am at all that, to Rocky it's a boring topic. Meanwhile, he's utterly shocked and amazed by humanity.

"*You hear light, question?*" Rocky says. (He puts a little quaver on the first note of his sentence when he's surprised or impressed.)

"Yes. I hear light."

While we chat, he uses his many hands to assemble some complicated-looking piece of equipment. It's almost as big as he is. I recognize several parts on it as things he's been repairing these past few days. He can hold a conversation and work on delicate machinery at the same time. I think Eridians are much better at doing multiple tasks than humans are.

"*How, question?*" he asks. "*How can you hear light, question?*"

I point to my eyes. "These are special body parts that focus and detect light. They send the information to my brain."

"*Light gives you information, question? Enough information to understand room, question?*"

"Yes. Light gives information to humans like sound gives information to Eridians."

A thought occurs to him. He stops working on his device entirely. *"You hear light from space, question? You hear stars, planets, asteroids, question?"*

"Yes."

"Amaze. What about sound, question? You can hear sound."

I point to my ears. "I hear sound with these. How do you hear sound?"

He gestures all over his carapace and arms. *"Everywhere. Tiny receptors on outer shell. All report back to brain. Like touch."*

So his whole body is a microphone. His brain must be doing some serious processing. It has to know the exact position of the body, sense the time difference between sound hitting different parts of it . . . man, that's interesting. But hey, my brain gives me an entire 3-D model of my surroundings just from two eyeballs. Sensory input is really impressive across the board.

"I can't hear as well as you," I say. "Without light, I can't understand the room. I can hear you talk, but no more."

He points to the divider. *"This is wall."*

"This is a special wall. Light passes through this wall."

"Amaze. I give you many choices for wall when first build. You choose this because light pass through, question?"

It seems like so long ago—back when the divider was a mosaic of hexagons of different textures and colors. I'd picked the clear one, of course.

"Yes. I chose this because light passes through."

"Amaze. I gave choices for different ♫♩♩♪♫ of sound. Never thought of light."

I glance at the laptop to check what that mystery word was. I almost never have to look at the laptop now. Still, once in a while there's a chord I just don't remember. The computer reports that word was "qualities." Okay, I can't fault myself for not knowing it. That one doesn't come up very often.

"Just good luck," I say.

"Good luck," he agrees. He makes a few more adjustments to the device, puts his tools back in his bandolier, then says, *"I am done."*

"What is it?"

"Device keeps me alive in small room." He looks happy. I think. He's holding his carapace just a little higher than usual. *"Wait."*

He disappears back into his ship, leaving the device behind. He returns with several plates of transparent xenonite. Each plate is a pentagon about a centimeter thick and a foot across. I hate myself for thinking in hybrid units like that. But that's what my brain came up with.

"I make room now," he says.

He assembles the pentagons edge to edge, using some kind of thick liquid glue from a tube to hold them together. Soon, he has two halves of a dodecahedron assembled. He holds them toward me proudly and places them together. *"Room."*

The "room" is a geodesic sphere made of pentagons. The total diameter is about a meter. Easily big enough to contain Rocky.

"What's the purpose of that room?" I ask.

"Room and device keep me alive in you ship."

I raise my eyebrows. "You're coming into my ship?"

"Want to see human technology. Is allowed, question?"

"Yes! Allowed! What do you want to see?"

"Everything! Human science better than Eridian science." He points to the laptop floating beside me. *"Machine that think. Eridians no have that."* He points to my toolkit. *"Many machines there Eridians no have."*

"Yes. Come look at anything you want!" I point to the small airlock drawer in the divider wall. "How will you get it through that?"

"You leave tunnel. I make new divider wall. Bigger airlock."

He pulls the completed device—which I now realize is a life-support system—onto his carapace and straps it on. It covers the radiator slits at the top of his carapace.

"Is that blocking your radiator? Isn't that dangerous?"

"No. This make hot air into cold air," he says.

Air conditioning. Not what I think of when I see a species that lives comfortably at over 200 degrees Celsius. But we all have our tolerances.

He seals the globe around himself with glue. *"I test."*

He just floats there for a minute. Then, he says, *"Works! Happy!"*

"Great!" I say. "How does it work, though? Where does the heat go?"

"Easy," he says. He taps one small part of the device. *"Astrophage here. Astrophage take all heat hotter than ninety-six degrees."*

Ah, right. To humans, Astrophage is hot. To Eridians, it's quite cold. And it's the perfect air-conditioning medium. All Rocky has to do is run the air over some Astrophage-filled cooling fins or something.

"Clever," I say.

"Thank. You leave now. I make large airlock for tunnel."

"Yes yes yes!" I say.

I collect all my belongings in the tunnel, including the mattress clamped to the wall, and stuff them into the control room, then go into the control room myself and seal both airlock doors.

I spend the next hour tidying up. I wasn't expecting company.

CHAPTER 15

It's been a few hours. But I just have to know. How does he modify the tunnel?

He needs massive atmospheric pressure to stay alive. My hull can't handle that. And he can't handle being in a vacuum. So how does he make modifications?

I hear clinks and clanks from the other side of the airlock. This time I'm going to find out!

I enter the airlock and look through the porthole. The *Blip-A*'s hull robot has removed the old tunnel and is installing a new one.

Oh. Well. That's anticlimactic.

The old tunnel drifts off into space—its use is at an end, apparently. The robot places the new tunnel in position and administers xenonite glue along the edge of the *Blip-A*'s hull.

How did Eridians pilot a ship that traveled near the speed of light without using computers? Dead reckoning? They're pretty good at doing math in their heads. Maybe they never needed to invent computers. But still. No matter how good they are at math, there are limits.

The clunking stops. I peek out the window again. The tunnel has been fully installed.

It looks like the previous tunnel, except it has a much larger airlock section. Pretty much the entire divider wall is a cabinet large enough to hold Rocky with room to spare. It is not, however, large enough to hold me. I guess I won't be visiting the *Blip-A* anytime soon.

"Hmph," I say. I try not to let it bother me, but come on. *He* gets to see an alien spaceship. How come *I* don't get to see one?

Rocky's side of the tunnel no longer has the network of gripping bars. Instead, there is a metal stripe running along the long axis of the tunnel. It extends into the divider airlock and further into my side of the tunnel. It leads right up to my airlock door.

Opposite the metal stripe is what looks like a pipe. It's made of the same drab xenonite browns and tans that the tunnel wall is made of. And it's square. It also runs the long axis of the tunnel.

With a *whoosh,* Rocky's side of the tunnel fills with fog. Then a second *whoosh* fills my side. That's what the pipe was for, I guess. Delivering the appropriate atmosphere to both sides. I'm glad Rocky has a supply of oxygen to work with.

The *Blip-A* door opens, and Rocky emerges, encased in his geodesic ball. He wears something like overalls with a bandolier across the bottom of his carapace. The AC unit is on his back. Two of his hands hold metal blocks. The other three are free. One of them waves to me. I wave back.

The spaceball (what else should I call it?) floats into the airlock and then sticks to the metal plate.

"What?" I say. "How . . ."

Then I see it. The ball didn't magically move. Those blocks Rocky is holding are magnets. Fairly powerful ones, I guess. And the metal strip is obviously magnetic. Probably iron. He rolls the ball along the metal line and into the divider airlock. He manipulates metal controls through the xenonite shell with his magnets. It's mesmerizing to watch.

After some hissing and the sound of pumps, he repels a plate away, which opens up the door on my side of the airlock. From there, he rolls along the metal line to my door. I open it.

"Hello!"

"Hello!"

"So . . . do I carry you around? Is that the plan?"

"Yes. Carry. Thank."

I gingerly grab the ball, worried it might be hot. But it isn't. Among other things, xenonite is an excellent insulator. I pull him through and into the ship.

Rocky is *heavy*. Much heavier than I thought he would be. If there were gravity, I probably wouldn't be able to lift him at all. As it is, he has a lot of inertia. It takes a lot of oomph to pull him along. It's like pushing a motorcycle in neutral. Seriously—he's as heavy as a motorcycle.

I shouldn't be surprised. He told me all about his biology and how it uses metals. Heck, his blood is mercury. Of course he's heavy.

"You are very heavy," I say. I hope he doesn't take that to mean *Hey, fatty! Go on a diet!*

"My mass is one hundred sixty-eight kilograms," he says.

Rocky weighs over 300 pounds!

"Wow," I say. "You weigh a lot more than me."

"What is you mass, question?"

"Maybe eighty kilograms."

"Humans have very small mass!" he says.

"I'm mostly water," I say. "Anyway. This is the control room. I operate the ship from here."

"Understand."

I push him ahead of me down the tunnel to the lab. He skitters around within his ball. He tends to shift around when he's looking at something new. I think it helps him get a better "view" of things with his sonar. Kind of like a dog tilting its head to get more information about a sound.

"This is my lab," I say. "All the science happens here."

"Good good good room!" he squeals. His voice is a full octave higher than normal. *"Want to understand all!"*

"I'll answer any questions you have," I say.

"Later. More rooms!"

"More rooms!" I say dramatically.

I push him along into the dormitory. I give us a very slow velocity so he can take it all in from the center of the room. "I sleep here. Well, I used to. Then you made me sleep in the tunnel."

"You sleep alone, question?"

"Yes."

"I also sleep alone many times. Sad sad sad."

He just doesn't get it. A fear of sleeping alone is probably hardwired in his brain. Interesting . . . that might have been the beginning of their pack instinct. And a pack instinct is required for a species to become intelligent. That weird (to me) sleep pattern could be the reason I'm talking to Rocky right now!

Yeah, that was unscientific. There are probably a thousand things that led to them being sapient and stuff. The sleep thing is likely just one part of it. But hey, I'm a scientist. I have to come up with theories!

I open a panel to the storage area and push his ball partially inside. "This is a small room for storage."

"Understand."

I pull him back out. "That's all the rooms. My ship is much smaller than yours."

"You ship has much science!" he says. *"Show me things in science room, question?"*

"Sure."

I take him back up to the lab. He shifts around in the ball, taking it all in. I float us to the center of the room and grab the edge of the table.

I push the ball against the lab table. I think it's steel, but I'm not sure. Most lab tables are. Let's find out.

"Use your magnets," I say.

He pushes one of his magnets against the pentagon face touching the table. With a *clunk* the magnet takes hold. He's now anchored in place.

"Good!" he says. He uses his magnets on one face after another to

roll across the table and back. It's not graceful, but it gets the job done. At least I don't have to hold him in place.

I nudge away from the table and float to the edge of the room. "There's a lot here. What do you want to know about first?"

He starts to point in one direction, then stops. Then he picks a new thing, but stops there too. Like a kid in a candy shop. Finally, he settles on the 3-D printer. *"That. What is that, question?"*

"It makes small things. I tell the computer a shape, and it tells this machine how to make it."

"I can see it make small thing, question?"

"It needs gravity."

"That is why your ship rotates, question?"

"Yes!" I say. Wow, he's quick. "The rotation makes gravity for science things."

"You ship no can rotate with tunnel attached."

"Right."

He thinks it over.

"You ship has more science than my ship. Better science. I bring my things into you ship. Release tunnel. You make you ship spin for science. You and me science how to kill Astrophage together. Save Earth. Save Erid. This is good plan, question?"

"Uh . . . yes! Good plan! But what about your ship?" I tap his xenonite bubble. "Human science can't make xenonite. Xenonite is stronger than anything humans have."

"I bring materials to make xenonite. Can make any shape."

"Understand," I say. "You want to get your things now?"

"Yes!"

I've gone from "sole-surviving space explorer" to "guy with wacky new roommate." It'll be interesting to see how this plays out.

"Have you met Dr. Lamai?" Stratt asked.

I shrugged. "I meet so many people these days I honestly don't know."

The carrier had a sick bay, but that was for the crew. This was a special medical center set up on the second hangar bay.

Dr. Lamai pressed her hands together and bowed her head slightly. "It is a pleasure to meet you, Dr. Grace."

"Thanks," I said. "Um, you too."

"I've put Dr. Lamai in charge of all things medical for the *Hail Mary*," Stratt said. "She was the lead scientist for the company that developed the coma technology we're going to use."

"Nice to meet you," I said. "So you're from Thailand, I assume?"

"Yes," she said. "The company did not survive, unfortunately. Because the technology only works on one in every seven thousand people and thus has limited commercial potential. I am very happy that my research may yet help humanity."

"Understatement," said Stratt. "Your technology might *save* humanity."

Lamai averted her eyes. "You compliment me too much."

She led us into her lab. A dozen bays were each full of slightly different apparatus experiments, each connected to an unconscious monkey.

I looked away. "Do I have to be here?"

"You'll have to excuse Dr. Grace," Stratt said. "He's a bit . . . tender on certain topics."

"I'm fine," I said. "I know animal testing is necessary. I just don't like to stare at it."

Lamai said nothing.

"Dr. Grace," Stratt said. "Stop being an asshole. Dr. Lamai, please bring us up to speed."

Lamai pointed to a set of metal arms over the nearest test monkey. "We developed these automated coma-monitoring and care stations when we believed we would have tens of thousands of patients. It never came to pass."

"Do they work?" Stratt asked.

"Our original design was not intended to be fully independent. It would handle everything routine, but if it encountered a problem it could not solve, a human doctor would be alerted."

She walked along the line of unconscious monkeys. "We are making significant progress on the fully automated version. This armature is run by extremely high-end software being developed in Bangkok. It will care for a subject in a coma. It watches their vitals, applies whatever medical care is needed, feeds them, monitors their fluids, and so on. It would still be better to have an actual doctor present. But this is a close second."

"Are they artificial intelligence of some kind?" Stratt asked.

"No," said Lamai. "We do not have time to develop a complicated neural network. This is a strictly procedural algorithm. Very complex, but not AI at all. We have to be able to test it in thousands of ways and know exactly how it responds and why. We can't do that with a neural network."

"I see."

She pointed to some diagrams on the wall. "Our most important breakthrough was, unfortunately, the undoing of our company. We successfully isolated the genetic markers that indicate long-term coma resistance. We can run a simple blood test to find out. And, as you know, once we tested this on the general population, we learned that very, very few people actually have those genes."

"Couldn't you still help those people, though?" I asked. "I mean, sure it's only one in seven thousand people, but it's a start, right?"

Lamai shook her head. "Unfortunately, no. This is an elective procedure. There is no pressing medical need to be unconscious throughout chemotherapy. In fact, it adds a small amount of risk. So there just would not be enough customers to sustain a company."

Stratt rolled up her sleeve. "Test my blood for the genes. I'm curious."

Lamai was briefly taken aback. "V-Very well, Ms. Stratt." She walked over to a rolling supply cart and got a blood-draw kit. Someone this important wasn't used to doing actual medical grunt work. But Stratt was Stratt.

Still, Lamai was no slouch. She got the needle into Stratt without delay and on the first try. The blood flowed into the tube. When the blood draw was complete, Stratt rolled down her sleeve. "Grace. You're up next."

"Why?" I asked. "I'm not volunteering."

"To set an example," she said. "I want everyone on this project, even tangentially related, to get tested. Astronauts are a rare breed, and only one in seven thousand of them will be coma-resistant. We might not have enough qualified candidates. We need to be ready to expand the pool."

"It's a suicide mission," I said. "It's not like we'll have a line of people saying, 'Oh, me! Please! Please me! Pick me!'"

"Actually, we do have that," Stratt said.

Lamai poked me in the arm. I looked away. I get a little queasy when I see my blood squirting into a tube. "What do you mean, we have that?"

"We've already had tens of thousands of volunteers. All with the complete understanding that it's a one-way trip."

"Wow," I said. "How many of them are insane or suicidal?"

"Probably a lot. But there are hundreds of experienced astronauts on the list too. Astronauts are brave people, willing to risk their life for science. Many of them are willing to *give* their life for humanity. I admire them."

"Hundreds," I say. "Not thousands. We'll be lucky if even one of those astronauts qualifies."

"We're already counting on a lot of luck," said Stratt. "May as well hope for some more."

Shortly after college, my girlfriend Linda moved in with me. The relationship only lasted eight months beyond that and was a total disaster. But that's not relevant right now.

When she moved in, I was shocked by the sheer volume of random junk she felt necessary to bring into our small apartment. Box after box of stuff she had accumulated over decades of never throwing anything out.

Linda was absolutely Spartan compared to Rocky.

He's brought in so much crap we don't have places to store it all.

Almost the entire dormitory is full of duffel-bag things made of a canvas-like material. They are random muddy colors. When visual aesthetic doesn't matter, you just get whatever colors the manufacturing process makes. I don't even know what's in all of them. He doesn't explain. Every time I think we might be done, he brings more bags in.

Well, I say "he" brings them in, but it's me. He hangs out in his ball, magnetically attached to the wall, while I do all the work. Again, this is very reminiscent of Linda.

"This is a lot of things," I say.

"Yes yes," he says. *"I need these things."*

"A lot of things."

"Yes yes. Understand. Things in tunnel is last things."

"Okay," I grumble. I float back to the tunnel and grab the last few soft boxes. I maneuver them through the cockpit and lab down to the dormitory. I find a spot to cram them. There's very little space left. I vaguely wonder how much mass we just added to my ship.

I manage to keep the area near my bunk clear. And there's a spot on the floor that Rocky picked out as his sleeping locale. The rest of the room is a mad tangle of soft boxes taped to each other, the wall, the other bunks, and anything else that would keep them from floating loose.

"Are we done?"

"Yes. Now detach tunnel."

I groan. "You made the tunnel. You detach it."

"How I detach tunnel, question? Me inside ball."

"Well, how do I do it? I don't understand xenonite."

He made a turning motion with two of his arms. *"Rotate tunnel."*

"Okay, okay." I grab my EVA suit. "I'll do it. Jerk."

"No understand last word."

"Not important." I climb into the suit and close the rear flap.

Rocky is surprisingly adept at doing things with a couple of magnets from inside a ball.

Each of his duffels has a metal pad on it. He's able to climb along the pile and rearrange it as needed. Occasionally, a bag he's using for purchase comes loose and he floats off. When that happens, he calls me and I put him back.

I hang on to my bunk and watch him do his thing. "Okay, step one. Astrophage sampling."

"Yes yes." He holds two hands in front of him and moves one around the other. *"Planet move around Tau. Astrophage go there from Tau. Same at Eridani. Astrophage make more Astrophage with carbon dioxide there."*

"Yes," I say. "Did you get a sample?"

"No. My ship had device for this. But device broke."

"You couldn't fix it?"

"Device not malfunction. Device broke. Fell off ship during trip. Device gone."

"Oh! Wow. Why did it break off?"

He wiggles his carapace. *"Not know. Many things break. My people make ship very hurry. No time to make sure all things work good."*

Deadline-induced quality issues: a problem all over the galaxy.

"I tried to make replacement. Failed. Tried. Failed. Tried. Failed. I put ship in path of Astrophage. Maybe some get stuck on hull. But robot on hull no can find any. Astrophage very small."

His carapace slumps down. His elbows are above the level of his breathing holes. Sometimes he dips his carapace when sad, but I've never seen him dip it this far.

His voice drops an octave. *"Fail fail fail. I am repair Eridian. I not science Eridian. Smart smart smart science Eridians died."*

"Hey . . . don't think of it like that . . ." I say.

"No understand."

"Uh . . ." I pull myself over to his pile of bags. "You're alive. And you're here. And you haven't given up."

But his voice remains low. *"I try so many times. Fail so many times. Not good at science."*

"I am," I say. "I'm a science human. You're good at making and fixing things. Together we'll figure this out."

He raises his carapace a bit. *"Yes. Together. You have device to sample Astrophage, question?"*

The External Collection Unit. I remember it from my first day in the control room. I didn't think about it much at the time, but that's got to be it. "Yes. I have a device for this."

"Relief! I try so long. So many times. Fail." He's quiet for a moment. *"Much time here. Much time alone."*

"How long were you here alone?"

He pauses. *"Need new words."*

I pull my laptop off the wall. We run into new words every day, but they're happening fewer and fewer times per day. That's something.

I launch the frequency analyzer and bring up my dictionary spreadsheet. "Ready."

"Seven thousand seven hundred and seventy-six seconds is ♩♫♩♪♪. Erid rotate one circle in one ♩♫♩♪♪."

I immediately recognize the number. I'd worked it out back when I was studying Rocky's clock. 7,776 is six to the fifth power. It's exactly how many Eridian seconds it takes to wrap an Eridian clock around to all zeroes again. They divided their day into a very convenient and (to them) metric number of seconds. I can follow that.

"Eridian day." I enter it into my dictionary. "A planet rotating once is a 'day.'"

"Understand," he says.

"Erid circles Eridani one time every 198.8 Eridian days. 198.8 Eridian days is ♫♩♪♫♪."

"Year," I say, and enter it. "A planet going around a star once is one year. So that's an Eridian year."

"We stay with Earth units or you get confused. How long is Earth day, question? And how many Earth days is one Earth year, question?"

"One Earth day is 86,400 seconds. One Earth year is 365.25 Earth days."

"Understand," he says. *"I am here forty-six years."*

"Forty-six years?!" I gasp. "*Earth* years?!"

"I am here forty-six Earth years, yes."

He's been stuck in this system for longer than I've been alive.

"How . . . how long do Eridians live?"

He wiggled a claw. *"Average is six hundred eighty-nine years."*

"*Earth* years?"

"Yes," he says a little sharply. *"Always Earth units. You are bad at math, so always Earth units."*

I can't even speak for a moment.

"How many years have you been alive?"

"Two hundred ninety-one years." He pauses. *"Yes. Earth years."*

Holy cow. Rocky is older than the United States. He was born around the same time as George Washington.

He's not even that old for his species. There are old Eridians out there who were alive when Columbus discovered (a bunch of people already living in) North America.

"Why you so surprised, question?" Rocky asks. *"How long do humans live, question?"*

CHAPTER 16

"T*his is Earth gravity, question?*" Rocky asks. His ball rests on the control-room floor next to the pilot seat.

I check the Centrifuge control screen. We are up to full rotational velocity and spool extension. The crew compartment has done the 180-degree turn correctly. The diagram shows the two halves of the ship at full separation. We are spinning smoothly in the void. The "Lab Gravity" value reads "1.00 g."

"Yes. This is Earth gravity."

He steps side to side, rolling his geodesic dome one face back and forth. "*Not much gravity. What is value, question?*"

"Nine point eight meters per second per second."

"*Not much gravity,*" he repeats. "*Erid gravity is 20.48.*"

"That's a lot of gravity," I say. But that's to be expected. He'd told me all about Erid before, including its mass and diameter. I knew their surface gravity had to be roughly double Earth's. Nice to have my calculations verified, though.

And side note: wow. Rocky's mass is 168 kilograms. That means on his homeworld he tips the scales at almost *800 pounds.* And that's his native environment, so I assume he can move around just fine.

Eight hundred pounds and can skitter around effortlessly. Mental note: Do not get in an arm-wrestling match with an Eridian.

"So," I say, leaning back in the pilot's seat. "What's the plan? Fly into the Petrova line and get some Astrophage?"

"Yes! But first I make xenonite room for me." He points down the hatchway toward the rest of the crew compartment. *"Mostly in sleep room. But tunnels in lab and small area in control room. Is okay, question?"*

Well, he can't just stay in a ball forever. "Yes, that's fine. Where is the xenonite?"

"Xenonite parts in bags in dormitory. Liquids. Mix. Become xenonite."

Like epoxy. But really, really strong epoxy.

"Interesting! Someday I want to know all about xenonite."

"I not understand science. I just use. Apology."

"That's okay. I can't explain how to make a thinking machine. I just use it."

"Good. You understand."

"How long will your xenonite construction take?"

"Four days. Could be five days. Why you ask, question?"

"I want to work fast."

"Why so fast, question? Slower is safer. Less mistakes."

I shift in my chair. "Earth is in a bad state. It's getting worse all the time. I have to hurry."

"Not understand," says Rocky. *"Why Earth so bad so fast, question? Erid go bad slower. Have at least seventy-two years before big problems."*

Seventy-two years? Man, I *wish* Earth had that kind of time. But seventy-two years from now Earth will be a frozen wasteland and 99 percent of the human population will be dead.

Why isn't Erid as badly affected? I furrow my brow. I only have to think for a moment before I have my answer: It's all about thermal energy storage.

"Erid is much hotter than Earth," I say. "And Erid is much larger with a much thicker atmosphere. So Erid has a whole lot more heat stored in its air. Earth is getting cold fast. Very fast. In fourteen more years, most humans will be dead."

His voice becomes monotone. It's a very serious intonation. *"Understand. Stress. Concern."*

"Yes."

He clicks two claws together. *"Then we work. We work now! Learn how to kill Astrophage. You return to Earth. You explain. Save Earth!"*

I sigh. I'm going to have to explain this eventually. May as well be now. "I'm not going back. I'm going to die here."

His carapace shudders. *"Why, question?"*

"My ship only had enough fuel for the trip here. I don't have enough to go home. I have tiny little probes that will return to Earth with my findings. But I will stay here."

"Why is mission like this, question?"

"This was all the fuel my planet could make in time."

"You knew this when you left Earth, question?"

"Yes."

"You are good human."

"Thanks." I try not to think about my impending doom. "So, let's collect Astrophage. I have ideas for how we can get some samples. My equipment is very good at detecting trace amounts—"

"Wait." He holds up a claw. *"How much Astrophage you ship need for return to Earth, question?"*

"Uh . . . just over two million kilograms," I say.

"I can give," he says.

I sit up in my chair. "What?!"

"I can give. I have extra. Can give that much and still have plenty for my return to Erid. You can have."

My heart skips a beat. "Seriously?! It's a lot of fuel! Let me repeat it: two million kilograms. Two times ten to the sixth power!"

"Yes. I have much Astrophage. My ship was more efficient than planned on trip here. You can have two million kilograms."

I fall back into my seat. I pant. I almost hyperventilate. My eyes well up. "Oh my God . . ."

"No understand."

I wipe away tears.

"You are okay, question?"

"Yes!" I sob. "Yes, I'm okay. Thank you! Thank you thank you!"

"I am happy. You no die. Let's save planets!"

I break down, crying tears of joy. I'm going to live!

Half the Chinese crew stood on the flight deck. Some were actually doing their jobs, but most were there to catch a look at humanity's saviors. The whole science team was there as well. The same set of usual suspects we had at our weekly status meetings. Stratt, me, Dimitri, Lokken, and our latest science addition, Dr. Lamai. Oh, and no science team would be complete without a gambling-addicted swindler, so Bob Redell was there too.

To be fair, Bob had done his job well. He had managed the Sahara Astrophage Farm magnificently. It's rare to find a scientist who is also a good administrator. It was no easy task, but the farm was generating Astrophage at the levels he'd promised.

The helicopter came in low and slow, then landed perfectly on the helipad. A ground crew rushed up to secure it. The rotors remained spinning and the cargo door opened.

Three people walked out, each dressed in blue jumpsuits, each bearing their country's flag on the shoulder. A Chinese man, a Russian woman, and an American man.

The ground crew ushered them to a safe distance, and the chopper took off again. Moments later, a second helicopter landed. Just like the first, this helicopter carried three astronauts. In this case, a Russian man, a Russian woman, and an American woman.

These six would be the prime and backup crews for the *Hail Mary.* Either of the helicopters could easily have carried all six astronauts, but Stratt had a very strict rule: Under no circumstances could any crewmember and their backup share a plane, helicopter, or car. Each position was specialized and would require years of specific training. We wouldn't want one car crash to ruin humanity's chances of survival.

The candidate pool wasn't deep. There just weren't many coma-resistant people out there who had "the right stuff" and were willing to go on a suicide mission.

Still, even with the reduced pool, the winnowing and selection process had been long, brutal, and filled with endless politicking by every government involved. Stratt stayed firm and insisted on only the best candidates, but some concessions had to be made.

"Women," I said.

"Yes," Stratt grumbled.

"Despite your guidelines."

"Yes."

"Good."

"No, it isn't." She frowned. "I got overruled by the Americans and Russians on it."

I folded my arms. "I never would have thought a woman would be so sexist against women."

"It's not sexism. It's realism." She righted a strand of hair that had blown into her face. "My guidelines were that all candidates must be heterosexual men."

"Why not all heterosexual women?"

"The *vast* majority of scientists and trained astronaut candidates are men. It's the world we live in. Don't like it? Encourage your female students to get into STEM. I'm not here to enact social equality. I'm here to do whatever's necessary to save humanity."

"Still seems sexist."

"Call it what you like. There's no room on this mission for sexual tension. What happens if there's some kind of romantic entanglement? Or dispute? People kill for less."

I looked across the deck to the candidates. Captain Yang welcomed them aboard. He took special interest in his countryman—the two were all smiles and handshakes.

"You didn't want a Chinese guy either. You thought their space program was still too young. But I hear you picked him to be the prime crew commander."

"He's the most qualified. So he's the commander."

"Maybe the Russians and Americans over there are qualified too. Maybe the people literally saving the world will keep it professional. Maybe cutting off literally half of the talent pool because you're afraid astronauts can't keep it in their pants isn't a good idea."

"We'll have to hope so. The Russian woman—Ilyukhina—is on the prime crew as well. She's a materials expert and by far the best candidate for the task. The science expert is Martin DuBois—the American man. Two men and one woman. Recipe for disaster."

I put my hand to my chest in mock surprise. "Goodness me! DuBois appears to be black! I'm surprised you allowed it! Aren't you afraid he'll ruin the mission with talk of rap music and basketball?"

"Oh, shut up," she said.

We watched the astronauts get surrounded by deck crew. They were absolutely starstruck—especially with Yáo.

"DuBois has three doctorates—physics, chemistry, and biology." Stratt pointed to the American woman. "Over there is Annie Shapiro. She invented a new kind of DNA splicing that's now called the Shapiro method."

"Seriously?" I said. "*The* Annie Shapiro? She invented three entire *enzymes* from scratch to splice DNA using—"

"Yes, yes. Very smart lady."

"She did it for her PhD thesis. Her *thesis*. Do you know how many people are on track for a Nobel Prize from research they did *in grad school*? Not many, I can tell you that much. And she's your *second* choice for the science expert?"

"She's the most talented DNA splicing specialist alive. But DuBois has strength in a huge variety of fields, and that's more important. We don't know what they're going to encounter out there. We need someone with a broad knowledge base."

"Amazing people," I said. "Best of the best."

"I'm glad you're impressed. Because you'll be training DuBois and Shapiro."

"Me?" I asked. "I don't know how to train astronauts!"

"NASA and Roscosmos will teach them the astronaut stuff," she said. "You're going to teach them science stuff."

"Are you kidding? They're way smarter than me. What would I teach them?"

"Don't sell yourself short," said Stratt. "You're the world's leading expert on Astrophage biology. You're going to impart every single thing you know about it to both of them. Here comes the prime crew."

Yáo, Ilyukhina, and DuBois walked over to Stratt.

Yáo bowed. He spoke with a very slight accent, but otherwise perfect English. "Ms. Stratt. It is an honor to finally meet you. Please accept my deepest gratitude for selecting me as the commander for this critical mission."

"Nice to meet you too," she said. "You were the most qualified. No thanks required."

"Hello!" Ilyukhina lunged forward and hugged Stratt. "I'm here to die for Earth! Pretty awesome, yes?!"

I leaned to Dimitri. "Are all Russians crazy?"

"Yes," he said with a smile. "It is the only way to be Russian and happy at the same time."

"That's . . . dark."

"That's *Russian*!"

DuBois shook Stratt's hand and spoke so softly as to be almost inaudible. "Ms. Stratt. Thank you for this opportunity. I won't let you down."

I and the other science leads all shook hands with the three astronauts. It was a disorganized affair, more like a cocktail mixer than a formal meeting.

In the middle of it all, DuBois turned to me. "I believe you're Ryland Grace?"

"Yeah," I said. "It's an honor to meet you. What you're doing is just . . . I can't even comprehend the sacrifice you're making. Or should I not talk about it? I don't know. Maybe we don't talk about it?"

He smiled. "It's on my mind quite often. We don't have to avoid the subject. Besides, you and I are birds of a feather, it would seem."

I shrugged. "I guess so. I mean, you're way more advanced than I am, but I do love cellular biology."

"Well, yes, that too," he said. "But I was talking about coma resistance. I hear you have the coma-resistance markers, just like me and the rest of the crew."

"I do?"

He raised his eyebrow. "They didn't tell you?"

"No!" I shot a look over to Stratt. She was busy talking to Embezzler Bob and Commander Yáo. "First I'm hearing of it."

"That's odd," he said.

"Why wouldn't she tell me?"

"You're asking the wrong person, Dr. Grace. But my guess is they only told Stratt and she only told people who needed to know."

"It's my DNA," I grumbled. "Someone should have told me."

DuBois deftly changed the subject. "In any event: I am looking forward to learning all about the Astrophage life-cycle. Dr. Shapiro—my counterpart on the backup crew—is also very excited. We shall be a classroom of two, I suppose. Do you have any experience teaching?"

"Actually, yes," I said. "A lot."

"Excellent."

I'm all smiles. It's been three days since I found out I won't die and I'm still all smiles.

Well, actually, I could still easily die. The trip home is long and dangerous. Just because I survived my coma on the way here, that doesn't mean I'll survive it on the way home. Maybe I can stay awake and just eat the feeding-tube slurry when my normal food runs out? I can do four years all alone, right? We were in comas to keep from killing one another. But solitary confinement is a whole different set of psychological damage. I should read up on it.

But not now. Right now I have to save Earth. My own survival is a problem for later. But it's a *problem,* not a hopeless guarantee of death.

The light on the Centrifuge screen blinks green.

"Gravity at full," I say with a smile.

We were back in zero g for a short time, but now I have the centrifuge going again. I had to "spin down" because I needed to use the engines. We can't have centrifugal gravity and propulsion at the same time. Just imagine firing up the spin drives while the ship is in two pieces connected by a hundred meters of cable. It's not a pleasant thought.

During the decades (gasp!) that Rocky's been here, he surveyed the system very well. He gave me all the information he'd accumulated. He cataloged six planets, noted their size, mass, positions, orbital characteristics, and general atmospheric makeup. He didn't have to travel around to do it. He just did astronomical observations from the *Blip*-A. Turns out Eridians are as curious about things as humans are.

And it's a good thing too. This isn't *Star Trek.* I can't just flip on a scanner and get all that information about a star system. It took Rocky months of observations to get things at this level of detail.

And more important, Rocky knows all about the local Petrova line. As expected, it goes to one specific planet—probably the one that has the most carbon dioxide. In this case, it's the third planet from the star, "Tau Ceti e." At least, that's what Earth calls it.

So that'll be our first stop.

Sure, we could fly the *Hail Mary* through any part of the Petrova line and get some Astrophage that way. But we'd only intersect the line for a few seconds. A solar system is not a static thing. We have to keep moving at least fast enough to maintain orbit around the star.

But Tau Ceti e is a nice, big planet in the widest part of the Petrova line. We can park the *Hail Mary* in orbit and be immersed in local Astrophage for half of every orbit. And we can stay there as long as we want, getting as much data as we need to about the Astrophage here and the dynamics of the Petrova line itself.

So we're on our way to the mysterious planet.

I can't just ask Mr. Sulu to plot a course. I spent two days doing math, checking my work, and rechecking my work before I figured out the exact angle and thrust to apply.

Sure, I have 20,000 kilograms of Astrophage left. And yes, that's quite a lot of fuel considering I can get 1.5 g's by spending 6 grams per second. And yes, Rocky's ship apparently has scads of Astrophage (I still don't understand how he has so much extra fuel). But I'm conserving fuel anyway.

I got us going a good head of steam and we're on course for Tau Ceti e. I'll do the orbital-insertion burn in about eleven days. While we wait, we may as well have gravity. So we're back to centrifuge mode.

Eleven days. Truly astonishing. The total distance we'll be traveling to get there is over 150 million kilometers. That's about the same as the distance from Earth to the sun. And we're doing it in eleven days. How? By having an absurd velocity.

I did three hours of thrust to get us going, and I'll do another three when we get to Tau Ceti e to slow down. Right now, we're cruising along at 162 kilometers per second. It's just ridiculous. If you left Earth at that speed, you'd get to the moon in forty minutes.

This entire maneuver, including the burn I'll have to do to slow down at the end, will consume 130 kilograms of fuel.

Astrophage. Crazy stuff.

Rocky stands in a bulb of clear xenonite in the floor of the control room.

"Boring name," Rocky says.

"What? What name is boring?" I ask.

He'd spent days building up the Eridian Zone throughout the ship. He even installed his own new tunnels from deck to deck. It's like having giant hamster Habitrails running everywhere.

He shifts his weight from one handhold to another. *"Tau Ceti e. Boring name."*

"Then give it a name."

"Me name? No. You name."

"You were here first." I unclip my seatbelts and stretch out. "You identified it. You plotted its orbit and location. You name it."

"This is you ship. You name."

I shake my head. "Earth-culture rule. If you're at a place first, you get to name everything you discover there."

He thinks it over.

Xenonite is truly amazing. Just a centimeter of transparent material separates my one-fifth atmosphere of oxygen pressure from Rocky's 29 atmospheres of ammonia. Not to mention my 20 degrees Celsius from Rocky's 210 degrees Celsius.

He's taken over more of some rooms than others. The dormitory is almost entirely his domain now. I insisted he move all his crap into his compartment, so we agreed he could have most of the space in there.

He also put a large airlock in the dormitory. He based it on the size of the *Hail Mary*'s airlock on the assumption that anything important in the ship would likely be small enough to fit through that. I can't ever go into his zone. My EVA suit would never stand up to his environment. I'd get squished like a grape. The airlock is really so we can pass items back and forth.

The lab is mostly mine. He has a tunnel leading up the side and another teeing off to run along the ceiling and ultimately through the ceiling into the control room. He can observe any of the scientific stuff I do. But in the end, Earth equipment wouldn't work in his environment, so it has to be in mine.

As for the control room . . . it's tight. Rocky put the xenonite bulb in the floor next to the hatchway. He really did try to keep the intrusion to a minimum. He assures me the holes he added to my bulkheads won't affect the ship's structural integrity.

"Okay," he finally says. *"Name is ♫♩♪♫."*

I don't need the frequency analyzer anymore. That was an A-below-middle-C major fifth, followed by an E-flat octave, and then a

G-minor seventh. I enter it into my spreadsheet. Though I don't know why. I haven't had to look at that thing in days. "What does it mean?"

"It is name of my mate."

I widen my eyes. That little devil! He never told me he had a mate! I guess Eridians don't kiss and tell.

We'd covered some biological basics during our travels. I explained how humans make more humans, and he told me where baby Eridians come from. They're hermaphrodites and they reproduce by laying eggs next to each other. Stuff happens between the eggs and one of them absorbs the other, leaving one viable egg that will hatch in one Eridian year—forty-two Earth days.

Laying eggs together is, basically, the Eridian equivalent of sex. And they mate for life. But this is the first I've heard of Rocky doing it.

"You have a mate?"

"Unknown," Rocky says. *"Mate possibly has new mate. I gone a long time."*

"Sad," I say.

"Yes, sad. But necessary. Must save Erid. You pick human word for ♫♩♩♪♫."

Proper nouns are a headache. If you're learning German from a guy named Hans, you just call him Hans. But I literally can't make the noises Rocky makes and vice versa. So when one of us tells the other about a name, the other one has to pick or invent a word to represent that name in their own language. Rocky's actual name is a sequence of notes—he told it to me once but it has no meaning in his language, so I stuck with "Rocky."

But my name is actually an English word. So Rocky just calls me the Eridian word for "grace."

Anyway, now I have to come up with an English word that means "Rocky's spouse."

"Adrian," I say. Why not? "Human word is 'Adrian.'"

"Understand," he says. He heads down his tunnel into the lab.

I put my hands on my hips and crane my neck to watch him leave. "Where are you going?"

"Eat."

"Eat?! Wait!"

I've never seen him eat. I've never even seen an orifice other than the radiator vents on top of his carapace. How does he get food in? For that matter, how does he lay eggs? He's been pretty cagey about it. He ate in his ship when we were connected. And I think he snuck a few meals here and there while I slept.

I scamper down the ladder into the lab. He's already halfway down his vertical tunnel, climbing the many handholds. I keep up, climbing my own ladder. "Hey, I want to watch!"

Rocky reaches the lab's floor and pauses. *"Is private. I sleep after eat. You watch me sleep, question?"*

"I want to watch you eat!"

"Why, question?"

"Science," I say.

Rocky shifts his carapace left and right a few times. Eridian body language for mild annoyance. *"Is biological. Is gross."*

"Science."

He wiggles his carapace again. *"Okay. You watch."* He continues downward.

"Yes!" I follow him down.

I squeeze into my little area of the dormitory. All I have these days is my bed, the toilet, and the robot arms.

To be fair, he doesn't have much room either. He has most of the volume, but it's laden with all his junk. Plus, he made an ad-hoc workshop in there and a life-support system out of parts from his ship.

He opens one of his many soft-sided bags and pulls out a sealed package. He tears it open with his claws and there are various shapes I can't identify. Mostly rocky material like his carapace. He sets about tearing them apart into smaller and smaller pieces with his claws.

"That's your food?" I ask.

"Social discomfort," he says. *"No talk."*

"Sorry."

I guess eating for them is something gross that is to be done in private.

He tears the rocky chunks off the food and exposes meat underneath. It's definitely meat—it looks just like Earth meat. Considering we are almost certainly descended from the same basic building blocks of life, I bet we use the same proteins and have the same general solutions to various evolutionary challenges.

Once again I'm struck by melancholy. I want to spend the rest of my life studying Eridian biology! But I have to save humanity first. Stupid humanity. Getting in the way of my hobbies.

He pulls all of the rocky chunks off the meat and sets that aside. Then he tears the meat up into small chunks. At all times, he keeps the food on the packaging it came in. It never touches the floor. I wouldn't want my food touching the floor either.

After a while, he has shredded the edible parts of his meal down as far as his hands can do it. Far more than any human would with their food.

Then he steps over to the other side of his compartment, leaving his food where it was. He pulls a flat, cylindrical container from a sealed box and places it under his thorax.

Then things . . . get gross. He did warn me. I can't complain.

The rocky armor on his abdomen splits and I see something fleshy rip open underneath. A few drops of shiny silver liquid dribbles out. Blood?

Then a gray blob plops out of his body into the pan. It lands with a damp-sounding splat.

He seals the pan and puts it back in the box it came from.

He returns to the food and flips over onto his back. The gaping abdominal hole is still open. I can see inside. There's soft-looking flesh in there.

He reaches over with a few of his hands and grabs some choice morsels of food. He brings them to his opening and drops them in. He repeats this process, slowly and methodically, until all the food is in his . . . mouth? Stomach?

There is no chewing. There are no teeth. As far as I can tell, there are no moving parts inside.

He finishes the last of his meal, then lets his arms fall limp. He lies spread-eagle on the floor, immobile.

I resist the urge to ask if he's okay. I mean, he looks dead. But this is probably just how Eridians eat. And poop. Yeah. I'm guessing that blob that came out earlier was what's left of his previous meal. He's a monostome—that is, the waste comes out the same opening that food goes into.

The opening in his abdomen closes slowly. A scab-like material forms where the break in the skin was. But I don't see it for long. The rocky abdominal covering folds back into place shortly thereafter.

"*I . . . sleep . . .*" he slurred. "*You . . . watch . . . question?*"

A food coma for Rocky is no small thing. This doesn't look voluntary at all. This is a biologically enforced post-meal siesta.

"Yes, I watch. Sleep."

"*Sle . . . ee . . . p . . .*" he mumbles. Then he conks out, still belly-up on the floor.

His breathing speeds up. It always does when he first falls asleep. His body has to dump all the heat in the hot circulatory system.

After a few minutes, he stops panting. Now I know he's well and truly asleep. Once he gets past the panting phase, I've never seen him wake back up in less than two hours. I can sneak off to do my own thing. In this case, I'll write down everything I just saw about his digestive cycle.

Step 1: Subject defecates from mouth.

"Yup," I say to myself. "That was pretty freaking gross."

CHAPTER 17

I wake up with Rocky staring at me.

It happens every morning now. But it never stops being creepy. How do I know that a pentagonally symmetrical creature with no eyes is "staring" at me? I just know. Something in the body language.

"You awake," he says.

"Yeah." I step out of bed and stretch. "Food!"

The arms reach up and hand me a hot box. I open it up and take a peek. Looks like eggs and sausage.

"Coffee."

The arms dutifully hand me a cup of coffee. It's kind of cool that the arms will hand me a cup when there's gravity, but a pouch when there isn't. I'll remember this when writing up the *Hail Mary*'s Yelp review.

I look to Rocky. "You don't have to watch me sleep. It's okay."

He turns his attention to a worktable in his partition of the dormitory. *"Eridian culture rule. Must watch."* He picks up a device and tinkers with it.

Ah, the c-word. "Culture." We have an unspoken agreement that cultural things just have to be accepted. It ends any minor dispute.

"Do it my way because it's how I was raised," basically. We haven't run into anything where our cultures clash . . . yet.

I eat my breakfast and drink my coffee. Rocky doesn't say anything to me during that time. He never does. Eridian courtesy.

"Trash," I say.

The arms collect my empty cup and meal package.

I head up to the control room and settle into the pilot's seat. I bring up the telescope view on the main screen. Planet Adrian sits in the center. I've been watching it grow larger and larger for the past ten days. The closer we get, the more I respect Rocky's astronomy skills. All of his observations on its motion and mass have been spot-on.

Hopefully his gravity calculation is right too. Or we'll have a very short and painful attempt to orbit.

Adrian is a pale-green planet with wispy white clouds in the upper atmosphere. I can't see the ground at all. Again, I'm amazed at the software that must have gone into this ship's computers. We are spinning around as we hurtle through space. But the image on-screen is rock solid.

"We're getting close," I say. Rocky is two floors below me, but I speak at a normal volume. I know he can hear it just fine.

"*You know air yet, question?*" Rocky calls out. Just as I know his hearing prowess, he knows my hearing limitations.

"I'll try again right now," I say.

I switch to the Spectrometer screen. The *Hail Mary* has been incredibly reliable in almost every way, but you can't expect everything to work perfectly. The spectrometer has been acting up. I think it has something to do with the digitizer. I've been trying it every day, and it keeps saying it can't get enough data to analyze.

I zero in on Adrian and give it another go. The closer we get, the more reflected light we'll get, and maybe it'll be enough for the spectrometer to tell me what Adrian's atmosphere is made of.

ANALYZING . . .

ANALYZING . . .

ANALYZING . . .

ANALYSIS COMPLETE.

"It worked!" I say.

"Worked, question?!" Rocky says, a full octave higher than normal. He scampers up his tunnels to the control-room bulb. *"What is Adrian air, question?"*

I read the results off the screen. "Looks like it's . . . 91 percent carbon dioxide, 7 percent methane, 1 percent argon, and the rest are trace gases. It's a pretty thick atmosphere too. Those are all clear gases, but I can't see the planet's surface."

"Normally you can see surface of planet from space, question?"

"If the atmosphere lets light through, yes."

"Human eyes are amazing organ. Jealous."

"Well, not amazing enough. I can't see Adrian's surface. When air gets really thick, it stops letting light through. Anyway, that's not important. The methane—that's weird."

"Explain."

"Methane doesn't last. It breaks apart very fast in sunlight. So how is methane present?"

"Geology creates methane. Carbon dioxide plus minerals plus water plus heat makes methane."

"Yes. Possible," I say. "But there's a lot of methane. Eight percent of a very thick atmosphere. Can geology make that much?"

"You have different theory, question?"

I rub the back of my neck. "No. Not really. It is odd, though."

"Discrepancy is science. You think about discrepancy. Make theory. You is science human."

"Yes. I'll think about it."

"How long until orbit, question?"

I switch to the Navigation console. We're right on course, and the orbital-insertion burn is scheduled for twenty-two hours from now. "Just under one day," I say.

"Excitement," he says. *"Then we sample Astrophage at Adrian. You ship sampler working well, question?"*

"Yes," I say, with no way to know if I'm telling the truth. There's no reason for Rocky to know I only vaguely understand the operation of my own ship.

I flip through the science instruments until I land on the controls for the External Collection Unit. I look at the diagram on the screen. It's simple enough. The sampler is a rectangular box. When activated, it will pivot up to be perpendicular to the hull. Then, doors on both sides of the rectangle will open up. Inside, there's a bunch of sticky resin—ready to catch anything that flies in.

That's it. Flypaper. Fancy space flypaper, but just flypaper.

"After collection, how sample enter ship, question?"

Simple doesn't mean convenient. As far as I can tell, there's no automated system to do anything with the sample. "I have to go get it."

"Humans are amaze. You leave ship."

"Yeah, I guess."

Eridians never bothered to invent spacesuits. Why would they? Space is devoid of sensory input to them. It would be like a human with scuba gear diving into an ocean of black paint. There's just no reason to do it. Eridians use hull robots for EVA work. The *Hail Mary* doesn't have one of those, so any EVA work has to be done by me.

"Amaze is wrong word," he says. *"Amaze is compliment. Better word is ♫♪♫♪."*

"What's that mean?"

"It is when person not act normal. Danger to self."

"Ah," I say, adding the new chord into my language database. "Crazy. My word for that is 'crazy.' "

"Crazy. Humans are crazy."

I shrug.

"Gosh darn it!" I said.

"Language!" came the voice over the radio. "Seriously, though, what happened?"

The sample vial fell gently away from my hand to the bottom of the pool. It took several seconds to fall 3 feet but, wearing this EVA suit at the bottom of the world's largest swimming pool, I had no chance of reaching out to grab it.

"I dropped vial number three."

"Okay," said Forrester. "That's three vials so far. We're going to have to work on the clamper tool."

"Might not be the tool. Might just be me."

The tool in my awkwardly gloved hand was far from perfect, but still pretty ingenious. It turned the clumsy pawing of an EVA suit glove into fine manipulation at the other end. All I had to do was squeeze a trigger with my index finger and the clamp constricted by 2 millimeters. If I squeezed a different trigger with my middle finger, it would rotate up to 90 degrees clockwise. My ring and pinkie fingers made it tilt forward up to 90 degrees.

"Stand by, I'm checking the video," said Forrester.

NASA's Neutral Buoyancy Lab at Johnson Space Center was a marvel of engineering in itself. The gigantic swimming pool was large enough to fit a full-size replica of the International Space Station inside. They used it to train astronauts on zero-g maneuvering while in EVA suits.

After countless meetings (that I was unfortunately forced to attend), the microbiology community convinced Stratt the mission needed custom-designed tools. She agreed, on the condition that none of them be mission-critical. She was resolute on having all the important stuff be off-the-shelf products with millions of hours of consumer testing.

And, being her little science lapdog, it fell to me to test out the IVME kit.

IVME was an acronym that stood for four words God never intended to be together: "in vacuo microbiology equipment." Astrophage lives in space. We could study them on Earth in our atmosphere all we wanted, but we wouldn't get the full picture of how they worked until we studied them in vacuum and in zero g. The crew of the *Hail Mary* would need these tools.

I stood in one corner of the NBL, the imposing figure of ISS behind me. Two scuba divers floated nearby, ready to rescue me in the event of an emergency.

NASA had sunk a metal lab table into the pool for me. The biggest problem wasn't making equipment that worked in vacuum—though they did have to completely redesign pipettes because there's no suction force in space. The problem was the ham-fisted EVA gloves the user had to wear. Astrophage may like vacuum, but human bodies certainly don't.

But hey, at least I was learning a lot about how Russian EVA suits worked.

Yes, Russian. Not American. Stratt listened to several experts and they all agreed the Russian Orlan EVA suit was the safest and most reliable. So that's what the mission would use.

"Okay, I see what happened," said Forrester through the headset. "You told the clamp to tilt yaw, but it released instead. The internal microcable wires must be tangled up. I'll be right there. Can you surface and bring the clamp with you?"

"Sure thing." I waved to the two divers and pointed upward. They nodded and helped me to the surface.

I got hoisted out of the pool by a crane assembly and placed on the deck nearby. Several techs came forward and helped me out of the suit. Though it was pretty easy—I just stepped out the back panel. Got to love chrysalis suits.

Forrester came from the control room next door and collected the tool. "I'll make some changes and we can try again in a couple of hours. I got a call while you were in the pool; you're needed in Building 30. Shapiro and DuBois have a couple-hour break while they reset the flight-control simulators. No rest for the wicked. Stratt wants you over there training them on Astrophage."

"Copy that, Houston," I said. The world might have been ending, but being at NASA's main campus was too awesome for me not to be excited.

I left the NBL and walked to Building 30. They would have sent a car if I'd asked, but I didn't want one. It was only a ten-minute walk. Besides, I loved walking around in my country's space history.

I walked in, through security, and onward to a small conference room they'd set up. Martin DuBois, in his blue flight uniform, stood and shook my hand. "Dr. Grace. Good to see you again."

His meticulous paperwork and notes were arrayed in front of him. Annie Shapiro's sloppy notes and wadded papers lay strewn on the table next to him, but her seat was empty.

"Where's Annie?" I asked.

He sat back down. Even while seated, he kept a firm, perfect posture. "She had to use the facilities. She should be back shortly."

I sat down and opened my backpack. "You know, you can call me Ryland. We're all PhDs here. I think first names are fine."

"I'm sorry, Dr. Grace. That is not how I was raised. However, you may call me Martin if you wish."

"Thanks." I pulled out my laptop and fired it up. "How have you been lately?"

"I have been well, thank you. Dr. Shapiro and I have begun a sexual relationship."

I paused. "Um. Okay."

"I thought it prudent to inform you." He opened his notebook and set a pen beside it. "There should be no secrets within the core mission group."

"Sure, sure," I said. "I mean. It shouldn't be a problem. You're the primary science position and Annie's the alternate. There's no scenario where you would *both* be on the mission. But . . . I mean . . . your relationship . . ."

"Yes, you are correct," DuBois said. "I will be setting out on a suicide mission in under a year. And if for some reason I am deemed unfit or unable, she will go on the suicide mission. We are aware of this, and we know this relationship can only end in death."

"We live in bleak times," I said.

He folded his hands in front of him. "Dr. Shapiro and I do not see it that way. We are enjoying very active sexual encounters."

"Yeah, okay, I don't need to know—"

"No need for condoms either. She is on birth control and we have both had extremely thorough medical examinations as part of the program."

I typed on my computer, hoping he'd change the subject.

"It's quite pleasurable."

"I'm sure it is."

"In any event, I thought you should know."

"Yeah, no, sure."

The door opened, and Annie trotted in.

"Sorry! Sorry! I had to pee. Like . . . so bad," said the world's smartest and most accomplished microbiologist. "My back teeth were floating!"

"Welcome back, Dr. Shapiro. I've told Dr. Grace about our sexual relationship."

I put my head in my hands.

"Cool," said Annie. "Yeah, we've got nothing to hide."

"In any event," said DuBois, "if I remember the previous lesson correctly, we were working on the cellular biology within Astrophage mitochondria."

I cleared my throat. "Yes. Today I'll be talking about the Astrophage's Krebs cycle. It's identical to what we find in Earth mitochondria, but with one additional step—"

Annie held up her hand. "Oh, sorry. One more thing—" She turned to DuBois. "Martin, we have about fifteen minutes of personal time after this lesson and before our next training exercise. Want to meet up in the bathroom down the hall and have sex?"

"I find that agreeable," said DuBois. "Thank you, Dr. Shapiro."

"Okay, cool."

They both looked to me, ready for their lesson. I waited a few seconds to make sure there was no more oversharing, but they seemed content. "Okay, so the Krebs cycle in Astrophage has a variant—wait. Do you call her Dr. Shapiro *while* having sex?"

"Of course. That's her name."

"I kind of like it," she said.

"I'm sorry I asked," I said. "Now, the Krebs cycle . . ."

Rocky's data about Planet Adrian was dead-on. It's 3.93 times Earth's mass and has a radius of 10,318 kilometers (almost double Earth's). It's plugging along around Tau Ceti with an average orbital velocity of 35.9 kilometers per second. Plus, he had the position of the planet correct to within 0.00001 percent. That data was all I needed to work out the insertion thrust needed.

It's a good thing those numbers were right. If they hadn't been, there would have been some serious scrambling when the orbital insertion went wrong. Maybe even some dying.

Of course, to use the spin drives at all, I had to take us out of centrifuge mode.

Rocky and I float in the control room, he in his ceiling bulb and me in the pilot's seat. I watch the camera-feed screen with a stupid grin on my face.

I'm at another planet! I shouldn't be this excited. I've been at another *star* for the past several weeks. But that's kind of esoteric. Tau Ceti is pretty much like the sun. It's bright, you can't get too close to it, and it even emits the same general range of frequencies. For some reason, being at a new *planet* is much more exciting.

The wispy clouds of Adrian coast by beneath us. Or, more accurately, the wispy clouds barely move at all and we zoom by overhead. Adrian has a higher gravity than Earth, so our orbital velocity is just over 12 kilometers per second—far more than what's needed to orbit Earth.

The pale-green planet that I've been watching for eleven days has a lot more detail now that we're on top of it. It's not just green. There are dark and light bands of green wrapping around it. Just like Jupiter and Saturn. But unlike those two gas-giant leviathans, Adrian is a rocky world. Thanks to Rocky's notes, we know the radius and mass, which means we know its density. And it's far too dense to be just gas. There's a surface down there, I just can't see it.

Man, what I wouldn't give for a lander!

Realistically, it wouldn't do me any good. Even if I had some way of landing on Adrian, the atmosphere would crush me dead. It'd be like landing on Venus. Or Erid, for that matter. Heck, in that case, I wish *Rocky* had a lander. The pressure down there might not be too much for an Eridian.

Speaking of Erid, Rocky's calibrating some kind of device in his control-room bubble. It looks almost like a gun. I don't think we've started a space war, so I assume it's something else.

He holds the device with one hand, taps it with another, and uses two more to hold a rectangular panel that is connected to the device by a short cable. He uses his remaining hand to anchor himself at a handhold.

He makes some more adjustments to the device with what looks like a screwdriver, and suddenly the panel springs to life. It was completely flat, but now has a texture to it. He waves the gun part left and right and the patterns on the screen move left and right.

"Success! It functions!"

I lean over the edge of the pilot's seat for a better look. "What's that?"

"Wait." He points the gun part at my external camera readout screen. He adjusts a couple of controls and the pattern on the rectangle settles into a circle. Looking closer, I see some parts of the circle are a little more raised than others. It looks like a relief map.

"This device hear light. Like human eye."

"Oh. It's a camera."

"♫♪♫," he says quickly. Now we have "camera" in our vocabulary.

"It analyze light and show as texture."

"Oh, and you can sense that texture?" I say. "Cool."

"Thank." He attaches the camera to the bulb wall and fixes its angle to point at my central screen. *"What are wavelengths of light humans can see, question?"*

"All wavelengths between 380 nanometers and 740 nanometers." Most people don't just know that off the top of their head. But most people aren't junior high schoolteachers who have giant charts of the visible spectrum on their classroom walls.

"Understand," he says. He turns a few knobs on his device. *"Now I 'see' what you see."*

"You're an amazing engineer."

He waves a claw dismissively. *"No. Camera is old technology. Display is old technology. Both were on my ship for science. I only modify to use inside."*

I think Eridians have a lot of modesty in their culture. Either that, or Rocky is one of those people who just can't take a compliment.

He points to the circle on his display. *"This is Adrian, question?"*

I check the exact region of Adrian he's pointing at, then compare to my screen. "Yes, and that part is 'green.' "

"I not have word for this."

Of course the Eridian language has no words for colors. Why would it? I never thought of colors as a mysterious thing. But if you've never heard of them before, I guess they're pretty weird. We have names for frequency ranges in the electromagnetic spectrum. Then again, my students all have eyes and they were still amazed when I told them "x-rays," "microwaves," "Wi-Fi," and "purple" were all just wavelengths of light.

"You name it then," I say.

"Yes yes. I name this color: middle-rough. My display pattern is smooth for high-frequency light. Rough for low-frequency light. This color is middle-rough."

"Understand," I say. "And yes, green is right in the middle of the wavelengths humans can see."

"Good good," he says. *"Is sample ready, question?"*

We've been in orbit for about a day now and I activated the sampler right when we got here. I flip to the External Collection Unit screen. It reads as fully functional and even reports how long it's been open: 21 hours and 17 minutes.

"Yeah, I guess so."

"You get."

"Ugh," I groan. "EVAs are so much work!"

"Lazy human. Go get!"

I laugh. He has a slightly different tone when he's joking around. It took a long time for me to identify. It's like . . . it's in the timing between words. They don't have the same cadence. I can't really put my finger on it, but I know when I hear it.

From the External Collection Unit screen, I order the sampler to close its doors and return to its flat configuration. The panel reports that it's been done, and I confirm it with hull cameras.

I climb into the Orlan EVA suit, enter the airlock, and cycle it.

Adrian is absolutely *gorgeous* in person. I stay out on the hull staring at the huge world for several minutes. Bands of dark and light green cover the orb, and the reflected glow from Tau Ceti is simply breathtaking. I could stare at it for hours.

I probably got to do this with Earth too. I wish I could remember. Man, I *really wish* I could remember that. It must have been every bit as beautiful.

"You out long time," comes Rocky's voice through the headset. *"You are safe, question?"*

I set up the EVA panel to always play my radio feed over speakers in the control room. Plus, I taped a headset microphone to Rocky's control-room bulb and set it to be voice-activated. All he has to do is talk and it broadcasts.

"I'm looking at Adrian. It's pretty."

"Look later. Get sample now."

"You're pushy."

"Yes."

I climb along the hull, bathed in Adrian-light. Everything has a light-green tinge to it. I find the sample collector right where it's supposed to be.

It's not as big as I expected. It's a half-meter square or so. There's a lever beside it with red and yellow stripes all around it. Text on the lever reads PULL LEVER TO RELEASE ECU—ПОТЯНУТЬ РЫЧАГ ЧТОБЫ ОСВОБОДИТЬ ECU—拉杆释放ECU.

I clip a tether to a convenient hole on the unit (presumably put there for this exact use), and pull the lever over to the open position.

The sampler floats free of the hull.

I work my way back across the hull to the airlock with the sampler in tow. I cycle my way back in and climb out of the suit.

"All is good, question?" Rocky asks.

"Yes."

"Good!" Rocky says. *"You inspect with science gear, question?"*

"Yes. Now." I bring up the Centrifuge panel. "Prepare for gravity."

"Yes, gravity." He grips handholds with three of his claws. *"For science gear."*

Once the centrifuge spins up, I get to work in the lab.

Rocky scurries into his tunnel in the lab ceiling and watches intently. Well, not "watches." Listens intently, I guess.

I lay the sampler on the lab table and open one of the panels. This is the side that faced Tau Ceti. I smile at what I see.

I crane my head to look up at Rocky. "This panel was white when we started; now it's black."

"Not understand."

"The sampler's color changed to the color of Astrophage. We got a lot of Astrophage."

"Good good!"

Over the next two hours, I scrape everything off of both halves of the sampler, putting each group in their own containers. Then I give each sample a good rinse with water and let the Astrophage settle to the bottom. I'm sure a lot of that sticky substance came with the Astrophage when I scraped it off, and I want it gone.

I perform a series of tests. First I run a few Astrophage through DNA-marker testing to see if they are identical to the Astrophage found at Earth. They are—at least, the markers I checked are identical.

Then I check overall population of each sample.

"Interesting," I say.

Rocky perks up. *"What is interesting, question?"*

"Both halves had approximately the same population."

"Not expected," he says.

"Not expected," I agree.

One side of the sampler pointed toward Tau Ceti, while the other pointed toward Adrian. Astrophage migrate to breed. For every frisky Astrophage that heads to Adrian with a twinkle in its eye, two should return. So, broadly speaking, there should be twice as many Astrophage going from Adrian to Tau Ceti as there are going the other direction. But that's not what's happening. The outgoing population is the same as the incoming population.

Rocky climbs along the tunnel that runs across the roof of the lab to get a better look. *"Flaw in counting, question? How you count, question?"*

"I measure total heat energy output of both samples." It's a surefire way to know how much Astrophage you're dealing with. Each one insists on being 96.415 degrees Celsius. The more of them there are, the more total heat will be absorbed by the metal plate I put them on.

He taps two claws together. *"That is good method. Population must be same. How, question?"*

"I don't know." I smear some of the "returning" Astrophage (that is, the Astrophage that was on the way from Adrian to Tau Ceti) onto a slide. I take it to a microscope.

Rocky scampers along his tunnel to keep up. *"That is what, question?"*

"Microscope," I say. "It helps me see very small things. I can see Astrophage with this."

"Amaze."

I take a look at the sample and gasp. There's a lot more than just Astrophage in there!

The familiar black dots of Astrophage are all over the sample. But so are translucent cells, smaller bacteria-looking things, and larger amoeba-like things. There are thin things, fat things, spiral things . . . too many to count. Too many *different kinds of things* to count. It's like looking at all the life in a drop of lake water!

"Wow!" I say. "Life! There's a whole bunch of life in here! Not just Astrophage. A bunch of different species!"

Rocky literally bounces off the tunnel walls. *"Amaze! Amaze amaze amaze!"*

"Adrian isn't just a planet," I say. "Adrian is a planet with life, like Earth or Erid! That explains where the methane comes from. Life makes methane!"

Rocky freezes. Then he shoots bolt-upright. I've never seen him raise his carapace so high. *"Life is also reason for population discrepancy! Life is reason!"*

"What?" I say. He's more excited than I've ever seen him. "How? I don't understand."

He taps the tunnel wall with his claw, pointing at my microscope. *"Some life on Adrian EATS Astrophage! Population in balance. Natural order. This explains all things!"*

"Oh my God!" I gasp. My heart just about beats out of my chest. "Astrophage has a predator!"

There's a whole biosphere at Adrian. Not just Astrophage. There's even an active biosphere within the Petrova line.

This is where it all started. Has to be. How else can we explain countless extremely different life-forms that all evolved to migrate in space? They all came from the same genetic root.

Astrophage was just one of many, many life-forms that evolved here. And with all life, there is variance and predation.

Adrian isn't just some planet that Astrophage infected. It's the Astrophage homeworld! And it's the home of Astrophage's predators.

"This is amazing!" I yell. "If we find a predator . . ."

"We take home!" Rocky says, two octaves higher than normal. *"It eat Astrophage, breed, eat more Astrophage, breed, eat more more more! Stars saved!"*

"Yes!" I press my knuckles against the tunnel wall. "Fist-bump!"

"What, question?"

I rap the tunnel again. "This. Do this."

He emulates my gesture against the wall opposite my hand.

"Celebration!" I say.

"Celebration!"

CHAPTER 18

The crew of the *Hail Mary* sat on the couch in the break room, each with their drink of choice.

Commander Yáo had a German beer, Engineer Ilyukhina had a distressingly large tumbler of vodka, and Science Specialist DuBois had a glass of 2003 Cabernet Sauvignon that he had poured ten minutes in advance to ensure it had time to breathe.

The break room itself had been a struggle to arrange. Stratt didn't like anything that wasn't directly related to the mission, and an aircraft carrier wasn't exactly overflowing with extra space. Still, with more than a hundred scientists from all over the world demanding a place to relax, she had relented. A small room in the corner of the hangar deck was built to house the "extravagance."

Dozens of people crowded into the room and watched the TV feed on the wall-mounted monitor. By silent agreement, the crew got to sit on the couch. The crew got all possible perks and privileges. They were sacrificing their lives for humanity. The least we could do was give them the best seats.

"And we're just minutes away from lift-off," said the BBC reporter. We could have watched American news, Chinese news, Russian news, it would have all been the same. The long shot of Baikonur

Cosmodrome interspersed with shots of the huge launch vehicle on the pad.

The reporter stood in the observation room overlooking Moscow's Mission Control Center. "Today's launch is the ninth in a total of sixteen launches for Project Hail Mary, but it is arguably the most important one. This payload contains the cockpit, lab, and dormitory modules. Astronauts on ISS are ready to receive the modules and will spend the next two weeks positioning them on the *Hail Mary*'s frame, which was built over the last several expeditions . . ."

Ilyukhina raised her vodka. "Do not fuck up my house, Roscosmos bastards!"

"Aren't they your friends?" I asked.

"They can be both!" She bellowed with laughter.

The countdown came on-screen. Less than a minute to go.

Yáo leaned forward and peered intently. It must have been hard—a military man of action forced to passively watch something so important play out.

DuBois saw Yáo's expression. "I'm certain the launch will go well, Commander Yáo."

"Mm," said Yáo.

"Thirty seconds to launch," said Ilyukhina. "I cannot wait that long." She downed her vodka and immediately poured herself another glass.

The assembled scientists pressed forward a bit as the countdown continued. I found myself pinned against the back of the couch. But I was too focused on the screen to care.

DuBois craned his neck to look back at me. "Will Ms. Stratt not be joining us?"

"I don't think so," I said. "She doesn't care about fun stuff like launches. She's probably going over spreadsheets in her office or something."

He nodded. "Then it's fortunate that we have you here. To represent her, in a way."

"Me? Represent her? How did you get that idea?"

Ilyukhina spun her head to face me. "You are number two, no? You are first officer of Project Hail Mary?"

"What? No! I'm just one of the scientists. Like all these guys." I gestured to the men and women behind me.

Ilyukhina and DuBois looked at each other and then back to me. "You honestly think this?" she said.

Bob Redell spoke up behind me. "You're not like the rest of us, Grace."

I shrugged at him. "Of course I am. Why wouldn't I be?"

"The point is," DuBois said, "you are, somehow, special to Ms. Stratt. I had assumed you two were engaged in sexual congress."

My mouth fell agape. "Wha—what?! Are you out of your mind?! No! No way!"

"Huh," said Ilyukhina. "Perhaps you should be? She is uptight. She could use good roll in hay."

"Oh my God. Is that what people think?" I turned to face the scientists. Most of them averted their eyes. "Nothing like that is going on! And I'm not her number two! I'm just a scientist—drafted into this project like the rest of you!"

Yáo turned around and stared at me for a moment. The room fell silent. He didn't speak much, so when he did, people paid attention.

"You are the number two," he said. Then he turned back to the screen.

The BBC announcer counted the last few seconds along with the on-screen timer. "Three . . . two . . . one . . . and we have lift-off!"

Flames and smoke surrounded the rocket on-screen, and it rose skyward. Slow at first, then picking up more and more speed.

Ilyukhina held her glass up for a few seconds and finally burst into cheers. "Tower is clear! Launch is good!" She gulped her vodka.

"It's only a hundred feet off the ground," I said. "Maybe wait till it reaches orbit?"

DuBois sipped his wine. "Astronauts celebrate when the tower is clear."

Without a word, Yáo took a sip of his beer.

"Why. Doesn't. This. Work?!" I hit my forehead with both palms at each word.

I flop into the lab chair, deflated.

Rocky watches from his tunnel above. *"No predator, question?"*

"No predator." I sigh.

The experiment is simple enough. It's a glass bulb full of Adrian's air. The air didn't actually come from Adrian, but the proportions of gases are based on the spectrograph of its atmosphere. The pressure is very low—one-tenth atmosphere, like the upper atmosphere of Adrian must be.

Also inside the bulb is our collected Adrian life-forms and some fresh Astrophage. I hoped that providing a bunch of nice, juicy Astrophage would make the predator population spike and I could isolate it from the sample once it was the dominant cell type present.

Didn't work.

"You are certain, question?"

I check my makeshift heat-energy indicator. It's just a thermocouple with part of it sticking in ice water and part of it attached to the bulb. Heat energy is provided by Astrophage and consumed by the ice. The resulting temperature of the thermocouple tells me how much total heat energy the Astrophage is giving off. If the temperature goes down, it means the Astrophage population went down. But that's not happening.

"Yeah, I'm sure," I say. "No change in Astrophage population."

"Maybe temperature of bulb no good. Too hot. Adrian upper atmosphere is probably much colder than you room temperature."

I shake my head. "Adrian air temperature shouldn't matter. The predator has to be able to handle Astrophage temperature."

"Ah. Yes. You are right."

"Maybe the predator theory is wrong," I say.

He clicks across the tunnel to the far side of the lab. He paces when he thinks. Interesting that humans and Eridians would both have that behavior. *"Predators is only explanation. Maybe predators no live in Petrova line. Maybe predators live further down in atmosphere."*

I perk up. "Maybe."

I look over to the lab monitor. I have it showing the external camera view of Adrian. Not for any scientific reason—just because it looks cool. Right this moment we're about to cross the terminator into the day side of the planet. The light of orbital dawn glows along an arc.

"Okay, let's say the predator lives in the atmosphere. What altitude?"

"What altitude is best, question? If you predator, where you go, question? You go to Astrophage."

"Okay, so what altitude are the Astrophage at?" The question answers itself. "Ah! There's a breeding altitude. Where air has enough carbon dioxide for Astrophage to breed."

"Yes!" He clatters back up his tunnel and stands above me. *"We can find. Easy. Use Petrovascope."*

I slam my fist into my palm. "Yes! Of course!"

Astrophage have to breed somewhere. Some partial pressure of carbon dioxide will be key. But we don't have to work that out or take any guesses. When an Astrophage divides, it and its offspring head back to Tau Ceti. And they use IR-light emission to make it happen. That means there will be a glow of Petrova-frequency light coming from all over the planet at that specific altitude.

"To the control room!" I say.

"Control room!" He scampers across the lab ceiling tunnel and disappears through his personal control-room entrance. I follow along beside but I'm not quite as fast.

I climb up the ladder, take the pilot's seat, and flip on the Petrovascope. Rocky has already taken up position in his bulb and points his camera at my main screen.

The entire screen glows red.

"What is this, question? No data."

"Wait," I say. I bring up the controls and options and start moving sliders. "We're inside the Petrova line. There's Astrophage all around us. Let me just change the setting to only show the brightest sources. . . ."

It takes a lot of manipulation, but I finally manage to get the brightness range set. What I'm left with are irregular blotchy areas of IR light coming from Adrian.

"I think this is our answer," I say.

Rocky gets closer to his textured screen to "see" what I'm looking at.

"Not what I expected," I say.

I thought it would just be a general layer of IR glow at a given altitude. But it's nothing like that. The clumps are basically clouds. And they don't match up with the wispy white clouds I can see with visible light. These are, for lack of a better term, IR clouds.

Or, more accurately, clouds of Astrophage that are emitting IR. For whatever reason, Astrophage breed much more in some areas than others.

"Unusual distribution," says Rocky, echoing my own thoughts.

"Yes. Maybe the weather affects breeding?"

"Maybe. Can you calculate altitude, question?"

"Yes. Wait."

I zoom and pan the Petrovascope until I'm looking at an Astrophage cloud right on the horizon of Adrian. The readouts show the camera's current angle with respect to the axes of the ship. I jot those angles down and switch to the navigation console. It tells me the angle of the ship relative to the center of our orbit. With that information, and a whole bunch of trigonometry, I can work out the altitude of the Astrophage clouds.

"The breeding altitude is 91.2 kilometers from the surface. The width is less than 200 meters."

Rocky folds one of his claws over the other. I know that body language. He's thinking. *"If predators exist, predators are there."*

"Agreed," I say. "But how do we get a sample?"

"How close can orbit get, question?"

"One hundred kilometers from the planet. Any closer and the ship will burn up in the atmosphere."

"This is unfortunate," Rocky says. *"Eight point eight kilometers away from breeding zone. No can get closer, question?"*

"If we hit the atmosphere at orbital speed, we die. But what if we slow down?"

"Slow down means orbit no good. Fall into air. Die."

I lean over the armrest to look at him. "We can use the engines to keep from falling into the atmosphere. Just thrust constantly away from the planet. Lower ourselves into the atmosphere, get a sample, and then leave."

"No work. We die."

"Why no work?"

"Engines give off enormous IR light. If you use in air, air become ions. Explosion. Destroy ship."

I wince. "Right, of course."

Back when Dimitri first tested a spin drive, it was only on for 100 microseconds and it melted a metric ton of metallic silicon behind it. And that test drive was one-thousandth the power of the *Hail Mary*'s engines. Everything works fine when I'm in a vacuum. But using the engines in air would create a fireball that makes a nuclear bomb look like a firecracker.

We sit in frustrated silence for a while. The salvation of both our worlds might be just 10 kilometers below us, and we can't get to it. There has to be a way. But how? We don't even need to be there. We just need to get a sample of the air there. Anything, no matter how small.

Wait a minute.

"How do you make xenonite again? You mix two liquids?"

Rocky is caught off guard by the question, but he answers. *"Yes. Have liquid and liquid. Mix. They become xenonite."*

"How much can you make? How much of those liquids did you bring?"

"I bring much. I use to make my zone."

I bring up a spreadsheet and start typing in numbers. "We need 0.4 cubic meters of xenonite. Can you make that much?"

"Yes," he says. *"Have enough liquids remain to make 0.61 cubic meters."*

"Okay. Then I have . . . an idea." I steeple my fingers.

It's a simple idea, but also stupid. Thing is, when stupid ideas work, they become genius ideas. We'll see which way this one falls.

The Astrophage breeding grounds are 10 kilometers into the atmosphere of Adrian. I can't fly the *Hail Mary* that low because the air is too thick and I'd burn up. I can't use the engines in the atmosphere because then all heck breaks loose and everything blows up.

So, it's time to go fishing. We're going to make a 10-kilometer-long chain, put a sampling device of some kind on the end (Rocky will make that), and drag it through the atmosphere. Easy enough, right?

Wrong.

The *Hail Mary* has to maintain a velocity of 12.6 kilometers per second to stay in orbit. Any slower and we'll decay and burn up. But if we drag a chain through the air at that velocity—even a xenonite chain—it'll get torn up and vaporized.

So we have to go slower. But going slower means falling toward the planet. Unless I use the engines to constantly maintain altitude. But if I do that, I'd be thrusting directly away from the chain and sample device. The exhaust from the engines will vaporize all of it.

So we'll thrust at an angle. Simple as that.

It'll look absolutely ridiculous. The *Hail Mary* will be tilted to 30 degrees from vertical, thrusting upward at that angle. Below it, the chain will dangle 10 kilometers into the air straight down. The atmosphere behind the thrusters will be in a constant state of ionized fire. It should be quite a show. But it'll be *behind* us and the chain will be passing through unaffected air.

All told, our lateral velocity will be just over 100 meters per second. The chain can handle that speed in the thin high-altitude air, no problem. I calculated that it'll only deflect about 2 degrees from vertical.

Once we feel like we have a sample, we skedaddle. What could possibly go wrong!

I say that ironically.

I'm not the greatest 3-D modeler, but I'm able to make a chain link in CAD reasonably well. It's not a normal oval link, though. It's mostly oval, but with a thin opening for another link to enter. Easy to assemble the links, but extremely unlikely for them to rattle apart. Especially when they're under tension.

I grab a block of aluminum and mount it in the mill.

"This will work, question?" Rocky asks from his ceiling tunnel.

"It should," I say.

I fire up the mill and it gets right to work. It drills out the mold for a chain link exactly the way I'd hoped.

I pull the workpiece out, dust off the aluminum shavings, and hold it up to the tunnel. "How's this?"

"Very good!" Rocky says. *"We will need many many many chain links. More molds means I can make more at one time. You can make many molds, question?"*

"Well." I look in the supply cabinet. "I have limited amounts of aluminum."

"You have many items in ship you no use. Two beds in dormitory, for instance. Melt them, make blocks, make more molds."

"Wow. You don't do anything by half-measure, do you?"

"No understand."

"I'm not going to melt a bunch of stuff. How would I even do that?"

"Astrophage. Melt anything."

"You got me there," I say. "But no. The heat would be too much for my life-support system to handle. That reminds me. Why do you have so much extra Astrophage?"

He pauses. *"Strange story."*

I perk up. Always up for a strange story. He clicks along his tunnel and sits in a slightly wider section. *"Science Eridians do much math. Calculate trip. More fuel mean faster trip. So we make much much much Astrophage."*

"How'd you make so much? Earth had a very difficult time making it."

"Was easy. Put in metal balls with carbon dioxide. Put in ocean. Wait. Astrophage double, double, double. Much Astrophage."

"Riiight. Because your oceans are hotter than Astrophage."

"Yes. Earth oceans are not. Sad."

When it comes to Astrophage manufacturing, Erid was born on third base. The whole planet is a pressure cooker. Twenty-nine atmospheres at 210 degrees Celsius means water is liquid on the surface. And their oceans are far, far hotter than the Astrophage critical temperature. They just put Astrophage in the water, let it absorb heat, and breed.

I'm jealous. We had to pave the Sahara Desert to breed up our Astrophage. All they had to do was throw it in the water. The stored heat energy of Erid's oceans is ridiculous. A whole bunch of water—multiples of Earth's total oceans—holding a temperature around 200 degrees Celsius or more. That's a lot of energy.

And that's why they can take a century or so to solve the problem while Earth is going to freeze in a few decades. It's not just their air storing heat. Their oceans store even more. Born on third base. Again.

"Science Eridians design ship and fuel requirements. Journey to take 6.64 years."

That trips me up for a moment. 40 Eridani is ten light-years away from Tau Ceti, so you can't get from one to the other in less than ten years from Erid's point of view. He must mean 6.64 years of time experienced by his ship thanks to time dilation.

"Strange things happen on trip. Crew sick. Die." His voice lowers. *"Now I know was radiation."*

I look down and give him a moment.

"Everyone sick. I alone to run ship. More strange things happen. Engines not work right. I am engine expert. I cannot figure out problem."

"Your engines failed?"

"No. Not fail. Thrust normal. But speed . . . not increase. No can explain."

"Huh."

He clatters back and forth as he talks. *"Then more strange: Reach halfway point earlier than should. Much earlier. I turn ship around. Thrust to slow down. But Tau get farther away. How? Still moving toward Tau but Tau moving away. Much confusion."*

"Uh-oh," I say. A thought creeps into my head. A very disturbing thought.

"I speed up. Slow down. Much confuse. But get here. Even with all mistakes and confusion, I get here in three years. Half of time science Eridian say should be. So much confuse."

"Oh . . . oh my . . ." I mumble.

"Much much much fuel remain. Much more than should have. No complain. But confuse."

"Yeah . . ." I say. "Tell me this: Is time on Erid the same as time on your ship?"

He cocks his carapace. *"Question make no sense. Of course time is same. Time is same everywhere."*

I put my head in my hands. "Oh boy."

Eridians don't know about relativistic physics.

They calculated their entire journey with Newtonian physics. They worked it all out by assuming they could just accelerate faster and faster and the speed of light wasn't an issue.

They don't know about time dilation. Rocky doesn't realize that Erid experienced a whole bunch more time than he did on that trip. They don't know about length dilation. The distance to Tau Ceti will actually increase as you slow down relative to it—even if you're still going toward it.

An entire planet of intelligent people put together a ship based on incorrect scientific assumptions, and by some miracle, the sole survivor of the crew was clever enough at trial-and-error problem solving to actually get it to its destination.

And out of that major screw-up comes my salvation. They thought they'd need a whole lot more fuel. So Rocky has boatloads to spare.

"Okay, Rocky," I say. "Get comfortable. I have a *lot* of science to explain."

He knocked twice and leaned into my office. "Dr. Grace? Are you Dr. Grace?"

It wasn't a large office, but you're lucky to have any personal space at all on an aircraft carrier. Before it held the high honor of being my office, the room was a storage locker for bathroom supplies. The crew had three thousand butts that needed daily wiping. I got to keep the room as my office until the next time we were in port. Then they'd fill it up with more supplies.

I was approximately as critical as toilet paper.

I looked up from my laptop. The short, somewhat disheveled man at the door waved awkwardly.

"Yeah," I said. "I'm Grace. You are . . . ?"

"Hatch. Steve Hatch. University of British Columbia. Nice to meet ya."

I gestured to the folding chair in front of the folding table I used as a desk.

He shuffled in, carrying a bulbous metal object. I'd never seen anything like it. He plunked it on my table.

I looked at the object. It was like someone had flattened a medicine ball, added a triangle to one end, and a trapezoid to the other.

He sat in the chair and stretched his arms. "Man, that was weird. I've never been on a helicopter before. Have you? Well, of course you have. How else would you get here? I mean, I guess you could have used a boat, but probably not. I hear they keep the carrier far away from land in case there's a disaster during Astrophage experiments. A boat would have been nicer, honestly, that helicopter ride almost made me puke. But I'm not complaining. I'm just happy to be involved."

"Um"—I gestured to the object on my desk—"what is this thing?"

He somehow became even more energetic. "Ah, right! That's a beetle! Well, a prototype for one, anyway. My team and I think we have most of the kinks worked out. Well, you never have *all* the kinks worked out, but we're ready for actual engine tests. And the university said we had to do those here on the carrier. Also the provincial government of British Columbia said it. Oh, and the national government of Canada said it too. I'm Canadian, by the way. But don't worry! I'm not one of those anti-American Canadians. I think you guys are all right."

"Beetle?"

"Yeah!" He picked it up and turned the trapezoid toward me. "This is how the *Hail Mary* crew will send us back the information. It's a little self-contained spacecraft that will automatically navigate itself back to Earth from Tau Ceti. Well, from anywhere, really. That's what me and my team have been working on for the past year."

I peek into the trapezoid and see a shiny glasslike surface. "Is that a spin drive?" I asked.

"Sure is! Man, those Russians know their stuff. We just used their designs and everything came out great. At least, I think it did. We haven't tested the spin drive yet. The tricky part is navigation and steering."

He turned the device around and faced the triangular head toward me. "This is where the cameras and computer are. No fancy-schmancy inertial-navigation nonsense. It uses ordinary visible light to see the stars. It identifies constellations and works out its orientation from that." He tapped the center of the bulbous carapace. "There's a little DC generator in here. As long as we have Astrophage, we have power."

"What can it carry?" I ask.

"Data. It's got a redundant RAID array with more memory storage than anyone would ever need." He knocked on the dome. It echoed slightly. "The bulk of this puppy is fuel storage. It'll need about 125 kilos of Astrophage to make the trip. Seems like a lot but . . . man . . . twelve light-years!"

I lifted the device and hefted it in my hands a couple of times. "How does it turn?"

"Reaction wheels inside," he said. "It spins them one way, the ship turns the other. Easy-peasy."

"Interstellar navigation is 'easy-peasy'?" I smiled.

He snickered. "Well, for what we have to do, yeah. It has a receiver that's constantly listening for a signal from Earth. Once it hears that signal, it'll broadcast its location and await instructions from the Deep Space Network. We don't have to be super accurate with the navigation. We just need it to show up within radio range of Earth. Anywhere within the orbit of Saturn or so will do just fine."

I nod. "And then scientists can tell it exactly how to get back. Clever."

He shrugged. "They'll probably do that, yeah. But they don't need to. They'll have it radio over all the data first thing. The information gets across. Then they can collect it later if they want. Oh, and we're making four of these. All we need is for one of them to survive the trip."

I turned the beetle this way and that. It was surprisingly light. A few pounds at most. "Okay, so there are four of these. How likely is each one to survive the trip? Is there at least a little system redundancy aboard?"

He shrugged. "Not that much, no. But it doesn't have to travel for nearly as long as the *Hail Mary* does. So stuff doesn't have to survive as long."

"It's going the same route, right?" I asked. "Why doesn't it take the same time?"

"Because the *Hail Mary*'s acceleration is limited by the soft, squishy humans inside. The beetle doesn't have that problem. Everything aboard is military-grade cruise-missile electronics and parts that can handle hundreds of g's of force. So it gets to relativistic speed much faster."

"Oh, interesting . . ." I wondered if this would make a good question for my students. I dismissed the idea immediately. It was absurdly complicated math no eighth grader would be able to handle.

"Yeah," Hatch said. "They accelerate at five hundred g's until they reach a cruising speed of 0.93 *c*. It'll take over twelve years to get back to Earth, but all told the little guys will only experience about twenty months. Do you believe in God? I know it's a personal question. I do.

And I think He was pretty awesome to make relativity a thing, don't you? The faster you go, the less time you experience. It's like He's inviting us to explore the universe, you know?"

He fell silent and stared at me.

"Well," I said. "This is really impressive. Good work."

"Thanks!" he said. "So can I have some Astrophage to test it?"

"Sure," I said. "How much you want?"

"How about a hundred milligrams?"

I drew back. "Easy there, cowboy. That's a lot of energy."

"All right, all right. Can't blame a guy for trying. How about one milligram?"

"Yeah, I can swing that."

He clapped. "Hell yeah! Astrophage comin' my way!" He leaned forward to me. "Isn't it amazing? Astrophage, I mean? It's like . . . the coolest thing ever! Again, God's just *handing* us the future!"

"Cool?" I said. "It's an extinction-level event. If anything, God's handing us the apocalypse."

He shrugged. "I mean, maybe a little. But man. Perfect energy storage! Imagine a battery-powered household. Like—you have a double-A battery, but full of Astrophage. That'd last your house about a hundred thousand years. Imagine buying a car and never having to charge it up? The entire concept of power grids is going to end. And it'll all be clean, renewable energy once we start breeding the stuff on the moon or something. All it needs is sunlight!"

"Clean? Renewable?" I said. "Are you suggesting Astrophage will be . . . *good* for the environment? Because it won't be. Even if *Hail Mary* finds a solution, we're looking at a mass extinction. Twenty years from now, a whole bunch of species on Earth will be extinct. And we're working hard to make sure humans aren't one of them."

He waved off my comment. "Earth's had five mass extinction events in the past. And humans are clever. We'll pull through."

"We'll starve!" I said. "Billions of people are going to starve."

"Naaaah," he said. "We're already stockpiling food. We've got a bunch of methane in the air to hold in the solar energy. It'll be all right. As long as *Hail Mary* succeeds."

I just stared at him for a moment. "You are, without a doubt, the most optimistic person I've ever met."

He gave me a double thumbs-up. "Thanks!"

He picked up the beetle and turned to leave. "Come on, Pete, let's get you some Astrophage!"

"Pete?" I asked.

He looked over his shoulder. "Sure. I'm naming them after the Beatles. The British rock group."

"I take it you're a fan?"

He turned back to face me. "Fan? Oh, yes. I don't want to exaggerate, but *Sgt. Pepper's Lonely Hearts Club Band* is the greatest musical accomplishment in the history of mankind. I know, I know. Many would disagree. But they're wrong."

"Fair enough," I said. "But why Pete? Aren't the Beatles named John, Paul, George, and Ringo?"

"Sure. And that's what we'll call the ones aboard the *Hail Mary*. But this fella is for testing in low Earth orbit. I get a whole SpaceX launch just for me! Isn't that amazing! Anyway, I named him after Pete Best—he was the drummer for the Beatles before Ringo."

"Okay, I didn't know that," I said.

"Now you do. I'm gonna get that Astrophage now. I've got to make sure these beetles will be able to . . . 'Get Back.' "

"Okay."

He frowned. " 'Get Back.' It's a song. It's by the Beatles."

"Sure. Okay."

He spun on his heel and left. "Some people got no appreciation for the classics."

I was left confused in his wake. Pretty sure I wasn't the first.

CHAPTER 19

Rocky was dumbfounded by relativity. For the first couple of hours, he simply refused to believe me. But then, as I showed more and more about how it explained his trip, he came around. He doesn't like it, but he accepts that the universe uses rules that are much more complicated than we can see.

And since then, we've spent an eternity making chain.

I made molds as fast as I could and Rocky cranked out links as fast as xenonite would set. It was a good system—one with a geometric progression of results. Every new mold I made added one to the number of links Rocky could make per batch.

Chain, chain, chain.

If I never see another chain again in my life, it will be too soon. Ten kilometers of chain—each link just 5 centimeters long. That's *two hundred thousand* links. Each one connected by hand or claw. It worked out to each of us working eight hours per day for *two weeks* doing nothing but connecting links.

I saw chain whenever I closed my eyes. I dreamed of chain every night. One of my dinner packets was spaghetti and all I could see were smooth, white chains instead of noodles.

But we got it done.

Once we had all the links made, we assembled them in parallel. We both made ten-meter lengths that we linked into twenties, and so on. At least we could be efficient that way. The tricky part was putting it all somewhere. Ten kilometers is a *lot* of chain.

The lab ended up being sort of a holding area. And even then, it just wasn't big enough. Rocky—ever the talented engineer—made large spools that could just barely fit through the airlock. With a whole bunch of EVAs, I mounted them to the hull. Then I stored the chain on them in 500-meter chunks. But of course, to do EVAs I had to spin down the centrifuge. So everything from that point on was in zero g.

Ever assemble chain in zero g? It's not fun.

The final assembly of those 500-meter chunks was challenging, to say the least. I had to connect all twenty of them together while wearing my EVA suit. Fortunately, I had the manipulator device from the IVME. NASA didn't intend for it to be a chain-making tool, but that's what I used it for.

Now Rocky and I float in the control room. He's in his bulb and I'm in my pilot's seat.

"Status of probe?" I say.

Rocky checks his readouts. *"Device is functioning."*

Rocky did a good job on the sampler probe. At least, I think he did. Engineering isn't my forte.

The sampler is a steel sphere, 20 centimeters across. It has a nice, thick ring on top that connects to the chain. Small holes perforate the sphere along its equator. They lead to a hollow inner chamber. There's a pressure sensor in there and a few actuators. The pressure sensor knows when the probe is at the right altitude, and will trigger the actuator to seal off the chamber. It's a simple matter of rotating the inner chamber shell a few degrees to deliberately misalign the holes in the outer sphere. That misalignment, along with some well-placed gaskets, will seal the local air in the chamber.

He also added a thermometer and heater in there. Once the sampler seals, the heater will maintain whatever temperature the air inside started at. Simple stuff, really, but I hadn't thought of it. Life can be pretty picky about temperature ranges.

The only remaining piece is a small radio transmitter that broadcasts a weird analog signal I wasn't able to read or decode with my equipment. Apparently it's a very standard Eridian data connection. But he has the receiver for it and that's what matters.

Just like that, with minimal complication, Rocky had made a life-support system for Adrian life-forms—a system that didn't need to know the conditions to provide in advance. It just maintains the status quo.

He really is a genius. I wonder if all Eridians are like that, or if he's special.

"I guess . . . we're ready?" I say. I'm not exactly brimming with confidence.

"*Yes,*" he quavers.

I strap myself into the pilot's seat. He uses three of his hands to grip handholds in his bulb.

I bring up the Attitude Control panel and initiate a roll. Once I have the ship pointed backward to our direction of travel and parallel to the ground below, I halt the rotation. Now we're hurtling along, butt-first, at 12 kilometers per second. I need that to be almost zero.

"Orientation is good," I say. "Initiating thrust."

"*Yes,*" says Rocky. He watches his readout screen intently. It shows him the textured version of my own screen, thanks to that camera he set up earlier.

"Here goes . . ." I fire up the spin drives. We go from zero g to 1.5 g's in under a second. I am pressed back in my chair and Rocky grabs a support with a fourth hand to stay steady.

As the *Hail Mary* slows down, our velocity can no longer keep us in orbit. I glance at the Radar panel and it confirms that we are losing altitude. I adjust the ship's attitude so we are pointing very slightly upward from horizontal. Just a fraction of a degree.

Even that small amount is too much! The radar shows us *gaining* altitude rapidly. I bring the angle back down. This is a sloppy, nasty, horrible way to fly a spacecraft, but it's all I have. There was no point to calculating this maneuver in advance. There are so many variables and ways to mess up the math I'd be flying on manual almost immediately anyway.

After a few more overcorrections, I get the feel for it. I increase the angle bit by bit as the ship slows down with respect to the planet.

"You tell when to release probe," Rocky says. His claw hovers over the button that will eject the spools and let the chain fall freely. We can only hope it doesn't get tangled.

"Not yet," I say.

The attitude screen shows we're at 9 degrees from the horizontal. I need to get us to 60. Something catches my eye off to the right. It's the external camera feed. The planet below is . . . glowing.

No. Not the whole planet. Just the bit right behind us. It's the atmosphere reacting with the IR blast from the engines. The *Hail Mary* is dumping hundreds of thousands of times more energy into that spot than Tau Ceti does.

The IR heats the air so much it ionizes and it's literally red hot. The brightness increases as our angle gets more severe. Then the affected area starts to grow. I knew it would be significant, but I had no idea it would be like this. We're leaving a red streak across the sky, destroying anything in the air. The carbon dioxide is probably being ripped apart from pure heat energy into particulate carbon and free oxygen. The oxygen might not even be forming O_2. That's a lot of heat.

"The engines are heating up Adrian's air a lot," I say.

"How you know, question?"

"Sometimes I can see heat."

"What, question?! Why you no tell me this, question?"

"It's related to sight . . . there's no time to explain it. Just trust me: We are making the atmosphere *very* hot."

"Danger, question?"

"I don't know."

"I no like that response."

We angle up and up and up. The glow behind us gets brighter and brighter. Finally, we reach the correct angle.

"Angle achieved," I say.

"Happy! Release, question?"

"Stand by. Velocity . . ."—I check the navigation console—"127.5 meters per second! Just what I calculated! Holy cow, it worked!"

I feel the pull of Adrian, tugging me into my seat.

This is one of those things I frequently have to explain to my students. Gravity doesn't just "go away" when you're in orbit. In fact, the gravity you experience in orbit is pretty much the same as you'd experience on the ground. The weightlessness that astronauts experience while in orbit comes from constantly falling. But the curvature of the Earth makes the ground go away at the same rate you fall. So you just fall forever.

The *Hail Mary* isn't falling anymore. The engines hold us up in the sky and our tilt makes us scooch forward at 127 meters per second—about 285 miles per hour. Fast for a car, but amazingly slow for a spaceship.

The air behind us glows so bright the external camera shuts down to protect its digitizer.

The Life Support panel comes up on my main screen, unprompted. EXTERNAL TEMPERATURE EXTREME, it warns.

"Air is hot," I call out. "Ship is hot."

"Ship no touch air," Rocky says. *"Why is ship hot, question?"*

"It's bouncing our IR back at us. And it's so hot now it emits its own IR. We're getting cooked."

"You ship is Astrophage-cooled, question?"

"Yes. Astrophage cools ship."

Astrophage conduits run all along the hull for just such an occasion. Well, not the occasion of "blasting a planet's atmosphere with so much IR light the results can melt steel" but the general situations where heat builds up. Mostly from the sun or Tau Ceti heating the ship up and the heat having nowhere to go.

"Astrophage absorb heat. We safe."

"Agree. We safe. And we ready. Drop probe!"

"Drop probe!" He slams his claw on the Drop button.

I hear the scrape and clink of the spools sliding off the hull one at a time and falling toward the planet below. Twenty spools in all, each one drops and unwinds before the next is released. Our best effort at keeping the chain from getting tangled.

"Spool Six away . . ." Rocky reports.

The Life Support panel blinks its warning again. I mute it again. Astrophage lives on stars. I'm sure a little reflected IR light won't be too much heat for it to handle.

"Spool Twelve away . . ." Rocky says. *"Sampler signal good. Sampler detecting air now."*

"Good!" I say.

"Good good," he says. *"Spool Eighteen away . . . air density increase . . ."*

With the external cameras offline, I can't see any of what's going on. But Rocky's readings are right in line with our plan. Right now, the chain is unfurling as it falls. Our angled engines keep us in the sky, but nothing keeps the chain from falling straight down.

"Spool Twenty away. All spools released. Air density of sampler is almost Astrophage breeding ground level . . ."

I watch Rocky with bated breath.

"Sampler has closed! Seal is airtight, heater is on! Success success success!"

"Success!" I yell.

It's working! It's actually working! We have a sample of Adrian air from the Astrophage breeding zone! If there are any predators, they *have* to be there, right? I hope so.

"Step two now." I sigh. This is not going to be fun.

I unhitch my restraints and climb out of the chair. Adrian's 1.4 g's of gravity pulls me down at a 30-degree angle. The whole room feels tilted because, actually, it *is* tilted. This isn't engine thrust I'm feeling. It's gravity.

One point four g's isn't too bad. Everything's a bit harder, but not unreasonably so. I climb into the Orlan EVA suit. This is going to be difficult, to say the least. I have to go outside and do an EVA while *completely under the effects of gravity*.

Needless to say, absolutely no part of the EVA suit, the airlock, or my training was remotely designed for this possibility. Who would have thought I would have to tromp around on the ship in full gravity? More than full, in fact?

Yet however much gravity there may be, there's still no air. Worst of all worlds. But there's no other way. I have to get the sample.

Right now, the sampler hangs at the end of a 10-kilometer chain, which is just dangling in the air. There's no easy way for us to get it back to the ship.

When planning this all out, my first thought was to thrust away from the planet, then collect the sampler when we're back to zero g. Problem is, there's literally no way to do that without vaporizing the sampler. Any path I try to take to get the ship out of Adrian's gravity—or even into a stable orbit—will mean using the spin drives. They'd push the ship along, which would make the chain and sample lag behind us and into the IR blast behind the ship. And then the sampler, everything in it, and the chain all become individual, very hot atoms.

The next idea I had was to make a huge spool that could winch up the chain. But Rocky informed me he'd never be able to make a spool big enough and strong enough to bring up the entire 10-kilometer length.

Rocky had a pretty clever thought: The sampler could climb the chain when it was done. But after some experimenting he ditched the idea. He said the risks just weren't worth it.

So we have . . . this other plan.

I grab a special winch Rocky designed and attach it to my suit's tool belt.

"Be careful," says Rocky. *"You are friend now."*

"Thanks," I say. "You are friend also."

"Thank."

I cycle the airlock and look outside.

This is a strange experience. Space is black. The planet is majestic below me. Everything looks like it should when in orbit. But there's gravity.

A red glow from the planet peeks out around the edges of the *Hail Mary*. I'm no dope—I oriented the ship to make sure it would shield me from the deadly heat bouncing up off the atmosphere.

The airlock door is "up." I have to pull myself—and a hundred pounds of gear—up and through that opening. And I have to do it in 1.4 g.

It takes me a full five minutes. I grunt. I say a bunch of not-really-profane things, but I get it done. Soon I'm standing on top of my ship. One misstep and I'll fall to my death. I wouldn't have to wait long for it either. As soon as I fell below the ship, the engines would punch my ticket.

I attach a tether to the handrail at my feet. Will a zero-g tether save me if I fall? It's not mountain-climbing gear. It wasn't made for this. Better than nothing, I guess.

I walk along the hull toward the chain anchor point. It's a large xenonite square that Rocky made. He explained in great detail how to adhere it to the hull. Looks like it did the job just fine. The chain is still attached.

I reach it and get down on my hands and knees. The gravity is absolutely brutal in this EVA suit. No part of this is how things are supposed to be.

I hook my (possibly worthless) tether to the nearest handrail and pull the winch from my tool belt.

The chain hangs away at a 30-degree angle and disappears into the planet below. It just goes so far away it's too thin for me to perceive after a kilometer or so. But I know from Rocky's readings it's the full 10 kilometers down, with a sample container full of potential salvation for two entire planets full of people.

I wedge the winch between the chain and the anchor plate. The chain doesn't budge—not even a millimeter. But that was expected. There's just no way human muscle could move something that heavy.

I hook the winch to the anchor plate. The casing of the winch is xenonite, so the xenonite-to-xenonite connection should have plenty of strength for what comes next.

I smack the winch a couple of times just to make sure it's properly seated. It is.

Then I press the activation button.

A gear pops out from the center of the winch, one cog catching a chain link through the center. The gear turns and drags the chain into the internal workings of the winch. Inside, it rotates the link 180 degrees, then slides it across its neighbor to release it.

When we made the chain, we did it with "trap" links that can connect without us having to seal each one. It's extremely unlikely that random movement would separate the links. But the winch is deliberately designed to do just that.

Once the link is freed, the winch ejects it out the side and repeats the process for the next link.

"The winch works," I say through my radio.

"Happy," comes Rocky's voice.

It's simple, straightforward, elegant, and solves all the problems. The winch is powerful enough to lift the chain. It separates the links and lets them fall into the planet below. Having a long length of chain dangling down next to the one we're pulling up would be a disaster. Imagine earbud wires getting tangled, then multiply that by 10 kilometers.

No, each link will take its own path to oblivion below and the rising chain will be unaffected.

"When winch get to link two hundred sixteen, you increase speed."

"Yes."

I have no idea how many links it's done so far. But it's plugging along nicely. Probably about two links per second. A safe, slow beginning. I watch for two minutes. That's probably about right. "All good. At least two hundred sixteen links now."

"Increase speed."

Two links per second may seem like a good clip, but it would take about thirty hours to raise the chain at that rate. I don't want to be out here that long and we definitely don't want to stay in this risky constant-thrust situation for that long. I press the control lever forward. The winch speeds up. Everything seems fine, so I put it in the final position.

Now the links fly out of the winch faster than I can count and the chain rises at a brisk pace.

"The winch is at maximum speed. All is good."

"Happy."

I keep my hand on the control lever and my eyes on the chain. If that sampler gets to the winch, everything will go south. The sample container will be torn apart, all the samples will die, and we'd have to make *another* chain.

I don't want to do that. Lord, I cannot express how much I don't want to do that.

I squint into the distance, ever vigilant. Boredom is a real problem here. I know it will take quite a while to pull up this whole chain, but I have to be ready for the sampler.

"Sample device radio signal strong," Rocky says. *"Getting closer. Be ready."*

"I'm ready."

"Be very ready."

"I am very ready. Be calm."

"Am calm. You be calm."

"No, *you* be cal—wait. I see the sampler!"

The end of the chain, with the sampler attached, rushes up toward me from the planet below. I grab the control lever and slow the winch. The sampler climbs slower and slower until it's at a crawl. All but the last few links of the chain fall to their doom and the sampler is finally within reach. I stop the winch.

Rather than risk stupidly dropping the big orb, I grab the top remaining link of the chain and unhitch it from the winch. Now I have a ball and chain. I hang on to the chain for dear life and clip it to my belt. I still don't let go. I'm not taking any chances with this.

"Status, question?"

"I have the sampler. Returning."

"Amaze! Happy happy happy!"

"Don't be happy until I'm inside!"

"Understand."

I take two steps and the ship shudders. I fall to the hull and grab two handrails.

"What the heck was that?!"

"I not know. Ship move. Sudden."

The ship shudders again, this time it's a steady pull. "We're thrusting the wrong direction!"

"Get inside fast fast fast!"

The horizon rises in my view. The *Hail Mary* isn't maintaining her angle anymore. She's tilting forward. That is absolutely not supposed to be happening.

I clamber from handhold to handhold. I don't have time to attach the tether each step. I just have to hope I don't fall.

Another sudden jerk and the hull slips sideways under my feet. I fall on my back but I keep my death grip on the sampler chain. What is going on?! No time to think. I have to get inside before the ship capsizes and kills me.

I cling to the handholds for dear life and crawl to the airlock. Thank God it's still facing more or less up. I hold the sampler to my chest and fall inside. I land headfirst. Good for me the Orlan helmet is so sturdy.

I squirm to my feet as best I can in the clunky spacesuit. I reach up, grab the outer hatch, and slam it closed. I cycle the airlock and get out of the suit as fast as I can. I'll leave the sampler in the airlock for now. I need to know what the heck is wrong with the ship.

I half climb, half fall into the control room. Rocky is in his bulb.

"Screens flash many colors!" he yells over the din. He points his camera here and there, watching the feed on his textured screen.

A metallic groan screams from somewhere down below. Something is bending and doesn't want to. I think it's the hull.

I get in the control seat. No time to strap in. "Where's that noise coming from?"

"All around," he says. *"But loudest at starboard dormitory wall segment. It bending inward."*

"Something's tearing the ship apart! Got to be the gravity."

"Agree."

But that bothers me in the back of my mind. This ship was *made* for acceleration. It endured four years at 1.5 g's. Surely it can handle this similar force? Something doesn't add up.

Rocky grabs several of his handholds for support. *"We have sampler. We leave now."*

"Yeah, let's get out of here!" I throw the spin-drive controls to full. The ship can pull up to 2 g when push comes to shove. And I think push has definitely come to shove.

The ship lurches forward. This is not a graceful, well-executed burn. This is nothing short of panicked flight.

The efficient way to leave a gravity well is laterally, to take advantage of the Oberth effect. I try to keep us more or less level to the ground below. I'm not trying to get away from Adrian. I just want to get into a stable orbit that doesn't need engines to maintain. I need velocity, not distance.

I need to keep the drives at full power for ten minutes. That should get us the 12 kilometers per second we need to stay in orbit. I just need to point a little above the horizon and thrust.

At least, that's what I want. But it's not happening. The ship keeps yawing forward and drifting laterally. What is going on?!

"Something wrong," I say. "She's fighting me."

Rocky has no trouble hanging on. He has many multiples of my strength. *"Engine damage, question? Much heat from Adrian."*

"Maybe." I check the Nav console. We're gaining velocity. That's something, at least.

"Hull bending in big room below dormitory," Rocky says.

"What? There's no room below—oh." He can sense the whole ship with his echolocation. Not just the habitable area. So when he says "big room below the dormitory," he means the fuel tanks.

Oh dear.

"Turn off engines, question?"

"We're going too slow. We'll fall into the atmosphere."

"Understand. Hope."

"Hope." Yes, hope. That's all we have at this point. Hope that the ship doesn't wreck itself before we get into a stable orbit.

The next several minutes are the tensest of my life. And, if I may say so, I've had some pretty tense moments these past few weeks. The hull continues to make horrible noises, but we're not dead, so I guess it didn't breach. Finally, after what seems like *a whole lot more* than ten minutes, our velocity is enough to stay in orbit.

"Velocity good. Stopping engines." I slide the spin-drive power sliders to zero. I let my head fall back to the headrest in relief. Now we can take our time and figure out what went wrong. No need to use the engines to . . .

Wait.

My head fell back into the headrest. It *fell* back into the headrest.

I hold my arms out in front of me, then relax them. They fall down and to the left.

"Uh . . ."

"Gravity still here," says Rocky, echoing my own observations.

I check the Nav console. Our velocity is good. We're in a stable orbit around Adrian. Well, actually it's ugly as heck—the apogee is 2,000 kilometers farther from the planet than perigee. But it's an orbit, darn it. And it's stable.

I check the Spin Drive panel again. All three drives are at zero. No thrust at all. I delve into the diagnostics screen and confirm that each of the 1,009 revolver triangles spread throughout the three drives is stationary. They are.

I let my arm fall again. It does the same strange movement. Down and to the left.

Rocky does a similar motion with one of his arms. *"Adrian gravity, question?"*

"No. We're in orbit." I scratch my head.

"Spin drive, question?"

"No. It's offline. There's zero thrust."

I let my arm fall again. This time it hits the armrest of the seat.

"Ow!" I shake my hand. That really hurt.

I let it fall again as an experiment. It fell faster this time. That's why it hurt.

Rocky pulls several tools from his jumpsuit bandolier and drops them one at a time. *"Gravity increasing."*

"This doesn't make any sense!" I say.

I check the Nav panel again. Our speed has increased considerably since I last looked. "Our velocity is increasing!"

"Engines on. Only explanation."

"Can't be. The spin drives are off. There's nothing to accelerate us!"

"Force increasing," he says.

"Yes," I say. I'm having trouble breathing now. Whatever we're at, it's much higher than a g or two. Things are getting out of hand.

With all my strength, I reach to the screen and cycle through panels. Navigation, Petrovascope, External View, Life Support . . . each one seems completely normal. Until I reach "Structure."

I'd never paid a lot of attention to the Structure panel. It's just a gray outline of the ship. But now, for the first time, it has something to say.

There's an irregular red blotch on the port fuel tank. Is that a hull breach? It could be. The fuel tanks are outside the pressure vessel. They could have a huge hole in them and we wouldn't lose air.

"There's a hole in the ship . . ." I say. I struggle to switch back to the external cameras.

Rocky watches my screen with his camera and texture pad. He's doing fine—no problems at all from the tremendous forces.

I angle the cameras around to look at the affected hull.

And there it is. A massive hole in the port side of the ship. It must be 20 meters long and half as wide. The edges of the hole tell the tale—the hull melted.

It was the blowback from Adrian's atmosphere. Not a physical explosion, but pure, unadulterated infrared light reflected off the air.

The ship tried to warn me that the hull got too hot. I should have listened.

I thought the hull couldn't melt. It was cooled by Astrophage! But of course it can melt. Even if Astrophage is a perfect heat absorber (and it may be), the heat has to conduct through the metal before it can be absorbed. If the outer layer of the hull reaches its melting point faster than the heat can transmit through the thickness of the hull, the Astrophage can't do anything about it.

"Confirmed. Hull breach. Port fuel tank."

"Why thrust, question?"

It all comes together. "Oh crap! The Astrophage in the fuel bay! It's exposed to space! That means it can see Adrian! My fuel is migrating to Adrian to breed!"

"Bad bad bad!"

That's where the thrust is from. Trillions and trillions of horny little Astrophages, all ready to breed. And then, all at once, they see Adrian. Not just a source of carbon dioxide, but their ancestral homeland. The planet they evolved over billions of years to seek out.

As each new sheet of Astrophage rushes out of the ship and toward Adrian, the next layer of Astrophage gets exposed. The ship is being pushed along by the IR thrust from the departing Astrophage. Fortunately, the rest of the Astrophage behind them are present to absorb the energy. But in absorbing that energy they absorb the momentum.

It's far from a perfect system. It's a chaotic, sputtering explosion. Any second now, this could degenerate into a much larger and less directed plume of IR and we'll be vaporized. I have to make this stop.

I can jettison fuel bays! I saw that feature on my first day in the control room! Where the heck was it . . . ?

It takes all the strength I have to lift my arm to the screen, but I manage to bring up the Astrophage panel. It shows a map of the ship and the fuel-bay area is broken up into nine rectangles. I don't have time to cross-reference these rectangles to the part of the bad hull. I grunt, force my arm forward, and tap one that I think is in the right place.

"Throwing . . . away . . . bad . . . fuel bay . . ." I say through clenched teeth.

"Yes yes yes!" Rocky says, cheering me on.

The Fuel Pod screen pops up: ASTROPHAGE 112.079 KG. Next to that, a button labeled "Jettison." I punch it. A confirmation dialog pops up. I confirm.

A sudden jerk of acceleration hurls me to the side. Even Rocky is unable to hold position. He slams into the side of his bulb but quickly rights himself and clamps onto his handholds with all five hands.

The hull groans louder than before. The acceleration has not stopped and my vision grows foggy. The pilot's seat begins to bend. I'm about to black out, so we're probably at 6 g or more.

"Thrust continues," Rocky quavers.

I can't reply. I can't get any sound out at all.

I *know* the fuel bay I jettisoned was in the affected area. There must be more than one breached bay. No time for subtlety. In a few seconds the force will be too strong for me to reach the screen at all. If there's a second breached bay, it'll be adjacent to the bay I just ditched. But there are two adjacent bays. I pick one at random. Fifty-fifty shot. With herculean effort, I tap its icon, the Jettison button, and confirm.

A jolt rocks the ship and I'm thrown around like a rag doll. In my ever-darkening peripheral vision I see Rocky curled up into a ball, bouncing against the walls, leaving silver blood splatters wherever he hits.

If anything, the force is worse than before. But wait . . . now it's the other direction.

Instead of being pulled back into my seat, I'm now being pulled away from it, my body pressing into the restraints.

The Centrifuge screen, of all things, comes to the foreground. EXCESSIVE CENTRIFUGAL FORCE WARNING, it blinks.

"Nnnng," I say. I meant to say *Oh God,* but I can't breathe anymore.

All that fuel blasting out into space . . . it didn't politely leave along the ship's long axis. It blew out at an angle, spinning us like a top. And the exploding fuel bays probably made things even worse.

Well, I stopped the fuel leak, at least. There are no new thrust vectors acting on the ship. Now I just have to deal with the spin. I manage to get a breath in. The centrifugal force is less than the uncontrolled thrust force, but it's still monumental. But hey, at least it pulls my arms toward the screen instead of away from it.

If I can get the spin drives back online, maybe I can cancel the—

My seat finally gives out. I hear the pops as the anchor points shear off. I fall forward, into the screen, still strapped to the metal seat, which crushes me from behind.

The chair probably doesn't weigh much in normal gravity. Maybe 20 kilograms. But with this much centripetal force, it's like having a cement block on my back. I can't breathe.

This is it. The weight of the chair is so much I can't inflate my lungs. I get dizzy.

Mechanical suffocation, it's called. It's how boa constrictors kill their prey. What an odd thing to think as my last thought.

Sorry, Earth, I think. There. Much better last thought.

My lungs, now full of carbon dioxide, panic. But the adrenaline rush doesn't give me the strength I need to escape. It just keeps me awake so I can experience death in more detail.

Thanks, adrenal glands.

The groaning of the ship has stopped. I guess anything that was going to break has broken and all that's left is stuff that can handle the stress.

My eyes water. They sting. Why? Am I crying? I have personally failed my entire species and they're all going to die because of it. It's a good reason to cry. But this isn't emotional. It's pain. My nose hurts too. And not from physical pressure or anything. Something burns at my nasal passages from the inside.

Something probably broke open in the lab. Some nasty chemical. Just as well I can't breathe. I probably wouldn't like the smell.

Then, out of nowhere, I can breathe again! I don't know how or why, but I gasp and wheeze in my newfound freedom. I immediately fall into a violent coughing fit. Ammonia. Ammonia everywhere. It's overpowering. My lungs scream and my eyes water over. Then there's a new smell.

Fire.

I roll around to see Rocky hovering over me. Not in his compartment. He's in the control room!

He has slashed my restraints and pulled the chair free. He shoves it to the side.

He stands over me, wobbling. I can feel the heat radiating from his body just inches away. Smoke billows out of the radiator slits atop his carapace.

His knees buckle and he collapses onto the screen next to me, destroying it. The LCD unit blacks out and the plastic bezel melts.

I see a trail of smoke leading up the tunnel to the lab and beyond.

"Rocky! What have you done!"

The crazy bastard must have used the large airlock in the dormitory! He came into my partition to save me. And he'll die because of it!

He shivers and folds his legs under himself.

"Save . . . Earth . . . Save . . . Erid . . ." he quavers. Then he slumps down.

"Rocky!" I grab his carapace without thinking. It's like putting my hands on a burner. I jerk away. "Rocky . . . no . . ."

But he is motionless.

CHAPTER 20

Rocky's body heats up the whole room.

I can barely move, the force of the centrifuge is so great.

"Nnnn!" I groan, pushing myself up off the cracked monitor. I drag myself across the shards to the next monitor over. I try not to lift too much of my body up at a time—I have to save my strength.

I slide my finger onto the monitor from the edge and tap the screen-select buttons at the bottom. I've got one chance at this.

I remember the navigation controls. The manual-control section has a button to zero out all rotation. That's mighty tempting right now, but I can't risk it. The fuel bay is wide open, I've jettisoned a couple of pods, and I have no idea what other damage may have been done. The last thing I want to do is fire up any spin drives—even the little ones that do attitude control.

I bring up the Centrifuge screen. It blinks red and white, still angry about the excessive tumble the ship is undergoing. With effort, I dismiss the warning, then enter into manual mode. There are a bunch of "hey, don't do this" kind of dialogs, but I dismiss them all. Soon I have direct control over the cable spools. I set them spinning at max speed.

The room spins and tilts in weird ways. My inner ears and my eyes are not enjoying the discrepancy. I know it's because the two halves of the ship are separating and that has nasty effects on the forces I feel here in the control room. But logic doesn't do any good in this situation. I turn my head and vomit on the wall.

After a few seconds, the force reduces dramatically. Much more manageable now. Less than 1 g, actually. All thanks to the magic of centrifuge math.

The force you feel in a centrifuge is inverse to the square of the radius. By spooling out the cables, I made the radius go from 20 meters (half the length of the ship) to 75 meters (distance from the control room to the center of mass with full cable extension). I don't know how much force I was dealing with before, but now it's one-fourteenth as much as it was.

I'm still pinned against the monitor, though not nearly as hard. I estimate about half a g. I can breathe again.

Everything feels upside down. I used the centrifuge in manual mode, so it did exactly what I told it to do and nothing else: It extended the cables. It did *not* rotate the crew compartment to face inward. The centrifuge pushes everything toward the nose of the crew compartment. The lab is "up" from me now, and the dormitory is even farther "up."

I don't even know where the manual controls for the crew-compartment rotation are and I don't have time to look for them. For now, I'll have to work in upside-down land.

I bound to the airlock and open it up. Everything is a shambles inside, but I don't care. I untangle the wadded-up EVA suit and detach the gloves. I put them on.

Back in the control room, I stand on the consoles (the control panels are "down" now). I hope I'm not damaging things too much. I position myself over Rocky's body, grab both sides of his carapace with my gloved hands, and lift.

Good. God.

I put him back down. If I try to move him like that, I'll throw out my back. But I did lift him, however briefly. It felt like 200 pounds.

Thank god we're in one-half gravity. He'd weigh 400 pounds at full gravity.

I'll need more than my hands to lift him.

I throw off the gloves, bounce back to the airlock, and fling items aside until I find the safety tethers. I wrap two tethers under Rocky's carapace and loop them over my shoulders. I burn my arms in several places during the process, but I'll deal with that later.

I clip each tether to itself under my armpits. This won't be comfortable and it definitely won't look cool, but my hands will be free and I'll be lifting with my legs.

I reach through the hatchway to the lab with both hands and get ahold of the closest rung of the ladder. It's slow going at first. There's no ladder in the control room. Why would there be? No one thought it would be upside down.

My shoulders scream in pain. This is not a well-designed backpack with a properly distributed load. It's 200 pounds of alien held up by two thin straps digging into my collarbones. And I just have to hope the melting point of the nylon tethers is higher than Rocky's body temperature.

I grunt and grimace, one rung at a time, until I get my feet into the lab. I use the edge of the hatchway to brace my feet and pull Rocky up with the straps.

The lab is a disaster. Everything is in piles all over the ceiling. Only the table and chairs remain on the floor above me—they're bolted to the floor. And, thankfully, most of the more delicate equipment is bolted to them. However, that delicate off-the-shelf lab equipment *wasn't* designed to be rattled around like popcorn and subjected to 6 or 7 g's. I wonder how many things are hopelessly broken.

The gravity is less up here. I'm closer to the center of the centrifuge. The higher I get the easier things will be.

I kick lab supplies and equipment out of my way and drag Rocky to the dormitory hatchway. I repeat the painful process I just did a moment ago. The force is less, but it still hurts. Again, I use the hatchway as a bracing point to pull Rocky into the room.

My little section of the dormitory barely fits us both. Rocky's section is a mess, just like the lab. His workbench wasn't bolted in place, so it's on the ceiling now.

I drag him across the ceiling and I get up on my bunk. It has swiveled completely around, thanks to its rocking pivot mounting. It's a handy platform for reaching the airlock between my zone and Rocky's.

The airlock door sits open on my side. He used it to come save me.

"Man, why did you do that?!" I grouse.

He could have let me die. He should have, really. He could handle the centripetal force, no problem. He could have taken his time, whipped up an invention, and used it to get back control of the ship. Yeah, I know, he's a good guy and he saved my life, but this isn't about us. He has a planet to save. Why risk his life and his whole mission for me?

The airlock door doesn't reach the ceiling, so I'll have to play "The Floor Is Lava" to get in.

I hop into the airlock from my bunk, then use the straps to pull Rocky in with me. I start to climb back out and that's when I see the airlock-control panel.

Or, rather, I see the destroyed box that was once the airlock-control panel.

"Oh, come *on*!" I yell.

Both sides of the airlock had control panels, so either Rocky or I could operate it as needed. But now mine are ruined—probably smacked by some debris flying around during the chaos.

I have to get him back into his environment, but how? I have an idea. It's not a good idea. There's an emergency valve in the airlock chamber itself that can let air in from Rocky's side.

It's there to cover a very specific edge case. There's no way I can ever enter Rocky's area of the ship. I certainly can't handle his environment, and my EVA suit would be crushed like a grape. But Rocky can come into my area with his homemade ball-spacesuit thing. So, just to be extra safe—just in case there was an emergency while

Rocky was in his ball in the airlock—there's a relief valve that will let the air from his side vent in. It's a large iron lever, so it can be manipulated with the magnets Rocky carries with him while in the ball.

I look at the lever in the airlock. I glance at the airlock's door to my compartment and its spinning-wheel lock. I look back to the lever, then back to the door.

I coil my muscles and mentally count to three.

I pull the lever and leap toward my compartment.

Blazing-hot ammonia floods the airlock and dormitory. I slam the airlock door behind me and spin the wheel lock. I hear hissing on the other side but I don't see anything. I might never see anything again.

My eyes burn like they're on fire. My lungs feel like a hundred knives are having a dance-off. My skin is numb all along my left side. And my nose—forget it. The smell is so overpowering my sense of smell just gives up.

My throat completely closes off. My body wants *nothing* to do with the ammonia.

"Com . . ." I wheeze. "Com . . . pu . . . ter . . ."

I want to die. Pain is everywhere. I climb into my bunk.

"Help!" I wheeze.

"Multiple injuries," says the computer. "Excessive eye mucus. Blood around the mouth, second-degree burns. Breathing distress. Triage result: intubate."

The mechanical arms, which thankfully don't seem to have any problem with being upside down, grab me and something is shoved violently down my throat. I feel a poke on my good arm.

"IV fluids and sedation," the computer reports.

And then I'm out like a light.

I wake up covered in medical equipment and pain.

There's an oxygen mask on my face. My right arm has an IV and my left arm is bandaged from wrist to shoulder. It hurts like heck.

Everything else hurts too. Especially my eyes.

But at least I can see. That's good.

"Computer," I say with a raspy voice. "How long have I been asleep?"

"Unconsciousness lasted six hours, seventeen minutes."

I take a deep breath. My lungs feel like they're coated in tar. Probably phlegm or some other gunk. I look over to Rocky's area. He's right where I left him in the airlock.

How can I tell if an Eridian is dead? When Rocky sleeps all movement stops. But that's also presumably what happens when an Eridian dies.

I spot a pulse-ox monitor on my right index finger.

"Compu—" I cough. "Computer: What is my blood oxygen content?"

"Ninety-one percent."

"It'll have to do." I take the mask off and sit up in bed. My bandaged arm stings with every movement. I pull the various things off of my body.

I open and close my left hand. It's working. The muscles are only a little bit sore.

I got hit with a quick blast of very hot, very high-pressure ammonia. Most likely, I have chemical burns in my lungs and on my eyes. And probably a physical burn on my arm. My left side took the brunt of the blast.

Twenty-nine atmospheres of pressure at 210 degrees Celsius (over 400 degrees Fahrenheit!). That must be what a grenade feels like. Side note: With no one manning the helm, it's pure luck we didn't crash into the planet.

The ship is either in a stable orbit or we escaped Adrian's gravity entirely. I shake my head. It's truly ridiculous how much power I have sitting in the fuel bay. To not even know if I'm still near a *planet* . . . wow.

I'm lucky to be alive. There's no other way to put it. Anything I do beyond that moment is a gift from the universe to me. I step off the bed and stand in front of the airlock. Gravity is still at one-half g and everything is still upside down.

What can I do for Rocky?

I sit on the floor opposite his body. I put my hand on the airlock wall. That feels too melodramatic, so I pull it back. Okay, I know the very basics of Eridian biology. That doesn't make me a doctor.

I grab a tablet and swipe through various documents I've made. I don't remember everything he told me, but at least I took copious notes.

When severely wounded, an Eridian body will shut down so it can try to work on everything at once. I hope Rocky's little cells are doing their thing in there. And I hope they know how to fix damage done by: (1) dropping air pressure to one twenty-ninth what he evolved to live in, (2) being suddenly exposed to a bunch of oxygen, and (3) being almost 200 degrees colder than his body expects.

I shake off the worry and return to my notes.

"Ah, here!" I say.

There's the information I need: Those capillaries in his carapace radiator are made of deoxidized metal alloys. The ambient circulatory system pumps his mercury-based blood through those vessels and air passes over them. In Erid's oxygen-free atmosphere, this makes perfect sense. In ours, it makes a perfect tinderbox.

A bunch of oxygen just passed over very hot metal pipes no thicker than a human hair. They burned. That's the smoke I saw coming out of Rocky's vents. His radiator was literally on fire.

Jesus.

The whole organ must be completely full of soot and other combustion products. And the capillaries will be coated in oxides, which ruin heat conductivity. Heck, oxides are *insulators*. The worst-possible outcome.

Okay. If he's dead, he's dead. I can't do any further harm. But if he's alive, I have to help. There's no reason not to try.

But what do I do?

So many pressures. So many temperatures. So many air mixtures. I have to keep track of them all. My own environment, Rocky's environment, and now the Adrian Astrophage breeding-ground environment too.

But first: gravity. I'm sick of living in *The Poseidon Adventure*. Time to right this ship.

I make my way back "down" to the control room. The center panel is ruined, but the others work fine. And they're interchangeable anyway. I'll mount a replacement in the middle when I have time.

I bring up the Centrifuge screen and poke around at the controls a bit. I finally find the manual controls for the crew-compartment rotation. They were buried pretty deep in the options; I'm glad I didn't try to find them during the crisis.

I order the crew compartment to rotate. Very, very slowly. I set the rate at 1 degree per second. It takes three minutes to turn around. And I hear a lot of thunks, clunks, and crashes from the lab. I don't care about any of that. I just want to make sure Rocky doesn't get further injured. This slow rate should make his body slide along the airlock ceiling, then along the wall, and finally to the floor. That's the plan, anyway.

Once the rotation is complete, things are back to feeling normal, albeit at half a g. I go back down to the dormitory to check on Rocky. He's now on the airlock floor, and still right-side up. Good. He slid rather than tumbled.

I really want to work on Rocky, but I have to make sure the adventure that may have killed him wasn't in vain. I grab the sample container from the ship's airlock. I'm kind of glad I left it there, honestly. It got cushioned from the crazy sudden accelerations by the EVA suit wadded up with it.

Rocky had the foresight to put readouts on the sampler to tell us what the temperature and pressure inside were. They're analog dial indicators in Eridian base-six numerology. But I've seen enough of that to be able to translate. The inside of the ball is minus 51 degrees

Celsius with a pressure of 0.02 atmospheres. And I know from my spectrometry earlier what the atmospheric makeup is.

Okay, that's the environment I have to duplicate.

I sort through what's left of the lab. It's slow going because I only have minimal use of my left arm. But I can use it to help slide things aside, at least. Just no heavy lifting for now.

I find a vacuum container that's only a little broken. It's a drum-shaped glass cylinder about a foot in diameter. I patch up the crack with epoxy and give it a test. It's able to pump the air out and maintain a vacuum. If it can maintain a vacuum, it can maintain 0.02 atmospheres.

I put the sample container inside.

The chemical-storage cabinet is still firmly anchored to the wall. I open it up. Everything is jumbled around inside, of course, but most containers look intact. I grab the small vial of Earth Astrophage.

There's about a gram in there, included in the supplies for testing purposes. I can always get more if I need it. All I have to do is cut any of the Astrophage-based coolant lines in the hull. But there's no need for that right now.

The sample is an oily sludge at the bottom of the vial. I open the vial and scoop it up with a cotton swab. (That gram of Astrophage has 100 trillion Joules of energy. Best not to think about it.)

I smear the Astrophage along the inner wall of the vacuum chamber and drop the cotton swab in next to the sample probe.

I pump all the air out of the vacuum chamber.

The chemistry supplies include several small cylinders of gases. Thankfully, steel cylinders are tough, so they survived the game of cosmic pinball we just went through. I add gases into the vacuum chamber, one at a time, through the infeed valve. I want to replicate Adrian's atmosphere. I pump in carbon dioxide, methane, and even argon. I don't imagine the argon will matter—it's a noble gas, so it shouldn't react with stuff. But that's what I used to think about xenon, and that turned out to be wrong.

I don't have any way to chill the air in there to minus 50 degrees, so

I'll just have to hope whatever the life inside can handle Earth room temperature.

I hear a click just as I finish putting the argon in. It's the sampler. Just as Rocky designed them to do, the little valves opened when the outside pressure matched the pressure at the Astrophage breeding altitude on Adrian. Good old Rocky. Best engineer I've ever met.

Okay. I've made the sample as safe as I can. The air composition and pressure is as close to its native environment as I could get it, and there's plenty of Astrophage to eat. If there are any microscopic predators in there, they should be in good shape.

I wipe my brow with my bandaged arm, and immediately regret it. I wince in pain.

"How hard is it, Ryland?!" I seethe to myself. "Stop using your burned-up arm!"

I climb back down the ladder to the dormitory.

"Computer: païnkillers."

The arms reach up and hand me a paper cup with two pills in it and a cup of water. I take the pills without even checking what they are.

I look back at my friend and try to come up with a plan. . . .

It's been over a day since I shoved Rocky in that airlock and he still hasn't moved. But I haven't been wasting my time. I've been mad sciencing some inventions in the lab. This kind of gadget creation is really Rocky's forte, but I give it my best.

I thought about lots of different approaches. But in the end, I think I should let Rocky's body heal itself as much as possible. I wouldn't feel comfortable trying to operate on a human, let alone an Eridian. His body should know what to do. I just have to let it.

That doesn't mean I'm going to do nothing at all, though. I have a guess as to what's going on. And if I'm wrong, my idea for treatment won't hurt him.

Right now, there's a bunch of soot and other combustion by-product crap in his radiator organ. So it probably doesn't work well. If he's alive at all, it'll take his body a long time to clear that out. Maybe too long.

So maybe I can help?

I hold the box in my hand. It's enclosed on five of six sides with the remaining side open. The walls are 4-inch-thick steel. It took me all day to repair the mill and get it working again, but once I did, milling up this box was a breeze.

Inside is a high-powered air pump. Simple as that. I can shoot high-pressure air really hard. I tested it out in the lab and it blew a hole in a 1-millimeter-thick sheet of aluminum from a foot away. It really works. I wish I could claim I'm a genius who made this all from scratch, but the reality is I only made the box. The pump is repurposed from a high-pressure tank.

Also in the box is a battery, a camera, some stepper motors, and a drill. I'll need all of these things for my plan to work.

I've cleaned up the lab, somewhat. Most of the equipment is ruined, but some might be fixable. I cross to the other side of the table, where I have another experiment.

I have a little chip of xenonite—some chaff left over from when we made two hundred thousand chain links. I used a generous application of epoxy to glue it to the tip of a roughed-up drill bit. It's been setting for over an hour. Should be done.

I pick up the bit and the xenonite comes with it. I use all my strength to try to pull them apart. I can't.

I nod and smile. This might work.

I do a few more tests with the box. My remote control for the motors works well enough. It's not true remote control. It's a bank of switches attached to a plastic container lid. I have wires from the switches going through a tiny hole in the steel, which is in turn filled up with resin. I can turn the power on or off to any of the components in there. That's my "remote control." I can only hope the motors don't have a problem with high heat or ammonia.

I bring everything to the dormitory and prep the epoxy. I stir it together and apply it generously to the edges of the steel box's open side. I press the box to the airlock wall and hold it in place. Then I just stand there for ten minutes, holding the box in place. I could have taped it to the wall or something while the epoxy set, but I need a really good seal and I don't want to take any chances. Human hands are better clamps than any tool I might have in the lab.

I gingerly release the box and wait for it to fall. It doesn't. I poke it a couple of times and it seems pretty solid.

It's five-minute epoxy, but I'll give it an hour to fully set.

I return to the lab. I may as well, right? Let's see what my little alien terrarium is up to.

Nothing much, as it happens. I don't know what I expected. Little flying saucers whizzing around in the chamber, maybe?

But the cylinder looks exactly like it did before. The sampler sits where I left it. The smear of Astrophage is unchanged. The cotton swab is . . .

Hey . . .

I hunker down and take a seat. I squint into the chamber. The cotton swab has changed. Just a little bit. It's . . . fluffier.

Sweet! Maybe there's something on there I could get a look at. I just need to get it under a microscope to—

Oh.

The realization dawns on me. I don't have any way to extract samples. I just plain overlooked that part.

"Dummy!" I smack my forehead.

I rub my eyes. Between the pain from my burns and the dopiness from the painkillers, it's hard to concentrate. And I'm tired. One thing I learned back in my graduate school days: When you're stupid tired, accept that you're stupid tired. Don't try to solve things right then. I have a sealed container that I need to get into eventually. I'll figure out how later.

I pull out my tablet and take photos of the container. Science rule number 1: If something is changing unexpectedly, document it.

Just to be more scientific, I point a webcam at the experiment and set up the computer to take a time-lapse at one frame per second. If anything is happening slowly, I want to know.

I head back to the control room. Where the heck are we?

Some work with the Nav console and I learn we're still in orbit. It's stable-ish. This orbit will probably decay over time. No rush, though.

I check all the ship's systems and do as many diagnostics as I can. The ship did pretty well, despite not being remotely designed to handle this situation.

The two fuel bays I jettisoned aren't around anymore, but the other seven look to be in good shape. There are cracks in the hull here and there, according to the diagnostics test. But they all seem to be internal. Nothing facing outside, which is good. I don't want my Astrophage to see Adrian again.

One of the micro-breaches is highlighted in red. I take a closer look. The breach's location has the computer in a tizzy. It's in the bulkhead between the fuel area and the edge of the pressure vessel. I can see the concern.

The bulkhead sits between the storage bay below the dormitory and Fuel Bay 4. I go take a look.

Rocky still hasn't moved. No surprise there. My steel box remains where I put it. I could probably use it now, but I'm resolved to wait the full hour.

I open up the storage panels and pull a bunch of boxes out. I climb into the storage area with a flashlight and toolkit. It's cramped—barely 3 feet tall. I have to crawl around in there for a good twenty minutes before I finally find the breach. I only spot it because there's a small frosty buildup around the edges. Air escaping into a vacuum gets really cold really fast. In fact, that ice probably helped slow the leak.

Not that it mattered. The leak is so small it would take weeks to be a problem. And the ship probably has a bunch of spare air in tanks anyway. Still, there's no reason to just let it leak. I apply a generous helping of epoxy on a small metal patch and seal the breach. I have to hold it for considerably more than five minutes before it sets. Epoxy takes a long time to set when it's cold, and the bulkhead is below freezing at that spot thanks to the leak. I considered getting a heat gun from the lab but . . . that's a lot of work. I just hold the patch for longer. It takes about fifteen minutes.

I climb back down and wince the whole time. My arm hurts non-stop now. It's a constant sting. It's been less than an hour, but the painkillers aren't doing the job anymore.

"Computer! Painkillers!"

"Additional dose available in three hours and four minutes."

I frown. "Computer: What is the current time?"

"Seven-fifteen P.M., Moscow Standard Time."

"Computer: Set time to eleven P.M. Moscow Standard Time."

"Clock set complete."

"Computer: painkillers."

The arms hand me a package of pills and a bag of water. I gobble them down. What a stupid system. Astronauts trusted to save the world but not to monitor their painkiller doses? Stupid.

Okay. It's been long enough. I turn my attention back to the box.

First I'll need to drill a hole in the xenonite. And that's where all hell will break loose if things go bad. The general idea here is for the drill inside the box to put a hole in the xenonite and for the box to contain the pressure that rushes in. But you never know. The box might not be held on tight enough.

I wear a medical breathing mask and eye protection. If there's going to be a jet of superheated, high-pressure ammonia in this room, I need to not die from it.

Earlier I filed down a metal rod to be sort of a spike. The full radius is a little bigger than the drill bit I have readied in the steel box. I hold the spike and hammer at the ready. If the pressure blows the box off, I'll hammer the spike into the hole and hope it plugs the gap.

Of course, the pressure might not blow the box off entirely. It might just spurt out around the edges of the glue joint. If that happens, I'll have to smack the box with the hammer until it comes off, then drive in the spike.

Yes, it's ridiculously dangerous. But I just don't know if Rocky will survive without help. Maybe I'm being emotional instead of rational. But so what?

I clench the hammer and spike. Then I activate the drill.

It takes so long for that drill to get through the xenonite, I actually calm down out of boredom. It's only 1 centimeter, but it's like trying to grind down diamond. I'm lucky the drill bit is hard enough to do anything at all. The camera feed from inside shows slow and steady progress. Instead of drilling like wood or metal, this is more like glass. It breaks off in chips and chunks.

Finally, the bit breaches to the other side. It is immediately launched back into the box and bent sideways by the pressure. There's a *whump* as Eridian air rushes into the little box. I squint my eyes. Then, after a few seconds, I open them again.

If the box was going to blow off, it would have done so right then. My seal held. For now anyway. I breathe a sigh of relief.

But I don't take the mask or goggles off. You never know when the seal might give out.

I check the camera screen. This will take careful aim, so I was very clever in making sure a camera could—

The camera feed is dead.

A pain in my wrist takes over and I pull it away.

Ah. Yeah. Webcams aren't designed to work at 210 degrees Celsius and 29 atmospheres. And my solid steel box, well, it's solid steel. Steel is an *excellent* heat conductor. I can't even touch it now it's so hot.

I'm still stupid. First the Adrian sample container, and now this. I want to sleep, but Rocky is more important. At least being stupid isn't permanent. I'll press on. I know I shouldn't, but I'm too stupid to take that into consideration.

Okay, the camera is dead. I can't see into the box. But I can still see Rocky in the airlock because the xenonite is clear. I'll have to work with what I've got here.

I fire up the high-pressure pump. It still works—at least, it's making noise. It should be shooting a very high-pressure jet of air in

Rocky's direction. At 29 atmospheres, air acts almost like water. You can really knock stuff around with it. But ammonia is clear. So I have no idea where it's going.

I adjust the angle of the jet with the servo controls. Are they working? I have no idea. The pump is too loud for me to hear if the servos are doing anything. I sweep left and right, inching down and up in a pattern.

Finally, I spot something. One of the levers in the airlock wiggles a bit. I zero in on it. It gets pushed back several inches.

"Gotcha!" I say.

Now I know where it's pointed. I do some guesswork and aim for Rocky's carapace vents. Nothing happens, so I do a grid search, back and forth, up and down, until I get a result.

And oh, what a result it is!

I hit the sweet spot. All of a sudden, Rocky's carapace vents belch out black smoke. The nasty dust and debris that built up when he was on fire. It's intensely satisfying. Like that feeling when you blast an air duster into an old computer.

I sweep back and forth, trying to hit each vent one by one. The latter vents don't cause nearly the commotion as that first one. I think they all lead to the same organ—like a human's mouth and nose do. Multiple orifices for redundancy and safety.

After a few minutes, no more sooty dust is coming out. I shut off the pump.

"Well, buddy," I say. "I've done all I can. I just hope you can do the rest."

I spend the rest of the day working on a secondary and tertiary containment box. I glue them in place over my device. The Eridian air will have to breach three seals to get into my compartment now. That will have to do.

I hope Rocky wakes up.

CHAPTER 21

"We can do this in private," I said. "I can meet with you one at a time."

The three astronauts sat on a couch in front of me. I'd commandeered the breakroom and locked the door for this meeting. Yáo sat in the center, looking stern as always. DuBois was to his left, his back arched to provide perfect posture. Ilyukhina slouched to Yáo's left, sipping a beer.

"No need for individual meetings," said Yáo. "There's no room on this mission for secrets."

I shifted in my chair. Why did Stratt send me to do this job? I'm not a people person and I don't know how to approach delicate matters. She said something about the crew liking me more than anyone else. Why? Maybe I just seemed friendly and pleasant because I was usually standing next to Stratt.

In any event, launch was just a month away and I had to get this information.

"Okay," I said. "Who wants to go first?"

DuBois raised his hand. "I can start if that's amenable to everyone."

"Sure." I did a quick test-scribble with my pen. "So . . . how would you like to die?"

Yeah. Awkward topic. But one that had to be covered. These three were going to give their lives just so the rest of us could have a fighting chance. The least we could do was help them die on their own terms.

DuBois handed me a crisp piece of paper. "I've detailed my request in this document. I believe you'll find everything in order."

I took the paper. There were bullet points, charts, and some references at the bottom. "What am I looking at here?"

DuBois pointed somewhere at the middle of the page. "I would like to die by nitrogen asphyxiation. All my research shows it is among the least painful ways to die."

I nodded and took some notes.

"That paper includes a list of the equipment I will need to ensure my death. It's well within my personal-item mass allowance."

I furrowed my brow, mostly to hide the fact that I had no idea what to say.

He folded his hands on his lap. "It's a simple matter of a nitrogen tank and a universal connector to the EVA suit. I can wear the suit and have it pump in nitrogen instead of oxygen. The suffocation reflex comes from excess carbon dioxide in the lungs, not lack of oxygen. The suit's systems will continuously remove the carbon dioxide that I exhale, leaving only nitrogen behind. I will simply get tired and perhaps a bit lightheaded. Then I will lose consciousness."

"All right." I tried to remain professional. "How about if the EVA suit isn't available?"

"Subsection four details the backup plan. If I cannot use the EVA suit, I will use the ship's airlock. The volume of the airlock will be sufficient to ensure the carbon-dioxide buildup isn't unpleasant."

"Okay." I wrote a few more notes down. Though I hardly had to. His paper was very thorough. "We'll make sure there's a tank with plenty of nitrogen, and a backup tank as well just in case the first one leaks."

"Excellent. Thank you."

I set the paper aside. "Ilyukhina? How about you?"

She set her beer down. "I want heroin."

Everyone looked at her. Even Yáo blanched a little.

"Sorry, what?" I said.

"Heroin." She shrugged. "I have been good girl all my life. No drugs. Limited sex. I want to experience massive pleasure before I die. People die from heroin all the time. Must be very nice."

I rubbed my temples. "You want to die . . . from a heroin overdose?"

"Not immediately," she said. "I want to enjoy. Start with normal effective dose. Get high. Addicts all agree first few uses are best. Then downhill from there. I want to feel those first few doses. Then overdose when time is right."

"I guess . . . we can do that," I said. "Death by overdose can be really unpleasant, though."

She waved the concern away. "Have doctors work out best dose schedule for me. Correct amount to maximize pleasantness on earlier doses. Then lethal dose can have other drugs inside to make sure I die without pain."

I wrote down her request. "Okay. Heroin. I don't know where we'll get it, but we'll work it out."

"You have entire world working for you," she said. "Get pharma company to make me heroin. Cannot be hard."

"Right. I'm sure Stratt can make a call or something."

I sighed. Two down, one to go. "All right. Commander Yáo? How about you?"

"I want a gun, please," he said. "A Type-92 handgun. Standard Chinese military-issue. Store the ammunition in a dry, sealed plastic container for the trip."

At least that made some sense. Quick and painless. "A gun. Got it. That's easy enough."

He looked back and forth to his crewmates. "I will be the last to die. If anything goes wrong with either of your methods, I will be on-hand with the weapon. Just in case."

"Very considerate," said DuBois. "Thank you."

"Don't shoot me if I look like I'm having a good time," Ilyukhina said.

"Understood," said Yáo. He turned back to me. "Will that be all?"

"Yeah," I said, already standing. "This has been very awkward, thanks. I'm going to . . . go be somewhere else now."

I writhe in my bed. The burns on my arm hurt more than ever. The painkillers barely do anything. I'm beginning to wonder if I can find Ilyukhina's heroin.

I won't, I won't. But I definitely *would* if this were still a suicide mission.

Focus on that. This is no longer a suicide mission. If I play my cards right, I save the world *and* go home.

The pain subsides somewhat. It comes and goes. When I get a chance, I'll take a look at whatever books I have on burns. I'd at least like to know when it'll stop hurting.

Tap.

"Huh?" I mumble.

Tap.

I look at the source of the noise. It's Rocky tapping on the airlock wall.

"Rocky!" I fall out of my bunk and roll onto my right side before landing. I scrabble along the floor to the airlock wall. "Rocky, buddy! Are you okay?!"

I hear a low thrum from within him.

"I don't understand. Speak louder."

"Sick . . ." he mumbles.

"Yeah, you're sick. You came into my air. Of course you're sick! You almost died!"

He tries to lift himself from the floor, then slumps back down. *"How I return here, question?"*

"I moved you."

He taps the ground with a claw, annoyed. *"You touch me air, question?"*

"A little, yeah."

He points to my left arm. *"Skin on arm is not smooth. Damage, question?"*

I guess he can see right through the bandages with his sonar. Must be pretty ugly under there. I kind of figured that would be the case, but now I know. "Yeah. But I'll be fine."

"You damage self to save me. Thank."

"You did the same thing. Is your radiator organ okay? You were on fire and got full of soot and oxides."

"It healing." He points to the soot all along the wall and floor. *"This come from inside me, question?"*

"Yes."

"How it leave me, question?"

I preen a little. Why shouldn't I? It was no easy task and I got it done. I point to the now-triply-covered steel box on the airlock wall. "I made a device to blow air at you. I aimed at your radiator vents and all that nasty stuff came out."

He's quiet for a moment. Then, still a little wobbly, he says, *"How long was that stuff inside me, question?"*

I run through the day in my mind. "About . . . two days."

"You almost kill me."

"What?! How?! I blew all the soot out of your radiator!"

He shifts his weight a little. *"Black substance is not soot. My body make this. It cover damage while body repairs."*

"Oh . . ." I say. "Oh no . . ."

I didn't blow soot out of his radiator. I blew the scabs off his wounds! "I'm so sorry! I was trying to help."

"Is okay. If you did earlier I die. But I heal enough before you do it. Removing help a little. Thank."

I put my head in my hands. "Sorry," I say again.

"No say sorry. You save me when you put me here. Thank thank thank." He tries to stand again, but only rises for a second before collapsing. *"I am weak. I will heal."*

I step back and sit on my bunk. "Would you be more comfortable in zero g? I can turn off the centrifuge."

"No. Gravity help heal." He adjusts his legs into sort of a bed for his carapace to rest on. Probably a comfortable sleeping pose. *"Sample container is safe, question?"*

"Yes. It's in the lab now. I made an Adrian environment in a sealed container and put some Astrophage in along with the sample container. I'll see how it's doing in a bit."

"Good," he says. *"Human light sense very useful."*

"Thanks," I say. "But my human brain wasn't as useful. I don't have a way to get the sample out of the container."

He tilts his carapace slightly. *"You seal sample and can no access sample, question?"*

"Yes."

"Usually you not stupid. Why stupid, question?"

"Humans are stupid when we need sleep. And when we take medicine to stop pain. I'm tired and drugged right now."

"You should sleep."

I stand up. "I will in a bit. But first I have to stabilize our orbit. Our apogee and perigee are . . . well, it's not a good orbit."

"Adjust orbit while stupid. Good plan."

I snicker. "New word: 'sarcasm.' You say opposite of true meaning to make point. Sarcasm."

He chimes the word for "sarcasm" in his language.

Between exhaustion and drugs, I sleep like a baby. I wake up feeling a million times better, but my burns feel a million times worse. I look at the bandages. They're new.

Rocky is at his workbench, tinkering with his tools. He's cleaned up his area. It looks good as new. *"You are awake, question?"*

"Yeah," I say. "How are you feeling? Are you healing?"

He wiggles a claw. *"Much more heal needed. But some heal complete. Cannot move much."*

I plop my head back on the pillow. "Same."

"Robot arms do things to you arm while you sleep."

I point to the bandages. "It changed the cloth. It's important for human healing to change the cloth."

He pokes at his latest invention with various tools.

"What's that?"

"I go to lab to see device that store Adrian life. I made device now to collect sample from inside and not let you air in." He holds up a large box. *"Put you vacuum chamber in this. Close this. This make Adrian air inside."*

He opens the top and points to a couple of hinged rods. *"Control these from outside. Gather sample. Seal you device. Open my device. Have sample. Do human science with sample."*

"Smart," I say. "Thanks."

He gets back to work.

I lie in my bunk. There are a bunch of things I want to do, but I need to take it slow. I can't risk another "stupid day" like yesterday. I almost ruined the sample and killed Rocky. I'm smart enough now to know I'm stupid. That's progress.

"Computer: coffee!"

After a minute, the arms hand me a cup of java.

"Hey," I say, sipping my coffee. "How come you and I hear the same sounds?"

He keeps working on the armatures inside his device. *"Useful trait. Both evolve. Not surprising."*

"Yeah, but why the same frequencies? Why don't you hear much higher frequencies than I can? Or much lower?"

"I do hear much higher frequency and much lower frequency."

Didn't know that. But I should have figured that was the case. It's an Eridian's primary sensory input. Of course he'll have a wider range than I do. That still leaves one unanswered question, though.

"Okay, but why is there overlap? Why don't you and I hear completely different frequency ranges?"

He puts the tool in one of his hands down, which leaves two hands still plugging away on his device. With the newly free hand, he scrapes his workbench. *"You hear this, question?"*

"Yes."

"That is sound of predator approaching you. That is sound of prey running away. Sound of object touching object very important. Evolve to hear."

"Ah! Yes."

It's obvious now that he points it out. Voices, instruments, bird-calls, whatever—they can all be wildly different sounds. But the sound of objects colliding isn't going to have much variance from planet to planet. If I bang two rocks together on Earth, they're going to make the same noise as if I bang them together on Erid. So we're all selected-for by being able to hear it.

"Better question," he says. *"Why we think same speed, question?"*

I shift over to lie on my side. "We don't think at the same speed. You do math way faster than I can. And you can remember things perfectly. Humans can't do that. Eridians are smarter."

He grabs a new tool with his free hand and gets back to tinkering. *"Math is not thinking. Math is procedure. Memory is not thinking. Memory is storage. Thinking is thinking. Problem, solution. You and me think same speed. Why, question?"*

"Hmm."

I ponder it for a while. It's a really good question. How come Rocky isn't a thousand times smarter than me? Or a thousand times dumber?

"Well . . . I have a theory for why we're about the same intelligence. Maybe."

"Explain."

"Intelligence evolves to gives us an advantage over the other animals on our planet. But evolution is lazy. Once a problem is solved, the trait stops evolving. So you and me, we're both just intelligent enough to be smarter than our planet's other animals."

"We are much much smarter than animals."

"We're as smart as evolution made us. So we're the minimum intelligence needed to ensure we can dominate our planets."

He thinks it over. *"I accept this. Still not explain why Earth intelligence evolve same level as Erid intelligence."*

"Our intelligence is based on the animals' intelligences. So what is animal intelligence based on? How smart do animals have to be?"

"Smart enough to identify threat or prey in time to act."

"Yes, exactly!" I say. "But how long is that time? How long does an animal have to react? How long will the threat or prey take to kill the animal or escape? I think it's based on gravity."

"Gravity, question?" He sets the device down entirely. I've got his undivided attention.

"Yeah! Think about it. Gravity is what determines how fast an animal can run. Higher gravity, more time spent in contact with the ground. Faster movement. I think animal intelligence, ultimately, has to be faster than gravity."

"Interesting theory," Rocky says. *"But Erid have double Earth gravity. You and I same intelligence."*

I sit up on my bed. "I bet our gravities are so close to the same, astronomically, that the intelligence needed is almost the same. If we met a creature from a planet with one one-hundredth of Earth's gravity, I bet it would seem pretty stupid to us."

"Possible," he says. He gets back to work on his gadget. *"Another similarity: You and me both willing to die for our people. Why, question? Evolution hate death."*

"It's good for the species," I say. "A self-sacrifice instinct makes the species as a whole more likely to continue."

"Not all Eridians willing to die for others."

I chuckle. "Not all humans either."

"You and me are good people," Rocky says.

"Yeah." I smile. "I suppose we are."

Nine days until launch.

I paced around my room. It was pretty bare, but I didn't mind. The portable unit was a small mobile home complete with a kitchenette.

Better than most people got. The Russians had their hands full erecting dozens of temporary shelters a few miles from Baikonur Cosmodrome. But then, I guess we all had our hands full lately.

Anyway, I'd barely used my bed since we'd arrived. There just always seemed to be some new issue or problem. Nothing major. Just . . . issues.

The *Hail Mary* was complete. Over 2 million kilograms of spacecraft and fuel in a nice, stable orbit—four times the mass of the International Space Station, and put together in one-twentieth the time. The press used to keep track of the total cost, but around the $10 trillion mark, they gave up. It just didn't matter. It wasn't about efficient use of resources anymore. It was Earth versus Astrophage, and no price was too high.

ESA astronauts had been on the ship for the past few weeks, putting it through its paces. The test crew reported about five hundred problems that we'd been mopping up for the past few weeks. None of them were showstoppers.

This was happening. The *Hail Mary* was going to launch in nine days.

I sat at the table that served as my desk and shuffled through papers. I signed off on some and set others aside for Stratt to look at tomorrow. How did I end up an administrator? We all had to accept changes to our lives, I guess. If this was my part to play, then so be it.

I set the papers down and looked out the window. The Kazakhstani steppes were flat and featureless. People generally don't build launch facilities next to anything important. For obvious reasons.

I missed my kids.

Dozens of them. Hundreds, really, over the course of a school year.

They didn't swear at me or wake me up in the middle of the night. Their squabbles were usually resolved within a few minutes, either by a teacher-enforced handshake or detention. And, somewhat selfish, but here it is: They looked up to me. I missed being that respected.

I sighed.

My kids would have a rough time even if the mission worked. It would take thirteen years for the *Hail Mary* to get to Tau Ceti, and (presuming the crew found an answer to our problems) another thirteen years for the beetles to get back to us. That's over a quarter century before we would even know what to do. My kids wouldn't be kids anymore when it was over.

"Onward," I mumbled, and grabbed the next problem report. Why was it on paper instead of just an email? Because Russians do things a certain way and it's easier to work with them than to complain about it.

The report was from the ESA crew about anomalies in Slurry Pump Fourteen of the medical feeding transport system. Pump Fourteen was only part of the tertiary system and it was still 95 percent effective. But there was no reason to put up with that. We still had 83 kilograms of unclaimed launch mass. I made a note to include a spare slurry pump—it was only 250 grams. The crew could install it before leaving orbit.

I set the paper aside and saw a brief flash out my window. Probably a jeep driving on the dirt road that led to the temporary shelters. I got headlights through my window from time to time. I ignored it.

The next paper in my stack was all about potential ballast issues. The *Hail Mary* kept its center of mass along its long axis by pumping Astrophage around as needed. But we still wanted to keep things as balanced as possible anyway. The ESA crew had rearranged several supply bags in the storage compartment to more adequately balance—

The window shattered as a deafening explosion shook the room. Glass shards nicked my face as a shockwave knocked me clean out of my chair.

After that: silence.

And then: sirens in the distance.

I got to my knees, and then to my feet. I opened and closed my mouth a few times to pop my ears.

I stumbled to the door and opened it. The first thing I noticed was that the small triplet of steps that once led to my door were several feet away. Then I saw the freshly disturbed earth between the steps and my door and I understood what happened.

The steps are anchored into the ground with four-by-fours sunk deep like fence posts. My portable has no such support.

My whole house moved and the stairs stayed put.

"Grace?! Are you okay?!" It was Stratt's voice. Her portable was next to mine.

"Yeah!" I say. "What the heck was that?!"

"I don't know," she said. "Hang on."

Shortly after, I saw the bobbing of a flashlight. She came to me, wearing a bathrobe and boots. She was already on her walkie-talkie. *"Eto Stratt. Chto sluchylos'?"* she demanded.

"Vzryv v issledovatel'skom tsentre," came the reply.

"The research center blew up," she said.

Baikonur was a launch facility, but they did have some research buildings. They weren't laboratories. They were more like classrooms. Astronauts generally spent a week before launch at Baikonur, and they usually wanted to study and prepare right up to launch day.

"Oh God," I said. "Who was there? Who was there?!"

She pulled a wad of papers from her robe pocket. "Hang on, hang on . . ." She rifled through the papers, throwing each to the ground as she moved on to the next. I knew what they were at a glance—I'd been seeing them every day for a year. Schedule charts. Showing where everyone was and what they were doing at all times.

She stopped when she reached the page she was looking for. She actually gasped. "DuBois and Shapiro. They're scheduled to be there doing some Astrophage experiments."

I put my hands on my head. "No! No, please no! The research center is five kilometers away. If the blast did this much damage to us here—"

"I know, I know!" She flicked on her walkie-talkie again. "Prime crew—I need your locations. Call them in."

"Yáo here," came the first reply. "In my bunk."

"Ilyukhina here. At officers' bar. What was that explosion?"

Stratt and I waited for the response we hoped would come.

"DuBois," she said. "DuBois! Check in!"

Silence.

"Shapiro. Dr. Annie Shapiro. Check in!"

More silence.

She took a deep breath and let it out. She clicked the walkie-talkie on one more time. "Stratt to transport—I need a jeep to take me to Ground Control."

"Copy," came the reply.

The next few hours were, frankly, chaos. The entire base was put on lockdown for a while and everyone's ID was checked. For all we knew, some doomsday cult wanted to sabotage the mission. But nothing turned up amiss.

Stratt, Dimitri, and I sat in the bunker. Why were we in a bunker? The Russians were taking no chances. It didn't look like a terrorist attack, but they were securing the critical personnel just in case. Yáo and Ilyukhina were off in some other bunker. The other science leads were in other bunkers as well. Spread everyone out so there's no single place to attack that would be effective. There was a grim logic to it. Baikonur was built during the Cold War, after all.

"The research buildings are a crater," said Stratt. "And there's still no sign of DuBois or Shapiro. Or the fourteen other staff that worked there."

She pulled up pictures on her phone and showed them to us.

The photos told a story of utter destruction. The area was lit up with powerful floodlights the Russians had set up and the place was swarming with rescue personnel. Though there was nothing for them to do.

Virtually nothing was left. No debris, limited wreckage. Stratt swiped through photo after photo. Some were close-ups of the ground. Round, shiny beads dotted the area. "What's up with the beads?" she said.

"Metal condensate," Dimitri said. "It means metals were vaporized, then condensed like raindrops."

"Jesus," she said.

I sighed. "There's only one thing in those labs that could create enough heat to vaporize metal: Astrophage."

"I agree," said Dimitri. "But Astrophage does not just 'explode.' How could this happen?"

Stratt looked at her wrinkled schedule pages. "According to this, DuBois wanted more experience with Astrophage-powered electrical generators. Shapiro was there to observe and assist."

"That makes no sense," I said. "Those generators use a tiny, tiny bit of Astrophage to make electricity. Nowhere near enough to blow up a building."

She put her phone down. "We've lost our primary and secondary science specialists."

"This is nightmare," said Dimitri.

"Dr. Grace. I want a short list of possible replacements."

I stared with my mouth agape. "Are you made of stone or something?! Our friends just died!"

"Yes, and everyone else will die, too, if we don't make this mission happen. We have nine days to find a replacement science specialist."

I well up. "DuBois . . . Shapiro . . ." I snuffled and wiped my eyes. "They're dead. They're *dead* . . . oh God . . ."

Stratt slapped me. "Snap out of it!"

"Hey!"

"Cry later! Mission first! You still have that list of coma-resistant candidates from last year? Start looking through it. We need a new science specialist. And we need them *now*!"

"Gathering sample now . . ." I say.

Rocky watches me from his tunnel in the lab ceiling. His device works just as it should. The clear xenonite box has a couple of valves and pumps that let me control the inside environment. The vacuum chamber is inside with its lid open. The box even has climate control, keeping the inside temperature a chilly minus 51 degrees Celsius.

Rocky admonished me for leaving the sample at (human) room temperature for so long. He had a lot to say on that subject, actually. We had to add "reckless," "idiot," "foolish," and "irresponsible" to our shared vocabulary just so he could fully express his opinion on the matter.

There was another word he threw around a lot, but he declined to tell me what it meant.

Three days off the painkillers and I'm a lot smarter than I was. At least he understands that much—I wasn't just some stupid human. I was a human with *enhanced* stupidity.

Rocky refused to give me the box I'm using until I slept three times without using the drugs. My arm hurts so bad right now, but he's got a point.

Rocky healed a fair bit in that time too. I have no idea what's going on inside his body. He looks the same as ever, but he's moving around much better than before. Not full-speed, though. Neither am I. We're the walking wounded, honestly.

By agreement, we've kept the gravity at one-half g.

I open and close the claws in the box a few times. "Look at me. I'm an Eridian now."

"Yes. Very Eridian. Hurry and get sample."

"You're no fun." I grab the cotton swab and bring it to a waiting glass slide. I rub it across the slide, leaving a noticeable smear, then return it to the vacuum chamber. I seal up the chamber, put the slide in a little clear xenonite container, and seal the box.

"Okay. That should do it." I turn the valves to let my air in, then open the box from above. The slide is safe in its xenonite container. The galaxy's smallest little spaceship. At least, from the point of view of any Adrian life that may be present.

I walk to the microscope station.

Rocky follows along in the tunnel above. *"You certain you can see light so small, question?"*

"Yes. Old technology. Very old." I put the container on the tray and adjust the lenses. The xenonite is plenty clear enough for the microscope to see through.

"Okay, Adrian, what do you have for me?" I put my face to the eyepieces.

The most obvious thing is the Astrophage. As usual, they're jet-black, absorbing all light. That's expected. I adjust the backlight and focus. And I see microbes everywhere.

One of my favorite experiments with the kids is to have them look at a drop of water. A drop of water, preferably one from a puddle outside, will be swarming with life. It always goes over well, except for the occasional kid who then refuses to drink water for a while.

"Lots of life in here," I say. "Different kinds."

"Good. Expected."

Of course there would be. Any planet that has life will have it everywhere. That's my theory, at least. Evolution is extremely good at filling every nook in the ecosystem.

Right now I'm looking at hundreds of unique life-forms, never before seen by humans. Each one an alien race. I can't help but smile. Still, I have work to do.

I pan around until I find a nice clump of Astrophage. If there's a predator to be had, it'll be where the Astrophage is. Otherwise it'd be a pretty bad predator.

I flick on the microscope's internal camera. The image appears on a little LCD screen. I adjust the screen and set it recording.

"This could take time," I say. "Need to see interaction between—*whoa!*"

I shove my face back to the microscope to get a better look. It only took seconds before the Astrophage fell under attack. Am I incredibly lucky, or is this life-form just that aggressive?

Rocky skittered back and forth above me. *"What, question? What happen, question?"*

The monster lurches toward the clump of Astrophage. It's an amorphous blob, like an amoeba. It presses itself against its much-smaller prey and begins to envelop the entire clump of them by oozing around both sides.

The Astrophage wriggle. They know something is wrong. They try to escape but it's too late. They can only sputter a short distance before they stop. Normally, Astrophage can accelerate to near light speed in seconds, but these can't. Maybe a chemical excretion by the monster that disables them somehow?

The encirclement completes, and the Astrophage are surrounded. A few seconds later, the Astrophage become cell-like in appearance. No longer featureless black, their organelles and membranes are starkly visible in the microscope's light. They have lost their ability to absorb heat and light energy.

They're dead.

"Got it!" I say. "I found the predator! It ate Astrophage right in front of me!"

"Found!" Rocky cheers. *"Isolate."*

"Yes, I'll isolate it!" I say.

"Happy happy happy!" he says. *"Now you name."*

I grab a nano-pipette from the supply. "I don't follow."

"Earth culture. You find. You name. What is name of predator, question?"

"Oh," I say. I'm not feeling creative at the moment. This is too exciting to take my attention away from. It's an amoeba from Tau Ceti. "Taumoeba, I guess."

Taumoeba. The savior of Earth and Erid.

Hopefully.

I should have a bolo tie. Maybe a cowboy hat. Because I'm a rancher now. And I'm running about 50 million head of Taumoeba on my ranch.

Once I isolated a few Taumoeba from the Adrian air sample, Rocky built a breeder tank and we let them get to work. It's just a xenonite box full of Adrian air and a few hundred grams of Astrophage.

As far as we can tell, Taumoeba is very resilient to temperature variations. Good thing, too, because I let it sit at room temperature that one day.

Drugs are bad.

In retrospect, it makes sense that they'd be robust on temperature. They live in a negative-51-degree-Celsius environment, and eat Astrophage, which is always 96.415 degrees Celsius. Hey, everyone likes a hot meal, right?

And boy, do they breed! Well, I gave them a mother lode of Astrophage to work with. It's the same as throwing yeast into a bottle of sugar water. But instead of making booze, we're making more Taumoebas. Now that we have enough to experiment with, I get to work.

If you take a goat and put it on Mars, what happens? It dies immediately (and horribly). Goats didn't evolve to live on Mars. Okay, so what happens if you put a Taumoeba on a planet other than Adrian?

That's what I want to find out.

Rocky watches from his tunnel above the main worktable as I simulate a fresh new atmosphere in my vacuum chamber.

"No have oxygen, question?" he asked.

"No oxygen."

"Oxygen dangerous." He's been a little edgy since his internal organs caught fire.

"I breathe oxygen. It's okay."

"Can explode."

I pull my goggles off and look up at him. "There's no oxygen in this experiment. Calm down."

"Yes. Calm."

I get back to work. I turn a valve to let a small bit of gas into the vacuum chamber. I check the pressure gauge to make sure that—

"Again confirm: No oxygen, question?"

I jerk my head up to glare at him. "It's just carbon dioxide and nitrogen! Only carbon dioxide and nitrogen! Nothing more! Don't ask me again!"

"Yes. No ask again. Sorry."

Can't blame him, I guess. Being on fire sucks.

We have two planets to deal with here. No, not Earth and Erid. Those are just the planets we live on. The planets we care about right now are Venus and Threeworld. That's where Astrophage is breeding out of control.

Venus, of course, is the second planet in my solar system. It's about Earth's size with a thick carbon-dioxide atmosphere.

Threeworld is the third planet in Rocky's home system. At least, Threeworld is what I call it. The Eridians don't have a name for it, even in their own language. Just a designation: "Planet Three." They didn't have ancient people looking up at astronomical bodies and naming them after gods. They only discovered other planets in their system a few hundred years ago. But I don't want to say "Planet Three" all the time, so I've named it Threeworld.

The hardest part about working with aliens and saving humanity from extinction is constantly having to come up with names for stuff.

Threeworld is a tiny little planet—only about the size of Earth's moon. But unlike our airless neighbor, Threeworld somehow has an atmosphere. How? I have no idea. The surface gravity is only 0.2 g's, which shouldn't be enough. Yet somehow, Threeworld manages to hang on to a thin atmosphere. According to Rocky, it's 84 percent carbon dioxide, 8 percent nitrogen, 4 percent sulfur dioxide, and a bunch of trace gases. All with a surface pressure less than 1 percent of Earth's.

I check the readouts and nod approvingly. I do a visual inspection of the experiment inside. I'm pretty proud of myself for this idea.

A thin coat of Astrophage sits on a glass plate. I coated the plate by shining IR light through the glass and attracting Astrophage from the other side. It's the same way the spin drive does it. The result is a uniform layer of Astrophage that's just one cell thick.

Then I seeded the slide with Taumoeba. As they eat the Astrophage, the currently opaque slide will become more and more transparent. It's a hell of a lot easier to measure light level than a quantity of microscopic organisms.

"Okay . . . the chamber has Venus's upper atmosphere duplicated. As good as I can, anyway."

I figure the breeding zone of Astrophage is based mainly on the air pressure. Basically, they have to aero-brake from near light speed when they hit the planet. But being so small that doesn't take very long and of course they gobble up all the heat that's created.

The end result is that Astrophage come to rest when the air is 0.02 atmospheres thick. So, going forward, that'll be our standard for pressure. Venus's atmosphere is 0.02 atmospheres at around the 70 kilometer mark, and the temperature there is about minus 100 degrees Celsius (thanks, infinite supply of reference material!). So that's the temperature I have the Venus analog experiment set to. Rocky's temperature-control system works perfectly, of course, even down to ultra-low temperatures.

"Good. Now Threeworld."

"What temperature is Threeworld's air at the 0.02 atmosphere altitude?"

"Minus eighty-two degrees of Celsius."

"Okay, thanks," I say. I move to the next chamber. It has an identical setup of Astrophage and Taumoeba. I let in the appropriate gases to simulate Threeworld's atmosphere and temperature at the 0.02-atmosphere pressure area. I get the relevant information from Rocky's perfect memory. It's not much different from Venus or Adrian. Mostly carbon dioxide with some other gases running around. No surprise there—Astrophage go for the biggest concentration of CO_2 they can see.

It's a good thing these planets aren't covered in helium or something. I don't have any of that aboard. But carbon dioxide? That's easy. I make that stuff with my body. And nitrogen? Thanks to DuBois and his preferred method of death, there's a whole bunch aboard.

Threeworld does have some sulfur dioxide, though. Four percent of the total atmosphere. It's enough that I didn't want to approximate it away, so I had to make some. The lab has quite a selection of reagents, but no sulfur dioxide gas. However, it does have sulfuric acid in solution. I recovered some copper tubing from a broken cooling coil in the freezer and used it as a catalyst. Worked like a charm to create the sulfur dioxide I needed.

"Okay, Threeworld's done," I say. "We'll wait an hour and check results."

"We have hope," says Rocky.

"Yes, we have hope," I say. "Taumoeba are very sturdy. They can live in a near vacuum, and they seem comfortable in extreme cold. Maybe Venus and Threeworld are habitable for them. They're good enough for Taumoeba's prey, so why not for Taumoeba?"

"Yes. Things are good. All is good!"

"Yeah. For once, everything's going great."

Then the lights go out.

CHAPTER 22

Total darkness.

No lights. No monitor glow. Not even the LEDs on the lab equipment.

"Okay, stay calm," I say. "Stay calm."

"Why not be calm, question?" Rocky asks.

Well, of course he didn't notice the lights go out. He doesn't have eyes. "The ship just shut down. Everything stopped working."

Rocky scuttles a bit in his tunnel. *"You equipment quiet now. My equipment still working."*

"Your equipment gets electricity from your generator. Mine's powered by my ship. All the lights are off. There's nothing working at all!"

"This is bad, question?"

"Yes, it's bad! Among other problems, I can't see!"

"Why ship turn off, question?"

"I don't know," I say. "Do you have a light? Something you can shine through the xenonite into my side?"

"No. Why would I have light, question?"

I bungle in the darkness, feeling my way around the lab. "Where's the ladder to the control room?"

"Left. More left. Continue . . . yes . . . reach forward . . ."

I get my hand on a rung. "Thanks."

"Amaze. Humans helpless without light."

"Yes," I say. "Come to the control room."

"Yes." I hear him skitter through his tunnel.

I climb up and it's just as dark. The entire control room is dead. The monitors are off. Even the airlock window provides no relief—that part of the ship happens to be facing away from Tau Ceti at the moment.

"Control room also have no light, question?" says Rocky's voice—presumably from his bulb in the ceiling.

"Nothing—wait . . . I see something. . . ."

Off in one corner of one panel, there's a small red LED. Definitely glowing, though not very bright. I sit in the pilot's seat and squint at the control. The seat wobbles a bit. My repair job on it was subpar, but it's anchored back to the floor again, at least.

Instead of the usual flat-panel displays found all over the control room, this one little section has physical buttons and an LCD display nearby. The light is coming from a button.

Obviously, I push it. What else would I do?

The LCD display comes to life. Some highly pixelated text appears, stating: PRIMARY GENERATOR: OFFLINE. SECONDARY GENERATOR: OFFLINE. EMERGENCY BATTERIES: 100%.

"Okay, how do I use the batteries . . . ?" I mumble.

"Progress, question?"

"Hang on." I peer all around the LCD panel until I finally spot it. A little switch, covered by a plastic safety shield. It's labeled "Batt." It'll have to do. I lift the shield and flick it.

Dim LEDs light up the control room—nowhere near as nicely as the normal lights do. The smallest control screen—and only that screen—comes to life. The *Hail Mary* mission patch shows on the center of the screen and the words "Loading Operating System . . ." appear at the bottom.

"Partial success," I say. "My emergency battery engaged. But my generators are offline."

"Why no work, question?"

"I don't know."

"You air is okay, question? No power, no life support. Humans turn oxygen into carbon dioxide. You will use all oxygen and become harmed, question?"

"It's okay," I say. "The ship's pretty big. It'll take a long time for the air to be a problem. It's more important that I find the cause of this failure."

"Machines break. Show me. I fix."

Not a bad idea, actually. Rocky seems to be able to do pretty much anything. Either he's gifted, or all Eridians are like that. Either way, I'm incredibly lucky. Still . . . how well would he do working on human technology?

"Maybe. But first I need to figure out why two generators would both die at the same time."

"Good question. More important: Can you control ship without power, question?"

"No. I need power to do anything."

"Then, most important: How long until orbit decays, question?"

I blink a couple of times. "I . . . don't know."

"Work fast."

"Yeah." I point at the screen. "First I have to wait for my computer to wake up."

"Hurry."

"Okay, I'll wait faster."

"Sarcasm."

The computer finishes its boot process and brings up a screen I've never seen before. I can tell it means trouble, because the word "TROUBLE" is in large type across the top.

Gone are the pleasant user-interface buttons and widgets from before the blackout. This screen is just three columns of white text on a black background. The left is all Chinese characters, the middle is Russian, and the right is English.

I guess under normal operation, the ship changes language based on who is reading the screen. And this "safe boot"–equivalent screen doesn't know who will be reading it so it's in all our languages.

"What is happen, question?"

"This screen came up with information."

"What is wrong, question?"

"Let me read!"

Rocky can be a real pain in the butt when he's worried. I read the status report.

EMERGENCY POWER: ONLINE

BATTERY: 100%

ESTIMATED TIME REMAINING: 04D, 16H, 17M

SABATIER LIFE SUPPORT: OFFLINE

CHEMICAL ABSORPTION LIFE SUPPORT: ONLINE. !!!LIMITED DURATION, NON-RENEWABLE!!!

TEMPERATURE CONTROL: OFFLINE

TEMPERATURE: 22°C

PRESSURE: 40,071 PA

"The ship's keeping me alive, but not doing anything else right now."

"Give me generator. I fix."

"First I need to find it," I say.

Rocky slumps. *"You not know where you ship parts are, question?!"*

"The computer has all that information! I can't remember all that!"

"Human brain useless!"

"Oh, shut up!"

I climb down the ladder to the lab. The emergency lighting is on in here too. Rocky follows along in his tunnel.

I reach down, grab my tool bag, and continue onward to the next ladder. He continues following me.

"Where you go, question?"

"The storage area. It's the only place I haven't completely searched. And it's the very bottom of the crew compartment. If the generator is accessible to the crew, that's where it'll be."

Once in the dormitory, I crawl into the storage space. My arm hurts. I climb around to inspect the bulkhead with the fuel bay. My arm hurts more.

At this point, my arm just always hurts, so I try to ignore it. But no more painkillers. They just make me too stupid. I lie back in the storage compartment and let the pain subside a bit. There must be access panels in here, right? I can't remember the exact layout of the ship, but critical equipment is probably inside the pressurized area. For this very reason. Right?

How do I find it, though? I'd need x-ray vision to know where—oh, hey!

"Rocky! Are there any doors in here?"

He is silent for a moment. He taps on the wall a few times. *"Six small doors."*

"Six?! Ugh. Tell me where the first one is." I put my hand on the compartment ceiling.

"Move hand toward your feet and left . . ."

I follow his directions to the first door. Man, they're hard to see. The emergency lighting in the dormitory is meager to start with, and the small amount getting into the compartment is dismal.

The panel is secured with a simple flat-head screw that controls a latch. I turn it with a stub screwdriver from my toolkit. The panel swings open to reveal a pipe with a valve on it. The label reads PRIMARY OXYGEN SHUTOFF. Definitely don't want to mess with that. I close the cabinet.

"Next door."

One by one, he leads me to each door and I check what's behind it. I know he can sonar-sense the shapes behind the doors but that's no good. I'd rather just look at what's there than have him describe what he senses in our limited shared language.

Behind the fourth door, I find it.

It's a lot smaller than I expect it to be. The whole cubby is about 1 cubic foot. The generator itself is in an irregularly shaped black casing and I only know it's a generator because it's labeled as such. I see two thick pipes with shutoff valves on them, as well as several fairly normal-looking electrical wires.

"Found it," I say.

"Good," comes Rocky's voice from the dormitory. *"Take out and give to me."*

"I want to look at it first."

"You bad at this. I fix."

"The generator might not survive your environment!"

"Mmm," he grumbles.

"If I can't fix it, you can talk me through it."

"Mmm."

The two pipes with shutoff valves must be the Astrophage supply lines. I look a little deeper into the cubby and find labels. One is "fuel" and the other is "waste." Clear enough.

I use a wrench to unscrew the hose bib on the "waste" line. As soon as it comes loose, a dark liquid drips out. Not much—just what was between the shutoff valve and my end of the hose. It must be whatever fluid we use to carry away dead Astrophage. I got some on my hand—it feels slimy. Maybe it's oil. It's a good idea, actually. Any liquid will do, oil is lighter than water, and it won't corrode the pipes.

Next I unscrew the "fuel" line. It, too, sloshes brown liquid out. But this time, it smells awful.

I wince and bury my face in my arm. "Ugh! God!"

"What is problem, question?" Rocky calls out from below.

"The fuel smells bad," I say. Eridians don't have a sense of smell. But while it took a long time to explain sight to Rocky, smell was easy. Because Eridians do have a sense of taste. When you get down to it, smell is just tasting at range.

"Is natural smell or chemical smell, question?"

I take another halting sniff. "Smells like rotted food. Astrophage doesn't normally smell bad. It doesn't normally have an odor at all."

"Astrophage is alive. Maybe Astrophage can rot."

"Astrophage can't rot," I say. "How could it rot—OH NO! OH GOD NO!"

I wipe my hand across the foul-smelling gunk, then wriggle out of the compartment. Then, keeping my gunky hand in the air and not touching anything, I climb up the ladder to the lab.

Rocky clatters along in his tunnel. *"What is wrong, question?"*

"No, no, no, no . . ." I say with a squeak at the end. My heart is about to beat right out of my throat. I think I'm going to puke.

I smear some gunk onto a glass slide and shove the slide into the microscope. There's no power for the backlight, so I grab a flashlight from the drawer and shine it at the plate. It'll have to do.

I look through the eyepieces and my worst fears are realized. "Oh God."

"What is problem, question?!" Rocky's voice is a full octave higher than normal.

I grab my head with both hands, smearing foul gunk on myself but I don't even care. "Taumoeba. There are Taumoeba in the generator."

"They damage generator, question?" Rocky says. *"Give me generator. I fix."*

"The generator isn't broken," I say. "If there are Taumoeba in the generator, it means there are Taumoeba in the fuel supply. Taumoeba ate all the Astrophage. We have no power because we have no fuel."

Rocky raises his carapace so fast he clunks it against the roof of his tunnel. *"How Taumoeba get into fuel, question?!"*

"There are Taumoeba in my lab. I didn't keep them sealed off. I didn't think to. Some probably got loose. The ship has a bunch of cracks, holes, and leaks ever since we almost died at Adrian. Some small hole in a fuel line somewhere must have let Taumoeba in. It only takes one."

"Bad! Bad bad bad!"

I start to hyperventilate. "We're dead in space. We're stuck here forever."

"Not forever," Rocky says.

I perk up. "No?"

"No. Orbit decay soon. Then we die."

I spend the whole next day examining the fuel lines I can get to. It's the same story everywhere. Instead of Astrophage suspended in oil, it's Taumoeba and (let's call it what it is) a lot of Taumoeba poop. Mostly methane with a bunch of other trace compounds. I guess that explains the methane in Adrian's atmosphere. Circle of life and all that.

There's some live Astrophage here and there, but with the overwhelming population of Taumoeba in the fuel they won't live long. It's pointless to try to salvage this. It'd be the same as trying to separate good meat from the botulism infecting it.

"Hopeless," I say, slamming the latest fuel sample onto the lab table. "The Taumoeba is everywhere."

"I have Astrophage on my side of partition," Rocky says. *"Approximately two hundred sixteen grams remaining."*

"That wouldn't power my spin drive for long. Thirty seconds or so. And it probably wouldn't live long enough. There's Taumoeba everywhere on my side of the partition. Keep your Astrophage safe on your side."

"I make new engine," Rocky says. *"Taumoeba turn Astrophage into methane. React with oxygen. Make fire. Make thrust. Get to my ship. Much Astrophage there."*

"That's . . . not a bad idea." I pinch my chin. "Use Taumoeba farts to propel ourselves through space."

"No understand word after Taumoeba."

"It's not important. Hang on, let me do the math. . . ."

I pull up a tablet—the computer screen in the lab is still offline. I don't remember the specific impulse of methane, but I do know that a hydrogen-oxygen reaction is about 450 seconds. Call that the best-case scenario. I had 20,000 kilograms of Astrophage, so pretend that's all methane now. The ship has a dry mass around 100,000 kilograms. I don't know if I even have enough oxygen for this reaction, but ignore that for now. . . .

Concentration is a constant struggle. I'm groggy and I know it.

I type away on the calculator app, then shake my head. "It's no good. The ship would get less than 800 meters per second velocity. We can't escape Adrian's gravity with that, let alone cross 150 million kilometers of the Tau Ceti system."

"Bad."

I drop the tablet on the table and rub my eyes. "Yes. Bad."

He clicks along his tunnel to hover above me. *"Give me generator."*

I slump my shoulders. "Why? What good would it do?"

"I clean and sterilize. Remove all Taumoeba. I make tiny fuel tank with my Astrophage. Seal generator airtight. Give back to you. You hook up to ship. Power restored."

I rub my aching arm. "Yeah. It's a good idea. If the generator doesn't melt in your air."

"If melt, I fix."

A few hundred grams of Astrophage isn't enough to fly around the galaxy, but it's more than enough to power the ship's electrical system for . . . I don't know . . . the rest of my life at least.

"Okay. Yeah. That's a good idea. At least we'll have the ship back online."

"Yes."

I trudge to the hatch. "I'll get the generator."

I really shouldn't be using tools in my state, but I press on. I go back to the dormitory, get into the crawlspace, and detach the generator. Or maybe it's the backup generator. I don't know. In any event, it turns Astrophage into electricity and that's the point.

I get back into the dormitory proper and put the generator in our airlock there. Rocky cycles the airlock and brings the generator to his workbench. Two claws get to work on it right away. A third points to my bunk. *"I work on this now. You sleep."*

"Make sure you don't get Taumoeba in your Astrophage over there!"

"My Astrophage in sealed xenonite container. Is safe. You sleep now."

Everything aches, especially my bandaged arm. "I can't sleep."

He points more firmly. *"You tell me humans need to sleep eight hours every sixteen hours. You no sleep for thirty-one hours. You sleep now."*

I sit on my bunk and sigh. "You make a good point. I should at least try. It's been a hard day. Night. Whatever. A hard day's night." I lie back in the bunk and pull the blanket over me.

"That sentence make no sense."

"It's an Earth saying. From a song." I close my eyes and mumble. ". . . and I've been working like a dog . . ."

A moment passes while I drift off . . .

"Whoa!" I shoot bolt-upright. "The beetles!"

Rocky is surprised enough to drop the generator. *"What is problem, question?"*

"Not a problem! A solution!" I leap to my feet. "The beetles! My ship has four smaller ships aboard called beetles! They're made to take information back to Earth!"

"You tell me this before," Rocky says. *"But they use same fuel, correct? Astrophage all dead now."*

I shake my head. "They use Astrophage, yeah, but each beetle is self-contained and sealed. They don't share air, fuel, or anything else with *Hail Mary*. And each beetle has 120 kilograms of fuel aboard! We have plenty of Astrophage!"

Rocky waves his arms in the air. *"Enough to get us to my ship! Good news! Good good good!"*

I wave my arms in the air too. "Maybe we won't die here after all! I need to do an EVA to get beetles. I'll be right back." I hop off the bunk and head to the ladder.

"No!" Rocky says. He skitters over to the partition and taps the divider. *"You sleep. Human no function well after no sleep. EVA dangerous. Sleep first. EVA next."*

I roll my eyes. "All right, all right."

He points back to my bunk. *"Sleep."*

"Yes, *Mom.*"

"Sarcasm. You sleep. I watch."

"This doesn't seem like a good idea anymore," I say into my radio.

"Do task," Rocky replies mercilessly.

I slept well and woke up ready to face the day. I had a nice breakfast. I got some stretches in. Rocky presented me with a sealed, fully functional generator that will last basically forever. I installed it and got the ship's power back on without a hitch.

Rocky and I chatted about the best way to use the beetles to get back to the *Blip-A*. Everything seemed like a good idea until just this moment.

I stand in the airlock, all suited up for an EVA, looking out onto the vast nothingness of space. Planet Adrian reflects its pale-green light at me, illuminating the ship. Then it drifts off out of view. I'm in darkness. But not for long. Because the planet shows up again in the top of my vision twelve seconds later.

The *Hail Mary* is still spinning. That's kind of a problem.

The ship has little Astrophage-powered thrusters on the sides to spin up and spin down for the artificial gravity. They don't work, of course. They're full of Taumoeba poo just like everything else. So here I am on *another* EVA that has to deal with gravity. But instead of Adrian's gravity, it's centripetal force threatening to fling me off into the void.

One death is as good as another. So why is this worse than my little Adrian sampler adventure? Because this time I have to balance on the nose of the ship. One false move could lead to death.

When I got the sampler, I stayed close to the hull, kept well tethered, and had lots of handholds all around just in case I lost my footing.

But the beetles are stored in the nose of the ship.

The nose is oriented toward the other half of the ship, thanks to the way the centrifuge system works. That puts the beetles at the "top" of the crew compartment from the point of view of the centripetal gravity. I have to get up there, open the nose, and get the little ships out. All while hoping I don't slip. There are no tether points at the nose. So I'll have to clip on to a point lower down. Which means if I fall, I'll have time to pick up a good head of steam before the tether goes taut. Will it hold? If not, the force of the centrifuge will fling me off into space and I'll become Adrian's newest moon.

I quadruple-check the tethers. I ran two of them, just for safety. They're firmly anchored to a hard point in the airlock and also to my suit. They should be able to handle the force if I fall.

"Should."

I step out, grab the top of the airlock, and pull myself upward. I'd never be able to do this with all my gear on at full gravity.

The angle of the nose cone is shallow enough that I don't slide off. I check the tethers again, then crawl up the nose toward the top. The centrifuge action shoves me to the side as I go. I have to stop every couple of feet and let friction with the hull zero out my lateral motion.

"Status, question?"

"Making progress," I say.

"Good."

I reach the nose. The artificial gravity is weakest here, being closest to the center of rotation. That's a nice little benefit.

The universe lazily revolves around me every twenty-five seconds. For half the time, Adrian fills my entire view below. Then I get a few seconds of Tau Ceti's burning brightness. Then nothing. It's a little disconcerting but not too bad. Just mildly annoying.

The beetle hatch is just where it should be. I'm going to have to be careful here. I don't want to damage anything.

This was all designed to be a suicide mission. They didn't care about the *Hail Mary* getting home. The mechanism inside has pyros to blow off this hatch. Then the beetles can launch and find their way back to Earth. Good system, but I need this hatch intact for when I go home. It's all for the aerodynamics.

Yes, aerodynamics.

The *Hail Mary* has always looked like something out of a Heinlein novel. Shiny silver, smooth hull, sharp nose cone. Why do all that for a ship that'll never have to deal with an atmosphere?

Because of the interstellar medium. There's a teeny, tiny amount of hydrogen and helium wandering around out there in space. It's on the order of one atom per cubic centimeter, but when you're traveling near the speed of light, that adds up. Not only because you're hitting a whole bunch of atoms but also because those atoms, from your inertial reference frame, weigh more than normal. Relativistic physics is weird.

Long story short: I need the nose intact.

The entire panel and pyro assembly is attached to the hull with six hex bolts. I pull a socket wrench from my tool belt and get to work.

As soon as I unscrew the first bolt, it slides down the slope of the nose cone and falls away into the unknowable distance.

"Um . . ." I say. "Rocky, you can make screws, right?"

"Yes. Easy. Why, question?"

"I dropped one."

"Hold screws better."

"How?"

"Use hand."

"My hand's busy with the wrench."

"Use second hand."

"My other hand's on the hull to keep me steady."

"Use third han—hmm. Get beetles. I make new screws."

"Okay."

I get to work on the second bolt. This time I'm very careful. I stop using the wrench halfway through and do the rest by hand. The fat fingers of the EVA suit are awful for this. It takes ten minutes just for this one bolt. But I get it done and, most important, I don't drop it.

I put it in a pouch on my suit. Now Rocky will know what I need him to duplicate.

I unscrew the next four bolts with the wrench and let them fall away. I suppose they'll be in orbit around Adrian for a while, but not forever. The tiny amount of drag we're getting up here will slow them down bit by bit until they fall into Adrian's atmosphere and burn up.

One bolt remains. But first, I lift up the opposite corner of the assembly enough to make a finger-width gap. I slip a tether in through a vacant bolt hole and clip it to itself. Then I clip the other end of the tether to my belt. Now I have four different tethers attached to me. And I like it that way. I may look like space Spider-Man, but who cares?

I still have two more tethers coiled on my tool belt ready to go if needed. There's no such thing as too much tether.

I unscrew the final bolt and the assembly slides down the nose. I let it past me and it halts at the end of the tether. It bounces a few times and knocks into the hull, then sways.

I look into the compartment. The beetles are right where they're supposed to be, each in their own cubbies. The four little ships are identical except for a small engraved name on each bulbous little fuel bay. They're labeled "John," "Paul," "George," and "Ringo," of course.

"Status, question?"

"Recovering beetles."

I start with John. A little clamp holds it in place, but I easily force it open. Behind the probe is a compressed air cylinder with a nozzle pointed outward. That's how they're supposed to be launched. They'd need to be far away from the ship before they start up their spin drives. Even an adorable little baby spin drive will vaporize anything behind it.

John comes out pretty easily. The probe is bigger than I remember—almost the size of a suitcase. Of course, everything seems bigger when you're holding it on an EVA with awkward gloves.

Ol' John weighs a lot too. I don't know if I could even lift it in

Earth's gravity. I tie it off to the backup tether, then reach in to get Paul.

Rocky can work fast when he needs to. And he needs to.

We're in a questionable orbit around Adrian. Now that the computers and guidance systems are all back online, I can see the orbit. It's not pretty. Our orbit is still highly elliptical, and the closest part of it is way too close to the planet.

Every ninety minutes, we touch the tippy-tippy-top of the atmosphere. It's barely an atmosphere at that altitude. Just a few confused air molecules bouncing around. But it's enough to slow us down just a teeny, tiny bit. That slowdown makes us dip a little deeper into the atmosphere on the next pass. You can see where this is going.

We scrape the atmosphere every ninety minutes. And I honestly don't know how many times we can get away with it. For some reason, the computer doesn't have models for "oddly elliptical orbits around the planet Adrian."

So yeah. Rocky is in a hurry.

It takes him just two hours to disassemble Paul and understand most of how he works. This was no easy task—before we passed Paul into Rocky's area of the ship, we had to make a special "cooling box." The beetles have plastic parts inside that would melt in Rocky's air. A big lump of Astrophage took care of that. Astrophage may be too hot for humans to touch, but it's cool enough that plastic won't melt, and of course it has no problem absorbing the extra heat and keeping things at 96 degrees Celsius.

Paul has a lot of electronics and circuitry inside. Rocky doesn't follow that too well—Eridian electronics isn't nearly so advanced as Earth's. They haven't invented the transistor yet, let alone IC chips. Working with Rocky is like having the world's best engineer from 1950 on the ship with me.

Seems odd that a species could invent interstellar travel before inventing the transistor, but hey, Earth invented nuclear power, television, and even did several space launches before the transistor.

An hour later, he's bypassed all the computer controls. He doesn't need to understand them to bypass them—it's just a matter of knowing what wires to directly apply voltage to. He jerry-rigged the spin drive to be activated by an audio-driven remote control. Pretty much everywhere humans use radio for short-range digital communication, Eridians use sound.

He repeats the process for Ringo and John. This time it's much faster, because there's no research effort. That leaves George unmodified. The little beetles don't have much thrust, so the more of them we use the better, but I have to draw a line somewhere. I want to keep one safely in reserve, unmodified, ready to fulfill its original mission.

Thanks to Rocky, I might just survive this suicide mission, but there are no guarantees. The *Hail Mary* is in bad shape, to say the least. Several fuel tanks are gone, there's damage and leaks all over the place. There are Taumoeba sneaking around waiting to eat whatever replacement fuel Rocky gives me. I can count at least a hundred ways the trip home might fail. So, before I set out, I'm going to send George on his way with all my findings and some Taumoeba aboard. I would much rather have kept two in reserve, but we need three beetles to be able to vector the thrust so we can angle the ship whatever direction we need.

Rocky passes the three modified beetles through the dormitory airlock to my side.

"You mount on hull," he says. *"Aim forty-five degrees out away from centerline of ship."*

"Understand." I sigh. Another EVA on a spinning ship. Yay.

But what else can I do? We can't zero the rotation without thrust.

I do the EVA. The only hard part is getting to the right place. The airlock is near the nose, and I need to mount the beetles on the rear section. And the ship is currently divided into two halves connected by nothing but five cables. But the designers of the *Hail Mary* thought of this. There are loops all along the cables that you can attach a tether to.

I'm getting better at the extremely odd skill set of EVAs in nonzero gravity. And unlike my death dance on the nose of the ship, the rear has lots of handles. Mounting the beetles is easy enough. I attach them to handles on the hull to immobilize them while Rocky's xenonite glue sets and makes a permanent bond.

In the end, I have John, Paul, and Ringo evenly spaced in a ring around the hull, each one angled so their engine points 45 degrees away from the long axis of the ship.

"Beetles set," I say into my radio. "Inspecting damaged area."

"Good," Rocky replies.

I make my way to the spot that was ruined by the fuel-tank rupture. There isn't much to see—I jettisoned the bad tanks at the time. A rectangle of missing hull plates shows an opening where the tanks once were. The area surrounding the hole tells a tale of trauma. Black scorch marks mar the otherwise shiny hull plates. There's clear and obvious warping on two of the neighboring panels.

"Some panels are bent. Some have burn marks. Not too bad."

"Good news."

"Burn marks are odd, don't you think? Why burn marks?"

"Much heat."

"Yeah, but no oxygen. This is space. How did it burn?"

"Theory: Many Astrophage in tanks. Some probably dead. Dead Astrophage have water. Dead Astrophage not immune to heat. Water and much much heat become hydrogen and oxygen. Oxygen and heat and hull becomes burn marks."

"Yeah," I say. "Good theory."

"Thank."

I get back across the space rope bridge that is the cabling, then inside the airlock without incident. Rocky waits for me in his ceiling bulb in the control room.

"All is well, question?"

"Yes," I say. "Controls for John, Paul, and Ringo are good?"

He holds identical control boxes in three of his hands. Each has a wire leading to a wall-mounted speaker/microphone attached to the hull. He taps a readout box with a fourth hand. *"Communication established. All beetles function and ready."*

I strap myself into the command chair. This next bit is going to be uncomfortable.

We put the beetles at 45-degree angles from the ship centerline so we can use them to angle the ship as needed. It also lets us control the ship's rotation. But we can only use the beetles when the ship is in one piece. So first I have to pull the halves together.

Conservation of rotational inertia being what it is, that means the ship is going to spin really fast. In fact, it'll spin exactly as fast as it was when Rocky had to save me last time. We haven't gained or lost any inertia in that time.

I bring up the Centrifuge panel on the main control screen. Well, it's just above the original main screen. That main screen got wrecked in the Adrian adventure. But this one's good enough.

"You are ready?"

"Yes."

"The g-forces will be strong," I say. "Easy for you, but hard for me. I might fall unconscious."

"Unhealthy for human, question?" There's a hint of quaver at the end.

"A little unhealthy. If I pass out, don't worry. Just get the ship stable. I'll wake when we stop spinning."

"Understand." Rocky holds the three controls at the ready.

"Okay, here goes." I put the centrifuge into manual mode and bypass three warning dialogs. First, I rotate the crew compartment 180 degrees. Just like last time, I take it slow. But unlike last time, I have everything battened down. So as the world turns around and gravity changes directions, the lab and dormitory aren't thrown into disarray.

Now I feel half a g pushing me toward the control panels. The nose is facing away from the rest of the ship again. I order all four spools to spool in without regard to ship rotation rate. The icons on the ship show the contraction as ordered and the force of my body into the restraints increases.

After just ten seconds, the forces are at 6 g's and I can barely breathe. I gasp and squirm.

"You are not healthy!" Rocky squeaks. *"Undo this. We make new plan."*

I can't speak, so I shake my head. I feel the skin of my face stretch away from my cheeks. I must look like a monster right now. The periphery of my vision fades to black. This must be the tunnel vision I've heard about. It's a good name.

The tunnel gets dimmer and dimmer until eventually it's all black.

I wake up moments later. At least, I think it's moments later. My arms float freely and only my restraints keep me from drifting out of my chair.

"Grace! You are okay, question?"

"Uh." I rub my eyes. My vision's blurry and I'm still groggy. "Yeah. Status?"

"Rotation rate is zero," he says. *"Beetles hard to control. Correction: Beetles easy to control. Ship powered by beetles hard to control."*

"You got it done, though. Good job."

"Thank."

I release my restraints and stretch out. Nothing seems to be broken or wounded other than my burned arm from before. It actually feels great to be back in zero g. I'm achy everywhere as a rule. Lots of physical labor and I'm still recovering from injuries. Getting that pesky gravity out of the way puts less stress on my body.

I cycle through screens on the monitor. "All systems are okay. At least, nothing's damaged further than before."

"Good. What is next action, question?"

"Now I do math. A whole lot of math. I have to calculate the thrust duration and angle to get us back to your ship using the beetles as engines."

"Good."

CHAPTER 23

I came to the meeting on time. At least, I thought I did. The email said 12:30. But when I got there, everyone was already seated. And silent. And they were all staring at me.

For the time being, we had a media blackout about the accident. The whole world was watching this project—their only hope for salvation. The last thing we needed was for people to know the primary and backup science specialists were dead. Say what you will about the Russians, they know how to keep a secret. All of Baikonur was on lockdown.

The meeting room, a simple trailer the Russians had supplied, had a great view of the launch pad. I could see the Soyuz through the window. Old technology, to be sure, but easily the most reliable launch system ever made.

Stratt and I hadn't spoken since the night of the explosion. She suddenly had to head up an ad-hoc disaster inquiry. It couldn't wait until later—if the accident was caused by some procedure or equipment that was going to be on the mission, we needed to know. I wanted to be involved but she wouldn't let me. Someone had to keep dealing with various minor *Hail Mary* issues being reported by the ESA team.

Stratt stared right at me. Dimitri fiddled with some papers—

probably a design for a spin-drive improvement. Dr. Lokken, the fiery Norwegian who designed the centrifuge, drummed her fingers on the table. Dr. Lamai wore her lab coat as always. Her team had perfected a fully automated medical robot and she'd probably be in line for a Nobel Prize someday. If Earth lived that long. Even Steve Hatch, the crazy Canadian who invented the beetle probes, was present. He, at least, didn't look awkward. He just typed away on a calculator. He didn't have papers in front of him. Just the calculator.

Also present were Commander Yáo and Engineer Ilyukhina. Yáo looked dour as ever, and Ilyukhina had no drink in her hand.

"Am I late?" I asked.

"No, you're just in time," Stratt said. "Have a seat."

I sat in the only empty chair.

"We think we know what happened at the research center," Stratt began. "The whole building is gone, but all their records were electronic and stored on a server that handles all of Baikonur. Fortunately, that server is in the Ground Control Building. Also, DuBois—being DuBois—kept meticulous notes."

She pulled out a paper. "According to his digital diary, his plan for yesterday was to test an extremely rare failure case that could happen in an Astrophage-powered generator."

Ilyukhina shook her head. "Should have been me testing this. I am responsible for ship maintenance. DuBois should have asked me."

"What was he testing, exactly?" I asked.

Lokken cleared her throat. "One month ago, JAXA discovered a possible failure state for the generator. It uses Astrophage to make heat, which in turn powers a small turbine with state-change material. Old, reliable technology. It runs on a tiny amount of Astrophage—just twenty individual cells at a time."

"That seems pretty safe," I said.

"It is. But if the moderator system on the generator's pump fails, *and* there's an unusually dense clump of Astrophage in the fuel line right at that moment, up to one nanogram of Astrophage could be put into the reaction chamber."

"What would that do?"

"Nothing. Because the generator also controls the amount of IR light shined on the Astrophage. If the chamber temperature gets too high, the IR lights turn off to let Astrophage calm down. Safe backup system. But there is a possible edge case, extremely unlikely, that a short in this system could make the IR lights turn on at full power and bypass the temperature safety interlock entirely. DuBois wanted to test this very, very unlikely scenario."

"So what did he do?"

Lokken paused and her lip wobbled a bit. She steeled herself and pressed on. "He got a replica generator—one of the ones we use for ground testing. He modified the feed pump and IR lights to force that crazy edge case to happen. He wanted to activate an entire nanogram of Astrophage at once and see how it damaged the generator."

"Wait," I said. "One nanogram isn't enough to blow up a building. At worst it could melt a little bit of metal."

"Yeah," said Lokken. She took a deep breath and let it out slowly. "So you know how we store tiny quantities of Astrophage, right?"

"Sure," I said. "In little plastic containers suspended in propylene glycol."

She nodded. "When DuBois requisitioned one *nanogram* of Astrophage from the research center's quartermaster, they gave him one *milligram* by mistake. And since the containers are the same and the quantities are so small, he and Shapiro had no way of knowing."

"Oh God." I rubbed my eyes. "That's literally a million times the heat-energy release than they were expecting. It vaporized the building and everyone in it. God."

Stratt shuffled her papers. "The simple truth is this: We just don't have the procedures or experience to manage Astrophage safely. If you asked for a firecracker and someone gave you a truck full of plastic explosive, you'd know something was wrong. But the difference between a nanogram and a milligram? Humans just can't tell."

We were all silent for a moment. She was right. We'd been playing around with Hiroshima-bomb levels of energy like it was nothing. In any other scenario it would have been madness. But we didn't have a choice.

"So are we going to delay the launch?" I asked.

"No, we've talked it over and we all agree: We can't delay the *Hail Mary*'s departure. It's assembled, tested, fueled, and ready to go."

"It is the orbit," Dimitri said. "It is in tight orbit at 51.6 degrees' inclination so Cape Canaveral and Baikonur can get at it easy. But is also in shallow orbit which is decaying. If it does not set out within next three weeks, we have to send entire mission up just to re-boost it to higher orbit."

"The *Hail Mary* will leave on schedule," said Stratt. "Five days from now. The crew will have two days of preflight checks, so that means the Soyuz has to launch in three days."

"Okay," I said. "What about the science expert? I'm sure we have hundreds of volunteers all over the world. We can give the selectee a crash course in the science they'll need to know—"

"The decision's been made," Stratt said. "Really, the decision made itself. There's no time to train a specialist in everything they need to know. There's just too much information and research to learn. Even the most brilliant scientists wouldn't be able to glean all of it in just three days. And remember, only about one in seven thousand people have the gene combination to be coma-resistant."

Right around then I got a sinking feeling. "I think I see where this is going."

"As I'm sure you know by now, your tests came up positive. You are that one in seven thousand."

"Welcome to crew!" Ilyukhina said.

"Wait, wait. No." I shook my head. "This is insane. Sure, I'm up to speed on Astrophage, but I don't know *anything* about being an astronaut."

"We will train you as we go." Yáo spoke quietly, but with confidence. "And we will do the hard tasks. You will be utilized only for science."

"I just mean . . . come on! There has to be someone else!" I looked to Stratt. "What about Yáo's backup? Or Ilyukhina's?"

"They're not biologists," said Stratt. "They're incredibly skilled people with a nose-to-tail expertise on the *Hail Mary,* its operations, and how to repair damage. But we can't train someone in all the cellular biology they need to know in the time we have. It would be like asking the world's best structural engineer to do brain surgery. It's just not their field."

"What about other candidates on the list? The ones that didn't make the original cut?"

"There's no one as qualified as you. Frankly, we're lucky—lucky beyond our wildest dreams—that you happen to be coma-resistant. Do you think I kept you on the project for so long because I needed a junior high schoolteacher around?"

"Oh . . ." I said.

"You know how the ship works," Stratt continued. "You know the science behind Astrophage. You know how to use an EVA suit and all the specialized gear. You've been present for every major scientific or strategic discussion we've had about the ship and its mission—I made sure of it. You have the genes we need, so I made *damn* sure you had the skills we need. God knows I didn't want it to come to this, but here we are. You've been the tertiary science specialist all along."

"N-No, that can't be right," I said. "There's got to be other people. Much more talented scientists. And, you know, people who actually *want* to go. You must have made a list, right? Who's the next candidate after me?"

Stratt picked up a piece of paper in front of her. "Andrea Cáceres, a distillery worker from Paraguay. She's coma-resistant, and holds a bachelor's degree in chemistry with a minor in cellular biology. And she volunteered for the mission back during the first call for astronauts."

"Sounds great," I said. "Let's give her a call."

"But you've had years of direct training. You know the ship and the mission inside and out. And you're a world-leading expert on Astrophage. We'd only have a few days to get Cáceres up to speed. You know how I operate, Dr. Grace. More than anyone else. I want to give *Hail Mary* every possible advantage. And right now, that's you."

I looked down at the table. "But I . . . I don't want to die. . . ."

"Nobody does," said Stratt.

"It must be your decision," said Yáo. "I will not have someone on my crew who is there against their will. You must come of your own volition. And if you refuse, we will bring in Ms. Cáceres and do our best to train her up. But I urge you to say yes. Billions of lives are on the line. Our lives matter little when compared against such tragedy."

I put my head in my hands. The tears started to come. Why did this have to happen to me? "Can I think about it?"

"Yes," Stratt said. "But not for very long. If you say no, we have to get Cáceres here in a hurry. I want your answer by five P.M. tonight."

I stood and shuffled out of the room. I don't think I even said goodbye. It's a dark and depressing feeling to have all your closest colleagues get together and decide you should die.

I checked my watch—12:38 P.M. I had four and a half hours to decide.

The spin drives of the *Hail Mary* are incredibly overpowered for its current mass. When we left Earth, the ship weighed 2.1 million kilograms—most of it being fuel. Now the ship only weighs 120,000 kilograms. About one-twentieth its departure weight.

Thanks to the *Hail Mary*'s relatively low mass, the scrappy little beetles are able to collectively give me 1.5 g's of thrust. Except that the ship wasn't designed to have a bunch of thrust coming in at 45-degree-angle force pushing arbitrary EVA handles on the hull. If we fire up the beetles at full power, they'll just rip free of the handles and ride off into the Tauset.

Rocky was mindful of that when he zeroed out our rotation. Now we have that under control and I can do EVAs in zero g like God intended. I 3-D print a model of the *Hail Mary*'s internal skeleton and give it to Rocky for his perusal. In under an hour, he not only has a solution but has fabricated the xenonite struts to implement it.

So I do another EVA. I add the xenonite supports to the beetles. For once, everything goes according to plan. Rocky assures me that the ship can now handle full thrust from the beetles and I don't doubt him for a second. The guy knows engineering.

I type in a bunch of calculations into a complicated Excel spreadsheet that's probably got errors in it somewhere. It takes me six hours to put together. I finally come up with what I think is the right answer. At least, it should put us close enough that we can see the *Blip-A*. Then we can fine-tune our vectors from there.

"Ready?" I say from the pilot seat.

"Ready," Rocky says in his bulb. He holds the three control boxes in his hands.

"Okay . . . John and Paul to 4.5 percent."

"John and Paul, 4.5 percent, confirmed," he says.

Sure, Rocky could have made controls for me to use, but this is better. I have to watch the screen closely and pay attention to our vectors. Best to have someone give their full attention to the beetles. Besides, Rocky's a ship's engineer. Who better to run our makeshift engines?

"John and Paul to zero. Ringo to 1.1 percent," I say.

"John and Paul zero. Ringo 1.1."

We make numerous tweaks to the thrust vectors bit by bit to angle the ship roughly the direction I want. We finally achieve what I hope is the right direction.

"Here goes nothing," I say. "All ahead full!"

"John, Paul, Ringo 100 percent."

I'm thrown back into my seat as the ship lurches forward, with 1.5 g's of gravity taking over as we accelerate in a straight line (maybe) toward the *Blip-A* (hopefully).

"Maintain thrust for three hours," I say.

"Three hours. I watch engines. You relax."

"Thanks, but no time for rest. Want to use gravity while I can."

"I stay here. Tell me how experiments go."

"Will do."

I'm shooting for another eleven-day transfer. It takes 130 kilograms of fuel to make that happen—about a quarter of what the beetles have aboard (if you include George, who is sitting on the lab table full of Astrophage). That should give us enough left over to correct whatever idiotic mistakes I made in my trajectory math.

We'll get up to cruising speed in three hours, then we'll coast for most of eleven days. I don't want to deal with spinning up or spinning down the centrifuge. Yes, it can be done—Rocky proved it when he zeroed us out before. But it was a delicate process with lots of guessing and opportunities for spinning out of control. Or worse—getting the cables tangled up.

So, for the next three hours I have 1.5 g's to work with. After that it'll be zero g for a while. Time to hit the lab.

I climb down the ladder. My arm hurts. But less than it has. I've been changing the bandages every day—or rather, Dr. Lamai's medical marvel machine has been doing it. There's definitely scarring all over the skin. I'm going to have an ugly arm and shoulder for the rest of my life. But I think the deeper layers of skin must have survived. If they hadn't, I probably would have died of gangrene by now. Or Lamai's machine would have amputated my arm when I wasn't looking.

It's been a while since I had to deal with1.5 g's. My legs don't approve. But I'm used to this sort of complaint at this point.

I walk to the main lab table, where the Taumoeba experiments are still in progress. Every part of them is firmly mounted to the table. Just in case we have more unexpected adventures in acceleration. Of course, it's not like I'm short on Taumoeba. I have a bunch of them *where my fuel used to be.*

I check the Venus experiment first. The cooling mechanism whirs slightly, keeping the inside temperature correct for Venus's extreme upper atmosphere. I originally intended to let the Taumoeba in there incubate for only an hour, but then the lights went off and we had other priorities. So now it's been four days. If nothing else, they've had plenty of time to do their thing.

I gulp. This is an important moment. The small glass slide inside had a one-cell-thick layer of Astrophage. If the Taumoeba are alive and dining on Astrophage, light will be able to get through. The more light I see through that slide, the fewer Astrophage are still alive on it.

I steel myself, take a deep breath, and look inside.

Jet-black.

My breathing becomes unsteady. I fish a flashlight out of my pocket and shine it from behind. No light gets through at all. My heart sinks.

I sidestep over to the Threeworld Taumoeba experiment. I take a look at the slide in there and see the same thing. Completely black.

Taumoeba can't survive Venus or Threeworld's environment. Or, at the very least, they aren't eating. The pit of my stomach feels like it's going to melt.

So close! We were so close! We have the answer right here! Taumoeba! A natural predator to the thing that's ruining our worlds! And it's hearty too. It can survive and thrive in my fuel tanks, obviously. But not in Venus or Threeworld's air. Why the heck not?!

"What you see, question?" Rocky asks.

"Failure," I say. "Both experiments. The Taumoeba are all dead."

I hear Rocky punch the wall. *"Anger!"*

"All this work! All of it for nothing. Nothing!" I slam my fist to the table. "I gave up so much for this! I sacrificed so much!"

I hear Rocky's carapace clunk to the ground in his bulb. A sign of deep depression.

We're both quiet for a time; Rocky slumped in his bulb and me with my face buried in my hands.

Finally, I hear a scrape. It's Rocky pulling his carapace off the floor. *"We work more,"* he says. *"We no give up. We work hard. We are brave."*

"Yeah, I guess so."

I'm not the right guy for this job. I'm a last-second replacement because the actually qualified people blew up. But I'm here. I may not have all the answers, but I'm here. I must have volunteered, believing at the time that it was a suicide mission. Doesn't help Earth, but it's something.

Stratt's trailer was twice the size of mine. Privileges of rank, I suppose. Though to be fair, she needed the space. She sat at a large table covered in papers. I could see at least six different languages in four different alphabets on the paperwork before her, but she didn't seem to have a problem with any of them.

A Russian soldier stood in one corner of the room. Not exactly at attention, but not relaxed either. There was a chair next to him, but he'd apparently elected to stand.

"Hello, Dr. Grace," Stratt said without looking up. She pointed to the soldier. "That's Private Meknikov. Even though we know the explosion was an accident, the Russians aren't taking any chances."

I looked to the soldier. "So he's here to make sure imaginary terrorists don't kill you?"

"Something like that." She looked up. "So. It's five o'clock. Have you made your decision? Are you going to be the *Hail Mary*'s science specialist?"

I sat opposite her. I couldn't meet her gaze. "No."

She scowled at me. "I see."

"It's . . . you know . . . the kids. I should stay here for the kids." I squirmed in my seat. "Even if the *Hail Mary* finds the answer, we're going to have almost thirty years of misery."

"Uh-huh," she said.

"And, um, well, I'm a teacher. I should teach. We need to raise a strong, solid generation of survivors. Right now we're soft. You, me, the whole Western world. We're the result of growing up in unprecedented comfort and stability. It's the kids of today that'll have to make the world of tomorrow work. And they're going to inherit a mess. I can really do a lot more by preparing kids for the world that's to come. I should stay here on Earth where I'm needed."

"On Earth," she repeated. "Where you're needed."

"Y-Yeah."

"As opposed to on the *Hail Mary,* where you could be instrumental in solving the entire problem because you're completely trained for the task."

"It's not like that," I said. "I mean. It's a little like that. But look, I'm no good on a crew. I'm not some intrepid explorer."

"Oh, I know," she said. She clenched her fist and looked to the side for a moment. Then back to me with a burning gaze I'd never seen before. "Dr. Grace. You're a coward and you're full of shit."

I winced.

"If you really cared so much about the children, you'd get on that ship without hesitation. You could save billions of them from the apocalypse instead of preparing hundreds of them for it."

I shook my head. "It's not about that—"

"Do you think I don't know you, Dr. Grace?!" she yelled. "You're a coward and you always have been. You abandoned a promising scientific career because people didn't like a paper you wrote. You retreated to the safety of children who worship you for being the cool teacher. You don't have a romantic partner in your life because that would mean you might suffer heartbreak. You avoid risk like the plague."

I stood up. "Okay, it's true! I'm afraid! I don't want to die! I worked my ass off on this project and I deserve to live! I'm *not* going, and that's final! Get the next person on the list—that Paraguayan chemist. She *wants* to go!"

She slammed her fist on the table. "I don't care who *wants* to go. I care who's most qualified! Dr. Grace, I'm sorry, but you are *going* on that mission. I know you're afraid. I know you don't want to die. But you're going."

"You're out of your darn mind. I'm leaving now." I turned to the door.

"Meknikov!" she shouted.

The soldier deftly stepped between me and the door.

I turned back to her. "You have got to be kidding."

"It would have been easier if you'd just said yes."

"What's your plan?" I jerked a thumb at the soldier. "Hold me at gunpoint for four years during the trip?"

"You'll be in a coma during the trip."

I tried to dart past Meknikov, but he stopped me with arms of iron. He wasn't rough about it. He was just monumentally stronger than I was. He held me by the shoulders and faced me toward Stratt.

"This is crazy!" I yelled. "Yáo will never go for this! He specifically said he doesn't want anyone on his ship against their will!"

"Yeah, that was a curveball. He is annoyingly honorable," Stratt said.

She picked up a checklist that she'd written in Dutch. "First, you're to be held in a cell for the next few days until the launch. You'll have no communication with anyone. Right before launch, you'll be given a very strong sedative to knock you out and we'll load you into the Soyuz."

"Don't you think Yáo will be a little suspicious about that?"

"I'll explain to Commander Yáo and Specialist Ilyukhina that, due to limited astronaut training, you were worried that you'd panic during the launch so you elected to be unconscious for it. Once aboard the *Hail Mary*, Yáo and Ilyukhina will secure you into your medical bed and start your coma procedure. They'll take care of all the prelaunch prep from there. You'll wake up at Tau Ceti."

The first seeds of panic started to grow. This lunacy might actually work. "No! You can't do that! I won't do it! This is insane!"

She rubbed her eyes. "Believe it or not, Dr. Grace, I kind of like you. I don't respect you very much, but I do think you're a fundamentally good man."

"Easy for you to say when you're not the one being murdered! You're *murdering* me!" Tears rolled down my face. "I don't want to die! Don't send me off to die! Please!"

She looked pained. "I don't like this any more than you do, Dr. Grace. If it's any consolation, you'll be hailed as a hero. If Earth survives this, there'll be statues of you all over the place."

"I won't do it!" I choked on bile. "I'll sabotage the mission! You kill me?! Fine! I'll kill your mission! I'll scuttle the ship!"

She shook her head. "No, you won't. That's a bluff. Like I said, you're fundamentally a good man. When you wake up, you'll be good and angry. I'm sure Yáo and Ilyukhina will be pretty mad about what I did to you too. But in the end, you three will be out there and you'll do your job. Because humanity depends on it. I'm ninety-nine percent sure you'll do the right thing."

"Try me!" I screamed. "Go on! Try me! See what happens!"

"But I can't rely on ninety-nine percent, can I?" She glanced at her paper again. "I always assumed the American CIA would have the best interrogation drugs. But did you know it's actually the French? It's true. Their DGSE has perfected a drug that causes retrograde amnesia that lasts for long periods of time. Not just hours or days, but weeks. They used it during various anti-terror operations. It can be handy for a suspect to forget he was ever interrogated."

I stared at her in horror. My throat hurt from yelling.

"Your med bed will give you a nice dose of it before you wake up. You and your crewmates will just assume it's a side effect of the coma. Yáo and Ilyukhina will explain the mission to you and you'll roll right into getting to work. The French assure me the drug doesn't erase trained skills, language, or anything like that. By the time your amnesia wears off, you guys might have already sent the beetles back. And if not, my guess is you'll be too far invested in the project to give up."

She nodded to Meknikov. He dragged me out the door and frog-walked me down the path.

I craned my neck back toward the door and screamed, "You can't do this!"

"Just think of the kids, Grace," she said from the doorway. "All those kids you'll be saving. Think of them."

CHAPTER 24

Oh.

Okay.

I see how it is.

I'm not some intrepid explorer who nobly sacrificed his life to save Earth. I'm a terrified man who had to be literally dragged kicking and screaming onto the mission.

I'm a coward.

All that came to me in a flash. I sit on the stool and stare at the lab table. I went from nearly hysterical to . . . this. This is worse. I'm numb.

I'm a coward.

I've known for a while that I'm not the best hope for saving mankind. I'm just a guy with the genes to survive a coma. I made my peace with that a while ago.

But I didn't know I was a coward.

I remember the emotions. I remember that feeling of panic. I remember it all now. Sheer, unadulterated terror. Not for Earth or humanity or the children. For myself. Utter panic.

"God damn you, Stratt," I mumble.

What ticks me off the most is that she was right. Her plan worked perfectly. I got my memory back, and now I'm so committed to the mission I'm still going to give it my all. Plus, come on, of course I was going to give it my all. What else would I do? Let 7 billion people die to spite Stratt?

At some point, Rocky came through his tunnel to the lab. I don't know how long he's been there. He didn't have to come—he could "see" everything going on from the control room with his sonar sense. Still, there he is.

"You are very sad," he says.

"Yeah."

"I am sad also. But we not be sad for long. You are scientist. I am engineer. Together we solve."

I throw up my arms in frustration. "How?!"

He clicked along the tunnel to the closest point above me. *"Taumoeba eat all your fuel. Therefore Taumoeba survive and breed in fuel-tank environment."*

"So?"

"Most life no can live outside its air. I die if not in Erid air. You die if not in Earth air. But Taumoeba survive when not in Adrian air. Taumoeba stronger than Erid life—stronger than Earth life."

I crane my neck to look up at him. "True. And Astrophage are also pretty tough. They can live in vacuum and on the surface of stars."

He tapped two claws together. *"Yes yes. Astrophage and Taumoeba from same biosphere. Probably evolve from common ancestor. Adrian life is very strong."*

I sit up. "Yeah. Okay."

"You have idea already. Not question. I know you. You have idea already. Tell idea."

I sigh. "Well . . . Venus, Threeworld, and Adrian all have a bunch of carbon dioxide. The Astrophage breeding zone in all three is where pressure is 0.02 atmospheres. So maybe I'll start with a chamber full of pure carbon dioxide at 0.02 atmospheres and see if Taumoeba survives that. Then add in more gases one at a time to see what the problem is."

"Understand," says Rocky.

I get to my feet and dust off my jumpsuit. "I need you to make me a test chamber. Clear xenonite with valves so I can let air in and out. Also, I need to be able to set temperature to minus 100 degrees Celsius, minus 50 degrees Celsius, or minus 82 degrees Celsius."

I could use my own equipment, but why not take advantage of superior material and craftsmanship?

"Yes yes. I make now. We are team. We fix this. No be sad." He skitters down the tunnel toward the dormitory.

I check my watch. "The main thrust ends in thirty-four minutes. After that's done, let's use the beetles to put ourselves in centrifuge mode."

Rocky pauses. *"Dangerous."*

"Yeah, I know. But we need gravity for the lab and I don't want to wait eleven days. I want to make good use of time."

"Beetles arranged for thrust, not rotation."

It's true. Our propulsion right now is, to say the least, rudimentary. We don't have servos or gimbals to vector our thrust. We're like a sixteenth-century nautical ship, but we're using beetles for sails. Actually, scratch that. The nautical ship could at least control the angle of their sails. We're more like a paddlewheel boat with a broken rudder.

It's not all bad, though. We have some slight attitude control by deciding how much each engine thrusts. It's how Rocky zeroed out our rotation before. "It's worth the risk."

He skitters back up the tunnel to face me. *"Ship will rotate off-axis. No can unspool centrifuge cables. Would tangle."*

"We'll create the needed rotation first, then shut off beetles, then unspool cables."

He draws back. *"If ship not unspooled, force is too much for human."*

That does present a problem. I want 1 g of gravity for the lab when the ship is fully unspooled in two halves. To get that much rotational inertia with the ship in one piece means spinning it *very* fast. Last time we did that, I passed out in the control room and Rocky almost died saving me.

"Okay . . ." I say. "How about this: I'll lay down in the storage room under the dormitory. That's the closest to the center of ship I can get. The force will be smallest there. I'll be okay."

"How you operate centrifuge controls from storage room, question?"

"I'll . . . umm . . . I'll bring the lab's control screen down there with me. I'll run data and power extension cables from the lab to the storage room. Yeah. That should work."

"What if you unconscious and no can operate controls, question?"

"Then you cancel the rotation and I'll wake up."

He shimmies back and forth. *"No like. Alternate plan: Wait eleven days. Get to my ship. Clean out you ship fuel tanks. Sterilize—make sure no Taumoeba. Refill with fuel from my ship. Then can use all functions of you ship again."*

I shake my head. "I don't want to wait eleven days. I want to work now."

"Why, question? Why no wait, question?"

He's completely right, of course. I'm risking my life and maybe the structural integrity of the *Hail Mary*. But I can't just sit around for eleven days when there's so much work to do. How do I explain "impatience" to someone who lives seven hundred years?

"Human thing," I say.

"Understand. Not actually understand, but . . . understand."

The spin-up went as planned. Rocky selected Ringo to do the spinning work, leaving John and Paul offline. George is still safely aboard the ship in case I need him.

The g-forces during the spin-up were rough—I won't lie. But I stayed awake long enough to manually deal with the centrifuge steps. I'm getting pretty good at it now. Since then, it's been a nice, level 1 g.

Yeah, it was impatient and a little risky, but thanks to that, I've had seven days of hardcore science since then.

Rocky delivered on the testing apparatus as promised. As always, everything worked flawlessly. Instead of a small, annoying glass vacuum chamber, I had something resembling a large fish tank. Xenonite doesn't care if there's a bunch of air pressure on a large, flat panel. "Bring it on," says xenonite.

I have, shall we say, an inexhaustible supply of Taumoeba. The *Hail Mary* is currently the Taumoeba party bus. All I have to do is open the fuel line that used to lead to the generator when I want more.

"Hey, Rocky!" I call out from the lab. "Watch me pull a Taumoeba out of a hat!"

Rocky climbs up his tunnel from the control room. *"I assume that is Earth idiom."*

"Yeah. Earth has entertainment called 'television' and—"

"Do not explain, please. You have findings, question?"

Just as well. It would take a long time to explain cartoons to an alien. "I have some results."

"Good good." He hunkers down into a comfortable sitting position. *"Tell findings!"* He tries to hide it, but his voice is just a touch higher in pitch than normal.

I gesture to the lab apparatus. "This functions perfectly, by the way."

"Thank. Tell about findings."

"My first experiment was Adrian's environment. I added Taumoeba and a slide covered in Astrophage. The Taumoeba survived and ate it all. No surprise there."

"No surprise. Is their native environment. But proves equipment works."

"Exactly. I did more tests to learn Taumoeba's limits. In Adrian air, they can live from minus 180 degrees Celsius to 107 degrees Celsius. Outside that range they die."

"Impressive range."

"Yes. Also, they can survive in a near vacuum."

"Like your fuel tanks."

"Yeah, but not a *total* vacuum." I frown. "They need carbon dioxide. At least a little bit of it. I made an Adrian environment but put argon in instead of carbon dioxide. The Taumoeba didn't eat anything. They stayed dormant. Eventually they starved to death."

"Expected," he says. *"Astrophage need carbon dioxide. Taumoeba from same ecology. Taumoeba also need carbon dioxide. How they get carbon dioxide in fuel tanks, question?"*

"I had the same question!" I say. "So I did a spectrograph of my fuel-bay sludge. There's a bunch of CO_2 gas dissolved into the liquid."

"Astrophage probably have carbon dioxide inside. Or decomposition creates carbon dioxide. Some percentage died in fuel tanks over time. Not all cells are perfect. Defects. Mutations. Some die. Those dead Astrophage put carbon dioxide in tanks."

"Agreed."

"Good findings," he says. He starts climbing back down.

"Wait. I have more. Much more."

He stops. *"More, question? Good."*

I lean against my lab table and pat the tank. "I made Venus in the tank. But not quite Venus. Venus's air is 96.5 percent carbon dioxide and 3.5 percent nitrogen. I started with just the carbon dioxide. The Taumoeba were fine. Then I added the nitrogen. And the Taumoeba all died."

He raises his carapace. *"All die, question? Sudden, question?"*

"Yes," I say. "In seconds. All dead."

"Nitrogen . . . unexpected."

"Yeah, very unexpected!" I say. "I repeated experiment with Threeworld's air. Carbon dioxide only: The Taumoeba were fine. I added in the sulfur dioxide: The Taumoeba were fine. I added the nitrogen: Boom! All the Taumoeba died."

He taps a claw absently on the tunnel wall. *"Very very unexpected. Nitrogen harmless to Erid life. Nitrogen required by many Erid life."*

"Same with Earth," I say. "Earth's air is seventy-eight percent nitrogen."

"Confusing," he says.

He's not alone. I'm just as baffled as he is. We're both thinking the same thing: If all life evolved from a single source, how can nitrogen be critical to two biospheres and toxic to a third?

Nitrogen is utterly harmless and nearly inert in its gaseous state. It's usually content to be N_2, which barely wants to react with anything. Human bodies ignore the stuff despite every breath being 78 percent nitrogen. As for Erid, their atmosphere is mostly ammonia—a nitrogen compound. How could a panspermia event ever seed Earth and Erid—two nitrogen-riddled planets—if a tiny amount of nitrogen kills that life?

Well, the answer to that is easy: Whatever the life-form was that caused the panspermia, it didn't have a problem with nitrogen. Taumoeba, which evolved later, does.

Rocky's carapace sinks. "*Situation bad. Threeworld air is eight percent nitrogen.*"

I sit on the lab stool and cross my arms. "Venus's air is 3.5 percent nitrogen. Same problem."

He sinks farther and his voice drops an octave. "*Hopeless. Cannot change Threeworld air. Cannot change Venus air. Cannot change Taumoeba. Hopeless.*"

"Well," I say. "We can't change Threeworld or Venus's air. But maybe we can change Taumoeba."

"*How, question?*"

I grab my tablet from the workbench and scroll through my notes about Eridian physiology. "Do Eridians have diseases? Sicknesses inside your bodies?"

"*Some. Very, very bad.*"

"How does your body kill diseases?"

"*Eridian body is closed,*" he explains. "*Only opening happen when eat or lay egg. After opening seals, area inside made very hot inside with hot blood for long time. Kill any disease. Disease can only get into body through wound. Then is very bad. Body shut down infected area. Heat with hot blood to kill disease. If disease fast, Eridian die.*"

No immune system at all. Just heat. Well, why not? The hot circulatory system of an Eridian boils water to make the muscles move. Why not use it to cook and sterilize incoming food too? And with heavy oxides—basically rocks—as skin, they don't get many cuts or abrasions. Even their lungs don't exchange material with the outside. If any pathogens do get in, the body seals the area off and boils it. An Eridian body is a nearly impenetrable fortress.

But a human body is more like a borderless police state.

"Humans are very different," I say. "We get diseases all the time. We have very powerful immune systems. Also, we find cures for diseases in nature. The word is 'antibiotics.'"

"No understand," he says. *"Cures for diseases in nature, question? How, question?"*

"Other life on Earth evolved defenses against the same diseases. They emit chemicals that kill the disease without harming other cells. Humans eat those chemicals and they kill disease but not our human cells."

"Amaze. Erid no have this."

"It's not a perfect system, though," I say. "Antibiotics work very well at first, but then over the years, they become less and less effective. Eventually they barely work at all."

"Why, question?"

"Diseases change. Antibiotics kill almost all the disease in the body, but some survive. By using antibiotics, humans are accidentally teaching diseases how to survive those antibiotics."

"Ah!" Rocky says. He raises his carapace a tad. *"Disease evolves defense against chemical that kills it."*

"Yes," I say. I point at the tank. "Now think of Taumoeba as disease. Think of nitrogen as antibiotic."

He pauses, then raises his carapace back to its proper location. *"Understand! Make environment barely deadly. Breed Taumoeba that survive. Make more deadly. Breed survivors. Repeat, repeat, repeat!"*

"Yes," I say. "We don't need to understand why or how nitrogen kills Taumoeba. We just need to breed nitrogen-resistant Taumoeba."

"Yes!" he says.

"Good!" I slap the top of the tank. "Make me ten of these, but smaller. Also provide a way for me to get Taumoeba samples without interrupting the experiment. Make a very accurate gas injection system—I need exact control over the nitrogen quantity in the tank."

"Yes! I make! I make now!"

He skitters down to the dormitory.

I check the results of the spectrograph and shake my head. "No good. Complete failure."

"Sad," Rocky says.

I put my chin in my hands. "Maybe I can filter out the toxins."

"Maybe you can concentrate on Taumoeba." There's a special warble that Rocky does when he's being snarky. That warble is especially present right now.

"They're coming along fine." I glance over to the Taumoeba processing tanks arrayed along one side of the lab. "Nothing to do but wait. We've had good results. They're already up to 0.01 percent nitrogen and surviving. The next generation might be able to go as high as 0.015."

"This is waste of time. Also waste of my food."

"I need to know if I can eat your food."

"Eat your own food."

"I've only got a few months of real food left. You have enough aboard your ship to feed a crew of twenty-three Eridians for years. Erid life and Earth life use the same proteins. Maybe I can eat your food."

"Why you say 'real food,' question? What is non-real food, question?"

I checked the readout again. Why does Eridian food have so many heavy metals in it? "Real food is food that tastes good. Food that's fun to eat."

"You have not-fun food, question?"

"Yeah. Coma slurry. The ship fed it to me during the trip here. I have enough to last me almost four years."

"Eat that."

"It tastes bad."

"Food experience not that important."

"Hey." I point at him. "To humans, food experience is very important."

"Humans strange."

I point at the spectrometer readout screen. "Why does Eridian food have thallium in it?"

"Healthy."

"Thallium kills humans!"

"Then eat human food."

"Ugh." I walk over to the Taumoeba tanks. Rocky had outdone himself. I can control the nitrogen content to within one part per million. And so far, things are looking good. Sure, this generation can only handle a smidgen of nitrogen, but it's a smidgen more than the previous generation could do.

The plan is working. Our Taumoeba are developing nitrogen resistance.

Will they ever be able to handle the 3.5 percent needed for Venus? Or the 8 percent for Threeworld? Who knows? We'll just have to wait and see.

I'm using percentages here to track the nitrogen. I can only get away with that because in all cases, Astrophage breed where the air is 0.02 atmospheres of pressure. So, since the pressure is always the same across all experiments, I can just track the percent of nitrogen.

The *proper* way to do it would be to track "partial pressure." But that's annoying. I'd just end up dividing by 0.02 atmospheres and multiplying by it again later when dealing with data.

I pat the top of Tank Three. It's been my lucky tank. Out of twenty-three generations of Taumoeba, Tank Three made the strongest strain nine times. Pretty good, considering she's got nine other tanks to compete with.

Yes, Tank Three is a "she." Don't judge me.

"How long until we reach the *Blip-A*?"

"Seventeen hours until reverse-thrust maneuver."

"Okay, let's spin down the centrifuge now. Just in case we run into trouble and need extra time to fix something."

"Agree. I go to control room now. You go to storage locker and lie flat. Do not forget control panel with long extension cords."

I glance around the lab. Everything is firmly secured. "Yeah, okay. Let's do it."

"John, Ringo, Paul off," says Rocky. *"Velocity is orbital."*

There is no "stationary" in a solar system. You're always moving around something. In this case, Rocky reduced our cruise velocity to put us in a stable orbit about 1 AU from Tau Ceti. That's where he left the *Blip*-A.

Rocky relaxes in his control-room bulb. He clamps the boxes to their wall mounts. Now that the engines are off we're back to zero g, and the last thing we want is for the "make ship thrust" button to be floating around unattended.

He grabs a couple of handholds and centers his carapace over the texture monitor. As always, it shows him my center monitor feed with colors represented as textures.

"You in control now." He's done his job. Now it's my turn.

"How long until the flash?" I ask

Rocky pulls an Eridian clock off the wall. *"Next flash is three minutes, seven seconds."*

"Okay."

Rocky's no dope. He left his ship set up to turn on its engines for a fraction of a second every twenty minutes or so, giving us a much-needed beacon. It's easy enough to math out where the ship *should* be. But gravity from other planets, inaccurate measurement of last known velocities, inaccuracies in our estimate of Tau Ceti's gravity . . . they all add up to make slight errors. And a slight error on the location of something orbiting a star is a pretty big distance.

So rather than hoping we can see Taulight reflect off the ship when we get to where it should be, he just set it up to flash the engines now and then. All I have to do is watch with the Petrovascope. It'll be an *extremely* bright flash.

"What is current nitrogen tolerance, question?"

"Tank Three had some survivors at 0.6 percent nitrogen today. I'm breeding them up now."

"What spacing, question?"

It's a conversation we've had dozens of times. But it's fair for him to be curious. His species depends on it.

The "spacing," as we've come to call it, is the difference in how much nitrogen each of the ten tanks receives. I don't just do the same thing in every tank. With each new generation, I try ten new percentages of nitrogen.

"I'm being aggressive—0.05 percent increments."

"Good good," he says.

All ten tanks are breeding Taumoeba-06 (named for the nitrogen percent it can withstand). Tank One is the control, as always. It has 0.6 percent nitrogen in the air. Taumoeba-06 should have no problem in there. If it does, it means there was a mistake in the previous batch and I have to go back to an earlier strain.

Tank Two has 0.65 percent nitrogen. Tank Three has 0.7. And so on all the way up to Tank Ten with 1.05 percent. The heartiest survivors will be the champions, and will move on to the next round. I wait a few hours just to make sure they can breed for at least two generations. Taumoeba has a ridiculously fast doubling time. Fast enough to eat all my fuel in a matter of days, as it happens.

If we get to Venus or Threeworld nitrogen percentages, I'll do much more thorough testing.

"Flash is soon," Rocky says.

"Copy."

I bring up the Petrovascope on the center monitor. Normally, I'd have it off to the side, but the center is the only one Rocky can "see." As expected, there's just background light in the Petrova frequency courtesy of Tau Ceti. I pan and tilt the camera. We deliberately positioned ourselves closer to Tau Ceti than the *Blip-A* should be. So I'm looking more or less directly away from the star. That should minimize the background IR and give me a good view of the flash.

"Okay. I think I have it pointed roughly toward your ship."

Rocky concentrates on his texture monitor. *"Understand. Thirty-seven seconds until flash."*

"Hey. What's is your ship's name, anyway?"

"Blip-A."

"No, I mean, what do you call it?"

"Ship."

"Your ship has no name?"

"Why would ship have name, question?"

I shrugged. "Ships have names."

He points to my pilot's seat. *"What is name of you chair, question?"*

"It doesn't have a name."

"Why does ship have name but chair no have name, question?"

"Never mind. Your ship is the *Blip-A*."

"That is what I said. Flash in ten seconds."

"Copy."

Rocky and I each fall silent and stare at our respective screens. It took me a long time to notice the subtleties, but I can now tell when Rocky is paying attention to something specific. He tends to angle his carapace toward it and pivot ever so slightly back and forth. If I follow the line he's pivoting on, that's usually what he's examining.

"Three . . . two . . . one . . . now!"

Right on cue, a few pixels on-screen blink white.

"Got it," I say.

"I not notice."

"It was dim. We must be far away. Hang on . . ." I switch to the Telescope screen and pan to where the flash came from. I sweep back and forth with small movements until I catch a slight discoloration in the blackness. Taulight reflecting off the *Blip-A*. "Yeah, we're pretty far away."

"Beetles have much fuel remaining. Is okay. Tell me angle change."

I check the readouts at the bottom of the screen. All we have to do is align the *Hail Mary* with the current telescope angle. "Rotate yaw plus 13.72 degrees. Rotate pitch minus 9.14 degrees."

"Yaw plus one three mark seven two. Pitch minus nine mark one four." He grabs the beetle controls from their holders and gets to work. By flicking on and off the beetles in sequence, he angles the ship toward the *Blip-A*.

I zero the telescope and zoom in to confirm. The difference between background space and the ship is so small as to be barely perceivable. But it's there. "Angle correct."

He focuses hard on his texture screen. *"I no detect anything on-screen."*

"Light difference is very very small. Need human eyes to detect. Angle is good."

"Understand. What is range, question?"

I switch to the Radar screen. Nothing. "Too far for my radar to see. At least ten thousand kilometers."

"Accelerate to what velocity, question?"

"How about . . . three kilometers per second? Will get to the *Blip-A* in an hour or so."

"Three thousand meters per second. Standard acceleration rate is acceptable, question?"

"Yes. Fifteen meters per second per second."

"Two hundred second thrust. Begin now."

I brace for gravity.

CHAPTER 25

We did it!

We actually did it!

I have Earth's salvation in a little tank on the floor.

"Happy!" Rocky says. *"Happy happy happy!"*

I'm so giddy I might throw up. "Yes! But we're not done yet."

I strap myself into my bunk. A pillow tries to float away, but I snag it in time and wedge it under my head. I'm all wired up, but if I don't go to sleep soon, Rocky will start hassling me. Sheesh—you almost ruin a mission *one time* and all of a sudden you have an alien-enforced bedtime.

"Taumoeba-35!" Rocky says. *"Took many many generations but finally success!"*

It's a weird feeling, scientific breakthroughs. There's no Eureka moment. Just a slow, steady progression toward a goal. But man, when you get to that goal it feels good.

We linked the ships back up together weeks ago. Rocky was pretty stoked to have access to his much larger ship again. First thing he did was set up a tunnel directly from his portion of the *Hail Mary* to the *Blip-A*. It meant another hole in my hull, but at this point I trust

Rocky to do any engineering task. Heck, if he wanted to do open-heart surgery on me, I'd probably let him. The guy is amazing at this stuff.

With the ships linked, I can't have the *Hail Mary*'s centrifuge going, which means we're back to zero g. But now that we're just breeding Taumoeba in tanks, I can live without my gravity-dependent lab equipment for now.

Over the weeks, we watched generation after generation of Taumoeba become more and more nitrogen-resistant. And now, today, we finally have Taumoeba-35: a strain of Taumoeba that can survive 3.5 percent nitrogen in a 0.02 atmosphere overall air pressure—the same situation found on Venus.

"You. Be happy now," Rocky says from his workbench.

"I am, I am," I say. "But we need to get to 8 percent so it can survive on Threeworld. Until then, we're not done."

"Yes yes yes. But this is moment. Important moment."

"Yeah." I smile.

He fiddles with some kind of new gadget. He's always working on one thing or another. *"Now you make exact Venus atmosphere in one tank and do detailed tests on Taumoeba-35, question?"*

"No," I say. "We'll keep going until we get to Taumoeba-80. It should work on Venus and Threeworld. I'll test everything then."

"Understand."

I turn to face his side of the room. The whole "watching me sleep" thing doesn't creep me out anymore. If anything, it's comforting. "What are you working on?"

The device is clamped to his workbench to keep it from drifting away. He works on it from many angles with many hands holding many tools. *"This is Earth electricity unit."*

"You're making a power converter?"

"Yes. Convert from Eridian prime-sequence electric amplitude to inefficient Earth direct-current system."

"Prime sequence?"

"Would take long time to explain."

I make a mental note to ask about it later. "Okay. What will you use that for?"

He puts down two tools and picks up three more. *"If all plans work, we make good Taumoeba. I give you fuel. You go Earth and I go Erid. We say goodbye."*

"Yeah, I guess," I mumble. I should be happier about surviving a suicide mission, returning home a hero, and saving my entire species. But saying goodbye to Rocky forever will be hard. I put it out of my mind.

"You have many portable thinking machines. I ask favor: You give one to me as gift, question?"

"A laptop? You want a laptop? Sure, I have a bunch of them."

"Good good. And thinking machine have information, question? Science information from Earth, question?"

Ah, of course. I'm an advanced alien race with knowledge far beyond Eridian science. I think the laptops have terabyte drives. I could copy the entire contents of Wikipedia over to him.

"Yes. I can do that. But I don't think a laptop will work in Eridian air. Too hot."

He points to the device. *"This is just one part of thinking-machine life-support system. System will give power, keep Earth temperature, Earth air inside. Many redundant backups. Make sure thinking machine not break. If break, no Eridian can fix."*

"Ah, I see. How will you read the output?"

"Camera inside convert from Earth light readout to Eridian texture readout. Like camera in control room. Before we leave, you explain written language to me."

He certainly knows enough English to look up any words he doesn't know. "Yeah, sure. Our written language is easy. Kind of easy. There are only twenty-six letters, but many strange ways to say them. Well, I guess there are actually fifty-two symbols because capital letters look different even though they're pronounced the same. Oh, and then there's punctuation . . ."

"Our scholars will solve. You just get me started."

"Yes. I'll do that," I say. "I want a gift from you too: xenonite. Solid form and liquid pre-xenonite form. Earth scientists will want that."

"Yes, I give."

I yawn. "I'm going to sleep soon."

"I watch."

"Good night, Rocky."

"Good night, Grace."

I fall asleep easier than I have in weeks. I have Taumoeba that can save Earth.

Modifying an alien life-form. What could possibly go wrong?

Back when I was a kid, like most kids, I imagined what it would be like to be an astronaut. I imagined flying through space in a rocket ship, meeting aliens, and just generally being awesome. What I didn't imagine was cleaning out sewage tanks.

But that's pretty much what I'm doing today. To be clear, it's not my poop I'm cleaning. It's Taumoeba poop. Thousands of kilograms of Taumoeba poop. Each of my seven remaining fuel bays has to be cleared out of all that gunk before I can put new fuel in.

So, on the one hand, I'm shoveling poop. On the other, at least I'm in an EVA suit while I do it. I've smelled this stuff before. It's not great.

The gunky methane and decomposing cells aren't a problem. If that were all I had to deal with, I'd just ignore it. Twenty thousand kilograms of gunk in a two-million-kilogram tank? Barely worth paying attention to.

The problem is there's probably surviving Taumoeba in there. The contamination ate all the available fuel several weeks ago, so they've mostly starved by now. At least, according to recent samples I checked. But some of the little bastards will probably still be alive. And the last thing I want to do is feed them 2 million kilograms of fresh Astrophage.

"Progress, question?" Rocky radios.

"Almost done with Fuel Bay Three."

Fully inside the tank, I scrape black gunk off the walls with a homemade spatula and fling it out through a one-meter-wide hole in the side. Where'd the one-meter-wide hole come from? I made it.

The fuel tanks have no human-sized entry hatches. Why would they? Valves and piping lead in and out, but the largest of them is only a few inches wide. I don't have anything to flush the tanks with—I left my "ten thousand gallons of water" collection back home. So for each tank I have to cut a hole, clean the gunk out, and then reseal it.

I have to say, though, the cutting torch Rocky made for me works like a charm. A little Astrophage, an IR light, some lenses, and I have a freakin' death ray in my hands. The trick is keeping the output low. But Rocky put extra safeties in. He made sure the lenses had some impurities and they *aren't* made of transparent xenonite. They're IR-permeable glass. If the light output from the Astrophage inside gets too high, the lenses will melt. Then the beam will defocus and the cutter will be useless. I'd have to sheepishly ask Rocky to make me another one, but at least I wouldn't cut my leg off.

So far, that hasn't happened. But I wouldn't put it past me.

I scrape a particularly stubborn crust of gunk off the wall. It floats away and I use the scraper to bat it out the hole. "Status on breeder tanks?" I ask.

"Tank Four still have live Taumoeba. Tank Five and higher all dead."

I shuffle forward in the tank. It's narrow enough that I can hold position by putting both boots on one side of the cylinder and a hand on the opposing side. This leaves my remaining hand free to scrape sludge. "Tank Four was 5.25 percent, right?"

"Not right. Five point two zero percent."

"Okay. So we're up to Taumoeba-52. Doin' good."

"How is progress, question?"

"Slow and steady," I say.

I flick a wad of gunk off into the void. I wish I could just flush the tanks with nitrogen and call it a day. After all, this Taumoeba has no nitrogen resistance at all. But it wouldn't work. The gunk is several centimeters thick. No matter how much nitrogen I pumped in, there would be some Taumoeba it doesn't get to—shielded by a centimeter-thick wall of their brethren.

All it takes is one survivor to start an infestation when I refill the tanks with Rocky's spare Astrophage. So I have to muck the tanks out as best I can before doing the nitrogen cleanse.

"You fuel tanks are big. You have enough nitrogen, question? I can give ammonia from Blip-A *life support if you need."*

"Ammonia wouldn't work," I say. "Taumoeba doesn't have a problem with nitrogen compounds. Just with elemental N_2. But don't worry, I'm fine. I don't need as much nitrogen as you think. We know 3.5 percent at 0.02 atmospheres will kill natural Taumoeba. That's a partial pressure of less than 1 Pascal. These fuel bays are only 37 cubic meters each. All I need to do is to squirt a few grams of nitrogen gas in here and it'll kill everything. It's amazingly deadly to Taumoeba."

I put my hands on my hips. An awkward pose in the EVA suit and it causes me to float away from the wall, but it fit the situation. "Okay. Done with Fuel Bay Three."

"You want xenonite patch for hole now, question?"

I float out of the fuel bay and into space. I pull on my tether to bring me back to the hull. "No, I'll do all the cleaning first, then close them up in a separate EVA."

I use the handholds to get to Fuel Bay Four, anchor myself in place, and fire up the Eridian AstroTorch.

Xenonite makes for some pretty darn good pressurized gas containers.

My fuel bays are all freshly cleaned and resealed. I gave them all about a hundred times as much nitrogen as it takes to kill any natural Taumoeba hanging around. And then I just let it stay there for a while. I'm taking no chances.

After a few days of sterilizing, it's time for a test. Rocky gives me a few kilograms of Astrophage to work with. I remember when "a few kilograms of Astrophage" would have been a godsend to everyone on *Stratt's Vat*. But now it's just, "Oh hey. Here's a few quadrillion Joules of energy. Let me know if you want more."

I divide the Astrophage into seven roughly equal blobs, vent the nitrogen, and squirt one blob into each fuel bay. Then I wait a day.

During this time, Rocky is aboard his ship plugging away on a pumping system to transfer Astrophage from his fuel tanks to mine. I offer to help, but he very politely declines. What good could I do aboard the *Blip-A* anyway? My EVA suit can't handle the environment in there, so Rocky would have to build me a whole tunnel system . . . it's not worth it.

I really *want* it to be worth it. It's an alien freakin' spaceship! I want to see the inside! But yeah. Got to save humanity and stuff. That's the priority.

I check the fuel bays. Any live Taumoeba will have found the Astrophage and snacked on it. So if the Astrophage is still there, the bay is sterile.

Long story short: Two of the seven bays weren't sterile.

"Hey, Rocky!" I yell from the control room.

He's aboard the *Blip-A* somewhere, but I know he can hear me. He can always hear me.

After a few seconds, the radio crackles to life. "*What, question?*"

"Two fuel bays still have Taumoeba."

"*Understand. Not good. But not bad. Other five are clean, question?*"

I steady myself with a handhold in the control room. It's easy to float off when you're concentrating on conversation. "Yeah, the other five seem good."

"*How Taumoeba in bad two bays survive, question?*"

"I probably didn't clean them well enough. Some gunk remained and shielded live Taumoeba from the nitrogen. That's my guess."

"*Plan, question?*"

"I'm going back into those two, scraping them down some more, and I'll sterilize them again. I'll leave the other five sealed for now."

"*Good plan. Do not forget to purge fuel lines.*"

With all the tanks infected, it's safe to assume the fuel lines (currently sealed off) will also be infected. "Yes. They'll be easier than the tanks. I just need to blow high-pressure nitrogen through them. It'll clean out the chunks and sterilize the rest. Then I'll test them the same as the fuel bays."

"Good good." He says. *"What is status of breeder tanks, question?"*

"Still making good progress. We're up to Taumoeba-62 now."

"Someday we find out why nitrogen was problem."

"Yeah, but that's for other scientists. We just need Taumoeba-80."

"Yes. Taumoeba-80. Maybe Taumoeba-86. Safety."

When you think in base six, arbitrarily adding six to things is normal.

"Agreed," I say.

I enter the airlock and climb into the Orlan EVA suit. I grab the AstroTorch and attach it to my tool belt. I turn on the helmet radio and say, "Beginning EVA."

"Understand. Radio if problem. Can help with my ship hull robot if you need."

"I shouldn't need it, but I'll let you know."

I seal the door behind me and start the airlock cycle.

"Screw it," I say. I press the final confirmation button to jettison Fuel Bay Five.

The pyros pop and the empty tank floats off into the nothingness of space.

No amount of scrubbing, cleaning, nitrogen-purging, or anything else could get the Taumoeba out of Fuel Bay Five. No matter what I did, they survived and chowed down on the test Astrophage I put in afterward.

At a certain point, you just have to let go.

I cross my arms and slump into my pilot's seat. There's no gravity to properly slump with, so I have to make a conscious effort to push myself into the seat. I'm pouting, darn it, and I intend to do it right. I'm missing a total of three of my original nine fuel bays. Two from our adventure over Adrian, and another one just now. That's about 666,000 kilograms of fuel storage I no longer have.

Do I have enough fuel to get home? Sure. Any amount of fuel that can make me escape Tau Ceti's gravity is enough to *eventually* get home. I could get home with just a few kilograms of Astrophage if I didn't mind waiting a million years.

It's not about getting there. It's about how long it'll take.

I do a ton of math and I get answers I don't like.

The trip from Earth to Tau Ceti took three years and nine months. And it was done by accelerating constantly at 1.5 g's the entire time—which is what Dr. Lamai decided was the maximum sustained g-force a human should be exposed to for almost four years. Earth experienced something like thirteen years during that time, but time dilation worked in our favor for the crew.

If I do the long trip home with just 1.33 million kilograms of fuel (which is all my remaining tanks can hold), the most efficient course is a constant acceleration of 0.9 g's. I'd be going slower, which means less time dilation, which means I experience more time. All told, I'll experience five and a half years on that trip.

So what? It's only an extra year and a half. What's the big deal?

I don't have that much food.

This was a suicide mission. They gave us food to last several months, and that's about it. I've been working my way through the food stores at a reasonable rate, but then I'll have to rely on coma slurry. It won't taste good but it's nutritionally balanced, at least.

But again, this was a suicide mission. They didn't give us enough coma slurry to get home either. The only reason I have any at all is because Commander Yáo and Specialist Ilyukhina died en route.

All told, I have three months of real food left and about forty months' worth of coma slurry. That works out to be just barely enough food to survive the trip home with full fuel and a bit to spare. But nowhere near enough to last the five and a half years of a slower trip.

Rocky's food is useless to me. I've tested it over and over. It's chock-full of heavy metals ranging from "toxic" to "highly toxic." There are useful proteins and sugars in there that my biology would love to make use of, but there's just no way to sort out the poison from the food.

And there's nothing here for me to grow. All my food is freeze-dried or dehydrated. No viable seeds or plants or anything. I can eat what I have and that's it.

Rocky clicks along his tunnel to the control-room bulb. He goes in and out of the *Blip-A* so often now I often don't know what ship he's on.

"You make angry sound. Why, question?"

"I'm missing a third of my fuel bays. The trip home will take more time than I have food."

"How long since last sleep, question?"

"Huh? I'm talking about fuel here! Stay focused!"

"Grumpy. Angry. Stupid. How long since last sleep, question?"

I shrug. "I don't know. I've been working on the breeder tanks and fuel bays . . . I forget when I last slept."

"You sleep. I watch."

I gesture violently to the console. "I have a serious problem here! I don't have enough fuel storage to survive the trip home! It's 600,000 kilograms of fuel. It would take 135 cubic meters of storage! I don't have that much space!"

"I make storage tank."

"You don't have enough xenonite for that!"

"Don't need xenonite. Any strong material will do. Have much metal aboard my ship. Melt, shape, make tank for you."

I blink a couple of times. "You can do that?"

"Obvious I can do that! You are stupid right now. You sleep. I watch and also design replacement tank. Agree, question?" He starts down the tube toward the dormitory.

"Huh . . ."

"Agree, question?!" he says, louder.

"Yeah . . ." I mumble. "Yeah, okay . . ."

I've done a lot of EVAs now. But none were as tiring as this one has turned out to be.

I've been out here for six hours. The Orlan is a tough old suit and it can handle it. The same can't be said about me.

"Installing final fuel bay now," I wheeze. Almost there. Stay on target.

Rocky's ad-hoc fuel bays are perfect, of course. All I had to do was detach one of my existing bays and give it to him for analysis. Well, I gave it to his hull robot. However he uses that robot to measure stuff, it does a good job. Every valve connection is in the right place and the right size. Every screw threading is perfectly spaced.

All told, he made three perfect copies of the fuel bay I gave him. The only difference is the material. My original bays were made of aluminum. Someone on Stratt's team had suggested a carbon-fiber hull but she shot that down. Well-tested technology only. Humanity had sixty-odd years of testing aluminum-hulled spacecraft.

The new bays are made of . . . an alloy. What alloy? Dunno. Rocky doesn't even know. It's a mishmash of metals from non-critical systems aboard the *Blip-A*. Mostly iron, he says. But there's at least twenty different elements all melted together. It's basically "metal stew."

But that's okay. The fuel bays don't need to hold pressure. They only have to keep the Astrophage aboard the ship—nothing else. They do need to be strong enough to not break apart from the weight of the fuel inside when the ship accelerates. But that's not hard. They could literally be made out of wood and be just as effective.

"You are slow," he says.

"You are mean." I ratchet the large cylinder into place with straps.

"Apologies. I am excited. Breeder Tanks Nine and Ten!"

"Yeah!" I say. "Fingers crossed!"

We're up to Taumoeba-78 as of the most recent generation. That strain is breeding away in the tanks while I work on these fuel bays.

The spacing is 0.25 percent, which means for the first time ever, some breeder tanks actually have 8 percent or more nitrogen inside.

As for installing the tanks . . . sheesh. I've learned that the first bolt is the hardest. The fuel bay has a lot of inertia and it's hard to keep aligned with the hole. Also, the original mounting system for the bay is gone. The pyros saw to that. They never figured I'd be adding in new bays after jettisoning old ones. The pyros don't just open a clamp. They shear the bolts clean off. And they don't care about the damage to the mounting points.

I spend a lot of time un-suiciding this suicide mission.

While the threaded mounting holes are in reasonable shape, every one of them has a sheared-off bolt to deal with. With no bolt head, they're a real pain in the patoot to unscrew. I've found that the best approach is to bring sacrificial steel rods and the AstroTorch. Melt the bolt a little, melt the rod a little, and weld them together. The result is ugly but it gives me a lever arm with enough torque to remove the bolt. Usually.

When I can't remove the bolt, I just start melting stuff. Can't be stuck if it's liquid.

Three hours later, I finally have all the new fuel bays installed . . . sort of.

I cycle the airlock, climb out of the Orlan, and enter the control room. Rocky is in his bulb waiting for me.

"It went well, question?"

I wiggle my hand back and forth—a gesture interestingly common to both humans and Eridians and with the same meaning. "Maybe. I'm not sure. A bunch of the bolt holes were unusable. So the bays aren't connected as well as they should be."

"Danger, question? Your ship accelerate at 15 meters per second per second. Will tanks hold, question?"

"I'm not sure. Earth engineers often double requirements for safety. I hope they did this time. But I will test to be sure."

"Good good. Enough talk. Check breeder tanks, please."

"Yeah, yeah. Let me get some water first."

He bounces and skitters down his tube to the lab. *"Why humans need water so much, question? Inefficient life-forms!"*

I chug a full liter bag of water I'd left in the control room before the EVA. It's thirsty work. I wipe my mouth and let the bag float off. I push off the wall to float down the tunnel to the lab.

"Eridians need water, too, you know."

"We keep inside. Closed system. Some inefficiencies inside, but we get all water we need from food. Humans leak! Gross."

I laugh as I float into the lab where Rocky is waiting. "On Earth, we have a scary, deadly creature called a spider. You look like one of those. Just so you know."

"Good. Proud. I am scary space monster. You are leaky space blob." He points to the breeder tanks. *"Check tanks!"*

I kick off the wall and float over to the breeders. This is the moment of truth. I should check them one at a time starting with Tank One, but to heck with that. I go straight to Tank Nine.

I shine a penlight into the tank and get a good look at the glass slide that was earlier covered in Astrophage. I check the tank readouts, then check the slide again.

I grin at Rocky. "Tank Nine's slide is clear. We have Taumoeba-80!"

He absolutely explodes with noise! His arms flail, his hands clatter against the tunnel walls. It's just random notes in no discernable order. After a few seconds he calms down. *"Yes! Good! Good good good!"*

"Ha-ha, wow. Okay. Easy there." I check Tank Ten. "Hey, Tank Ten is also clear. We have Taumoeba-82.5!"

"Good good good!"

"Good good good, indeed!" I say.

"Now you do much testing. Venus air. Threeworld air."

"Yes. Absolutely—"

He shifts back and forth from one tunnel wall to the other. *"Exact same gases in each test. Same pressure. Same temperature. Same death 'radiation' from space. Same light from nearby star. Same same same."*

"Yes. I'll do that. I'll do all of that."

"Do now."

"I need rest! I just did an eight-hour EVA!"

"Do now!"

"Ugh! No!" I float over to his tunnel and face him through the xenonite. "First I'm going to breed up a bunch more Taumoeba-82.5. Just to make sure we have enough for testing. And I'll make several stable colonies of it in sealed containers."

"Yes! And some on my ship too!"

"Yes. The more backups the better."

He bounces back and forth some more. *"Erid will live! Earth will live! Everyone live!"* He curls the claws of one hand into a ball and presses it against the xenonite. *"Fist me!"*

I push my knuckles against the xenonite. "It's 'fist-bump,' but yeah."

There has to be liquor somewhere. I can't imagine Ilyukhina going on a suicide mission without insisting on some booze. I can't imagine her going across the street without some booze, honestly. And after looking through every box in the storage compartment, I finally find it—the personal kits.

The box has three zipped duffels. Each one is labeled with a crewman's name. "Yáo," "Ilyukhina," and "DuBois." I guess they never replaced DuBois's personal kit, because I never got a chance to make mine.

Still a little mad about how that played out. But maybe I'll get a chance to tell Stratt my feelings on the topic.

I pull the kits into the dormitory with me and Velcro them to the wall. Deeply personal belongings of three people who are now dead. Friends who are now dead.

I may have a somber moment later and spend some time looking at all these bags have to offer. But for now, this is a time of celebration. I want booze.

I open Ilyukhina's bag. There are all sorts of random knickknacks inside. A pendant with some Russian writing on it, a worn old teddy bear she probably had as a kid, a kilogram of heroin, some of her favorite books, and there we are! Five 1-liter bags of clear liquid labeled водка.

It's Russian for "vodka." How do I know that? Because I spent months on an aircraft carrier with a bunch of crazy Russian scientists. I saw that word a lot.

I zip up her bag and leave it Velcroed to the wall. I fly through to the lab where Rocky waits in his tunnel.

"Found it!" I say.

"*Good good!*" His usual jumpsuit and tool-belt bandolier are nowhere to be seen. He has an outfit on I've never seen before.

"Well, well, well! What have we here?" I say.

He juts out his carapace with pride. It's covered with a smooth cloth underlayment that supports symmetrical rigid shapes here and there. Almost like armor, but not as fully covering, and I don't think they're metal.

The top hole, where his vents are, is ringed with rough gems. Definitely jewelry of some kind. They're faceted, similar to how Earth jewelry might be cut, but the quality is horrible. They're blotchy and discolored. But they're really big and I bet they sound great to sonar.

The sleeves leading off the shirt stop about halfway down his arms and are similarly ornamented at the cuffs. Each shoulder is connected to its neighbors by loose braided cords. And for the first time I've ever seen, he has gloves on. All five hands are covered in coarse, burlap-like material.

This outfit would severely limit Rocky's ability to move freely, but hey, fashion isn't about comfort or convenience.

"You look great!" I say.

"*Thank! This is special clothing for celebration.*"

I hold up a liter of vodka. "This is special liquid for celebration."

"*Humans . . . eat to celebrate?*"

"Yeah. I know Eridians eat in private. I know you think it's gross to see. But this is how humans celebrate."

"*Is okay. Eat! We celebrate!*"

I float over to the two experiments mounted to the lab table. Inside one is an analog of the atmosphere of Venus. Inside the other is the atmosphere of Threeworld. In both cases, I made them as precise as I could. I used the best reference data I have, which is considerable thanks to my collection of every human reference book ever and Rocky's knowledge about his own system.

In both cases, Taumoeba have not only survived but thrived. They breed as fast as ever, and even the smallest amount of Astrophage injected into either experiment gets eaten immediately.

I hold the bag of vodka up. "To Taumoeba-82.5! Savior of two worlds!"

"You will give that liquid to the Taumoeba, question?"

I unclip the fastener on the straw. "No, it's just a thing humans say. I am honoring Taumoeba-82.5." I take a sip. It's like fire in my mouth. Ilyukhina apparently liked her vodka strong and rough.

"Yes. Much honoring!" he says. *"Human and Eridian work together, save everyone!"*

"Ah!" I say. "That reminds me: I need a life-support system for Taumoeba—something that feeds them just enough Astrophage to keep the colony alive. It has to be completely automatic, has to work on its own for several years, and it has to weigh less than a kilogram. I need four of them."

"Why so small, question?"

"I'm going to put one on each beetle. Just in case something happens to the *Hail Mary* on the way home."

"Good plan! You are smart! I can make these for you. Also, today I finish fuel-transfer device. Can give you Astrophage now. Then we both go home!"

"Yeah." My smile fades.

"This is happy! Your face opening is in sad mode. Why, question?"

"Going to be a long trip and I'll be all alone." I haven't decided if I want to risk a coma on the way home. I may have to for my own sanity. Total solitude and nothing to eat but chalky, nasty coma slurry might just be too much. For the first part of the trip, at least, I definitely plan to stay awake.

"You will miss me, question? I will miss you. You are friend."

"Yeah. I'm going to miss you." I take another swig of vodka. "You're my friend. Heck, you're my best friend. And pretty soon we're going to say goodbye forever."

He tapped two gloved claws together. They made a muffled sound instead of the usual click that comes along with the dismissive gesture. *"Not forever. We save planets. Then we have Astrophage technology. Visit each other."*

I give a wry grin. "Can we do all that within fifty Earth years?"

"Probably not. Why so fast, question?"

"I only have fifty years or so left to live. Humans don't"—I hiccup—"don't live long, remember?"

"Oh." He's quiet for a moment. *"So we enjoy remaining time together, then go save planets. Then we are heroes!"*

"Yeah!" I straighten up. I'm a little dizzy now. I've never been much of a drinker, and I'm hitting this vodka harder than I should. "We're the moss imporn't people in the gal'xy! We're awesome!"

He grabs a nearby wrench and raises it in one of his hands. *"To us!"*

I raise the vodka. "To ush!"

"Well. This is it," I say from my side of the connector.

"Yes," says Rocky on his side. His voice is low, despite his attempts to keep it high.

The *Hail Mary* is all fueled up: 2.2 million kilograms of Astrophage. A full 200,000 kilograms more than she left Earth with. Rocky's replacement tanks were, of course, more efficient and had more volume than my originals.

I rub the back of my neck. "I assume our people will meet up again. I know humans will want to learn all about Erid."

"Yes," he says. *"Thank you for laptop. Centuries of human technology all for our scientists to learn about. You have given greatest gift in history of my people."*

"You tested it in that life-support system you built for it, right?"

"Yes. That is stupid question." He grips a handle on his side to keep in place.

Rocky had removed his direct connecting tunnel and resealed the *Hail Mary*'s hull. He put the airlock-to-airlock connector in place to finish packing up.

At my request, he left the xenonite walls and tunnels in the *Hail Mary* in place, but with a few meter-wide holes in them here and there so I can use the space. The more xenonite Earth scientists have to study the better, I figure.

The ship still smells a little like ammonia. I guess even xenonite isn't completely immune to gas permeation. It'll probably smell that way for a while.

"And your farms?" I say. "You double-checked them all?"

"Yes. Six redundant Taumoeba-82.5 colonies, each in separate tanks with separate life-support systems. Each with Threeworld simulated atmosphere. Your farms are functioning, question?"

"Yeah," I say. "Well, it's just my ten breeder tanks. But now I have them all set up with Venus's atmosphere. Oh, and thanks for the mini-farms, by the way. I'll install them in the beetles during my trip. I won't have much else to do."

He glances at a notepad. *"These numbers you gave me. You are certain these are the times for me to turn around and the times for me to reach Erid, question? They are so soon. So fast."*

"Yeah, that's time dilation for you. Weird stuff. But those are the correct values. I checked them four times. You'll reach Erid in under three Earth years."

"But Earth is almost same distance from Tau Ceti, and you will take four years, question?"

"I'll *experience* four years, yes. Three years and nine months. Because time won't be as compressed for me as it is for you."

"You have explained before, but again . . . why, question?"

"Your ship accelerates faster than mine. You'll be moving closer to the speed of light."

He wiggles his carapace. *"So complicated."*

I point toward his ship. "All the information about relativity is in the laptop. Have your scientists take a look."

"Yes. They will be very pleased."

"Not when they find out about quantum physics. Then they'll be really annoyed."

"Not understand."

I laugh. "Don't worry about it."

We're both quiet for a while.

"I guess this is it," I say.

"It is time," he says. *"We go save homeworlds now."*

"Yeah."

"You face is leaking."

I wipe my eyes. "Human thing. Don't worry about it."

"Understand." He pushes himself along to his airlock door. He opens it and pauses there. *"Goodbye, friend Grace."*

I wave meekly. "Goodbye, friend Rocky."

He disappears into his ship and closes the airlock door behind him. I return to the *Hail Mary*. After a few minutes, the *Blip-A*'s hull robot detaches the tunnel.

We fly our ships nearly parallel but with a few degrees' difference in course. This ensures neither of us vaporizes the other with the back blast from our Astrophage engines. Once we have a few thousand kilometers of separation, we can aim in any direction we want.

Hours later, I sit in the cockpit with my spin drives offline. I just want one last look. I watch the point of IR light with the Petrovascope. That's Rocky, headed back to Erid.

"Godspeed, buddy," I say.

I set course for Earth and fire up the spin drives.

I'm going home.

CHAPTER 26

I sat in my cell, staring at the wall.

It wasn't a dingy jail cell or anything. If anything, it looked kind of like a college dorm room. Painted brick walls, desk, chair, bed, en-suite bathroom, et cetera. But the door was steel and the windows were barred. I wasn't going anywhere.

Why did the Baikonur launch facility have a jail cell handy? I don't know. Ask the Russians.

That launch would be today. Soon, some muscular guards would come through that door along with a doctor. He'd inject me with something and that'd be the last time I'd see Earth.

Almost on cue, I heard the clink of the door being unlocked. A braver person might have seen that as an opportunity. Charge the door and maybe get past the guards. But I'd given up hope of escape long ago. What would I do? Run into the Kazakhstani desert and take my chances?

The door opened and Stratt walked in. The guards closed the door behind her.

"Hey," she said.

I glared at her from my bunk.

"The launch is on schedule," she said. "You'll be on your way soon."

"Whoopee."

She sat in the chair. "I know you won't believe this, but it wasn't easy for me to do this to you."

"Yeah, you're really sentimental."

She ignored the barb. "Do you know what I studied in college? What my undergraduate degree was in?"

I shrugged.

"History. I was a history major." She drummed her fingers on the desk. "Most people assume I had a science major or business management. Communications, maybe. But no. It was history."

"Doesn't seem like you." I sat up on my bunk. "You don't spend a lot of time looking backward."

"I was eighteen years old and had no idea what to do with my life. I majored in history because I didn't know what else to do." She smirked. "Hard to imagine me like that, eh?"

"Yeah."

She looked out the barred window toward the launchpad in the distance. "But I learned a lot. I actually liked it. People nowadays . . . they have no idea how good they have it. The past was unrelenting misery for most people. And the further back in time you go, the worse it was."

She stood and meandered around the room. "For fifty thousand years, right up to the industrial revolution, human civilization was about one thing and one thing only: food. Every culture that existed put most of their time, energy, manpower, and resources into food. Hunting it, gathering it, farming it, ranching it, storing it, distributing it . . . it was all about food.

"Even the Roman Empire. Everyone knows about the emperors, the armies, and the conquests. But what the Romans *really* invented was a very efficient system of acquiring farmland and transportation of food and water."

She walked to the other side of the room. "The industrial revolution mechanized agriculture. Since then, we've been able to focus our energies on other things. But that's only been the last two hundred years. Before that, most people spent most of their lives directly dealing with food production."

"Thanks for the history lesson," I said. "But if it's all the same to you, I'd like my last few moments on Earth to be a little more pleasant. So . . . you know . . . could you leave?"

She ignored me. "Leclerc's Antarctica nukes bought us some time. But not much. And there's only so many times we can dump chunks of Antarctica into the ocean before the direct problems of sea-level rise and ocean-biome death cause more problems than Astrophage. Remember what Leclerc told us: Half the global population will die."

"I know," I muttered.

"No, you don't know," she said. "Because it gets a lot worse."

"Worse than half of humanity dying?"

"Of course," she said. "Leclerc's estimate assumes all the nations of the world work together to share resources and ration food. But do you think that will happen? Do you think the United States—the most powerful military force of all time—is going to sit idly by while half their population starves? How about China, a nation of 1.3 billion people that's always on the verge of famines in the best of times? Do you think they'll just leave their militarily weak neighbors alone?"

I shook my head. "There'll be wars."

"Yes. There'll be wars. Fought for the same reason most wars in ancient times were fought for: food. They'd use religion or glory or whatever as an excuse, but it was always about food. Farmlands and people to work that land.

"But the fun doesn't stop there," she said. "Because once the desperate, starving countries start invading each other for food, the food production will go *down*. Ever heard of the Tai Ping rebellion? It was a civil war in China during the nineteenth century. Four hundred thousand soldiers died in combat. And *twenty million* people died from the resulting famine. The war disrupted agriculture, see? That's how massive in scale these things are."

She wrapped her arms around herself. I'd never seen her look so vulnerable. "Malnourishment. Disruption. Famine. Every aspect of infrastructure going to food production and warfare. The entire fabric of society will fall apart. There'll be plagues too. Lots of them. All over the world. Because the medical-care systems will be overwhelmed. Once easily contained outbreaks will go unchecked."

She turned to face me. "War, famine, pestilence, and death. Astrophage is literally the apocalypse. The *Hail Mary* is all we have now. I'll make any sacrifice to give it even the tiniest additional chance of success."

I lay down on my bunk and faced away from her. "Whatever lets you sleep at night."

She walked back to the door and knocked on it. A guard opened it up. "Anyway. I just wanted you to know why I'm doing this. I owed you that."

"Go to hell."

"Oh, I will, believe me. You three are going to Tau Ceti. The rest of us are going to hell. More accurately, hell is coming to us."

Yeah? Well, hell's coming back to you, Stratt. In the form of me. I'm hell.

I mean . . . I don't know what I'll say to her. But I definitely plan to say stuff. *Mean* stuff.

I'm eighteen days into my nearly four-year journey. I'm just now reaching Tau Ceti's heliopause—the edge of the star's powerful magnetic field. At least, the edge of where it's strong enough to deflect fast-moving interstellar radiation. From now on, the radiation load on the hull will be much higher.

Doesn't matter to me. I'm surrounded by Astrophage. But it's interesting to see the external radiation sensors go up and up and up. It's progress, at least. But in the grand scheme of things, I'm on a long road trip and my current status is "just walking out the front door of the house."

I'm bored. I'm by myself in a spaceship without much to do.

I clean and catalog the lab again. I might come up with some research experiments for either Astrophage or Taumoeba. Heck, I could write some papers while I'm on my way home. Oh, and there's the matter of the intelligent alien life-form I hung out with for a couple of months. I might want to jot a few things down about him too.

I do have a huge collection of video games. I have every piece of software that was available when we built the ship. I'm sure they can keep me busy for a while.

I check the Taumoeba farms. All ten of them are doing just fine. I feed them Astrophage from time to time, just to keep them healthy and breeding. The farms emulate Venus's atmosphere, so as the generations of Taumoeba go by, they'll get even better at Venusian life. After four years of this, by the time I drop them off at the planet, they'll be well suited for it.

And yes, I've already decided I'll drop them off. Why not?

I have no idea what kind of world I'll be returning to. Thirteen years have passed on Earth since I left, and they'll experience another thirteen before I get back. Twenty-six years. All my students will be adults. I hope they all survive. But I have to admit . . . some probably won't. I try not to dwell.

Anyway, once I get back to my solar system, I may as well swing by Venus and drop off the Taumoeba. Not sure how I'll seed it, but I have a few ideas. The simplest is just to wad up a ball of Taumoeba-infested Astrophage and throw it at Venus. The Astrophage will absorb the heat of reentry and the Taumoeba will be released into the wild. Then they'll have a field day. Venus must be Astrophage-central by now, and lord knows Taumoeba can get right to work once they find their prey.

I check my food stores. I'm still on schedule. I have another three months of real, edible food packs left, and then it'll be coma slurry from then on.

I'm reluctant to go back into a coma. I've got the genes to survive it, but so did Yáo and Ilyukhina. Why risk death if I don't have to?

Also, I can't be 100 percent sure I correctly reprogrammed the course navigation. I think it's right, and whenever I spot-check, I'm still on course toward home. But what if something goes wrong while I'm in a coma? What if I wake up and I missed the solar system by a light-year?

But between isolation, loneliness, and disgusting food, I may be willing to take those risks eventually. We'll see.

Speaking of loneliness, my thoughts turn back to Rocky. My only friend now. Seriously. He's my only friend. I didn't have much of a social life back when things were normal. Sometimes I'd grab dinner with other faculty and staff at the school. I'd have the occasional Saturday-night beer with old college friends. But thanks to time dilation, when I get home all those folks will be a generation older than me.

I liked Dimitri. He was probably my favorite of the whole *Hail Mary* gang. But who knows what he's up to now? Heck, Russia and the United States may be at war. Or they may be allies in a war. I have no idea.

I climb the ladder to the control room. I sit in the pilot's seat and bring up the Nav panel. I really shouldn't do this, but it's become a bit of a ritual. I shut off the spin drives and coast. Gravity immediately disappears, but I hardly notice. I'm used to it.

With the spin drives off, I can safely use the Petrovascope. I scan around in space for a bit—I know where to look. I quickly find it. The little dot of Petrova-frequency light. The *Blip-A*'s engines. If I were within a hundred kilometers of that light, my entire ship would be vaporized.

I'm on one side of the system and he's on the other. Heck, even Tau Ceti itself just looks like a lightbulb in the distance. But I can still clearly make out the *Blip-A*'s engine flare. Using light as a propellant releases a simply *absurd* amount of power.

Maybe that's something we could use in the future. Maybe Earth and Erid could communicate with massive releases of Petrova light thanks to Astrophage. I wonder how much it would take to make a flash visible from 40 Eridani. We could talk in Morse code or something. They have a copy of Wikipedia now. They'd work out what we're up to when they saw the flashes.

Still, our "conversation" would be slow. 40 Eridani is sixteen light-years away from Earth. So if we sent a message like "Hey, how ya doin'?" it would be thirty-two years before we got their reply.

I stare at the little point of light on the screen and sigh. I'll be able to track him for quite a while. I know where his ship will be at any given moment. He'll use the exact flight plan I gave him. He trusts my science as much as I trust his engineering. But after a few months, the Petrovascope won't be able to see the light anymore. Not because the light is too dim—it's a very sensitive instrument. It won't be able to see him because our relative velocities will cause a red-shift in the light coming off his drives. It won't be the Petrova wavelength anymore when it gets to me.

What? Would I do a ridiculous amount of relativistic math to calculate our relative velocity at any given moment as perceived by my inertial reference frame and then do Lorentz transformations to figure out when the light from his engines will drop out of the Petrovascope's perception range? Just so I know how much longer I can see my friend in the distance? Wouldn't that be kind of pathetic?

Yeah.

Okay, my sad little daily ritual is over. I turn off the Petrovascope and fire up the spin drives again.

I check my dwindling supply of real food. I've been "on the road" for thirty-two days now. According to my calculations, fifty-one days from now I'll be completely reliant on coma slurry.

I go to the dormitory. "Computer. Provide coma food substance sample."

The mechanical arms reach into their supply area and come back with a bag of white powder and drop it on the bunk.

I pick up the bag. Of course it's a powder. Why would they include the liquid in the long-term storage? The water system of the *Hail Mary* is a closed loop. Water goes into me, it comes out of me in various ways, and then it's purified and reused.

I take the package to the lab, open it up, and pour some powder in a beaker.

I add a little water, give it a stir, and it becomes a milky-white slurry. I give it a sniff. It doesn't really smell like anything. So I take a sip.

It takes effort, but I resist the urge to spit it out. It tastes like aspirin. That nasty pill-like taste. I'm going to have to eat this Bitter Pill Chow™ every meal for several years.

Maybe a coma isn't that bad.

I set the beaker aside. I'll deal with that misery when the time comes. For now, I'm going to work on the beetles.

I have four little Taumoeba farms, courtesy of Rocky. Each one is a steel-ish capsule no larger than my hand. I say "steel-ish" because it's some Eridian alloy of steel that humans haven't invented yet. It's much harder than any metal alloys we have, but not harder than diamond-cutting tools.

We went back and forth on the mini-farm casing. The obvious first choice was to make it out of xenonite. The problem is: How would Earth scientists get in? None of our tools would be able to cut it. The only option would be extremely high heat. And that risks harming the Taumoeba inside.

I suggested a xenonite container with a lid. Something that could be clamped down tight like a pressure door. I'd leave instructions on the USB stick on how to safely open it. Rocky rejected that idea right away. No matter how good the seal was, it wouldn't be perfect. Over the two years that the farm will experience during the trip, enough air could leak out to suffocate the Taumoeba inside. He insisted the whole farm be a single, completely sealed container. Probably a good idea.

So we settled on Eridian steel. It's strong, it doesn't oxidize easily, and it's extremely durable. Earth can cut it open with a diamond saw. And hey, they'll probably analyze it to learn how to make their own. Everyone wins!

His approach for the farms themselves was simple. Inside, there's an active colony of Taumoeba and a Venus-like atmosphere. Also, there's a coil of very thin steel-ish tubing full of Astrophage. The Taumoeba can only get at the outermost layer, so they have to work their way down the tube, which has a total length of about 20 meters. Some basic experimentation tells us that will last the small Taumoeba population several years. As for waste products—they'll just stew in their own poop. The capsule will gain methane and lose carbon dioxide over time, but it doesn't matter. Though it's a small volume by human standards, it's a vast, gigantic cavern to the tiny microbes inside.

The beetles have been a priority for me. I want them ready for launch at a moment's notice. Just in case there's a catastrophic problem with the *Hail Mary*. But I don't want to send them off if there isn't a mission-critical problem. The closer we are to Earth when they launch, the better their odds of making it there safely.

In addition to installing the mini-farms, I also have to refuel the little buggers. I'd used almost half their fuel supply when they served as ad-hoc engines for the *Hail Mary*. But they only need 60 kilograms of Astrophage each to be full. Barely a drop in the bucket compared to my supply of imported, Eridian-made Astrophage.

The hardest part is opening the beetle's little fuel bay. Like everything else around here, it wasn't intended for reuse. It's like adding fresh butane to a Bic lighter. It's just not meant for that. It's completely sealed. I have to clamp it into the mill and use a 6-millimeter bit to get in . . . it's a whole big thing. But I'm getting good at it.

I finished John and Paul yesterday. Today I'm working on Ringo and, time permitting, George. George will be the easiest. I don't need to refuel him—I never used him as an engine. I just have to attach the mini-farm.

Figuring out where to put the mini-farm was another matter. Even with its small size, it's too big to fit inside the little probe. So I epoxy it to the undercarriage. Then I spot-weld a small counterweight to the top of the beetle. The computer inside has very strong opinions about where the center of mass of the probe is. It's easier to add a counterweight than completely reprogram a guidance system.

Which brings us to the matter of weight.

The additional weight of the farm makes the beetles weigh a kilogram more than they should. That's okay. I remember countless meetings with Steve Hatch discussing the design. He's a weird little guy, but he's a heck of a rocket scientist. The beetles know their location in space by looking at the stars, and if they have less fuel than they expected to have, they taper their acceleration down as needed.

In short: They'll get home. It'll just take a little longer. I ran the numbers and it's a trivial difference in Earth time. Though the beetles will experience several additional months during the trip than the original plan.

I go to the supply cabinet and pull out the BOCOA (big ol' container of Astrophage). It's a lightproof metal bin with wheels. There are several hundred kilograms of Astrophage in there and I'm in 1.5 g's of gravity. That's why I added the wheels. You'd be amazed what you can do with a machine shop and a firm desire not to drag heavy stuff around.

I hold the handle with a towel because it's so hot. I wheel it over to the lab table, settle into the chair, and get ready for the methodical refueling process. I get the plastic syringe at the ready. With it, I can squirt 100 milliliters of Astrophage into that 6-millimeter hole per shot. That's about 600 grams. All told, I have to do it about two hundred times per beetle.

I open the BOCOA and—

"Ugh!" I wince and draw away from the container. It smells horrible.

"Uh . . ." I say. "Why does it smell like that?"

Then it hits me. I know that smell. It's the smell of dead, rotting Astrophage.

The Taumoeba are loose again.

CHAPTER 27

I leap from the stool, but I don't have a plan.

"Okay, don't panic," I tell myself. "Think clearly. Then act."

The BOCOA is still hot. That means there's a lot of living Astrophage still in there. I caught it early. That's good. Not because of the BOCOA—it's toast. I'll never be able to sort out the Taumoeba from the Astrophage in there. But it means that however the heck the Taumoeba got in there, this is very recent and hopefully hasn't reached the ship's fuel.

Yes. That's priority number one. Don't let Taumoeba into the fuel bays. Last time they got in was because of various microscopic leaks in the system. But it had to have gotten there from the crew compartments where I had brought it aboard. There isn't much overlap between the fuel system and the crew compartment. There's just one place that's the likely culprit for transfer.

Life support.

If the ship is too cold, it runs air across coils filled with Astrophage to warm it up. A breach in one of those coils would do it. Lucky for me I've had a big pile of 96°C Astrophage in the lab keeping the crew compartment so warm the ship has to use the air-conditioning system.

Okay, now I have a plan.

I scamper up the ladder to the control room. I bring up the Life Support panel and look at the logs. As I suspected, the heater hasn't been turned on in over a month. I deactivate the heater entirely. It shows as disabled, but I don't trust it.

I go to the primary breaker box. It's under the pilot's seat. I find the breaker for the heating system and flick it off.

"Okay," I say.

I get back in the seat and check the Fuel panel. The fuel bays all seem to be in good shape. The temperature is correct. It wouldn't take long for Taumoeba to run wild and eat everything in a fuel bay—I know that for darn certain. If they were affected, they'd be colder than that.

I bring up the spin-drive controls and shut the engines off. The floor drops out from under me as I return to weightlessness. I probably don't need to shut them off, but for now I don't want the fuel doing *anything*. If there's Taumoeba in a fuel line, I want it to stay there, not get pumped all over the ship.

"Okay . . ." I say again. "Okay . . ."

More thinking.

How did it get loose? I *sterilized* every part of this ship with nitrogen before getting a gram of Astrophage from Rocky. The only Taumoeba aboard are in the sealed mini-farms on the beetles and the sealed, *xenonite* breeder tanks.

No. No time for science questions. I can speculate on the cause later. Right now I have an engineering problem. I wish Rocky were here.

I always wish Rocky were here.

"Nitrogen," I say.

I don't know how the Taumoeba got out, but I need them dead. Taumoeba-82.5 can handle 8.25 percent nitrogen at 0.02 atmospheres. Maybe a little higher. But it definitely can't handle 100 percent nitrogen at the crew compartment's 0.33 atmospheres. That works out to be *two hundred times* its lethal dose of nitrogen.

I float to the breaker box and shut off everything related to life support. Immediately, the emergency alarm sounds and red lights turn on. I kick across the control room to the emergency system's breaker box and shut those all off as well.

The master alarm is annoying, so I silence it on the main interface panel.

I fly down to the lab and throw open my gas cylinder supply cupboard. I have about 10 kilograms of nitrogen gas in a single canister. Again, I owe my life to DuBois's preferred method of suicide.

I don't remember all the details about the life-support system, but I know it has manual overpressure valves. The ship simply will not allow more than 0.33 atmospheres. If all else fails (which it will, because I shut the emergency systems down), it'll vent excess pressure into space.

I can't just release the nitrogen and hope for the best. I want to get rid of the existing oxygen first. I'm through messing around with this stuff. I want 100 percent nitrogen in here. I want to make this ship so utterly toxic to Taumoeba that it has no chance of survival. Even if it's hiding under some goop somewhere—I want the nitrogen to suffuse through it. Nitrogen everywhere. Everywhere!

I grab the nitrogen cylinder, kick off the floor, and float back up to the control room. I throw open the airlock inner door and get into the Orlan suit faster than I ever have in the past. I boot everything up and don't even bother with the self-check. No time.

I leave the inner airlock door open and turn the manual emergency valve on the outer door. The ship's air hisses away into space. The primary and emergency life-support systems are powered down. They are unable to replace the lost gas.

Now I wait.

It takes a surprisingly long time for a ship to lose all its air. In movies, if there's a little breach everyone dies immediately. Or the muscular hero guy plugs the hole with his biceps or something. But in real life, air just doesn't move that fast.

The emergency valve on the airlock is 4 centimeters across. Seems like a pretty big hole to have in your spaceship, right?

It took twenty minutes for the ship's air pressure to drop to 10 percent of its original value. And it's dropping very slowly now. I think it's a logarithmic function. So in the middle of this emergency, I just have to stand here with my tank in my hand.

"Okay. Ten percent is close enough," I say. I close the airlock emergency valve to reseal the ship. Then I open the nitrogen tank.

So now, instead of listening to a hiss from the airlock, I listen to a hiss from the nitrogen tank.

Not much difference there.

Again. It's a bit of a wait. But not as long this time. Probably because the pressure inside that nitrogen tank was a lot higher than the pressure in the ship. Whatever. Point is, in short order the ship is back to 0.33 atmospheres of pressure. But it's almost entirely nitrogen.

Funny thing—I'd be perfectly comfortable if I took this EVA suit off. I'd breathe without any problems. Right up until I died. There's nowhere near enough oxygen for me to survive.

I want that nitrogen to permeate everything it can. I want it to get into every crevice. Wherever Taumoeba are lurking, I want them found and killed. Go forth, my N_2 minions, and cause destruction!

I head down to the lab and check out the BOCOA. I left in such a hurry I forgot to seal the vat. Fortunately, Astrophage is gunky stuff. Surface tension and inertia kept it inside. I close the lid and bring it up to the airlock. I jettison the whole thing.

I probably could have saved the surviving Astrophage in the vat. I could have bubbled nitrogen through the sludge to make sure it gets at all the little Taumoeba lurking inside. But why take the chance? I have over 2 million kilograms of Astrophage. There's no point in risking the whole mission just to save a few hundred.

I wait three hours. Then I flick the breakers back on. After a period of initial panic, the life-support system gets the air back to normal thanks to the ship's copious oxygen reserves.

I have to isolate every source of Taumoeba on this ship. Preferably before the life-support system finishes pumping out the nitrogen. Why not do it before getting back to normal air? Because it'll be a lot easier and faster without wearing the EVA suit. I need my hands to do this, not my hands inside bulky gloves.

I climb out of the Orlan and fly down to the lab, the nitrogen cylinder in hand.

First up: the breeder farms.

I put each of the ten farms in large plastic bins. I install a little valve on each bin (epoxy can do anything), and pump in nitrogen. If any of the farms have a leak, the nitrogen will get in and kill everything. Any farm that's behaving properly—keeping airtight—won't have any problems.

The bins are airtight to begin with, but I seal them with duct tape anyway, and I deliberately overpressurize them by just a little bit. The sides and tops bulge out. Now if any of the farms leak, it'll be visually apparent because the bulging will disappear.

Next up: the beetles and their mini-farms.

John and Paul already have their mini-farms installed. I put them in isolation bins just like I did with the breeder farms. I was working on Ringo when the poop hit the fan, so that mini-farm and the one intended for George are still uninstalled. I put the pair together in another isolation bin.

I tape everything to the walls. I don't want any of the bins to float around. They might bump into something sharp.

The lab is a shambles. I was halfway through disassembling Ringo when I shut off the spin drives. Tools, beetle parts, and all manner of other junk floats around the room. I'll have to clean all that up without the aid of gravity before I can even take a break.

"Well, this sucks," I mumble.

CHAPTER 28

It's been three days since the Great Taumoeba Escape. I've taken no chances.

I manually shut off all the fuel bays—completely segregating each one from the fuel system. Then, one tank at a time, I opened it, collected an Astrophage sample from the line, and checked it in the microscope for Taumoeba contamination.

Thankfully, all nine tanks passed the test. I brought the spin drives back online and I'm cruising along at 1.5 g's again.

I cobble together a "Taumoeba alarm" to alert me if this happens again. I should have done that in the first place, but hindsight is 20/20.

It's a slide of Astrophage—same as I used in the Taumoeba farms—with a light on one side and a light sensor on the other. The whole system is exposed to the open air of the lab. If Taumoeba get ahold of that Astrophage, they'll eat it, the slide will turn clear, and the light sensor will start beeping. So far, no beeping. The slide remains jet-black.

Now that things have calmed down and the problem is contained, I can start asking the million-dollar question: How did the Taumoeba get loose?

I put my hands on my hips and stare at the quarantine zone.

"Which one of you did this?" I say.

None of it makes sense. The farms worked for months without any hint of a leak. The mini-farms are hermetically sealed steel capsules.

Maybe some rogue Taumoeba was lurking on the ship since the last outbreak—back at Adrian. Somehow it didn't find any Astrophage until just now?

No. From our experiments, Rocky and I learned that Taumoeba can only last about a week without food before it starves to death. And they're not big on moderation. Either they wildly breed and consume all Astrophage to be found, or they aren't present at all.

One of these containers must be leaking. I can't just jettison everything—I need these Taumoeba to save Earth—so what do I do? I have to figure out which one is the problem.

I check each farm as best I can. Since they're in bins, I can't operate any of the controls, but I don't need to. They're fully automated. It's a pretty simple system—Rocky tends to find elegant solutions to complex problems. The farm monitors the air temperature inside. If it drops below 96.415 degrees Celsius, it means there's no more Astrophage because the Taumoeba ate it. So it pumps in a little more Astrophage. Simple as that. And the system keeps track of how often it has to feed them. From that it makes a very rough approximation of the Taumoeba population inside. It adjusts the Astrophage feed rate as needed to control that population and, of course, has a readout to tell us the current state.

I check each farm's readouts. Each one shows 96.415 degrees Celsius with a population estimate of 10 million Taumoeba. Exactly what they're supposed to read.

"Hm," I say.

The air pressure inside those farms is way lower than the nitrogen pressure surrounding them. If any of those farms had a leak, the nitrogen would get in and pretty soon the Taumoeba would all die. But they haven't. And it's been three days.

The breeder farms aren't leaking. It must be the mini-farms. But how the heck does a microbe work its way through half a centimeter of Eridian steel? Rocky knows what he's doing, and he knows all about Eridian steel. If it wasn't good for holding microbes in place, he'd know. They don't have Taumoeba on Erid, but they definitely have other microbes. This isn't new to them.

All of this leads me to something I would normally consider impossible: Rocky made an engineering mistake.

He *never* makes mistakes. Not when it comes to creating things. He's one of the most talented engineers on his entire planet! He *couldn't* have messed up.

Could he?

I need definitive proof.

I make more Astrophage test slides. They're super-handy for Taumoeba detection and easy to make.

I start with the bin containing the two mini-farms—the ones intended for George and Ringo. They certainly *seem* sealed. They're just capsule-shaped pieces of metal. All sorts of stuff going on inside, but smooth Eridian steel on the outside.

I peel the duct tape off one corner of the box, pry up the lid, and throw an Astrophage slide in, then reseal everything. Experiment number one: Make sure I didn't accidentally breed up some Super-Taumoeba that can live in pure nitrogen.

Another fun fact I've learned: Once Taumoeba get ahold of an Astrophage slide, it'll be crystal clear in a couple of hours. So I wait a couple of hours and the slide is still black. Okay, good. No Super-Taumoeba.

I unseal the bin, open the lid, and let it air out for a minute. Then I reseal it. The nitrogen content in there will be nominal now. Way less than Taumoeba-82.5 needs to worry about. If there's a leak in those mini-farms, the slide will tell the tale.

One hour, no results. Two hours, no results.

I take a sample of the air inside the bin just to be sure. The nitrogen level is nearly zero. So that's not an issue.

I seal it up again and give it another hour. Nothing.

The mini-farms aren't leaking. At least, the ones intended for

George and Ringo aren't. Maybe the leak was in one of the mini-farms I've already installed.

They're just glued to the outsides of John and Paul. They're not protected by the beetle's hull or anything. I repeat the Taumoeba detection experiment with John and Paul's bins.

I get the same result: no Taumoeba at all.

"Hm."

Okay, time for the ultimate test. I remove John, Paul, and the two uninstalled mini-farms from quarantine. I set them on the lab table next to my Taumoeba alarm. I'm pretty sure they're clean. But if they aren't, I want to know right away.

I turn my attention to the even less likely culprits: the breeder farms.

If Taumoeba can't escape Eridian steel, they definitely can't get through xenonite. One centimeter of that stuff can effortlessly hold in Rocky's 29 atmospheres of pressure! It's harder than diamond and also somehow not brittle.

But I need to be thorough. I repeat the Astrophage slide test with all ten of the breeder farm bins. There's no point in doing them one at a time. I pipeline the whole process. Now all ten of the farms are in sealed bins full of normal air and have an Astrophage slide inside.

It's been a long day. It's a good time to take a break and sleep. I'll leave them overnight to see what happens. I bring bedding up from the dormitory to the lab. If my Taumoeba-detector alarm goes off, I want to be darn sure it wakes me up. I'm too pooped to work up a louder solution. So I'll just bring my ears closer to the lab table and call it a night.

I drift off to sleep. It feels wrong to sleep without someone watching.

I wake up about six hours later. "Coffee."

But the nanny-arms are downstairs in the dormitory. So of course I get no response.

"Oh, right . . ." I sit up and stretch.

I get up and shuffle over to the quarantine zone. Let's see how those Taumoeba farm tests are doing.

I check the first farm's Astrophage slide. It's completely clear. So I move on to the next—

Wait. It's clear?

"Uh . . ."

I'm still not 100 percent awake. I wipe my eyes and take another look.

It's still clear.

Taumoeba got to the slide. It got out of the breeder farm!

I spin to the Taumoeba alarm on the lab table. It's not beeping, but I run over to get a visual. The Astrophage slide in it is still black.

I take a deep breath and let it out.

"Okay . . ." I say.

I return to the quarantine zone and check the other farms. Every single one of them has a clear slide. The farms are leaking. *All of them are leaking*. The mini-farms are fine. They're sitting on the lab table right next to the Taumoeba alarm.

I rub the back of my neck.

I've found the problem, but I don't understand it. Taumoeba are getting out of the farms. But how? If there was a crack in the xenonite, the overpressure of nitrogen would've gotten inside and killed everything. All ten farms have happy, healthy Taumoeba populations. So what gives?

I climb down to the dormitory and have breakfast. I stare at the xenonite wall that once housed Rocky's workshop. The wall is still there, but with a hole cut in it where I'd requested. I'm using the area mainly for storage.

I chew on a breakfast burrito, trying to ignore the fact that I'm one meal closer to coma slurry. I stare at the hole. I imagine I'm a Taumoeba. I'm millions of times larger than a nitrogen atom. But I can get through a hole the nitrogen atom can't. How? And where did the hole come from?

I'm starting to get a bad feeling. A suspicion, really.

What if Taumoeba can, for lack of a better description, work their way around the molecules of xenonite? What if there's no hole at all?

We tend to think of solid materials as magical barriers. But at the molecular scale they're not. They're strands of molecules or lattices of atoms or both. When you get down to the teeny, tiny realm, solid objects are more like thick jungles than brick walls.

I can work my way through a jungle, no problem. I may have to climb over bushes, weave around trees, and duck under branches, but I can make it.

Imagine a thousand tennis-ball launchers at the edge of that jungle aimed in random directions. How deep into the jungle will the tennis balls get? Most of them won't get past the first few trees. Some may get lucky bounces and go a little deeper in. Fewer still may get multiple lucky bounces. But pretty soon, even the luckiest tennis ball runs out of energy.

You'd be hard-pressed to find any tennis balls 50 feet into that jungle. Now, let's say it's a mile wide. I can make it to the other side, but there's just no chance a tennis ball can.

That's the difference between Taumoeba and nitrogen. The nitrogen is just moving in a line and bouncing off stuff like a tennis ball. It's inert. But Taumoeba is like me. It has stimulus-response capabilities. It senses its environment and takes directed action based on that sensory input. We already know it can find Astrophage and move toward it. It definitely has senses. But nitrogen atoms are ruled by entropy. They won't "exert effort" to do anything. I can walk uphill. But a tennis ball can only roll so far before it rolls back down.

That all seems really weird. How could Taumoeba, from the planet Adrian, know how to carefully navigate its way through xenonite, a technological invention from the planet Erid? It does not make sense.

Life-forms don't evolve traits for no reason. Taumoeba lives in the upper atmosphere. Why would it develop the ability to work its way through dense molecular structures? What evolutionary reason could there be to—

I drop my burrito.

I know the answer. I don't want to admit it to myself. But I know the answer.

I go back to the lab and perform a nerve-wracking experiment. The experiment itself isn't nerve-wracking. I'm just worried that the results will be what I expect.

I still have Rocky's AstroTorch. It's the only thing on the ship that can get hot enough to dissociate xenonite. There's plenty of xenonite to be had throughout the ship, thanks to Rocky's tunnel system. I cut into the dormitory divider wall. I can only cut a little bit at a time, then I have to wait for life support to cool things back down. The AstroTorch makes a *lot* of heat.

In the end, I have four rough circles, each a couple of inches across.

Yes, *inches*. When I'm stressed out, I revert to imperial units. It's hard to be an American, okay?

I take them up to the lab and put together an experiment.

I smear some Astrophage on one of the circles and put another circle on top of it. Astrophage sandwich. Delicious, but only if you can get through the xenonite "bread." I epoxy the two halves together. I make another identical sandwich.

And then I make another two similar sandwiches, but instead of xenonite, I use ordinary plastic discs that I cut from some mill stock.

Okay. Four hermetically sealed Astrophage samples—two with xenonite discs, two with plastic discs, all four of them sealed with epoxy.

I get two clear, sealable containers and set them up on the lab table. I put a xenonite sandwich and a plastic sandwich in each container.

In the sample cabinet, I have a few metal vials full of natural Taumoeba. The original stuff from Adrian, not the Taumoeba-82.5 version. I set the vial in one of the containers, open it up, and quickly seal the experiment. This is a very dangerous road to go down, but at least

I know how to contain a Taumoeba outbreak if it happens. As long as I have nitrogen I'm okay.

I go to Breeder Tank One in the quarantine zone. I use a syringe to get the Taumoeba-infected air from the bin, then immediately flood the bin with nitrogen. I tape over the hole made by the syringe.

Back to the lab table, I close up the other container and use the syringe to inject the Taumoeba-82.5 in. Again, I seal that hole with tape.

I rest my chin in my hands and peer into the two boxes. "Okay, you sneaky little punks. Let's see what you can do . . ."

It takes a couple of hours, but I finally see results. They're exactly what I expected and the opposite of what I'd hoped.

I shake my head. "Dang it."

The xenonite-covered Astrophage in the Taumoeba-82.5 experiment is gone. The plastic-covered Astrophage remains unchanged. Meanwhile in the other experiment, both Astrophage samples are unharmed.

What that means: The "control" samples (the plastic discs) prove Taumoeba can't get through epoxy or plastic. But the xenonite samples tell a different story. Taumoeba-82.5 can work its way through xenonite, but natural Taumoeba can't.

"I'm so stupid!" I smack myself on the head.

I thought I was oh so clever. All that time in the breeder tanks. Generation after generation of Taumoeba. I used evolution to my advantage, right? I made Taumoeba with nitrogen resistance! I'm so awesome! Let me know when I can pick up my Nobel Prize!

Ugh.

Yes, I made a strain of Taumoeba that could survive nitrogen. But evolution doesn't care what I want. And it doesn't do just one thing at a time. I bred up a bunch of Taumoeba that evolved to survive . . . in xenonite breeder tanks.

Sure, it has nitrogen resistance. But evolution has a sneaky way of working on a problem from every angle. So not only did they gain resistance to nitrogen, they figured out how to hide from nitrogen by sneaking into the xenonite itself! Why wouldn't they?

Xenonite is a complicated chain of proteins and chemicals I have no hope of understanding. But I guess Taumoeba has a way to worm its way in. There's a nitrogen apocalypse going on in the breeder farm. If you can get into the xenonite walls deep enough that the nitrogen can't reach, you get to survive!

Taumoeba can't get through ordinary plastic. It can't get through epoxy resin. It can't get through glass. It can't get through metal. I'm not even sure if it could get through a ziplock bag. But thanks to me, Taumoeba-82.5 can get through xenonite.

I took a life-form I knew nothing about and used technology I didn't understand to modify it. Of *course* there were unintended consequences. It was stupidly arrogant of me to assume I could predict everything.

I take a deep breath and let it out.

Okay, this isn't the end of the world. In fact, it's the opposite. This Taumoeba can permeate xenonite. No problem. I'll store it in something else. It's still nitrogen-resistant. It doesn't *need* xenonite to survive. I tested it thoroughly in my glass lab equipment back when we first isolated the strain. It'll still do its thing on Venus and Threeworld. Everything's fine.

I glance back at the breeder farms.

Yeah. Fine. I'll make a big farm out of metal. It's not hard. I have a mill and all the raw materials I need. And God knows I have time to spare. I'll salvage the operational equipment from a farm Rocky made. Only the casing is xenonite. Everything else is metals and stuff. I don't need to reinvent the wheel. I just need to put it on a different car.

"Yeah," I reassure myself. "Yeah, this is okay."

I just need to make a box that can maintain a Venusian atmosphere. All of the hard stuff is already done, thanks to Rocky.

Rocky!

I feel a sudden surge of nausea. I have to sit on the floor and put my head between my legs. Rocky has the same strain of Taumoeba aboard his ship. It's stored in xenonite farms like mine.

All critical bulkheads of his ship, including the fuel tanks, are made of xenonite. There's nothing standing between his Taumoeba and his fuel.

"Oh . . . God . . ."

CHAPTER 29

I made the new Taumoeba farm. Sheet aluminum and some basic milling on the CNC mill. It wasn't a problem.

Rocky's ship is the problem.

I've been watching his engine flare every day for the past month. Now it's gone.

I float in the control room. The spin drives are off, and the Petrovascope is set to maximum sensitivity. There's some random Petrova-wavelength light coming from Tau Ceti itself, as always. And even that's dim. The star, almost as bright as Earth's sun, now just looks like a fatter-than-usual dot in the night sky.

But aside from that . . . nothing. I'm way too far away to detect the Tau Ceti–Adrian Petrova line and the *Blip-A* is nowhere to be seen.

And I know right where it should be. Down to the milli-arc-second. And from here, its engines should be lighting up my scope. . . .

I ran the numbers again and again. Though I'd already proven my formulae correct by daily observations of his progress. Now there's nothing. No blip from the *Blip-A*.

He's derelict out there. His Taumoeba escaped their enclosure and wormed their way into his fuel bays. From there, they ate everything. Millions of kilograms of Astrophage gone in a matter of days.

He's smart, so he surely has the fuel compartmentalized. But those compartments are made of xenonite, right? Yeah.

Three days.

If the ship were damaged, he'd fix it. There's nothing Rocky can't fix. And he works fast. Five arms whipping around, often doing unrelated things. He could be dealing with a massive Taumoeba infection, but how long would that take? He has plenty of nitrogen. He can harvest as much as he wants from his ammonia atmosphere. Let's assume he did that as soon as he noticed the contagion.

How long would it take him to get things back online?

Not this long.

Whatever may have happened, if the *Blip-A* could be fixed, he would have fixed it by now. The only explanation for it still being dead in space is that it has no fuel. He wasn't able to stop the Taumoeba in time.

I put my head in my hands.

I can go home. I really can. I can return and spend the rest of my life a hero. Statues, parades, et cetera. And I'll be in a new world order where all energy problems are solved. Cheap, easy, renewable energy everywhere thanks to Astrophage. I can track down Stratt and tell her to shove it.

But then Rocky dies. And more important, Rocky's people die. Billions of them.

I'm *this close*. I just need to survive four years. Yeah, it'll be eating nasty coma slurry but I'll be *alive*.

My annoying logical mind points out the other option: Launch the beetles—all four of them. Each with their own Taumoeba mini-farm and a USB stick full of data and findings. Earth scientists will take it from there.

Then turn the *Hail Mary* around, find Rocky, and take him home to Erid.

One problem: It means I die.

I have enough food to survive the trip to Earth. Or I have enough to survive the trip to Erid. But even if the Eridians refuel the *Hail Mary* right away, there won't be enough food for me to survive the trip back to Earth from Erid. I'll have only a few months of food left at that point.

I can't grow anything. I don't have any viable seeds or living plant matter. I can't eat Eridian food. Too many heavy metals and other major toxins.

So that's what I'm left with. Option 1: Go home a hero and save all of humanity. Option 2: Go to Erid, save an alien species, and starve to death shortly after.

I pull on my hair.

I sob into my hands. It's cathartic and exhausting.

All I see when I close my eyes is Rocky's dumb carapace and his little arms always fidgeting with something.

It's been six weeks since I made my decision. It wasn't easy, but I'm sticking with it.

I have the spin drives off for my daily ritual. I bring up the Petrovascope and look out into space. I see nothing at all.

"Sorry, Rocky," I say.

Then I spot a tiny speck of Petrova light. I zoom in and search that area. A total of four little dots, barely visible, are on the monitor.

"I know you'd love a beetle to take apart, but I couldn't spare one."

The beetles, with much smaller spin drives, won't be visible for much longer. Especially with them zooming off toward Earth and me headed almost the opposite direction toward the *Blip-A*.

The Astrophage coils in the mini-farms will protect the Taumoeba from radiation, and I did thorough tests to make sure both the farms and the life inside could handle the massive acceleration that beetles use. They'll be back at Earth in a couple of years from their point of view. About thirteen years, from Earth's time frame.

I bring the spin drives back online and continue on course.

Finding a spaceship "somewhere just outside the Tau Ceti system" is no small task. Imagine being given a rowboat and told to find a toothpick "somewhere in the ocean." It's like that, but nowhere near as easy.

I know his course and I know he followed it. But I don't know when his engines conked out. I only checked up on him once a day. Right now, I'm smack-dab in the center of my "best guess" for his position and I've matched my best guess on his velocity. But that's only the beginning. I have a heck of a search ahead of me.

I wish I had tracked him more often. Because I don't know the exact time his engines died, the margin of error on my guess is about 20 million kilometers. That's about one-eighth the distance between the Earth and the sun. It's a distance so large it takes light a full minute to traverse it. That's the best I can do with the information I have.

Frankly, I'm lucky the error margin is so *small*. If the Taumoeba had escaped a month later, it would have been exponentially worse. And all this is going on at the edge of the Tau Ceti system. Barely the beginning of the trip. The distance between Tau Ceti and Earth is over *four thousand times* the width of the entire Tau Ceti system.

Space is big. It's . . . so, so big.

So yeah. I'm extremely lucky to have only 20 million kilometers to search.

"Hmm," I mumble.

This far away from Tau Ceti, his ship won't be reflecting much Tau-light. There's no chance I'd spot the *Blip-A* with my telescope.

Side note: I'm going to die.

"Stop," I say. Whenever I think about my impending death, I think about Rocky instead. He must have a sense of hopelessness right now. *I'm coming, buddy.*

"Wait . . ."

I'm sure he's sad, but he's also not one to mope for long. He'll be working on a solution. What would he do? His whole species is on the line and he doesn't know I'm coming. He wouldn't just kill himself, right? He'd do anything he could think of, even if it would have only a tiny percent chance of success.

Okay. I'm Rocky. My ship is dead. Maybe I rescued some Astrophage. The Taumoeba can't have gotten *all* of it, right? So I have some. Can I make my own beetle? Something to send back to Erid?

I shake my head. That would require a guidance system. Computer stuff. Way beyond Eridian science. That's why they had a crew of twenty-three on a massive ship in the first place. Besides, it's been a month and a half. If he were going to build a little ship, he'd be done by now and I would have seen its engine flare. Rocky moves fast.

Okay. No beetle. But he's got energy. Life support. Food enough to last him a long, long time (original crew of twenty-three, and it was always intended to be a round-trip voyage).

"Radio?" I say.

Maybe he'll make a radio signal. Something powerful enough to be heard on Erid. Just a small chance of detection, but something. Eridians have a long life-span. Waiting a decade or so for rescue wouldn't be that big a deal. Well, not on the life-or-death scale. If you asked me a few years ago I'd say it's not possible to send a radio signal ten light-years. But this is Rocky we're talking about, and he might have some rescued Astrophage to power whatever he creates.

It doesn't have to contain information. It just needs to be noticed.

But . . . no. There's just no way. Some back-of-the napkin math tells me that even with Earth's radio technology (which is better than Erid's), the strength of that signal at Erid would be way less than background noise.

Rocky will know that too. So there's no point.

"Hmm."

I wish I had better radar. Mine is good for a few thousand kilometers. Obviously that's nowhere near good enough. Rocky could probably whip something up if he were here. It's a little paradoxical, but I wish Rocky were here to help me save Rocky.

"Better radar . . ." I mumble.

Well, I have plenty of power. I have a radar system. Maybe I can work something out.

But you can't just add power to the emitter and expect things to go well. I'll burn it out for sure. How can I turn Astrophage energy into radio waves?

I shoot up from my pilot's seat. "Duh!"

I have everything I need for the best radar ever! To heck with my built-in radar system, with its measly emitter and sensors. I have spin drives and a Petrovascope! I can throw *900 terawatts* of IR light out the back of my ship and see if any of it bounces back with the Petrovascope—an instrument carefully designed to detect even the smallest amounts of that exact frequency of light!

I can't have the Petrovascope and engines on at the same time. But that's okay! Rocky is up to a light-minute away!

I work up a search grid. It's pretty simple. I'm smack-dab in the middle of my guesstimate on Rocky's location. So I have to search all directions.

Easy enough. I fire up the spin drives. I take manual control, which, as usual, requires me to say "yes," "yes," "yes," and "override" to a bunch of warning dialogs.

I throw the throttle to full and turn hard to port with the yaw controls. The force shoves me back into the seat and to the side. This is the astronavigational equivalent of doing donuts in the 7-Eleven parking lot.

I keep it tight—it takes me thirty seconds to do one full rotation. I'm roughly back where I started. Probably a few dozen kilometers off but whatever. I cut the engines.

Now I watch the Petrovascope. It's not omnidirectional, but it can cover a good 90-degree arc of space at a time. I slowly pan across space in the same direction I'd shined the engines and at the same rate. It's not perfect; I could get the timing wrong. If Rocky is very close or very far away this won't work. But this is just my first try.

I finish a full circle with the Petrovascope. Nothing. So I do another lap. Maybe Rocky is farther than I thought.

The second lap turns up nothing.

Well, I'm not done yet. Space is three-dimensional. I've only searched one flat slice of the area. I pitch the ship forward 5 degrees.

I do the same search pattern again. But this time, the plane of my search pattern is 5 degrees different from the last time. If I don't get a hit on this pass, I'll do another 5-degree tilt and try again. And so on until I get to 90 degrees, when I will have searched all directions.

And if *that* doesn't work, I'll start over, but with a faster pan rate on the Petrovascope.

I rub my hands together, take a sip of water, and get to work.

A flash!

I finally see a flash!

Halfway through my Petrova pan of the 55-degree plane. A flash!

I flail in surprise, which launches me out of the seat. I bounce around the zero-g control room and scramble back into position. It's been slow going up till now. I was as bored as a guy could be. But not anymore!

"Crud! Where was it! Okay! Relax! Calm down. *Calm down!*"

I put my finger on the screen where I saw the blip. I check the Petrovascope bearing, do some math on the screen, and work out the angle. It's 214 degrees' yaw in my current plane, which is 55 degrees off the Tau Ceti–Adrian orbital ecliptic.

"Gotcha!"

Time for a better reading. I strap on my now-worn and banged-up stopwatch. Zero g has not been kind to the little guy, but it still works.

I take the controls and angle the ship directly away from the contact. I start the stopwatch, thrust in a straight line for ten seconds, turn, and shut down the engines. I'm moving something like 150 meters per second away from the contact, but that doesn't matter. I don't want to zero out the velocity I just added. I want the Petrovascope.

I stare at the screen with the stopwatch ticking away in my hand. Soon, I see the blip again. Twenty-eight seconds. The spot of light remains for ten seconds, then disappears.

I can't guarantee it's the *Blip-A*. But whatever it is, it's definitely a reflection of my spin drives. And it's fourteen light-seconds away (fourteen seconds to get there, fourteen seconds to get back equals twenty-eight seconds). That works out to about 4 million kilometers.

No point in trying to work out the object's velocity by taking multiple readings. I don't have that kind of precision with my "finger on the screen" approach. But I have a heading.

I can cover 4 million kilometers in nine and a half hours.

I fist-pump. "Yes! I'm definitely going to die!"

I don't know why I said that. I guess . . . well, if I wasn't able to find Rocky, I'd set course for Earth. I'm surprised I put this much effort into it, actually.

Whatever. I set course for where I saw the blip and fire up the engines. I don't even need to account for relativity on this one. Just high-school physics. I'll accelerate half the way, then decelerate the other half.

I spend the next nine hours cleaning up. I'm going to have a guest again!

I hope.

Rocky will have to plug up all the holes he made in the xenonite walls. But that shouldn't be a problem.

That assumes the contact I got was the *Blip-A* and not just a random piece of debris in space.

I try not to think about it. Keep hope alive and all that.

I move all my junk out of the xenonite areas.

Once I'm done with that, I fidget a lot. I want to stop and do another sweep to confirm my heading, but I resist the urge. Just wait it out.

I stare at the aluminum Taumoeba farm in my lab. And the slide of Astrophage next to it in the Taumoeba alarm. Everything is going just fine. Maybe I could—

The timer beeps. I'm at the location!

I scramble up the ladder to the control room and shut off the spin drives. I have the Radar screen up before I even get in the chair. I do a full active ping and full power. "Come on . . . come on. . . ."

Nothing.

I settle into the seat and strap in. I thought something like this might happen. I'm a lot closer to the contact now, but still not in radar range. I just traveled 4 million kilometers. Radar range is less than a thousandth of that. So my precision isn't 99.9 percent. Big surprise.

Time for another Petrovascope sweep. But this time I don't have the luxury of a full light-minute between me and the contact, wherever it is. If I'm, say, 100,000 kilometers away, I'll have less than a second before the light comes back to me. And I can't use the Petrovascope with the spin drives on.

So now what?

I need to create a bunch of Astrophage light *without* turning off the Petrovascope. I look through the menu options and don't find anything. There's no way to have the scope on when the spin drives are running. It must be a physical interlock somewhere. Somewhere aboard this ship is a wire leading from the spin-drive controls to the Petrovascope. I could spend the rest of my life looking for that and have no success.

However, the main engines aren't the only spin drives I have.

The attitude-adjustment engines are little spin drives sticking out the side of the *Hail Mary*. They're what let me yaw, pitch, and roll the ship. I wonder if the Petrovascope cares about them?

I keep the scope on and do a quick roll to the left. The ship rolls and the scope stays active!

Got to love those edge cases! Though I'm sure someone on the design team thought of this case. They probably decided the comparatively small output from the attitude drives wouldn't hurt the scope. And, looking at the overall concepts, it makes sense. The engines and attitude drives all point away from the ship and thus away from the Petrovascope. The reason it shuts down when the main drives are on is because of reflected light off small amounts of cosmic dust. The reflected light from the far less powerful adjustment drives was deemed acceptable.

But those adjustment drives are still putting out enough light to vaporize steel. Maybe they'll be enough to light up the *Blip-A*.

I aim the Petrovascope parallel to the port-side yaw thruster. In fact, I can see the thruster itself in the bottom of the visible-light mode image. I fire it up.

There's definitely a visible glow in the Petrova spectrum. A general haze near the thruster, like turning on a flashlight in the fog. But after a few seconds the haze dies down. It's still there, just not as prevalent.

Probably dust and trace gases from the *Hail Mary* herself. Tiny particles of stuff drifting away from the ship. Once the thruster vaporized all the ones nearby, things calmed down.

I keep the thruster on, and let the ship rotate on its yaw axis as I watch the Petrovascope. Now I have a flashlight. The rotation rate of the ship increases faster and faster. I can't have that. So I activate the starboard-side yaw thruster as well. The computer complains up a storm. There's no sensible reason to tell the ship to rotate clockwise and counterclockwise at the same time. I ignore the warnings.

I do a full revolution and see nothing. Okay. Nothing new. I do a 5-degree pitch adjustment and try again.

On my sixth go-around—at 25 degrees from the Adrian ecliptic, I spot the contact. Still too far away to make out any detail. But it's a flash of light in response to my yaw thruster. I flick the thruster on and off a few times to gauge the response time. It's nearly instant—I'd say less than a quarter second. I'm within 75,000 kilometers.

I point toward the contact and fire up the drives. This time I won't go barreling in willy-nilly. I'll stop every 20,000 kilometers or so and take another reading.

I smile. It's working.

Now I just have to hope I haven't been chasing an asteroid all day.

With careful flying and repeated measurements, I finally have the object on radar!

It's right there on the screen. "BLIP-A."

"Oh, right," I say. I forgot that's how it got its name.

I'm 4,000 kilometers away—the very edge of radar range. I bring up the telescope view, but I can't see anything, even at the highest magnification. The telescope was made for finding celestial bodies hundreds or thousands of kilometers across, not a spaceship a few hundred meters long.

I creep closer. The object's velocity with respect to Tau Ceti is about right for Rocky's ship. Roughly the speed he would have gotten to around the time his engines died.

I could take a bunch of readings and do math to work out its course, but I have an easier plan.

I thrust for a few minutes here, a few minutes there, slowing down and speeding up until I match the object's velocity. It's still 4,000 kilometers away, but now the relative velocity to me is almost zero. Why do this? Because the *Hail Mary* is very good at telling me about its own course.

I bring up the Nav console and tell it to calculate my current orbit. After some stargazing and calculation, the computer tells me exactly what I wanted to hear: The *Hail Mary* is on a hyperbolic trajectory. That means I'm not in orbit at all. I'm on an escape vector, leaving Tau Ceti's gravity influence entirely.

And that means the object I'm tracking is also on an escape vector. You know what objects in a solar system *don't* do? They don't escape the star's gravity. Anything going fast enough to escape did so billions of years ago. Whatever this is, it's no normal asteroid.

"Yes yes yes yes . . ." I say. I kick the spin drives on and head toward the contact. "I'm comin', buddy. Hold tight."

When I'm within 500 kilometers, I finally get some resolution on the object. All I see is a highly pixelated triangle. It's four times as long as it is wide. It's not much information, but it's enough. It's the *Blip-A*. I know the profile well.

I have a bag of Ilyukhina's vodka handy for just such an occasion. I take a sip from the zip-straw. I cough and wheeze. Dang, she liked her liquor rough.

Rocky's ship sits 50 meters off my starboard side. I came up really carefully—I don't want to cross an entire solar system just to accidentally vaporize him with my engines. I've matched velocities to within a few centimeters per second.

It's been almost three months since we parted. From the outside, the *Blip-A* looks the same as it always has. But something is definitely wrong.

I've tried everything to communicate. Radio. Flashes of spin-drive light. Nothing gets a response.

I get a sinking feeling. What if Rocky's dead? He was all alone in there. What if all heck broke loose while he was in a sleep cycle? Eridians don't wake up until their bodies are ready. What if the life-support system went offline while he was asleep and he just . . . never woke up?

What if he died of radiation sickness? All that Astrophage that was protecting him from radiation turned into methane and Taumoeba. Eridians are very susceptible to radiation. It might have happened so fast he didn't have a chance to react.

I shake my head.

No. He's Rocky. He's smart. He'd have backup plans. A separate life-support system that he sleeps in, I bet. And he'd account for radiation—it killed his entire crew.

But why no response?

He can't see. He doesn't have windows. He'd have to actively look outside with the *Blip-A*'s sensory equipment to know I'm there at all. Why would he do that? He thinks he's hopelessly derelict in space.

EVA time.

I climb into the Orlan for what seems like the millionth time and cycle through the airlock. I have a nice long tether anchored to the airlock interior itself.

I look out into the vast nothingness before me. I can't see the *Blip-A*.

Tau Ceti is too far away to light things up. I only know where the ship is because it blocks the background stars. I'm just . . . out in space and a big chunk of it has no pinpricks of light.

There's no good way to do this. I'm just going to have to take a guess. I kick off the *Hail Mary*'s hull as hard as I can, aiming for the *Blip-A*. It's a big ship. I just have to hit any part of it. And hey, if I miss, the tether will bounce me back in the galaxy's first interstellar bungee jump.

I float across space. The blackness ahead of me grows. More and more stars disappear until I see nothing. I don't even have a sense of movement. I know logically I must have the same velocity as when I kicked off my ship. But there's nothing to prove it.

Then, I spot a faint blotchy tan glow ahead. I'm finally close enough to the *Blip-A* that my helmet lights are illuminating part of it. It gets brighter and brighter. I can see the hull more clearly now.

It's go time. I have just seconds to find something to grab on to. I know his hull has rails all over the place for that robot to get around. I'm hoping I'll be close enough to one to grab.

I spot a rail dead ahead. I reach out.

Slam!

I hit the *Blip-A* much harder than an EVA suit should. I shouldn't have kicked off the *Hail Mary* with so much gusto. I scrabble at the hull, grabbing for anything. My plan to grab a rail failed miserably, I got a hand on one but just couldn't keep a grip. I bounce and start drifting away. The tether gets tangled up behind and around me. It'll be a long climb back to my ship for another try.

Then I spot a weird, jagged protuberance on the hull a few meters away. An antenna, maybe? It's too far to reach with my hands, but maybe I can get it with the tether.

I'm drifting away from the hull at a slow but steady rate and I don't have a jetpack. It's now or never.

I tie a quick slipknot in the tether and throw it at the antenna.

And, I'll be gosh darned, I nailed it! I just wrangled an alien spaceship. I pull the loop tight. For a second, I worry it might break the antenna off, but then I see the blotchy tan texture. The antenna (if that's what it is) is made of xenonite. It's not going anywhere.

I pull myself along the tether to the hull. This time, with the antenna and tether to aid me, I manage to grab hold of a nearby robot rail.

"Whew," I say.

I take a moment to catch my breath. Now to put Rocky's hearing to the test.

I pull the biggest wrench I have from my tool belt. I rear back and smack the hull. Hard.

I smack it over and over. *Clank! Clank! Clank!* I hear the sound through my own EVA suit. If he's alive in there, that'll get his attention.

I push one end of the wrench against the hull and crouch down to bring my helmet in contact with the other end. I stretch my neck out in the helmet and push my chin against the faceplate.

"Rocky!" I yell as loud as I can. "I don't know if you can hear me! But I'm here, buddy! I'm on your hull!"

I wait a few seconds. "I have my EVA suit radio on! Same frequency as always! Say something! Let me know you're okay!"

I turn up my radio volume. All I hear is static.

"Rocky!"

A crackle. My ears perk up.

"Rocky?!"

"Grace, question?"

"Yes!" I've never been so happy to hear a few musical notes! "Yeah, buddy! It's me!"

"You are here, question?!" his voice is so high-pitched I can barely understand him. But I understand Eridian pretty well now.

"Yes! I'm here!"

"You are . . ." he squeaks. *"You . . ."* he squeaks again. *"You are here!"*

"Yes! Set up the airlock tunnel!"

"Warning! Taumoeba-82.5 is—"

"I know! I know. It can get through xenonite. That's why I'm here. I knew you'd be in trouble."

"You save me!"

"Yes. I caught the Taumoeba in time. I still have fuel. Set up the tunnel. I'm taking you to Erid."

"You save me and you save Erid!" he squeaks.

"Set up the darn tunnel!"

"Get back in you ship! Unless you want to look at tunnel from outside!"

"Oh, right!"

I wait eagerly by the airlock door, trying to watch the action play out through the little window. It's all happened before—Rocky attaching the airlock-to-airlock tunnel with the hull robot. But this time it was a little more challenging. I had to maneuver the *Hail Mary* into position because the *Blip-A* can't move at all. Still, we got it done.

A final clank, then a hiss. I know that sound!

I float into the airlock and check through the outer window. The tunnel is in place. He kept it all this time. Why not? It's an artifact from his species' first contact with alien life. I'd keep it too!

I turn the emergency relief valve. Air from my ship fills my half of the tunnel. Once it equalizes, I throw open the door and fly in.

Rocky waits for me on the other side. His clothes are a mess. Covered in the all-too-familiar gunky Taumoeba residue. And there are burns all along one side of his jumpsuit and two of his arms are in pretty bad shape. Looks like he had a pretty rough time. But his body language is sheer joy.

He bounces from handhold to handhold.

"I am very very very happy," he says with a high pitch.

I point to his bad arms. "Are you hurt?!"

"I will heal. Attempted many things to stop Taumoeba infestation. All failed."

"I succeeded," I say. "My ship isn't made of xenonite."

"What happen, question?"

I sigh. "The Taumoeba evolved to resist nitrogen. But it also evolved to get into xenonite to hide from nitrogen. The side effect is Taumoeba-82.5 can work its way through xenonite over time."

"Amaze. Now what, question?"

"I still have two million kilograms of Astrophage. Bring your stuff aboard. We're going to Erid."

"Happy! Happy happy happy!" He pauses. *"Need to make nitrogen wash. Make sure no Taumoeba-82.5 get into Hail Mary."*

"Yes. I have full faith in your abilities. Make a sterilizer."

He shifts from one set of bars to another. Those burned arms are hurting him, I can tell. *"What about Earth, question?"*

"I sent the beetles with the mini-farms. Taumoeba-82.5 can't get through Eridian steel."

"Good good," he says. *"I make sure my people take good care of you. They will make Astrophage maybe for you to go home!"*

"Yeah . . ." I say. "About that . . . I'm not going home. The beetles will save Earth. But I won't ever see it again."

His joyous bouncing stops. *"Why, question?"*

"I don't have enough food. After I take you to Erid, I will die."

"You . . . you no can die." His voice gets low. *"I no let you die. We send you home. Erid will be grateful. You save everyone. We do everything to save you."*

"There's nothing you can do," I say. "There's no food. I have enough to last until we get to Erid and then a few months more. Even if your government gave me the Astrophage to go home, I wouldn't survive the trip."

"Eat Erid food. We evolve from same life. We use same proteins. Same chemicals. Same sugars. Must work!"

"No, I can't eat your food, remember?"

"You say is bad for you. We find out."

I hold up my hands. "It's not just bad for me. It will kill me. Your whole ecology uses heavy metals all over the place. Most of them are toxic to me. I'd die immediately."

He trembles. "*No. You no can die. You are friend.*"

I float closer to the divider wall and talk softly. "It's okay. I made my decision. This is the only way to save both of our worlds."

He backs away. *"Then you go home. Go home now. I wait here. Erid maybe send another ship someday."*

"That's ridiculous. Do you really want to risk the survival of your entire species on that guess?"

He's silent for a few moments and finally answers. *"No."*

"Okay. Get that ball thing you use as a spacesuit and come on over. Talk me through how to patch up the xenonite walls. Then you can move your stuff in—"

"Wait," he says. *"You no can eat Erid life. You no have Earth life to eat. What about Adrian life, question?"*

I snort. "Astrophage? I can't eat that! It's ninety-six degrees all the time! It would burn me alive. Plus, I doubt my digestive enzymes would even work on its weird cell membrane."

"Not Astrophage. Taumoeba. Eat Taumoeba."

"I can't eat—" I pause. "I . . . what?"

Can I eat Taumoeba?

It's alive. It has DNA. Is has mitochondria—the powerhouse of the cell. It stores energy as glucose. It does the Krebs cycle. It's not Astrophage. It's not 96 degrees. It's just an amoeba from another planet. It won't have heavy metals like Eridian life evolved to have—they aren't even present in Adrian's atmosphere.

"I . . . I don't know. Maybe I can."

He points to his ship. *"I have twenty-two million kilograms of Taumoeba in fuel bays. How much you want, question?"*

I widen my eyes. It's the first time I've felt genuine hope in a long time.

"Settled." He puts his claw against the divider. *"Fist my bump."*

I laugh and put my knuckles against the xenonite. "Fist-bump. It's just 'fist-bump.' "

"Understand."

CHAPTER ∀ℓ

I finish off the last bite of my meburger and gulp down the vitamin-enriched soda. I put my dishes in the sink and check the clock on my kitchen wall. Wow, is it VℓIλλ already? I better hurry up.

My first few years on Erid were touch-and-go. Taumoeba kept me alive, but I became severely malnourished. The microbes gave me calories, but they weren't a balanced diet.

Those were painful days. I had scurvy, beriberi, and a raft of other maladies. Was it worth it? I still don't know. I might never know. There's no way to communicate with Earth. It's sixteen light-years away.

For all I know, the beetles may have malfunctioned or missed their target. I don't even know if the climatologists like Leclerc were right in their models for what would happen. The *Hail Mary* might have been hopeless from the get-go. Earth might already be a frozen wasteland with billions of corpses.

But I try to stay positive. What else have I got?

For what it's worth, the Eridians are fantastic hosts. They don't have a government, per se, but all the important entities agreed to do whatever it takes to keep me alive. After all, I played a critical role in saving their planet. And even if I hadn't, I'm a living, breathing alien.

Of course they're going to keep me alive. I'm of extreme scientific interest.

I live in a big dome in the middle of one of their "cities." Though "city" isn't quite the right word. A better description might be a "cluster."

I have grounds and everything. Thirty Eridians outside the dome maintain my life-support systems, or so I'm told. And my dome is very close to one of the larger science centers. Many of Erid's greatest minds collect there and thrum. That's sort of a song and discussion in one. But everyone talks at the same time and it's not really conscious on their part. Somehow the thrum leads to conclusions and decisions. The thrum itself is much smarter than any Eridian in it. In a way, Eridians can become ad-hoc neurons in a group mind. But they come and go as they please.

I'm particularly interesting, so pretty much every scientist on the planet came together to thrum up ways to keep me alive. I'm told it was the second-largest science-oriented thrum ever executed. (The largest, of course, was when they had to make a plan for dealing with Astrophage.)

Thanks to my Earth scientific journals, they know all my nutritional needs and how to synthesize the various vitamins in labs. Once they solved that, smaller, less-focused groups worked on making them taste better. That's more or less up to me, actually. Lots of taste tests. Glucose, common to both Eridian and Human biomes, comes up a lot.

The best thing, though, is they managed to clone my muscle tissue and grow it in labs. I can thank Earth science for that. They were nowhere near that technology when I first showed up. But that was sixteen years ago—they're catching up quite well.

Anyway, it means I can finally eat meat. Yes, that's right, I'm eating human meat. But it's my own meat, and I don't feel bad about it. Spend a decade eating nothing but odd-tasting, vaguely sweet vitamin shakes and then see if you'll turn down a burger.

I love meburgers. I eat one every day.

I grab my cane and head out. I'm not a young man anymore, and the high gravity of Erid has only made my bones degenerate faster. I think I'm fifty-three years old now, but I'm not sure. I've done a lot of time-dilated travel. I can accurately say seventy-one years have gone by on Earth since I was born, for what it's worth.

I leave through my front door and cross the grounds. There are no plants or anything—I'm the only thing on this planet that can survive my environment. But there are some very tasteful and aesthetically pleasing rocks. It's become a hobby of mine: making the grounds as pretty as possible. The Eridians just see a bunch of rocks, but I see all the colors.

They installed lights at the top of the dome that get brighter and dimmer on a twenty-four-hour cycle. I explained that's critical to my mood and they took my word for it. Though I did have to explain to this species of interstellar travelers how to make lightbulbs.

I make my way along the gravel pathway to one of the many "meeting" rooms at the dome's wall. Eridians value face-to-carapace communication as much as humans do, and this is a good compromise. My side is within my bubble environment. And on the other side of the 1-centimeter clear xenonite is a room that's out in Erid's natural atmosphere.

I hobble in. It's one of the smaller meeting rooms, really only suitable for a one-on-one conversation. But it's become our go-to spot for meeting up.

Rocky waits for me on the Eridian side. *"Finally! I've been waiting for ℓλ minutes! What took you so long?!"*

I can understand Eridian fluently now, of course. And Rocky is equally fluent in English comprehension.

"I'm old. Give me a break. It takes me a while to get ready in the morning."

"Oh, you had to eat, right?" Rocky says, a tinge of disgust in his voice.

"You told me not to talk about that in polite company."

"I'm not polite company, my friend!"

I snicker. "So what's up?"

He wiggles and jiggles. I've almost never seen him this excited. *"I just heard from the Astronomy hive. They have news!"*

I hold my breath. "Sol? Is it about Sol?!"

"Yes!" he squeals. *"Your star has returned to full luminance!"*

I gasp. *"Are you sure? Like, Iℓℓ percent certainty?"*

"Yes. The data was analyzed by a thrum of λV astronomers. It checks out."

I can't move. I can barely breathe. I start to tremble.

It's over.

We won.

Simple as that.

Sol—Earth's sun—has returned to its pre-Astrophage brightness. There's only one possible way that happens: Astrophage is gone. Or at least reduced in population so much that it doesn't matter.

We won.

We did it!

Rocky cocks his carapace. *"Hey, your face is leaking! I haven't seen that in a long-ass time! Remind me—does that mean you're happy or sad? 'Cause it can mean either one, right?"*

"I'm happy, of course!" I sob.

"Yeah, I thought so. Just checking." He holds a balled claw against the xenonite. *"Is this a fist-bump situation?"*

I press my knuckles to the xenonite as well. "This is a monumentally epic fist-bump situation."

"I guess your scientists got right on it," he says. *"If you account for the time it took your beetles to get there and the travel time for light to get from Sol to Erid . . . I think it took less than one of your years to get it done."*

I nod. It's still sinking in.

"So will you go home now? Or will you stay?"

The . . . entities . . . that make major decisions for Erid long ago offered to refuel the *Hail Mary*. It's still sitting in a nice, stable orbit around Erid, where it's been since Rocky and I first arrived all those years ago.

The Eridians could stock it up with food and supplies, help me make sure everything is working right, and send me on my way. But so far I haven't taken them up on it. It's a long, lonely journey, and until a minute ago I didn't even know if Earth was still habitable. Erid may not be where I'm from, but at least I have friends here.

"I . . . I don't know. I'm getting old and the trip is long."

"Speaking from a selfish perspective, I hope you stay. But that's just me."

"Rocky . . . that news about Sol . . . it . . . it makes my whole life have meaning. You know? I still can't . . . I can't . . ." I start sobbing again.

"Yeah, I know. That's why I wanted to be the one to tell you."

I check my watch. (Yes, the Eridians made me a wristwatch. They make anything I ask for. I try not to abuse it.) "I have to go. I'm late. But . . . Rocky . . ."

"I know," he says, tilting his carapace in what I've come to realize is a smile. *"I know. We'll talk more about it later. I have to get home anyway. Adrian is going to sleep soon, so I have to be there to watch."*

We both head toward our respective exits, but he pauses. *"Hey, Grace. Do you ever wonder? About other life out there?"*

I lean on my cane. "Sure, all the time."

He walks back in. *"I keep thinking about it. The theories are pretty hard to dispute. Some ancestor of Astrophage seeded Earth and Erid with life billions of years ago."*

"Yeah," I say. "And I know where you're going with this."

"Do you?"

"Yeah." I shift my weight from one leg to the other. Arthritis is starting to settle in my joints. High gravity isn't great for humans. "There are fewer than fifty stars as close to Tau Ceti as we are. But two of them ended up with life. It means life—at least, the life Tau Ceti puts out—might be a lot more common in our galaxy than we think."

"Think we'll find more of them? Intelligent species?"

"Who knows?" I say. "You and I found each other. That's something."

"Yeah," he says. *"It really is something. Go do your job, old man."*

"Later, Rocky."

"Later!"

I hobble out of the room and make my way along the perimeter of the dome. They made the whole thing out of clear xenonite because they thought that's what I would want. But it doesn't matter. It's pitch-dark outside all the time. Sure, I can shine a flashlight out there and occasionally see an Eridian going about his business. But I don't get sweeping vistas of mountains or anything. Just inky blackness.

My smile fades a little.

How bad did it get back on Earth? Did they work together to survive? Or did millions die in wars and famine?

They were able to collect the beetles, read my information, and implement a solution. A solution that would have involved a probe going to Venus. So there's definitely some advanced infrastructure still there.

I bet they did work together. Maybe it's just the childish optimist in me, but humanity can be pretty impressive when we put our minds to it. After all, everyone worked together to build the *Hail Mary*. That was no easy feat.

I hold my head up high. Maybe I will go home someday. Maybe I'll find out for sure.

But not right now. Right now, I've got work to do.

I continue along the path to the large double doors leading to another meeting space. And I have to say, it's my favorite one.

I step into the chamber. About one-fifth of the room is my Earth environment. The other side of the divider wall has thirty little Eridians bouncing around like idiots. Each one is no more than thirty Earth years old. The selection process for which ones get to attend . . . well . . . again, Eridian culture is complicated.

An Earthlike organ keyboard sits in the center of my area, oriented such that the operator faces the kids. The organ has quite a few more options than a typical keyboard found on Earth. I can apply inflection, tone, mood, and all the other little intricacies of spoken language. I settle into the comfortable chair, crack my knuckles, and start the class.

"All right, all right," I play. *"Everyone settle down and get in your seats."*

They scamper to their assigned desks and sit quietly, ready for the lesson to begin.

"Who here can tell me the speed of light?"

Twelve kids raise their claws.

ACKNOWLEDGMENTS

I'd like to thank the following people who helped me get the science as accurate as possible: Andrew Howell, for helping me with astronomy and stellar sciences. Jim Green, for explaining the basics of planetary science and how atmospheres work. Shawn Goldman, for telling me all about exoplanet detection. Charles Duba (who I actually went to high school with!), for explaining complex details about neutrinos. And finally, Cody Don Reeder, for giving me vital chemistry information and also being an all-around cool guy to exchange emails with.

On the book front, I'd like to thank my agent, David Fugate, for always having my back. Also, Julian Pavia, my editor on this book and so far all of my books. And Sarah Breivogel, who has handled publicity for my books since day one. And I'd like to thank my eclectic group of beta readers: My mother, Janet, who loves everything I do; Duncan Harris, who questions every plot point and keeps me honest; and Dan Snyder, who . . . wait. You never got back to me, Dan! What, am I not good enough for you!?

And I'd like to thank my wife, Ashley, for putting up with godknows how many conversations about possible plot and story structure ideas and always giving me wise feedback.

PHOTO BY AUBRIE PICK

ANDY WEIR built a career as a software engineer until the success of his first published novel, *The Martian,* allowed him to live out his dream of writing full-time. He is a lifelong space nerd and a devoted hobbyist of subjects such as relativistic physics, orbital mechanics, and the history of manned spaceflight. He also mixes a mean cocktail. He lives in California.

Andyweirauthor.com
Facebook.com/AndyWeirAuthor
X: @andyweirauthor

ABOUT THE TYPE

This book was set in Albertina, a typeface created by Dutch calligrapher and designer Chris Brand (1921–98). Brand's original drawings, based on calligraphic principles, were modified considerably to conform to the technological limitations of typesetting in the early 1960s. The development of digital technology later allowed Frank E. Blokland (b. 1959) of the Dutch Type Library to restore the typeface to its creator's original intentions.